THE
HOUSE
ON
THE
LAKE

CARA KENT

The House on the Lake
Copyright © 2023 by Cara Kent

CHAPTER ONE

THE SURGEON

Christopher Fleming appreciated privacy. More than that, he required tranquility. So when his bank account had informed him that it was time to purchase a vacation home, he avoided the gaudy new builds on the outskirts of Glenville's suburbia and opted for something far from the prying eyes and pandemonium of civilization.

Upon purchase, his wife, Kathleen, had taken it upon herself to name their new pride and joy. Constructed partly from Douglas fir and dark in color, she quickly settled on Black Douglas, which was coincidentally the name of her favorite scotch. Unbeknownst to her then, the whiskey's namesake was a vicious Scottish knight and feudal lord, though upon finding out, she doubled down on the name. Christopher thought it a somewhat macabre choice, on account of all the bloodshed, but he had made it a habit to remain on his wife's good side.

Much like the other more exclusive lake houses in Whitetail Forest, the entrance to Black Douglas was hard to find. It was further sequestered by the security gate disguised as forest undergrowth. Due to his infrequent visits over the past five years, he almost missed the turnoff but spotted the silver buzzer and keypad protruding from the faux leafage just in time.

Christopher veered left, leaned out the window, and pressed the button with a buzz. Despite hearing the receiver ring inside the house, there was no response, and the gate remained static. He tried again, and still, the gate didn't budge. Remembering that Kathleen had mentioned swimming in the lake before he left, he shrugged it off and typed in the gate code. It was 1994, the year of his son's birth, and as easy to remember as all their other security codes. Another buzz sounded, and the plastic wall of plants parted.

As Christopher parked his brand-new electric BMW—an indulgent birthday present, even by his standards—he looked up at the lake house. In doing so, every second of his life fell into place. All the late nights, narcissistic clients, sociopathic teachers, student loans, and competitive peers had been worth it because everywhere he looked, he saw another dream come true.

Though it had been impressive at the time of purchase, the recent renovations had elevated the house beyond belief. He had his wife's excellent taste to thank for that, and while she still grumbled at the odd, indiscernible blemish, to Christopher, the building was the pinnacle of perfection. His slack-jawed, wide-eyed wonder ceased most of Kathleen's gripes because nobody knew more about perfection than her plastic surgeon husband.

The house had been built in the late '70s, back when Christopher had still resided in Glenville, by a genius architect who tragically died shortly after construction at the age of thirty-three. Only four of his houses remained in North America, and Christopher counted himself lucky to own one-quarter of them.

Clad with umber timber and lined with black around the clusters of large, asymmetrical windows, Black Douglas was incredibly modern despite its advancing age. Though if you looked close enough, there were still hints of history in the slanted roof and interior brick feature walls. Christopher's favorite aspect was the wraparound veranda, which became a protruding waterside sundeck and dock at the back. However, today there was something he disliked. The size. Eight bedrooms and six bathrooms were not usually something he'd complain about, but on his fiftieth birthday, the expanse of furnished rooms felt hollow.

His son, Jason, had called him while Christopher milled about his old stomping grounds, picking up food for the barbecue. As it turned out, Jason couldn't make it last minute due to a work-related emergency. Christopher knew better than to press the nature of the crisis, but after failing to reschedule, his spirits were suitably crushed. He tried to be understanding, keeping the call upbeat, but as soon as he hung up, a storm began to brew.

He called Kathleen, who battened down the hatches with promises of drinks by the lake and delicious dinners, but even his beloved wife could do little to tamp the bluster. It was his fiftieth birthday, after all, and this family trip had been in talks for months. He knew, of course, how vital Jason's job was, but no Jason meant no Natalie, and without their mother, there was no way Christopher's toddler granddaughters were making it from Virginia to Washington.

As Christopher glanced back at the house and the bottle of champagne in the back seat, he sighed. He knew he owed it to both himself and his wife to lift his spirits. They hadn't been able to enjoy a romantic weekend together in quite some time due to his increasingly busy schedule, and he wasn't sure when they would next get the opportunity.

Plastering a smile on his face, Christopher exited the car, paper bags in hand, and made his way to the front door. He stopped, the happy expression melting from his lips when he noticed the door was ajar. He knew Kathleen was at home, but after years spent in an undesirable area of New York, she was not the kind of woman to leave the door unlocked.

I must've forgotten to latch the door, he thought as he shouldered his way in.

The house was quiet, and the lights were off, which would have been usual if not for Kathleen's preference for reading in the distant glass sunroom. Yet there was something eerie about the halls, rooms, and quarters that hadn't been there earlier.

He slipped off his polished oxfords, his expression still downturned, and he called out to his wife as he placed the bags on the console. She didn't respond despite how his voice carried, and his blood began to chill. Before he'd left, Kathleen had been wandering around with a chair and a small bucket of paint, touching up the cornices where she felt the professional painters hadn't sufficiently done their job. The chair had felt circles stuck to the bottoms of the feet to avoid scratching, making it liable to slip. He'd warned her about this, but Kathleen was hard of hearing when offered advice.

At the time, he'd laughed it off. After decades of being a ballerina, Kathleen was nimble with quick reflexes, but now he feared that her obsession with perfection had resulted in some terrible disaster.

He made his way into the kitchen and sniffed. It was pristine but smelled strongly of food despite there being no evidence of cooking. He crept around the kitchen bench, fearful of every hidden alcove, and saw that the chair had been returned to the breakfast nook. He exhaled, eliminating the possibility of discovering Kathleen surrounded by a pool of white-turned-pink paint.

Christopher slid the glass doors open and stepped out onto the back deck to check the lake. There were neither people nor boats, and the water was undisturbed. Drowning was a possibility, but her towel and sunscreen were nowhere to be seen.

Growing increasingly anxious, Christopher tried to call Kathleen's phone as she stalked through the house to the sunroom. That, too, was immaculate, undisturbed, and empty. The magazines were folded in a neat pile, Kathleen's bookmark was in the same place as yesterday's, and the pillows were perfectly fluffed.

He ducked his head out the back door to glance around the large yard at the side of the house. Everything was as it had been before he left, except the barbecue had been moved to the gazebo, and its lid was open. He stepped outside onto the verandah to get a better look. As he did so, a twig snapped underfoot, but not under *his* foot. The sound had come from the surrounding trees. Christopher froze, calming his own pumping heart enough to make out hushed voices coming from the same spot.

"Who's there?" he called out.

He took another step and opened his mouth to ask again when at least sixty people jumped out from the surrounding trees.

"Surprise!" they yelled in unison.

Christopher started, but then he realized what this was, and he began to laugh, his eyes darting around, unsure of where to land until he spotted Kathleen. She wore a tight yellow dress and a wide-brimmed straw hat that covered her strawberry-blonde waves in shadow. Her well-toned calves stuck out the bottom, and her feet were as bare and dirty as ever as she bounded across the grass. Her arms were raised, her face was bare, and her expression was cocky. She flashed a wink at him as he shook his head.

She was a goddess, sculpted into divine proportions by his own hands. Too beautiful to be believed but not too delicate to be touched. He picked her up into the air and twirled her. Once her feet were reunited with the wooden boards, she stood on her tiptoes and wrapped her arms around him.

"Happy birthday, darling," she whispered.

He kissed her cheek. "Thank you, my love. This is wonderful."

They pulled apart, and he looked around at all their friends and family and felt another pang of disappointment. Jason wasn't among them. The phone call hadn't been part of the ruse.

"I know," Kathleen said sadly. "But it's going to be a wonderful day."

Christopher nodded. "Of course it will. There's no party like a Kathleen Fleming party."

"You're damn right," Kathleen said, her grin widening as she looked past her husband and toward the back door.

Before Christopher could turn, two small pairs of arms wrapped around each of his legs, and he looked down to see his granddaughters' gap-toothed and freckled faces.

"Oh!" Christopher exclaimed. "I seem to have befriended two little monkeys. Do you bite, little monkeys?"

"No!" Charlotte and Marie replied in sync, outraged at the accusation.

"Phew," Christopher replied, pretending to wipe the sweat off his brow. "How did you monkeys get here? Did you swing here by vines through the jungle?"

"Grandad, that's not a jungle," Charlotte, the eldest, informed him. "That's a forest. There aren't any vines!"

"How silly of me. My mistake. So how did you get here?"

"We flew," Marie said, the *l* sound getting lost in translation.

"Flying monkeys, my, my," Christopher said. "I don't suppose a wicked witch sent you?"

"That's not a very nice thing to say about your daughter-in-law," a voice said from behind.

Christopher clumsily turned, the girls wrapped around his calves and balanced on top of his feet. Jason and Natalie stood in the doorway with their arms wrapped around each other. Natalie, a timid little thing, giggled quietly at Jason's joke.

Christopher narrowed his eyes. "Did my son just make a joke? No, it must be someone who looks like him."

"Consider that your birthday present," Jason said flatly, striding forward.

"Well, what an honor! Though frankly, the monkeys were gifts enough."

Jason shook his father's hand and gave him a brief hug and a pat on the back. Next up was Natalie, who gave him a gentle hug and a birthday card before darting back to her husband's side. Kathleen too sidled up to Christopher, and the pairs looked at each other fondly.

Doing so was like staring into a funhouse mirror. Unlike the athletic Kathleen, Natalie was a waif dressed in a conservative frock better suited for a grandma and white ankle socks that stuck out the top of her sensible T-strap shoes. Similarly, where Christopher was stout in height and slender in build, Jason was the opposite. Their ever-serious son was built in a manner that Kathleen described as akin to "a brick shithouse," an assessment that Christopher agreed with.

"You trickster!" Christopher enthused. "I really thought you weren't coming. Though I suppose working for the CIA would improve your lying capabilities."

"I think you're just becoming gullible, old man."

"Old man!"

"We are here for your fiftieth birthday party, right? Or have I got the wrong house? "Jason teased, dealing out another unusual joke.

"Fifty is the new thirty, I'll have you know."

"Does that mean thirty is the new ten? Because I don't think my boss will keep me around if that's the case."

"Okay, maybe we'll just knock ten years off."

"Ten years!" Charlotte pouted, holding up her fingers to count. "That makes me minus 6."

Christopher raised his eyebrows. "Wow. She clearly got all of Natalie's brains."

"Quite right," Natalie retorted, trying to pry her children from Christopher's legs. "They got all of their love of rough-housing from their daddy though."

With Jason's help, she succeeded, and Jason picked tiny two-year-old Marie up. "We'll be right back. Just going to unpack and put these two down for a nap," he said.

Charlotte started to whine, but Christopher interrupted her by dropping to her level and squeezing her hands. "Don't worry, honey. We'll put the party on hold until you return. After all, you are the guests of honor. If you go to sleep right away, I'll even let you blow out my candles if you like."

This seemed to do the trick, and Charlotte took off, forcing Natalie and Jason to jog after her.

Christopher chuckled and squeezed Kathleen. "How on earth did you pull this off? Where are all the cars?" he asked.

"Garage," Kathleen replied. "I know you never park in there. I bet you didn't even know it fits twelve."

"Twelve? My god."

They turned together and stepped down from the veranda onto the grass, ready to face another dream come true: all their favorite people in the world gathered in one place. Siblings, aunts, uncles, cousins, nieces, nephews, co-workers, employees, and friends greeted Christopher warmly as they sipped champagne and munched on hors d'oeuvres. Kathleen handed him a glass as he talked to a cousin he hadn't seen for six years, but instead of drinking it, he turned to the assembly and tapped the glass with his wedding ring.

"Thank you so much for coming!" he yelled to applause. "I'm fifty. Fifty! I'm two years older than the digital camera and one younger than the hacky sack. I've been all around the world. I've seen incredible things invented and invented some myself. Half a century of wisdom and joy. It's unbelievable. And what's even more unbelievable is that Kathleen has been with me for thirty-two years of this life, and it would not be half as blessed without her in it. So... a toast to my wife who organized this wonderful party and a big thank-you to all of you for coming. Please enjoy yourselves, and for those of you who enjoy a drink or two, please mind the lake. Cheers!"

"Cheers!" replied the crowd, and everyone drank deeply from their flutes as Christopher planted an exaggerated kiss on Kathleen, who playfully shoved him off and put her fists up.

Over the laughter, he heard the gate opening and tires on the tarmac driveway around the corner.

"More guests?" he asked.

Kathleen looked around at the group. "I don't think so. I suppose I must be forgetting somebody."

"Well, you are forty-nine, my dear. Getting on a bit."

Kathleen playfully punched him, but her expression was a little strained. "I wonder who I've forgotten."

Christopher sipped his champagne and craned his neck. "It'll be someone really important, and we'll both be embarrassed, I'm sure."

"Sounds about right."

Two figures rounded the corner on the verandah and made their way to the short set of stairs that led onto the grass. They stood side by side, and Kathleen gave a shuddering gasp. Christopher protectively wrapped an arm around her and pulled her several steps back, ready to run.

The intruders were dressed in black, their faces concealed by balaclavas, and they held a pistol in each of their right hands. Nobody but Kathleen and Christopher seemed to notice until the shorter one fired a shot in the air. All hope of directing the crowd toward safety vanished. Instead, pandemonium erupted, and everyone darted in different directions across the grass like billiard balls following a break shot.

It was clear that these strangers—who appeared from their physicality to be young men—were making a beeline for Christopher and anyone who got in their way was merely a barrier to be exterminated. When the first shot made contact with someone, and he fell to the ground clutching his stomach, the chaos and screaming worsened.

However, whether from shock or determination, Christopher and Kathleen stood their ground as the men shot their way through the crowd. It was only when they were a mere twenty feet away did Kathleen move, putting herself between the gunmen and her husband.

"My love," Christopher whispered, "they want me. And only me. I have to go with them to make this stop."

"No," she replied sternly.

"I love you. Please don't make me watch you die on my birthday."

Kathleen shook as if the words had jolted her. She turned, placed her hands on his cheeks, and kissed him hard. She pulled away, straightened his spectacles, and ran off into the woods as fast as she could.

She escaped just in time, and by the time the men reached him, Christopher could no longer see his wife, and many of the uninjured had joined her in the forest. The less lucky lay on the floor, either injured or with their hands over their heads.

"Don't follow us!" yelled one of the men as he roughly grabbed Christopher. "You will be shot."

To Christopher's immense relief, no one tried to be a hero and stayed put as he and the two men strode across the yard. He went peacefully and reached the driveway without injury. The gate was still open, held in place by large decorative rocks, and Christopher wondered how they'd got inside in the first place. Had somebody buzzed them in, or had they known the code? The latter idea made him feel unwell to the point of puking, but he held it back in his throat.

Their black van—which was cheap and poorly spray-painted—was parked haphazardly, the side door still open.

The vehicle's hungry mouth grew bigger as Christopher was dragged toward it. Just as the metal jaws were close enough to bite and the leather tongue of the seat close enough to lick, one of the shooters paused.

"Hey, check out this house, man. There's no way this guy's not rolling in it. Think there's any valuables inside?" he asked his partner.

"Probably. You really feel like risking it? Cops will be here any minute."

"Hell yeah, I'm not getting paid enough for this shit. No one said there'd be a goddamn mob here."

"Fine, I'll stay here with him and keep the van running. Be quick, or I'm leaving without you."

"You got it."

Christopher's moment of respite ended, and he was shoved roughly into the van and cuffed to the headrest of the rear-facing seat. He considered making small talk as the man secured him, but he saw the tarp, the tools, and the zip ties, and thought better of trying anything bold. Instead, he looked at his beautiful house and tried to keep calm. He closed his eyes, trying to record the start of his initially perfect party for posterity. He knew he'd need it in the coming days.

CHAPTER TWO

THE AGENT

G UNSHOTS. THE SOUND WAS UNMISTAKABLE, ESPE-
cially to Jason. He'd heard so many bullets fly in the
past ten years that he could even guess the make and
model. The first shot was a 9 mm Luger pistol, likely a Taurus
G2c. Cheap and cheerful. The second shot came from another
9 mm pistol, but this one sounded expensive. A Smith and
Wesson 1911 Performance Center. A dangerous piece in any
hands and incredibly deadly in the wrong ones.

Jason straightened from tucking Charlotte into the twin-
size bed, leaving the padded quilt loose. He composed himself
and looked down at his daughter, her teddy bear's head sharing

the pillow with her, and stroked her hair before turning to face Natalie. His wife was already shaking, but he didn't reach out to comfort her. His children were old enough to interpret body language, and he needed them to remain tranquil.

"Stay calm," Jason mouthed at Natalie, who nodded tearfully and stiffened.

"Are they doing fireworks without us?" Charlotte whined.

"No, they're not, sweetheart," Jason assured his daughter.

He turned and saw that she'd folded her arms. She looked so much like her mother, and on any other day, this mini-me act would be funny, but not this one. Today her hereditary stubbornness filled him with fear. He backed toward the bedroom door, opened it, and quickly checked that the hallway was clear.

"Hey, girls, I have a good idea," he said. "Because you don't seem very tired yet, how about we play a game of hide-and-seek before your nap? You and Mommy will go hide somewhere, and I'll come to find you."

"What about Grandpa? Isn't he going to get bored?" Charlotte asked.

"Grandpa won't get bored. He has so many friends here," Natalie promised.

Charlotte looked across the room silently, communicating with her little sister, and the two began to clap and giggle excitedly. The plan was a go, and Jason looked into his wife's wide, watery eyes and nodded. Natalie picked up Marie and set her on the ground as Charlotte clambered out of bed.

"Doesn't that sound like fun, girls?" Natalie asked, forcing an encouraging smile. "Come on, let's go hide while Daddy counts to one hundred."

"You better hurry," Jason warned. "You know I count fast."

"Okay, Daddy," Charlotte replied, running out of the room.

Natalie kissed his cheek, and he pulled her in close. "The attic," he whispered. "The trapdoor is steel and has a deadbolt. It doubles as a panic room."

"I love you," Natalie gasped before disappearing after their children.

Jason didn't say it back because saying your goodbyes was a jinx in situations like this, and this wouldn't be the last time they saw each other. Of that, he was sure.

As the three ran up the hallway, he called 911, told the operator that there were two shooters on site, that there were injured civilians, and relayed the address and gate code. The young woman sounded panicked. Maybe it was her first day, or maybe it was because things like this didn't happen in towns like Glenville.

As he spoke to the operator, he crossed the hallway into the oversized guestroom he and Natalie were occupying and retrieved his gun from the bathroom cupboard in the charcoal-tiled en suite. He knew his Glock 19 was loaded from the weight, but he checked anyway. As soon as the clip was reinserted, he heard a squeak from the section of the hallway floorboards that drove his mother insane. She'd ripped it up and put it all back again, and still, it squeaked. Today he was thankful her DIY skills had failed her.

He tilted the standing mirror in the corner to reflect a portion of the hallway, then positioned himself with his back to the side of the doorway and watched for the gunman. The man he was looking for appeared in the frame moments later. A portrait of death—dressed in black, his face covered, and his Taurus Luger pointing out in front of him.

Jason's stomach turned as the man swerved left first, pointing the pistol into his daughters' room. If they'd moved any slower or, God forbid, thrown a tantrum, who knows what could have happened. Jason had faced armed men countless times, but for the first time in a long time, he felt fear.

Jason padded toward the man—silently, despite his size—and raised the butt of his gun, intending to pistol-whip him. He intended to take him out without firing; however, as he lifted his arm, he caught sight of his own form towering over the other man. The security blind was lowered on the other side of the window. It was to help the girls sleep but had incidentally turned it into a mirror.

The man turned and pulled the trigger. His reaction time had nothing on Jason's, but was quick enough that when Jason jumped back into the hallway, the shot missed him by mere centimeters. He darted back into the guestroom and resumed his position by the doorway. He tried to remember how many times he'd heard the Luger fire. He counted seven, leaving his attacker with another four rounds. Jason had fifteen, which gave him an advantage, but he knew it only took one to the skull for the duel to be over.

Jason ducked around and fired at the man, who was similarly hiding behind the doorway of the opposite room. The bullet clipped the wooden frame, but the man stayed hidden. Jason pulled back and waited for a return shot, only to be met with the sound of running feet. He rounded the doorway and shot down the hallway at the man, who, unlike any assassin or hitman he'd ever met, was wearing dirty running shoes—though he noted that the shoes were expensive and trendy, aimed at people who called themselves sneakerheads.

Mid-twenties, Jason thought to himself as he pursued the man cautiously. *Male, Caucasian, blue eyes, five foot ten*, he added as he watched his prey run.

The man fled down the stairs and fired a shot behind him. From the angle of the gun, Jason didn't bother dodging and watched as the bullet hit a framed photo on the wall and shattered the glass. Jason carefully stepped over the debris and added, *Lousy shot*, to his assessment.

At the top of the stairs, Jason fired again. He missed intentionally, not yet ready to kill but desperate to detain. The round skimmed the top of the man's balaclava and planted a bullet in the plaster. The man bounded down the rest of the stairs like a baby deer stuck in a house—all lanky limbs and no coordination. Jason's intentions to scare him were working, but when the sounds of grief-stricken anguish seeped toward him from the yard, he adjusted his aim. Was somebody dead? His mother? His father?

Jason's face hardened, and he sped up, jumping down the stairs and firing another two shots. These pierced the man's shoulder and calf, and the perpetrator cried out in agony. It slowed him down, and his gun hung limply by his side.

Jason adjusted his aim again, pointing at the back of his skull. He could kill him. He'd done it before. It would be so easy, yet his questioning mind, the skilled interrogator, wanted to know more. Why here? Why his family? They were in the middle of nowhere under lock and key. This wasn't a robbery gone wrong. It was a hit.

Silhouetted in the front door, the man looked back at Jason with wide blue eyes and fired one last time. The bullet missed and hit a bust of Christopher square in the temple, cracking the marble and threatening to split the carving in twain.

"Stop," Jason commanded, holding his gun, prepared to make an easy killing shot.

The man sprang from the front step, Jason's resulting shot hitting him in the ass as he limped toward the black van. Jason stood in the doorway, finally ready to kill, as the man jumped into the open vehicle with another agonized yelp.

"Yeah, I'm really not being paid enough for this shit! Step on it!" the man exclaimed to the driver, who was obscured by tinted glass.

The van, which was already running, began to move, and as the vehicle turned to leave, Jason prepared himself to fire into the open side door. Just as the opportunity arose, he relieved the pressure on the trigger. There were two men in the back. One the invader and the other his father. He was handcuffed to the seat and called out to his son.

"I love you!" he yelled, his words cut off by the door slamming shut.

Once again, Jason didn't say it back, though he thought the words over and over in his head as the van sped away. Jason fired several shots into the back window and the wheels, but it did no good. There was no explosion, no halting, and Jason stood, hopeless, as the vehicle disappeared into the darkness of the forest.

Jason moved toward the garage, wanting to jump into his own car and take off in pursuit, but the sounds of anguish from the yard stopped him. Right now he was needed here, and he knew his father, ever selfless, would agree.

Blood pounding through his ears, Jason reentered the house, his expression stony and his grip on his gun tight enough to hurt. He wanted to hurt, wanted a distraction, wished a hit had landed so he'd have something to focus on.

The cries of children broke him from his haze, and he put the safety on and pocketed his gun as he squatted to hug his children.

"Why aren't you in the attic?" he asked sweetly while looking up at Natalie accusingly.

Natalie flinched. "They wanted to know why you hadn't come to find us. They were worried about you."

"Well, you really should've stayed in the attic," Jason chided.

"I heard the car take off, and ..." Natalie stuttered.

Jason nodded apologetically. It wasn't the time for arguing, and Jason reminded himself that his wife was not one of his work colleagues or a soldier. She was a stay-at-home mom, and the only violence she experienced was in the form of water pistols and hair-pulling.

"Hey, girls," Jason said, gesturing to all three of them to approach him. "It's okay. I'm okay."

"What were all those banging sounds?" Charlotte asked hesitantly as they embraced Jason.

Now that his heart was slowing, he could hear Marie suck her thumb and Natalie sniffle, and Jason sighed. He didn't know how to lie, so he told his children the truth. He figured they were bound to find out something terrible had happened when they realized Grandpa was gone and the cops showed up.

"There was a bad man in the house," he said, pulling them closer.

Charlotte gasped. "Did you catch him, Daddy?"

Jason looked up at Natalie. "No, I didn't."

"What if he comes back?" asked his daughter, her eyes welling with tears.

"He won't, I promise," Jason replied, continuing to tell the truth.

"But—"

Jason interrupted, his capacity for words running out. "Now, you girls stay inside with Mommy. I need to go check on everyone else."

"Did the bad man hurt anyone?"

"I don't know, sweetheart. That's why I have to go check, okay?"

"Okay," Charlotte said, pulling away and cradling her sister.

"That's my good, brave girl," he said, kissing each of them on the forehead before standing.

As he strode away, Natalie ran after him and wrapped her arms around his waist. He pulled free from her grasp, turned, and stroked her hair before continuing toward the yard. The sounds of sobbing increased, and the knot in his stomach tightened as he reached the veranda.

It was worse than he thought. He looked out at the chaos and carnage and froze, his hand gripping the wooden railing so tight it could've splintered. There were pools of blood on the perfectly mown grass in battlefield quantities. Trails of it led to motionless figures lying on their backs. Packs of mourners surrounded them, sobbing on their knees or clutching those who were still breathing tightly.

There was too much to look at or absorb, and his eyes flitted from a dead second cousin to a mortally wounded great-uncle. It was the worst thing he'd ever seen and all he could do to stop his knees from buckling as he descended the steps.

Despite everything, he exhaled when he saw his mother emerge from the cluster. She sprinted toward him, the front of her butter-colored dress covered in blood.

"Jason!" she wailed, her arms out.

He held out his own arms and let her embrace him tightly. They held each other for a minute, her rocking him despite their significant size difference.

"Are the girls and Natalie okay?" she asked.

"Yeah. They were hiding in the attic."

"Did they take your dad?"

"Yeah, I chased the guy out of the house. They took off in a van. I'm sorry I couldn't stop them."

She pulled back and looked up at him, her expression stern. "Don't you dare apologize."

"It's my job to stop men like that. It's my *job*."

"Honey, you're not at work. They caught you by surprise."

"It's not an excuse."

Her brow knitted, she reached up and grabbed his face, but with all the brusqueness of a schoolmarm with a cane. The pressure hurt and penetrated the all-encompassing numbness.

"Hey. I'm proud of you," she said. "You did your best. Now, snap out of it and help me. We have a lot of people down."

"Yes, ma'am."

17

She clapped his cheek. "Good boy. We can worry about your dad later. He can take care of himself for now."

"Mom."

"You don't know your father like I do," she snapped. "Now, come on."

Jason nodded and mimicked his mother's strides as they approached the nearest body—a young black man whom Jason didn't recognize but his mother clearly did. He was maybe twenty at the most, and his eyes were open and unseeing. A woman with graying curls—likely the young man's mother—was applying pressure to a gut shot that had clearly been profusely bleeding but had finally stopped. Kathleen knelt, comforted the sobbing bereaved mother, and stayed perfectly calm as the woman pawed at her desperately and coated her best dress with the young man's blood. As she held the woman, she reached out and closed the young man's eyelids.

CHAPTER THREE

THE DETECTIVE

"FASTER, FASTER, FASTER," HEATHER MUTTERED over the deafening siren as the SWAT team struggled to keep up.

Despite Gabriel's insistence that she keep her eyes on the road, Heather frequently glanced into the rearview mirror to monitor the driver's feeble attempts to traverse the muddy, rural roads. She could feel her blood pressure rising, and the leather steering wheel squeaked under her white-knuckle grip.

"You're going to lose them," Gabriel warned, twisting in his seat to watch the van try to keep up with Heather's 1977 Ford Granada.

"I should've driven the damn thing myself," Heather growled, turning a corner, and losing the SWAT team for the fourth time since entering the forest. "Maybe slow down a bit?" Gabriel asked, holding on to the grab handle for dear life.

Heather looked at him with disbelief. "There is an active shooter in Glenville and injured civilians, and you want me to slow down? They're the ones that need to speed up. I know that goddamn van can go faster than that. The ambulance too."

"I know. I get it," Gabriel said, adjusting the Velcro on his bulletproof vest. "But it's going to be damn near impossible to stop a shooter if we hit a moose and die."

Heather rolled her eyes. "I'm not going to hit a goddamn moo—"

"Watch out!"

At the very last second, Heather swerved out of the way of a doe leaping across the narrow stretch of road. The space between the seemingly suicidal creature and the car was so slim that Heather swore she heard its fur brush across the paint. Had it jumped out even two seconds sooner, it would have been embedded in the windshield.

Gabriel stared at her wide-eyed. "Are you kidding me?"

"We're almost there now," Heather replied, refusing to lift her foot from the accelerator.

It wasn't a lie, and she turned left through a tall, vegetation-covered gate and into a vast driveway that could have easily housed a dozen cars. Strangely, it was empty aside from one luxury BMW parked neatly on the right-hand side as if within invisible dividing lines. She figured the six-figure vehicle was unlikely to belong to the shooters, so the question was, where *was* their car? There was no way they could have made it on foot.

She turned the siren off and exited the car with her gun in hand. The house ahead was awe-inducing, but she wasn't breathless because of the architecture. What sucked the air from her lungs was the stillness. All she could hear was the wind in the leaves. There were no gunshots, no screaming, and no getaway van squealing.

Gabriel looked at her, all the anxiety and apprehension draining away as he listened to the breeze and lowered his gun.

20

She knew he was thinking the same thing she was. They were too late.

Heather groaned as the SWAT team finally caught up and pulled in. The back door banged open, and five local officers jumped out dressed in tactical gear. The group looked around wildly, their weapons drawn, and Heather approached them with a clenched fist.

"Eyes on the shooter?" one of them asked.

"No," Heather said. "I think they're gone. Just stay here and listen out for me on the walkie."

"Do you need us to check the area for threats?" asked a different officer, who sounded like she really wanted the answer to be no.

"That won't be necessary. Officer Silva and I will contact you if you're needed. For now, just move out of the ambulance's way."

The five officers seemed relieved by not having to jump into action, which aggravated Heather until she remembered they were not a professionally trained Seattle SWAT team. They were a group of nervous local police officers dressed in dusty riot gear. It wasn't their fault that Glenville wasn't equipped for something like this. Or at least, that's what she tried to tell herself.

Heather turned back to Gabriel, tilted her head toward the veranda, and then to the right. Gabriel nodded and strode forward with two hands on his gun. At least he was there and competent, Heather thought.

The hollow wooden structure drummed beneath their steel-toe boots as they rounded the corner, their guns pointing toward the ground at an angle. Their pace fell out of sync as the gut-wrenching cries of multiple people reached them, and they quickened their gait. They emerged out onto a larger section of the decking and looked out at the expansive yard. Before they could speak, the sobs turned to screams. Heather looked around for the cause of their fear before realizing it was them: armed strangers dressed in black. They hastily tucked their weapons away.

21

"Police!" Heather exclaimed, her hands raised. "We're here to help, my name is Detective Heather Bishop, and this is Officer Gabriel Silva."

Looking around, Heather knew that her variety of help was not what they needed. Without the assistance of a time machine, what lay before her was a job for the EMTs now. Bloodied, motionless bodies were dotted across the lawn, surrounded by mourners. Some of those who stood and stared at her looked to be injured, and their hopeless expressions made Heather feel as if she'd been the one to fire the gun.

"Is the shooter still on-site?" Gabriel asked and was met with small headshakes.

"The ambulance is on its way. If you're injured, please move to the driveway so they can help you as soon as they arrive," Heather requested. Even those who were bleeding seemed reluctant to move, so she added, "Officer Silva will escort you. You can trust him."

She leaned into Gabriel and whispered, "Call two more. All of these people need to go to the hospital."

Gabriel nodded and beckoned the wounded toward him with a kind but unsmiling expression. It seemed to do the trick, and half a dozen people trudged toward them with glassy eyes. They each stepped up onto the veranda with wobbly legs and weak knees and followed Gabriel around the corner. Heather heard him trying to console them as they went, but he received no verbal response.

"Is someone able to tell me what happened here?" Heather asked of the large crowd.

A large, stoutly built man stood up, revealing an ashen body of a young girl lying in the grass. She was evidently dead, and painful memories flashed before Heather's eyes of toe tags, open-casket funerals, and mourning parents.

She braced herself for a punch or a shove from the stony-faced figure and flinched when he stuck out his hand, only to realize it was there to shake. The man—who looked to be about thirty and sported a crew cut—was bloody but seemingly uninjured. She shook and found his grasp to be both steady and dry.

"Jason Fleming," he said, pausing as two SWAT team members emerged from the back door.

Heather clenched her jaw but tried to hide her irritation over the disobedience.

"Unfortunately, I think the need for a SWAT team has passed. Though they're welcome to check the house. It belongs to my parents."

"Understood. I'm sorry we didn't get here soon enough," Heather replied, struggling to keep her voice as steady as his.

"Don't apologize," Jason said sternly. "By the time I called you, the shots had already been fired. Many of the deceased were killed instantly."

Goosebumps rippled across Heather's heavily clothed flesh. It chafed, and her body temperature failed to regulate, leaving her both cold and sweating.

She swallowed hard. "How many are there? Deceased, I mean."

"Ten. Some local. Some not. I suppose that's something for your department to figure out."

His wording took her aback. It was as if he was expecting someone else—the more competent Seattle PD perhaps—to arrive and take over the case at hand, leaving the organization of the deceased to the local hicks. Perhaps he was on that force himself. There was something about his robotic but polite nature that screamed "not a civilian."

Heather cleared her throat. "Yes, it is. The locals will be taken to the funeral home, and those who are from out of state will be transported per the wishes of their wills and families. I can assure you, this will be handled with the utmost care and timeliness."

Whether Jason was reassured by her claims, it was impossible to tell. His face was a fortress, and Heather was growing unnerved by his unreadability. His grief, or lack thereof, was bordering on bizarre. She was well acquainted with the extreme sliding scale of human emotion, and though some might claim shock as an explanation, that didn't seem to be the case here. He was utterly neutral, and his pragmaticism in the face of a tragedy was both haunting and enviable.

"I can help with some of that. Several of the dead are our relatives. I can provide you with a list of their next of kin's contact details."

23

"Thank you, I appreciate that."

Jason made a subtle gesture that resembled a shrug. "There's no point in this being any harder than it has to be. I don't know the three locals though, but my mom will. I'll ask her when she's less busy."

"Where are you from?"

"Virginia. Dad was born in Glenville, but we rarely come out here. It's a long trip. Kids."

His expression darkened for the first time when he mentioned his father. There was something sore there that Heather feared agitating with a clumsy tongue, but she knew she had to press the subject.

"Is your father among the deceased?" Heather asked.

"No," Jason replied.

Heather noticed a hesitation and waited expectantly for him to continue until he reluctantly did.

"He was kidnapped by the shooters. I tried to stop them but was unable to."

Heather wanted to scream. A kidnapping only further complicated everything and added a ticking clock to locating the suspects.

"Do you have a description of the shooters or the vehicle they were driving?"

Jason hesitated again. "I do, but I want you to know that I will be handling my dad's rescue. Please do whatever you need to for the deceased and their family, but leave the killers to me."

Heather stared unblinking at him, almost at a loss for words.

"Sir, respectfully, I am the lead detective of this town and this case, and I cannot allow a civilian to hunt down two mass murderers and kidnappers in my stead. I am happy for you to help with the case, where appropriate, but vigilante justice is not something I can allow."

Jason sighed and retrieved something from his pocket. It was a little leather wallet not unlike the one in her back pocket, and he flipped it open to reveal a golden eagle CIA badge and blue ID, identifying him as an active CIA Intelligence Officer.

"Ah, I see," Heather said.

"Yeah," Jason replied as if that were that and pocketed his identification.

Heather thought for a second and straightened up. "Except for the fact that this crime happened on American soil and thus falls under the jurisdiction of the police and the FBI. Unless your dad is a foreign dignitary and you've failed to mention that?"

"He is not. He's a world-renowned plastic surgeon."

"Right. Impressive, but still not CIA business," she replied.

Jason raised an eyebrow, and she let the indignation go. So serene was his demeanor that it was easy to forget that he was having the worst day of his life.

Gently, avoiding eggshells, she continued, "Now, I understand that this is your family, and I am incredibly sorry for your losses, but respectfully, I'm going to need those descriptions. I know you don't believe me yet, but I will hunt these guys down. I'm no special agent, but I'm a damn good detective."

Something resembling an emotion flickered across Jason's face. Was it amusement? Irritation? Heather wasn't sure, but she stood tall all the same. She was more than sorry that he'd lost so much, but she was damned if she'd lay down and give up in the face of ten murders in her own town.

"Wow," Jason said at last.

"You thought I was going to give up a lot easier than that, didn't you?"

"I did. Most small-town cops would."

"Well, I'm not most cops, small-town or otherwise."

The same flicker appeared again. "You know, I think I've heard of you."

"Really?" Heather asked.

"Yeah. I knew I recognized your name. You solved the Warren case and helped bring down Francisco Medina."

"Yeah, that's me."

"Well, you weren't lying. You are a good detective."

"Thanks," Heather replied, a little embarrassed.

"Are you always this difficult?" he asked.

"My boss would say so," Heather retorted, unable to tell if he was joking.

"Great," Jason said dryly. "Are you ready for those descriptions?"

"Yep," Heather said, whipping out her tattered notebook.

Jason looked at the little book judgmentally but began to relay his report. "I didn't see the second shooter, the getaway driver, but I believe he was using a 9 mm Smith and Wesson 1911 Performance Center."

"How could you tell if you didn't see him?"

"I could hear it."

Heather nodded, impressed. "Okay, so the guy you did see?"

"He was approximately 170 pounds, Caucasian, about five-foot-ten, mid-twenties, and a sloppy shot. Used a Taurus G2c Luger. Definitely not a high-ranking professional."

"Low-level crook hired for a big job?"

"Isn't it your job to answer that?" Jason asked. Heather faltered, and he quickly continued, "From the way he told it, it was a much bigger job than they'd signed up for."

"How do you mean?"

"'I don't get paid enough for this shit,'" Jason said, using air quotes.

"What about the van?"

"No number plates, but it seemed to be some type of old Toyota that they'd sprayed black."

Heather nodded and scribbled, but before she could reply, Jason looked around, grabbed a business card from his pocket, snatched Heather's pen from her hand, and wrote down his number.

"I have to get back to everyone, but here's my number. Call me if you need any more information."

Heather took his card and her pen and handed him her own card in return. "Just in case," she said.

Jason pocketed it and turned to leave, but Heather called after him.

"Does your dad have any enemies?"

"Nope, but as you can probably tell, he has a lot of money, and that's pretty much the same thing."

"So you're thinking ransom?" Heather asked.

"It would be my main guess."

Heather looked past Jason to a woman wearing a blood-covered dress who was clearly waiting for him. "You go. Be with your family."

"Stay in touch."

"I plan to."

Something resembling a smile flickered at the corner of Jason's mouth before disappearing into the abyss of neutrality. He turned back to the beautiful woman, set in contrast against a backdrop of blood and death. It was like looking out at a battlefield, something Heather figured he must be used to seeing.

Heather walked back toward the driveway to call Tina with the bad news and warn her of the oncoming media frenzy. As she swapped her notebook for her phone, she took one last look at the scene and saw Jason wrap his arm around the woman in the yellow dress. They looked related, though she seemed too young to be his mother, and Heather noted that she was also not crying or panicking but doing her best to console those who were.

Heather thought that maybe her assessment of his cold demeanor had been unfair. In the face of ten dead bodies, perhaps the two weren't unfeeling. They were brave.

CHAPTER FOUR

THE DETECTIVE

T HE WITCHING HOUR STRUCK ON THE SWISS CHALET–
themed cuckoo clock, and a little man in lederhosen
emerged with his alpenhorn. His appearance was not
accompanied by the sound of a horn but instead was announced
by the more common bird call sound. This was undeniably disappointing. However, despite this glaring flaw, the clock still
ranked highly among Heather's recent garage sale discoveries.

She was conscious when the rhythmic chirps marked three
o'clock almost every night, but she was more than just awake
tonight. She paced the living room in increasingly speedy cir-

cles, slurping down black coffee and talking mostly to herself despite Gabriel's presence.

Her movements had become so frantic that he had joked with increasing concern about her wearing a groove into the carpet. Unlike Heather, Gabriel was usually fast asleep by this point. However, after the terrifying day they'd had, he found that sleep had been out of reach and showed up on Heather's doorstep just after midnight, confident she'd be in the same boat.

As usual, he'd brought a six-pack of beer with him, but it was all about coffee for Heather tonight, so he tentatively cracked his fifth one and moved to the window to smoke. Heather stopped pacing for just long enough to hand him a mug for the butt, each of her arms sporting a nicotine patch in preparation for the temptation her friend wrought.

"I thought you quit," she said.

"Not exactly. I'm allowed one if I'm drunk, or celebrating, or really happy, or really sad, or really stressed out, or—"

"So basically, every day of your life for any reason."

Gabriel shrugged and smirked. "At this point, yeah."

"Well, you'll probably need them in the coming days. It's going to get crazy around here. Luckily we don't have to deal with the FBI on top of the media."

"Wait, why is that a good thing? Surely we need all the help we can get."

"The problem is that they wouldn't be helping. They'd just take over and force me—and especially Jason—out. We deserve a chance to solve this ourselves and get justice."

"So why isn't the FBI coming? I mean, this is a big case. Seems like their sort of thing."

"Well, if you don't request assistance, and the murders or kidnapping doesn't involve the president or government officials or federal land, then it's essentially not their problem."

"Wait, seriously?" Gabriel asked, genuinely confused. "I thought they just sort of showed up in places."

Heather shrugged. "Sometimes they do, but mostly that only happens on TV."

"Huh," Gabriel said, looking mystified. "So what's the difference between the FBI and CIA?" He must've seen the weary look on Heather's face and quickly retreated. "I'll just Google it."

Heather chuckled and remembered that rural cops rarely tangled with the likes of the FBI and the CIA and that their inner workings, officers, and agents were as mystical as Bigfoot.

"Basically, one works domestically within the United States, and one works internationally and collects intelligence for law enforcement and the military," she said.

Gabriel hummed thoughtfully. "Are you sure you don't want to request help from the FBI? What if these guys hurt more people?"

Heather finally sat down, her heart pumping overtime, and cracked the last beer to take the edge off. She looked over at her corkboard, which was occupied once more after being empty for two weeks since she'd last solved a cold case for Julius. Two men in balaclavas were pinned smack-dab in the middle, illustrated to the best of the artist's ability based on the witness descriptions.

"They're not going to," she said.

"How can you possibly know that?"

"Because they only wanted Christopher Fleming. Everyone who died was just in the wrong place at the wrong time."

"What makes you think that more people won't be in the wrong place at the wrong time?"

"Because if they want to keep him hidden, they won't draw attention to themselves like that."

Gabriel nodded, lighting another smoke. "It would be pretty sloppy."

"And they are sloppy, but they're not idiots. They're going to make another mistake—I'm counting on it—but it's not going to be another mass shooting."

Gabriel furrowed his brow. "What if they already have?"

"What do you mean?"

"Before they showed up. What if they already made a mistake? I mean, someone in town must've seen them and their van. What if they asked for directions and showed their faces? Or stopped for lunch at the diner?"

Heather jumped to her feet and continued her pacing. "I mean, it would make sense. Sloppy criminals are going to be consistently so from beginning to end."

"So what do we do?" Gabriel asked eagerly.

Heather paced over to her laptop and began working on a profile for the van, using images from Google that matched Jason's description. She kept it simple, using four images of old, flat-faced black vans and listed off all she knew with her number at the bottom. She then did the same using the composite drawings of the killers and stocked her printer with a thick wad of paper.

After the printer spit out the first copy, Heather waved it around. "We're going to post these around town and see if anyone local knows anything."

"Awesome. I can go through the traffic cams after that if you want."

"We have traffic cams?"

"Gene got the funding a few years ago. We don't really use them much, but it helps sort out drunk drivers. Anyway, Tina has me on paperwork duty, so I can watch that at the same time."

"You angel," she said, clasping her hands together in prayer and striding toward Gabriel to grab his cheeks.

Gabriel laughed and tried to free himself from her coos and pinches. She was hardly kidding. Examining traffic cam footage was arduous at best, and she owed anyone who would do it in her stead a big favor.

"So canvassing tomorrow?" he asked, finally squirming away.

"Yeah. We'll put these flyers up and ask around, and I reckon before the day is out, we'll be flooded with calls."

"That's the thing about small towns. Everybody talks."

"And for once, it's a good thing," Heather said.

Gabriel looked at her doubtfully.

"Okay, admittedly, there's a little mass hysteria and a lot of gossip right now, but how often do we get dealt a perfect hand of cards?"

"Never."

"Exactly, and it's never stopped me from solving a case before."

Gabriel looked at Heather, bemused by her mania. "You seem very confident today."

"Glenville needs me to be. Jason too, even if he doesn't realize it yet."

Gabriel smirked. "Are you sure that Jason needs you?"

"What do you mean?"

"Come on. He's a CIA agent, and he's built like Batman."

"Just because he's CIA doesn't mean he's better than us," Heather retorted. "He just has nicer toys to play with and more intelligent peers."

"Hey!"

Heather shot him a withering look. "Not you."

"You need to be nicer to the squad."

"I am nice," she insisted. "I just can't help but think, what if my old Seattle squad had been with me today? Would we have been able to save some people?"

"Hey, a wise woman once told me to take my what-ifs and bury them out back in the dirt. I think it would be wise to follow her advice."

Heather smiled. "She sounds smart."

"She is. Sometimes," Gabriel teased.

Heather sighed and rested her head on her hand while sipping her warm beer. "I know I'm being harsh on everyone."

"You have been a little intense as of late."

"What can I say? I've got my groove back," Heather jested.

Gabriel didn't laugh. "Just be careful that you don't end up like Jason the robot… or worse, Julius."

"What's wrong with Julius?" Heather asked with a scoff.

"Does he do anything other than look at dead bodies and cry about his ex-wife?"

"You've only met him once."

"But I'm right."

"Now who's being harsh?" Heather asked quietly. "You know he's the most awarded forensic pathologist in the state? We should all strive for that kind of achievement."

"I thought you didn't care about awards?" Gabriel asked, looking around at the console table beneath the cuckoo clock that Heather had recently decorated with her varying awards and family photos.

"Maybe I realized my achievements mean something."

Gabriel hesitated. "All I'm saying is that you left the city for a reason. Don't let your nostalgia make you forget what that is."

Heather drained the rest of the beer and crushed the can before returning to her laptop now that most of the flyers had finished printing. It was time to flesh out the corkboard accordingly, and she decided to start with Dr. Christopher Fleming.

It wasn't hard to find a photo of him—after all, he had his own Wikipedia page, which she also printed out a section of to accompany the selected picture—and she couldn't help but smile at the man she'd never met. He had one of the kindliest faces she'd ever seen. Even more so than professional Santas and cookie-baking grandmas. She was admittedly surprised by how old he looked at only fifty, but his shock of white hair, thick spectacles, and laughter lines only made him more pleasant-looking. She also supposed premature aging came with the career choice of slicing open rich people on a daily basis.

Once his profile was printed, she moved on to Jason. There was only one photo of him that she could find. He was dressed in a suit and stood before an American flag with his jaw set and buzzcut freshly faded. He couldn't have been more dissimilar to his father, and it seemed strange that someone with such twinkly eyes could produce such an intimidating son. The photo led to his official CIA profile, which listed a few of his non-classified achievements as well as his educational background.

"Wow, he speaks four languages," she said in amazement.

Gabriel turned to her and pointed accusingly. "You're the one that thinks the CIA is better than us! You want to impress him."

"No, I don't. I just don't like being looked down on for being a small-town detective."

"Well, I, for one, am fine with being looked down upon," Gabriel said, rummaging around for more alcohol, which Heather was glad she didn't have.

"Really?"

"Yeah, don't get me wrong. I love what I do, but I like my small-town life and having days off and not ending up in shoot-outs every week. Imagine having to take down terrorists for your nine-to-five."

Heather nodded slowly; added the printouts of Jason, his father, and the van to her board; and joined Gabriel on the couch to look at it. It felt like something, but it was missing something. She stood again and tentatively picked up the list of victims and their next of kin's contact numbers. Her hands shook as she put the pin in, and her vision became bleary as she reread the list repeatedly, trying to memorize those who had lost their lives.

"Are you okay?" Gabriel asked.

"Yep."

"Okay. Well, in that case, I'm beat," he yawned.

"Yeah, me too," Heather whispered, though she didn't feel the same. The caffeine was still pumping through her system, and her heart was hammering. She removed the list from the corkboard, threw a blanket at Gabriel, and turned off the lights.

"Up at seven," she commanded. "We need to get these fly-ers out first thing."

Gabriel groaned. "That's like three hours from now. How about eight?"

"Six-thirty," she countered.

"Seven-thirty."

"Six it is. I'll buy you breakfast after we're done."

"Ugh. Fine. You know I liked you better when you were thirty-two."

"Good night, asshole."

"Night," Gabriel slurred, already half unconscious.

Heather crept toward the kitchen to pour herself another coffee, the list in one hand and her laptop in the other. There would be no two hours of sleep for her, not while the killers of ten were still out there with Christopher Fleming in their grasp.

CHAPTER FIVE

THE AGENT

AFTER WAKING TEN MINUTES BEFORE HIS USUAL FIVE o'clock alarm, Jason got up without disturbing Natalie and worked out in the fully equipped but underutilized gym for forty-five minutes. He finished off the hour by sitting in the steam room and then showered, shaved, ironed, and dressed. By six-thirty, he was ready to make himself useful.

His first objective was to clean up all of yesterday's party decorations and throw away any food that had been left out. Due to Kathleen's enthusiasm for hosting, this killed over ninety minutes. Yet by the time he threw away the last balloon at eight, everyone was still asleep, and the day stretched out long in front of him. So he moved on to another time-consuming task: prying the bullets from the walls and repainting and plastering the holes. This required a quick trip to the local hardware store, where he, fortunately, went unrecognized, and by eleven, the interior of Black Douglas was as good as new.

Then it was time to face the lawn.

Forensics had been surprisingly prompt and efficient the previous evening, and by dinnertime, Heather had cleared the scene for cleaning. She'd offered to send a crew over, but Jason had denied her admittedly helpful offer. Restoring his parents' pride and joy was something he needed to do himself, the same way he had rinsed his mother's hands clean of blood when he'd found her in the kitchen struggling with the smart tap.

He stood in the sunroom and looked out at the sun shining down on the congealed patches of reddish brown amongst the vivid green. He had a strong stomach but was glad to have delayed breakfast.

He attempted to wash away the remnants of death with the sprinkler system, but it did little good other than turning patches into sticky puddles. So donning a trash bag over his shirt, he grabbed the hose, unwound it to its full length, and blasted the gore away by hand. He pushed it off the yard and into the trees, hoping it wouldn't attract too many wild animals. The last thing they needed was a hungry bear patrolling the perimeter.

Once the job was done and the lawn was returned to the excellence of a bowling green, Jason finally stopped moving for long enough to eat. Muesli, fresh fruit, and Greek yogurt started him off, and then he made two slices of whole-grain toast topped with avocado and poached eggs. He ate it while standing at the kitchen counter staring out at nothing, and washed it down with orange juice.

He hardly tasted the meal. It was all cardboard to him this morning. He was far from a foodie at the best of times, but he liked what it could do for his body and his brain. If given the option, he would take a pill instead, but while scientists worked on that, he forced the grub down his gullet, knowing he needed to be on his A game.

After his stomach was satisfied, he brewed a black coffee with his father's coffeemaker. It was an overly-complicated device that cost more than most people's cars and, in Jason's opinion, wasn't worth the result. He was more accustomed to dumping instant coffee in the bottom of his mug, but what he cobbled together was drinkable, and he made his way to the veranda to look out at the untainted lake.

It was a beautiful view, and the morning breeze carried warmth on its breath as the sun bore down, but Jason hardly registered the temperature of the scorching coffee or the beams tanning his face.

Using their private, at-home-only phone numbers, he contacted his three closest friends and confidants at the CIA— Takahiro Nakamura, Bonnie Anderson, and Jessica Malloy— and informed them of what was happening and what he needed from them.

They already knew what had happened; watching the news was essentially a requirement for their roles. But despite their condolences, he could tell his request made them nervous. However, after some gentle pushing and a touch of guilt-tripping, one by one, they agreed to help him with his covert investigation.

Bonnie, who spent every day supporting officers and field agents—and essentially running the CIA with the other Directorates of Support—was the first to volunteer her time into looking into the killings and enthusiastically so. She could offer file access and help sort through information with her administration abilities and permissions. She was also friendly with various law enforcement agencies and was confident about also getting her hands on their files.

Takahiro—a Science, Technology, and Weapons Analyst— was hesitant but agreed as long as they were discreet. Jason promised that he would take the blame if any higher-ups found out that they were secretly investigating something outside of CIA jurisdiction. This seemed to comfort Takahiro, which was a relief to Jason as they needed his access to all the CIA technology more than they needed anything else, especially as none of the rest of them knew how to use it.

Jessica was the hardest to win over. She was a Paramilitary Operations Officer turned Field Agent and a tough nut to crack, but luckily, Jason knew just where to apply the pressure. A favor owed and a soft spot no one else knew about. After setting some boundaries about her time and abilities, she was in.

Operation Silver Scalpel was a go.

He thanked them profusely, taking extra time to suck up to Jessica. Her combat skills and tracking abilities would be vital once they closed in on these killers. Just as he was wrapping up the conversation with the three of them, a new call came through from an unknown number, and he hurriedly ended the call with his team to start a new one, much to Jessica's cut-off aggravation.

He expected an altered vocoder voice to come through, asking for ransom money, but instead, a young woman with a slightly raspy voice spoke.

"Jason Fleming?" she asked.

"Who is this?"

"It's Detective Heather Bishop. We met yesterday. I texted you. You sent me the contact details in return."

"I remember."

"Guess you didn't save my number," she joked, a little petulantly in his opinion.

"Guess not. How can I help you, Detective?"

"I have a lead on our killers."

Jason raised his eyebrows. "Really?"

"Yeah," Heather replied, unable to keep the smugness out of her voice. "The owner of The Black Bear Motel, Ursula Gromov, called me after I put some flyers up around town. The way she tells it, two guys in a black van stayed in her motel the night before last, though she only saw one of them. A lanky guy with brown hair."

"Any further description?"

Heather sighed. "Just that he was average-looking, though, as far as I can tell, it's who we're looking for."

"Any CCTV?"

"Unfortunately not. But even though she says the room has been cleaned, I've stayed at The Black Bear Motel before, and let's just say that my version of clean is not the same as Ursula's."

"So you think there might be DNA?"

"Maybe. Maybe not. But I think it's worth checking out before you leave town. CSI will sweep it once we've looked around."

"Understood."

"Meet in an hour?" she asked.

"I'll be there. Text me the address," Jason replied.

"See you then," Heather replied and hung up.

Jason had to admit that he liked the spunky detective—as challenging as she could be—a lot more than any other small-town law enforcement he'd met. Or any law enforcement in general. Though the FBI and the CIA didn't hate each other like they did in the movies, he had to admit their different approaches to investigation, jurisdictions, responsibilities, and opinions regarding their levels of importance caused a lot of butting heads.

He also recognized that if the FBI knew the CIA was sniffing around the case, they'd suddenly change their mind about it being of federal significance, so he was grateful she hadn't yet escalated the matter.

He thought it hopeful that Heather's determination came from the heart rather than pride or defensiveness. For now, at least, he was happy to have her on his side, and though he refused to get his hopes up about her "lead," he was retrospectively glad that his attempts to scare her from her own case had been futile.

He stood, considering grabbing another coffee before heading to the motel, when the squeals of two young girls echoing inside the house caused him to turn. His daughters, dressed in matching pink pajamas and fluffy socks, were running toward him at full tilt. He put his mug back on the table, squatted, and readied for impact. Once they were upon him, he scooped them up easily, balancing each on his shoulders and holding them steady with strong hands.

Natalie appeared in the doorway, looking tired and drawn but mostly fond. "Morning," she whispered.

"Morning," he said. "Want some breakfast?"

She shook her head. "No, I'm not hungry."

"What about these little monsters?" he asked.

The girls giggled and began to demand blueberry pancakes with increasing ferocity. With nearly an hour to spare, he was happy to oblige and carried the girls into the house. Natalie remained in the doorway, looking out at the water, as he placed Marie into her high chair and Charlotte on her big-girl seat.

Once the girls were situated and the ingredients were out, he wrapped his arms around his wife and peppered her with kisses, much to their daughters' disgust. He then led Natalie by the hand to the kitchen island, and as he cooked, he also made her a cup of chamomile, hoping she'd at least be able to consume that.

The smell of breakfast soon lured his mother from her bed, and she padded into the room wearing a white dressing gown and men's pajama set.

"Crap on a cracker. It's hot," she said, shucking the gown onto the floor and kicking it toward the wall with a bare foot. "What is it? Like eighty already?"

"Eighty-two," Jason confirmed.

"Wow. Well, I think we're going to have to go for a swim today. What do you think, girls?" Kathleen asked, rummaging around in a junk drawer for her menthol cigarettes.

Natalie shot her a look that said, "No swimming and no smoking inside," and Kathleen's grin faltered. The two got along okay most of the time, but Natalie had always found Kathleen to be too fun, especially for her age, and Kathleen, in turn, found Natalie to be a bit of a stick in the mud.

"How about we play in the sprinklers instead of the lake?" Kathleen asked as she moved toward the verandah, happy to compromise.

"Fine. I brought swimsuits," Natalie retorted with a forcibly happy tone. She didn't want to be the bad guy, which was an easy trap to fall into with always-fun Grandma in the room.

"Great! Now don't eat all those pancakes without me," Kathleen warned, pointing her smoke at the girls accusingly.

The girls giggled, Kathleen winked, and just as she was about to dip out through the door—cigarette in between her recently plumped and sculpted lips—she had a change of heart. She skidded toward the fridge with a flourishing spin—obtaining applause from her eldest granddaughter—and plucked an open bottle of champagne from the fridge pocket.

"Join me in the sun when you get the chance, Jason. Vitamin D will do you good," she said as she sauntered toward the sunroom instead of the lake, cigarette in one hand and booze in the other.

Jason frowned. His mother was fun, but rarely this "fun," and once his daughters had received their fill of food and attention, he headed outside with two small pancakes for his mom. He figured if she was going to day drink the blues away, she shouldn't do so on an empty stomach.

After putting the food down, he wandered through the house and onto the deck adjacent to the lawn. He pulled up a seat at the small two-seater table and watched as his mom sipped, smoked, and took bites in between the two former activities.

"Thanks, honey. Good job on the yard. Looks great. The girls and I will be able to have a nice frolic on that later." She paused to take a drag. "I could've done it myself, you know."

"I know."

"I'm not so old that I can't take care of you for a change. I'm still your mother. A mother should be the one to clean up these sorts of messes so her son doesn't have to look at them."

"Mom, you know what I do for a living."

She waved him off. "I know, I know. All the same, don't feel you have to worry about me."

"How are you doing today?"

Kathleen raised her shoulders and cocked her head from side to side. "You know, so-so. Bodies are getting shipped out today. Got a lot of funerals to pay for and organize."

"Pay for *and* organize?"

Kathleen shot him a sharp look. "Their deaths happened on my property because some bastards wanted to kidnap my husband. I owe them for inviting them."

"You didn't know that what happened would happen."

"But it did. And a lot of them are family. Now, I know you're tough, but don't get cold. It's not a good look."

Jason nodded curtly as if taking orders from an army sergeant. "Yes, ma'am. Do you need any help?"

Kathleen took a big swig from the bottle and shook her head as she wiped her mouth with the back of her hand. "Nope. Never do. All I need you to do is bring my husband back. Can you do that?"

"Yes, ma'am," he said again, more assertively this time.

"Good boy."

She flashed a bright smile and washed her large mouthfuls of pancake down with some more champagne. She'd be like this for a few days until she became too matted, unwashed, and drunk. Then she'd disappear into her room for an hour or two and reemerge as a new woman. It had happened before, a few times now, and Jason trusted her process.

He stood, kissed her on the top of the head, and told her he was heading into town. He didn't want to get her hopes up, so he didn't tell her what for, but she didn't seem to mind or notice much as he walked away. He looked over his shoulder as he reentered the house and saw her taut, hollow expression as she focused on the patch of grass where her aunt had died. Though it was near impossible, he forced his lips into an upward curl on his face as he returned to his daughters. He just hoped they wouldn't notice that the cheery expression didn't reach his eyes.

CHAPTER SIX

THE DETECTIVE

HEATHER SAT ON THE HOOD OF HER CAR AND BOBBED her knee in time to the hummingbird rattle of her heart. She missed the days when she could pass the time with a cigarette more than ever. Without them, everything felt too slow. Every two-minute delay became twenty, and every twenty minutes spent waiting felt like two hours. In this instance, the waiting was her own fault. She had run out of information to print and flyers to hang, leaving her to drift toward the motel fifteen minutes before the agreed-upon meeting time.

Wild, dark eyes darted around, examining the motel's exterior to keep her racing mind occupied. She'd never paid much attention to its nooks and crannies before. There had never been a reason to. It was a cheap place to sleep, and up until now, to Heather, that was all it was. She'd only stayed there once when pest control had informed her that her house needed to be bug-bombed for fleas, and though it had been far from a luxury resort—and the spare blankets had perhaps only perpetuated her pest problem—it certainly had its charm.

For starters, the complimentary breakfast buffet elevated it far above the world of roadside motels, and the cocktail meet-and-greets in the lounge were popular among older tourists—and older locals. Ursula herself, for all her sternness and rules, was a gracious and memorable host, and if her fur coats were any indicator, business was booming.

Sure, the utter lack of competition helped, but even if Glenville was a hotel hotspot, everyone would still choose The Black Bear. If you were presented with two places to stay—one generic and the other covered in wooden bear cutouts and painted to look like the seven dwarves' cottage from *Snow White*—which one would you choose? Heather was confident that every tourist with half a brain would choose the latter and be rewarded with a delicious cherry pie and mediocre White Russian for their troubles.

She was staring at the "head in the hole" standee of the Three Bears and Goldilocks when she heard a car pull into the empty parking lot. It was black, shiny, and seemingly three times taller than her Ford Granada. It screamed "CIA agent" just as badly as her mission brown sedan screamed "homicide detective." She couldn't help but chuckle at the juxtaposition as Jason parked beside her with pinpoint efficiency.

He hopped out of the car with his sunglasses on, and Heather gave him a small wave as he strode over. His face was even more unreadable than usual due to his hidden eyes, and once again, when he stuck out his hand, Heather innately flinched.

"Nice to see you again, Detective," he said.

"Same to you, *Detective*," Heather said, shaking his hand and hoping he didn't judge her jittery demeanor.

Jason cocked his head. "What are you talking about?"

"As of right now, you're my new consulting detective."

"Like Sherlock Holmes? Is that a real thing?"

"Not really, but most people around here take TV as fact, so no one outside the department will ever think twice about it."

"Whatever works."

Heather hesitated before asking, "You doing okay?"

"I'll be fine if this lead turns out to be something," Jason said curtly.

"Understood," Heather replied, knowing to leave that can of worms alone. "So… I've already spoken to Ms. Gromov. As you know, there is no CCTV on-site. Unfortunately, they also paid in cash, and she didn't ask for ID because they looked over eighteen."

"What about their names?"

Heather grimaced. "Kenny McCormick and Eric Cartman."

"I'm guessing you don't think those are their real names," Jason asked.

"Don't watch a lot of TV, huh?" Heather asked, receiving a blank stare in response. "They're characters from an adult cartoon show called *South Park*."

"Ah," Jason replied, clearly a little embarrassed.

"Well, at least it confirms their age. Anyone naming themselves after Cartman has to be a millennial."

"I already knew their ages."

Heather sucked her teeth. "Yeah. You did."

"So what now?"

Heather checked her watch. "Let's go look at the room."

Heather was starting to fear that she'd been overconfident about the lead and, in the same breath, was beginning to regret inviting Jason along. With no names, no footage, and no license plate, her faith in the motel was starting to wane, and as they walked to the room, she crossed her fingers that it wouldn't also be a bust. Because if it was, not only would she have dragged Jason away from his family for no reason, but she also stood to lose his confidence in her investigation before it had the chance to begin.

This is what you get for being cocky, she scolded herself. *None of this is about you. It's about getting justice.*

They walked along the row of motel rooms on the ground floor, heading toward the open door at the far end. Two young housekeepers watched them with intrigue while loading sheets into the cart. The bedding looked crisper than usual, the towels were neatly folded, the spray bottles full, and the women even wore gloves and hairnets.

"Crap," Heather muttered, her heart sinking.

"What was that?" Jason asked.

"Nothing."

Heather swerved into the room and began to search from top to bottom, starting with the doorframe itself. Jason followed her every step of the way, close enough that she could hear his steady breathing. The scrutiny made her palms sweat, and she was transported back to pop quizzes and teachers watching over her shoulder. Like Jason, she could never tell if she was doing a good job or if they were internally mocking her every move. Though his snort disguised as a cough when she checked behind a painting of a deer was a pretty good indicator.

The room was poorly lit, with two decently sized twin beds and a decidedly smoky aroma. There was a small fridge filled with overpriced water bottles that constantly buzzed, an ancient air conditioner that hacked up dust, a microwave from the early nineties, and a separate bathroom with a mildew problem. Despite this, the patchwork quilts, fake fireplace, and stacked log walls gave it a cozy feeling, and to Heather's dismay, it did seem to be cleaner than usual. There were vacuum marks on the carpet, the sheets were wrinkle-free, and there was a note of lemon and pine beyond the cigarettes.

Still, she persisted, and once all the most unlikely places were cleared, she moved onto cupboards and drawers. She had more hope for this stage but was only met with dust, dead flies, and a well-read Bible. Jason still lingered but was quickly losing interest and becoming increasingly distracted by his phone.

Trying not to seem frantic, Heather moved into the bathroom and suffocated the urge to tear the whole room apart. Jason watched idly from the doorway as she gutted the vanity table and tipped the freshly changed trash can upside down. When she lifted the toilet lid up and inspected the bowl, he cleared his throat.

"Look, Heather. We both want something to be here, but how about we call it a day? No harm, no foul."

Heather pushed past him back into the bedroom and began to move the furniture. Jason removed his sunglasses and watched Heather keenly as if he had discovered a new species of animal and wasn't sure whether it was a threat. Heather glowered at him as he refused to help her drag the armchairs, side tables, and chest of drawers around.

Her exhausting efforts were met with the discovery of more dust bunnies, bobby pins, and hair ties. She doubted the two young men would've used either, but left the furniture where it was so forensics could bag the items up.

Jason cleared his throat again. "It's been fascinating watching you work, Detective, but I think it's time for me to get back to my family."

"Just let me check one more place," Heather requested. "And then we can call it quits on The Black Bear."

"Deal."

Heather nodded, dropped to her knees, and blindly rummaged under the beds. When that also yielded no results, and Jason began to move toward the door, Heather disappeared underneath the left side bed. It wasn't as filthy as she feared, but it was cleaner than she'd hoped. From the look of the carpet, she figured the housekeepers likely vacuumed it once a week. There were chip crumbs, a penny, and a sprinkling of dust, but that was it.

Heather retreated and saw that Jason had left the room and was waiting for her outside. She held up one finger and scurried under the other bed.

"Heather, I'm going to go," he called out. "I'll be—"

Heather interrupted him by banging her head loudly on the edge of the bed, and she reemerged. "Ha!" she cried triumphantly as she waved around a small card.

"What is that?" Jason asked, removing his sunglasses and squinting.

"*This* is a loyalty card for… a café in Portland called Sunshine Sally's. Whoever it belongs to is a regular and is only one stamp away from a free drink."

"Okay."

"*So...* that means whoever took your father lives in Portland."

"How do you know it belongs to the kidnappers?"

"Well, from the look of things, no one has vacuumed under the bed for a week, though I'll check with the cleaners to confirm. That means that this card either belongs to our killers or the people who stayed before them. I'll check the log and ask Ursula to give me the contact details of the guests who stayed here within the time frame of the last under-the-bed cleaning session. Then using the process of elimination, I figure out who this card belongs to."

"And if it belongs to the killers, we've got our location."

Heather nodded, out of breath. "Yep."

"Huh. Well, color me impressed, Detective. You really left no stone unturned. Or, hotel bed, as it were And let me know what you unturn."

"You got it."

He paused thoughtfully. "I have no idea what you're doing in such a Podunk town, but thus far, you're proving yourself correct."

"About what?"

"Being a good detective. I'll even admit that I could do with your help. If you're interested, I've assembled a small team to help look into this—secretly, of course—and it would be beneficial to have someone on the ground investigating."

"I mean, I was going to investigate anyway."

"I know. This is more about mutual back-scratching. I need someone like you to report back to me, and you need me and my team because we can make your life easier. Technology, files, weapons, all at your fingertips."

"So all I have to do is keep you updated, and the CIA will help me solve this case?"

Jason nodded.

"Then I'm in," Heather said confidently.

"Great. Don't make me regret this."

"I won't," Heather insisted, her tone indignant.

With a flicker of what Heather had finally decided was amusement, Jason returned to his monstrous vehicle and disappeared behind the darkened glass. He peeled out of the parking lot with all the flashiness and skillfulness of a race car driver, and Heather watched until he was just a black dot in the distance before turning to the housekeepers and asking them about the beds.

They lied at first, claiming it had been cleaned that morning, but once Heather explained she was a cop, not a guest, they informed her that it had been six days since they'd cleaned under the beds. Timeline in place, Heather whistled as she made her way to the lobby to talk to Ursula.

Ursula had hosted cocktail hour earlier than usual on account of the tragedy, and it showed no sign of stopping despite going on hour three. This, fortunately, meant prying the logbook from her hands easier than it would usually have been.

The only other people who'd stayed in that room in the past six days were the Miller family, and with great relief, Heather saw that the area code of their phone number was for California. She called them all the same, just to thoroughly dot her i's and cross her t's for the day.

"Hello, Miller residence," came a chirpy woman's voice on the other end.

"Hello, my name is Detective Heather Bishop. I work for the Glenville, Washington Police Force."

"Oh, is everything okay?" the woman asked, her cheery voice darkening and adopting a waver.

"Don't worry, you're not in any trouble, we simply need to rule some things out for a case I'm investigating. Do you mind if I ask you a couple of quick questions?"

"Of course not. Please, go ahead, Detective."

"Do you recall staying at The Black Bear Motel in Glenville a few nights ago?" Heather asked.

"Yes. We were there for the nature hikes. My husband and I just love the outdoors."

"It's a great place for that."

"Yes. Gosh, I'm so glad we missed all the tragedy though," Mrs. Miller said before lowering her voice to a whisper. "Oh, is that what you're calling about?"

"Yes, ma'am. We believe the killers stayed in the same room you did just a few days later."

"Oh, gosh, how awful!" Mrs. Miller replied, her tone disgusted as if she might contract an urge to kill via close contact.

"We found a loyalty card under one of the beds and are just ruling out who it could belong to. Are you familiar with Sunshine Sally's Café?"

"Sunshine Sally's? No, I don't think so. Where is it?"

"Portland."

"Oh, then I've definitely never heard of it. I've never even been to Portland."

Heather wanted to punch the air and jump for joy, but instead, she thanked Mrs. Miller for her time and called Jason to tell him the good news. He didn't sound half as overjoyed as Heather felt, but she could tell there was some levity in his tone. As they wrapped up the call, the CSI team approached, and Heather resumed her seat on the bonnet of her hot car as they got to work.

After about forty minutes, the CSO—Lisa, one of the only locals who Heather truly trusted to do her job—approached. And even though the woman was wearing a mask, Heather knew it was bad news.

"How's it going, Lis?" Heather asked.

"Sorry, Heather, but the surfaces have been wiped clean, and even though there are plenty of fingerprints on the light switch and the lamp—"

"There's too many to single them out."

"Pretty much."

"What about the loyalty card?"

"Only partial."

Heather nodded and stood. "Well, keep going, and let me know if anything changes."

"Of course," Lisa replied.

Heather patted the roof of the car and dropped into her seat. It didn't matter if they didn't find anything else. Heather had gotten what she came for and more. They had a city. They had a favorite coffee shop. Soon the names and current location would follow, but for now, it was time to run a couple of errands and then spend the evening hunkered down with her trusty corkboard and faithful laptop.

CHAPTER SEVEN

THE DETECTIVE

HEATHER STEPPED BACK AND LOOKED AT HER CORK-board masterpiece as she called Portland's north precinct and asked for the captain. At the center of the display was a map of Portland and a red pushpin highlighted a particular location in the city's northeast. Attached to said pushpin was a strand of red string that led to a blown-up photocopy of the loyalty card from Sunshine Sally's.

Above the map were the composite drawings of the killers and the description of their van. Beneath it were the profiles she'd compiled on Christopher Fleming and his son, Jason. Finally, to the left was the list of victims, accompanied by photos and contact details. For once, there were no sleep-deprived ramblings or unreadable Post-it notes, just an organized compilation of the past twenty-four hours.

After a brief hold, the captain answered and introduced himself as Howard Lewis. A cursory search informed Heather that he was only thirty-one years old and the first African American to achieve the role in that particular precinct. What the internet didn't prepare Heather for was what a delight Howard was. He was earnest and somber in all the right places and insisted she call him Howie right off the bat.

Much to her chagrin, it soon became apparent that Howie was an admirer of her work. He rattled on about her lesser-known cases like a fangirl talking about her favorite pop star's B-sides. It was undeniably flattering, but Heather's cheeks burned as she tried to get a word in edgewise. It was understandable that the locals admired her, but the fact that her name had spread to decorated captains in other states made her feel uncomfortably akin to a celebrity.

When Howie finally got back on track, he promised her that he would put his best guys on the case. He praised them individually, naming names and listing accolades, clearly highly confident in his team's abilities. Between Howie and Jason's crew at the CIA, Heather felt on a roll like never before. Together they were going to catch these guys.

After she managed to wrap up the small talk and get off the phone with Howie, the next step was to call Tina. Heather hated talking on the phone, texting, or communicating in any manner that wasn't face-to-face. Yet in the past year, it felt like ninety percent of her job had become calling people.

Initially, she went straight to voice mail and immediately gave up to head to the station in person. Just as she put her phone into her pocket, though, the sheriff called her back. When Heather picked up, she was met with a deafening din and pulled the phone away from her ear. It sounded like thirty people speaking at once, and when the rabble didn't quiet down, Heather hung up and tried again to leave the house. Twenty seconds later, Tina called her again.

Third time's the charm, she thought before answering.

"Heather?" Tina asked.

"Hi. What the hell was that all about? Where are you?" Heather asked.

"I'm seeking refuge in the staff room. The media are here," Tina groaned, even though Heather knew she loved having her name in the headlines. Not to mention if she played her cards right through all this, she'd have no problem graduating from temporary to official sheriff come the November elections.

"Wow. Already?"

"Yep. It's a madhouse. Please tell me you've found something useful at Ursula's place. I'm sick of twiddling my thumbs in their face."

Heather wanted to remind her that it had scarcely been twenty-four hours but decided better of it. "Yes, but—and bear with me on this—you can't tell the media about this. I don't want these guys to know I'm onto them."

"Onto them how?"

"We have a location. At least we know where they live, and from what I've gathered about these guys, I think they're likely to return there rather than go on the run."

"Okay, I can work with that. I can just assure them that we're confident of a location. So where are they?"

"We're pretty sure they're in Portland. Near a café called Sunshine Sally's."

"Who's we?"

Heather hesitated, forgetting that Jason was not actually her consulting detective. "Me and Gabriel. I was running my theory past him, and he agreed."

"Okay. How'd you figure Portland out?"

"Loyalty card. Process of elimination. Long story."

"Anything else?"

"Not yet, but this a great start."

A knock banged on the staff room door, and Tina sighed. "It's a fine start. I have to get back to the mob, but how about you make yourself useful and go take a look at the deceased at Ellsworth's place? Probably won't tell you much, but it'll help me tick some boxes and allow the bodies to be buried."

"Sure, I can do that."

"Great. Good work today." The knock sounded again, and Tina groaned. "I'm coming!"

She hung up, and Heather patted her dogs good-bye before getting back in her car and heading over to the Ellsworth Family Funeral Home. She knew the way like the back of her hand, having seen Foster frequently over the past few months. Fortunately, up until now, it had never been for work purposes but solely to obtain some intellectual conversation and delve into his impressive collection of teas. Heather always looked forward to seeing the old man. He had stories like nobody else and, in telling them, had vastly expanded her knowledge of death and all that came with it. In fact, she now knew so much about embalming she was convinced she could take over for Foster if she ever fancied a change of career.

When she pulled up, the large front door of the Victorian Revival mansion was ajar as it always was when she arrived. Foster seemed to have a second sense about these things, and after one personal visit, she'd been permitted to enter his abode as and when she pleased.

She parked behind the beautiful hearse (reminded for the second time that day about how badly her car needed a wash), strode across the striped lawn, and stopped to smell the roses before entering the velvet-lined abode.

Just like that, she had stepped back in time, and it was as comforting as ever to travel to a time before her birth. Before the Paper Doll Killer, before Dennis Burke, and before yesterday's terrible events. She knew that the nineteenth century—and the latter decades to which the decor belonged—hadn't been any better than the 2020s regarding murder, but she had not investigated H. H. Holmes nor the Zodiac killer. Those crimes were different, intangible, so she allowed herself the comforts the past provided.

However, the luxurious kitchen and drawing room were not her destination today. The basement was, and it was a different story altogether. She'd last entered it seven months ago to examine the corpse of Roland Ellis, the missing mayor who'd died via acute cyanide poisoning during his plummet to earth. He'd died screaming, and though his face haunted her still, the reasons she hated the clinical cleanliness and all its sharp implements were much older than that.

As she stared at the little door, a key twisted in its lock, she started to think about that basement in Seattle with the little blue hand sticking out from the bathroom door and the plastic tarp on the floor. A blank paper doll had been leaning next to a box of tools accompanied by a pure-white puzzle piece, both marking the end of the game.

"Heather!" a deep, eloquent voice exclaimed.

Heather jumped and turned to see Foster Ellsworth standing at the top of the stairs.

His yellowing, piano-key grin melted into a somber expression. "I didn't mean to frighten you, my dear. Are you quite all right?"

"Yeah, I'm okay."

He drummed his long, gnarled fingers on the polished banister. "Cup of tea?" he offered.

"No, thank you. Maybe after."

"Of course," he said before hesitating again. "Ghastly business. Never seen anything like it. Ten dead. In our town. Three locals too." He shook his head sadly. "Just terrible."

"Have you—"

"Embalmed them? No, not yet. I'll get started after you leave, and then on they go to their places of forever slumber."

Heather nodded. "Let's get this over with then. Get them there as quickly as possible."

"Your wish is my command," Foster said kindly, descending the stairs dressed in a black-and-white suit that buttoned tightly at his liver-spotted, elongated neck.

Foster strode past Heather to open the door for her and swept out his arm to usher her in. Despite his hospitality, Heather's feet stayed glued to the spot. The basement was dark—the automatic lights untriggered by the lack of movement. She supposed this was a good thing. No horror movie moment here, but still, forcing herself forward felt like trudging through tar.

As she forced herself to the top step, Foster placed a hand on her arm and adopted a grave expression. "I must warn you, there's a young girl among them. She's badly damaged. Considering your history, might you invite the lovely Dr. Tocci down in your stead?"

Heather inhaled and exhaled shakily. "That won't be necessary."

She hesitated again, and Foster squeezed past her. "Well, at least let me enter first. I know the rule calls for ladies to do so, but considering the situation, this seems more chivalrous."

Heather nodded, and once Foster was halfway down and the lights turned on, she followed him into the basement. She realized his suggestion about requesting Julius's presence was a good one when the astringent wave of chemicals and embalming fluids hit her. It didn't smell foul, per se, but her sense of smell was tightly bound with memories, all of which were unpleasant.

She must've gagged unknowingly because Foster looked back at her sorrowfully.

"I'm afraid I finished work on a different body only an hour ago. The smell tends to linger. My apologies."

Heather shook her head. "It's fine."

"If you're sure."

Foster continued to descend the long staircase, glancing back at Heather encouragingly every few steps, and eventually, they finished the descent and entered the tiled room.

Three bodies lay in a row on wheeled steel slabs. From left to right, there was an adolescent black man, an elderly white woman, and a very young white girl. Heather's brain wanted to look away, but her eyes wouldn't stop staring.

White sheets covered their lower halves for modesty's sake, which Heather thought was a thoughtful touch on Foster's behalf. But she supposed he wasn't the same as the pathologists she had worked with. His job wasn't to slice, dice, and diagnose. He was a funeral director and embalmer. It was his job to make the dead comfortable.

Heather cleared her throat and looked at each ashen yet restful face. She pulled out her notebook and pointed to each body starting from the left.

"So that's Logan Green, Audrey Shepherd, and Susanna Barnes?" she asked.

"That's correct."

"Ages?"

"Twenty-six, sixty-two, and twelve, respectively."

"And the cause of death, I'm guessing, is all due to the gun-shot wounds."

"While I'm no Dr. Tocci when it comes to diagnosing death, yes, the catalyst of each death was the shooting. However, the causes of death vary a little among the three. Mr. Green died of blood loss due to his abdominal injury. Mrs. Sheperd was shot twice in her right lung."

"So asphyxiation."

"Pneumothorax," Foster corrected her.

"Right. And Miss Barnes?" Heather asked though she could see the answer written across the girl's forehead.

"Bullet to the brain," Foster said sadly. "At least it was quick."

It was a small comfort but a comfort all the same. "Did you know any of them?" Heather asked.

"Not the child, but Logan worked at the butcher's, and Mrs. Shepherd was the head librarian. I also arranged her parents' funerals some years back. I suppose she'll be buried with them."

"I've never seen any of them before today," Heather said apologetically.

"Not a big reader?" Foster enquired.

"Apparently not. And I buy my meat from the grocery store."

"Ah. Perhaps it's for the best that you didn't know them. I've heard tell that it can interfere with your particular job if you know the victim."

"It can. Does it interfere with yours?" Heather asked.

"No. In fact, I see it as an honor to be in charge of such an important transition for those I care about. I did my own father's embalming, you know. It seemed the right thing to do, considering he taught me everything I know."

Heather chewed her lip, imagining her own parents lying on the slab, blood bucket at their feet, and tubes in their necks. She thought about stuffing their cheeks with cotton, fusing their maxilla to their mandible, and placing plastic caps on their eyeballs. She shuddered involuntarily and realized she was perhaps overconfident about taking over the funeral home. It was much less painful to read about the processes in the medical tomes.

Foster placed a spindly hand on her shoulder. "It's only death, my dear. You'll understand when you're as old as me."

"I don't know if I'll ever be as old as you," Heather said. She repeated it back to herself in her head and spun around, her mouth open apologetically once she realized how insulting it sounded.

Foster chuckled warmly. "I don't know about that. You seem to be the scrappy sort. I'm sure you'll outlive us all."

"I've been getting pretty friendly with the reaper as of late."

"Well, you seem to be doing a fine job of outrunning him."

She looked back at the bodies and sighed. "Harder to do when he carries a gun."

Foster gave her a little squeeze. "Yes. It certainly is."

He removed his grip as Heather opened her notebook and stepped forward to inspect the bodies. She started with Logan Green. His stomach was a mess of sporadically aimed shots. And when she turned him onto his side—trying to ignore how cold his bruised flesh was—she could see that two of the three bullets hadn't left his body. Upon closer inspection of his front, she could see that the one that had exited through his back had pierced him at an extreme and odd angle, only clipping his organs by mere centimeters. Though the puncture seemed purposeful, it was clearly made blindly.

Mrs. Shepherd's wounds were cleaner, and though the two shooters apparently used the same ammo, she would guess these wounds were caused by the Smith and Wesson 1911 Performance Center and thus fired by the getaway driver. Oddly, there was another shot, too, embedded in the fat in her side. A non-fatal shot and a waste of a bullet. Heather blamed that one on the Luger and the man who'd failed to clip Jason during their shoot-out.

The little girl, Susanna, was hard to look at, but Heather forced herself to inspect the wound in her temple. She wondered if it had been aimed elsewhere—an adult's chest perhaps—or if these killers had indeed been happy to kill a child with a headshot. Heather hoped it was the former and that the guilt kept them up at night writhing, their skin covered in icy sweats and stress hives.

"What's your professional opinion?" Foster asked.

"That these guys had no idea what they were doing," Heather said, close to speechless by what she was looking at.

"Or at least one of them didn't. Whether he was panicked or just a lousy marksman, each possibility leads me to the same conclusion. That he's an amateur. Maybe they both are."

"I must say that would be my opinion too. The last time I saw bullet wounds of a similar variety was when I was in charge of a man who had been the victim of a burglary gone wrong. They had shot him in the dark while high on meth. Amateurs, desperate for money."

Heather nodded and put her notebook away. "How about that cup of tea?" she asked, turning to face Foster.

He didn't seem to hear her and despondently perched on a stool while looking at the bodies. "What has happened to Glenville?" he lamented. "Ten years ago, there was the odd crime, but never something like this. Now it seems with each passing year, the killing doubles. So much untimely death, so much darkness."

"I know," Heather whispered.

"Well," he said, looking up at Heather fondly. "At least we have you."

"Tea?" she prompted again, desperate to leave.

"Ah, of course," Foster said, getting to his feet and traipsing up the steps with his back hunched.

At least they have you, she thought bitterly as she continued to tear the dry skin from her lower lip.

It was hard for her to overlook the fact that her moving to Glenville felt like a catalyst. Sure, it could be a series of unfortunate coincidences, but she was starting to worry that it was more cosmic than that. If you'd asked her five years ago if a person could be bad luck, she would have said no. If you asked her today, she wasn't sure what the answer would be.

CHAPTER EIGHT

THE DETECTIVE

AFTER FOSTER HAD FINISHED GUIDING HEATHER through his photo album from 1979—primarily comprised of him and Ernie at various bizarre American roadside attractions—Heather drank the rest of her tea and excused herself. She was anxious to get back to work, and as much as he liked telling stories of his youth, Heather could tell Foster was too.

Deciding to use her time productively in the car, Heather looked up when Sunshine Sally's was due to close and, seeing that she had twenty minutes, called the number listed online.

"Hello, Sunshine Sally's," answered a bored-sounding girl with a terminal case of vocal fry.

"Hi, are you Sally?"

"Ma'am, there is no Sally," the girl droned. "That's just the name of the café."

"Oh, of course," Heather responded, feeling as embarrassed as she had when attempting to befriend the popular girls in high school. The drawl and the uninterested, flippant tone—it was all too familiar. "Are you the owner then?"

"Nope."

"Is the owner there?"

"Who's calling?"

"Detective Heather Bishop of the Glenville Police Department."

"Glenville? Where's that?"

Heather pinched the bridge of her nose. "It's a town in Washington."

"Okay."

"So is the owner there?"

The girl popped a bubble of chewing gum right into the receiver, waited a few drawn-out seconds, and then said, "Yeah."

"Can you put them on the phone?"

"I guess."

A scuffle sounded after that, and hushed voices argued until a new woman answered. Her voice was high-pitched, bubbly, and bright though a little out of breath.

"Hello? Are you there?" she chirped.

"Hi. I'm here. My name is Detective Heather Bishop. Nice to meet you."

"Hello, *Detective*," the woman replied loudly, addressing the girl in the distance with displeasure. "My name is Sally, and I am awfully sorry about the delay."

"Wait, your name is Sally? The girl who answered said there is no Sally."

Sally tutted. "That would be my niece, who's working here as punishment for breaking curfew. What her parents don't realize is that she's having the time of her life, and I'm losing business."

61

"I'm sorry to hear that."

"Oh, please don't be. How may I be of assistance, Detective?" Sally asked eagerly.

A true crime fan, Heather thought.

"I work for the Glenville Police Department and—"

"Oh. The shooting. I saw that on the news. How horrible."

"Yes, it is. And I believe you might have some information that could help me catch the killers."

"Me?" Sally questioned, her voice brimming with nervous excitement.

"Yes, ma'am. I believe the two suspects might be in Portland or at least from there. We found a loyalty card in their motel room for your café. It was almost complete. One more purchase before they're owed a free drink."

Sally gasped. "A killer customer?"

"Yes, ma'am."

"That's… wow. What do they look like?"

"That's what I'm hoping you can help us with. They were wearing balaclavas, but I'm wondering if our descriptions match any of your regulars and if you can tell us what their faces look like or if any names spring to mind."

"Sure. I'll try my best."

"Okay, they're both in their mid-twenties and white. One is around five-ten and of a slender build. The other is two inches shorter and more muscular. The taller one has blue eyes. Ring any bells?"

Sally hesitated. "I'm so sorry, Detective, but what you just described is seventy percent of my customer base. Do you have any more details than that? Hair color, maybe?"

"One has brown hair."

"Anything else?"

Heather cursed Ursula's bad memory. "I'm afraid not."

"Well, I'd love to help, but…"

"Don't worry about it," Heather replied. "Do you have an email address?"

"Sure." She provided an address with the same name as the shop.

"Great. I'll send you my personal number. Please contact me if anything comes to mind."

"Of course. I'll keep an eye out too, and if anyone who matches your description comes in, I'll send over some stills from the security cameras."

Remembering everyone in the city had security cameras restored a little hope, and Heather thanked Sally profusely for her time. "Thank you, Sally. That'd be extremely helpful."

"No problem, Detective. You have a nice night."

"You too."

Sally hung up, and Heather sighed wearily. She should've known the description would be a dead end. A generic and faceless man in a popular city coffee shop? It made perfect sense that nothing had come to mind. Sally probably saw four hundred skinny white guys every day, and judging from the pictures of the stunning woman online, they were likely all regulars.

Don't give up, she told herself firmly. It was still a good lead. It narrowed down their possible location to an incredibly small area of North America. Without that loyalty card, they could be in Texas or Wisconsin for all she knew. And though they may have fled to somewhere far away, their identities were tied up in those few blocks around Sunshine Sally's.

It's also only been twenty-four hours, the angel on her shoulder added.

But by seventy-two hours, your chances of finding him drop to almost nothing, said the devil.

Not if they want money, argued the angel.

If that is what they want, retorted the devil.

"Shut up, both of you," Heather murmured as she pulled into her driveway.

It was just after five, and she wracked her brains for anything else she could achieve today but came up blank. It had been a good day, she reminded herself again. She knew where they were from, where they'd stayed, where they'd likely returned to, whom they killed, and what type of killers they were. The deceased were on their way home, Jason had teamed her up with high-level CIA professionals, and both Howie and Sally were on the lookout for the suspects. It really had been as good of a day as it could be considering the dire conditions that had caused it, and it felt as if those were all the puzzle pieces this day was willing to spit out.

Still, it felt like a dour note to end on when the ball had been rolling so smoothly, but she promised herself that she'd occupy her evening accordingly. Research, research, research, and staring at the corkboard until something clicked. If that didn't work, there was always exercise to get her brain pumping and weave some of the loose strands together. If her dogs and her body were lucky, she'd decide on a late-night walk through the woods to clear her head and order some brain food from Sherwood's.

It always felt wrong indulging in comfort food or anything pleasant at times like these. Those ten people, that little girl, would never eat a cheeseburger again or watch trash TV under the comfort of a blanket, but she knew it wasn't wise to think like that. If she didn't turn her brain off, it would soon run out of battery. Gene had told her that a few weeks back, and she tried, failed, and sometimes succeeded in incorporating his advice into her schedule.

At least she could follow his gardening wisdom to a tee. Now there was an activity that didn't feel like an indulgent time-waster. It was nourishing, skill-honing, productive, and dragged her outside into the fresh air without the lure of nicotine. The periodic harvests also made for pleasant detours and rest stops when the tunnel to the light felt inordinately lengthy.

As she slunk inside, she received a text from Gabriel asking her to meet him at Sherwood's for a drink. As she had for the past few months, she quickly declined without any umming or ahhing. One drink at Sherwood's always turned into ten, and that certainly was a waste of time and brain cells.

Her dogs—who had taken to sleeping in her bed when she was gone—greeted her with melodic howls as she collapsed onto the couch. They skidded up the wooden hallway, finally gaining traction on the living room carpet, and fought to cover her in slobbery kisses. She laughed and struggled to shove them away.

"All right, all right. Walk time. Heard you loud and clear," Heather chuckled, pushing past the dogs and retrieving their tackles from the coat rack.

This triggered further happy howls as she clipped on their harnesses and leads and attached them to her hands-free walking belt. The three dogs—Fireball, Beam, and Turkey—comprised of a graying Pitbull, a grizzled Labrador mix, and a mutt of unknown origins. She'd adopted them simultaneously shortly after moving to town, glad to finally be free of her ex-husband's hatred of animals.

It had actually been Tina who'd signed the dogs over to Heather back when she'd had enough time to volunteer at the local shelter. Even though Heather could begrudgingly admit that Tina was a good sheriff most of the time, it was at that shelter, surrounded by abandoned animals, that she had really been in her element. Heather, who hadn't started working at the station yet, liked Tina a lot upon meeting her, and the two seemed to be hurtling toward friendship as they walked through the shelter.

After looking Heather up and down and assessing her strength and temperament, Tina led her to Fireball, née Harriet. Heather was sold from the first belly scratch, but when she looked into the pen next door and spotted the quaking bonded pair of mutts, she knew that the sassy Pitbull would not be the only dog going home with her. This triple adoption gave Heather cred with Tina for years but, sadly, did not last forever.

Maybe I should adopt another one, Heather thought, *and get bonus points with Tina for another three years.*

She opened the door, and as her three dogs pulled her out with enough force that she feared whiplash, she quickly changed her mind about making this trio a quad. Once they were deep into the woods and far away from the woods, Heather let Beam and Turkey run free but kept Fireball close to her side. The other two never strayed far, but Fireball was a wanderer, and when she did eventually come back, she was always covered in some form of smelly sludge. She didn't seem to mind that she could no longer run free and panted happily by Heather's side.

Halfway along the trail, Heather's phone buzzed in her pocket, and she prayed it was Sally calling her back post-epiphany. She was surprised but not altogether disappointed to see that it was Jason who was calling. She answered and heard a pair of young girls screaming in the background, which became muffled when a door was pulled closed. There was a creak of

65

leather and a rolling of wheels as Jason lowered himself into what sounded like an office chair.

"Hello, Heather?"

"Present," she said.

"Sorry, my daughters are having a pillow fight with Grandma."

"How are they doing?"

"Well, my mom is a master of distraction. I don't think the three of them have stopped moving for long enough to think about yesterday. My wife, on the other hand, is chewing her nails down to the bone."

"I know the feeling," Heather said.

"Huh, I figured you to be more of the 'can't stop moving type' than an anxious nail-biter."

"I'm both."

"That's reassuring," Jason replied, monotonous as ever.

"Hey, what can I say? Neurotics get the job done."

"If you say so. Speaking of the job?"

"Oh, um, I went to the funeral home."

"And?"

"Bleak," Heather said.

"Learn anything?"

"Luger user is a major rookie. Can't hit a target—moving or still—to save his life. His friend with the Taurus is a better shot but not by much. I don't think they meant to hit the little girl at all."

Jason sighed and took much longer to respond than usual, the sound of his daughters seeping through in his absence. "And the coffee shop?"

"Nothing yet. The description was too vague, but Sally was very cooperative, and she's going to keep an eye out for us. North Portland PD too."

"And your partner is going through the footage?"

"Yep," Heather replied.

"So what's next?"

"Honestly? I'm just waiting for something to fall in my lap."

"Well, instead of waiting for a miracle, how about you fly to Virginia with me tomorrow to meet the team? I'm flying back anyway with my family."

Heather didn't reply, so Jason continued.

"It would be good for them to know who's working on the ground for us, and it would be good for you to know who's providing your information. Due to the nature of this investigation, it's important to establish trust."

Heather hesitated. She knew Jason was right, but the last thing she wanted to do right now was fly across the country and abandon Glenville in the wake of its greatest tragedy. Not to mention she hated planes, and being in one for upward of five hours was not appealing.

"Are you there?" Jason asked.

"Yeah, I'm here. I mean, what if something happens here? Isn't my role being on the ground floor while you sit in your ivory tower with your futuristic gadgets?"

"See, this is why you need to come. You think I'm James Bond and—"

"Oh, do I now?" Heather laughed.

"What I mean is, your view of the CIA is warped. Come along so you can see for yourself. Plus, my family wants to meet the person who is going to get Grandpa back."

Heather hesitated again.

"Please don't make me beg you," Jason added. "It will be embarrassing for us both."

"Fine. I'll fly to Virginia. But I'm only staying one night."

"Fine by me. I'll buy you a first-class ticket and send a car to pick you up at nine."

"Oh, I'll just fly economy," Heather insisted.

"So you *are* always this difficult. Don't be a martyr. Let me buy you a ticket."

Heather relented. "Ugh. Okay."

"Have you flown first class before?" Jason asked as if he didn't already know the answer.

"No, Jason, I haven't. One ticket cost more than my car."

"Yeah, your car was actually what made me figure as such. And your phone."

"What's wrong with my phone?" Heather laughed.

"It has a broken screen and is six models behind, which I thought was impossible. You still have a Home button."

"If it ain't broke, don't fix it."

"But it *is* broken," Jason insisted.

"One man's trash is another man's treasure," Heather replied, barely repressing her laughter as Jason distanced himself from his phone to groan.

"So I'll see you tomorrow at the airport."

"I guess so."

"Thank you for your cooperation. I look forward to working together."

"Me too," she replied, not realizing he'd already hung up until she was met with dead air. "Son of a bitch," she scoffed in disbelief.

Heather turned around and made her way back to the house. It was time to pack and plan. Travel—and everything associated with it—was usually something she dreaded, but today she was grateful for the challenge to occupy the long hours ahead of her. This was not the type of trip where she could just chuck some basics in a bag and put on sweats in the morning. No, she needed to strategize. What she wore was vital.

This team that she was joining was comprised of observant, highly paid, well-educated professionals. The clearance rack at The Gap wasn't going to cut it. She was going to have to dig deep into her wardrobe for pieces of the past because tomorrow, she couldn't just be Heather, the small-town cop; she had to be Detective Bishop—the esteemed, decorated homicide specialist of Seattle.

It was time for a resurrection.

CHAPTER NINE

THE DETECTIVE

HEATHER SPOTTED JASON WAITING FOR HER AS THE pleasantly quiet driver pulled into the drop-off zone. He was as still and poised as the Queen of England's foot guards and wore an immaculate, monochromatic outfit. As if he couldn't look more like his occupation, his signature Wayfarers covered his eyes, a Bluetooth earpiece was in place, and his smartwatch was on his wrist. Passersby did double takes, looked around for the celebrity he must be guarding, and scrutinized Heather in turn when she exited the back seat.

Heather pulled her wallet out of her pocket as the driver popped the trunk with a button, but Jason was already way ahead of her. He swerved around her as she was struggling with the zipper, ducked into the passenger window, and paid before she could even calculate what was owed. He played with a black card, and she hurriedly shoved the crumpled bills into the bill-fold before he could see.

She succeeded just as he turned around and looked her up and down.

"Well, one of us is going to have to change," he said.

Heather glanced down at her clothing selection and real-ized that she had inadvertently chosen almost the exact same outfit as Jason was wearing. Black pants, white shirt, gray jacket. It was an outfit she used to wear to meetings in Seattle. Timeless, classic, bland.

She laughed sheepishly as she gathered her luggage from the trunk and tried to think of a funny retort. By the time she'd come up with something halfway decent, she looked up and saw that Jason had vanished. She looked around as she set her suitcase on the ground and swung her backpack onto her shoul-der, but sure enough, she'd been abandoned.

Through the front doors, she spotted him in the distance and shuffled after him as best she could, the wheel of her suit-case deciding now would be a great time to break. Cursing, she picked it up, the wheels and sharp edge of the fender repeatedly bashing and slashing at her thigh. Jason seemed oblivious to her struggles and easily pressed forward through the crowds as if also unaware of their meager presence.

His strong, confident stature made people move, but her struggle with her bags only made the mob want to trample her. They'd picked her out as a weak link, an airport newbie, and there was no right of way in this traffic jam. She watched Jason's stature, paused briefly to readjust her luggage, and tried to mimic his posture with her head held high. To her surprise, the sea began to part for her too, and she was able to catch up with him just as he disappeared down a passageway.

Now that no one was in her way, she jogged after him; but when he came to an abrupt halt, the added weight of her lug-gage compounded, propelling her forward. Fortunately, she put on the brakes just in time, and she narrowly avoided a nasty collision. Jason turned, that increasingly familiar faintly amused look on his face, and he gestured for her to drop her bags. To their left was a glass door and a sign that welcomed them to the Alaska Lounge.

"We're here," he said.

"Yeah, no thanks to you."

"You handled it, didn't you?"

"Were you testing me?" Heather huffed.

"A little. It's clear that you're a good investigator, but aside from you tearing that motel room apart, I wasn't sure about your physicality. Externally, you seem to be in good shape, but it's hard to tell with the police. Half of your kind are complete marshmallows."

"Not everyone needs to be an action hero."

"No, but you do."

"You're not going to make me run an assault course when we get there, are you?" Heather grumbled.

"Now there's an idea," Jason said wryly.

"I run four miles a day, asshole," Heather quipped.

"Impressive. Weights?"

"Sometimes."

"Up sometimes to three times a week. Shooting range?"

"Whenever I can." Heather paused. "And what about you? How much do you run?"

"Five miles a day."

Heather rolled her eyes. "Of course you do."

Jason exhaled through his nose in a manner that was almost a laugh and inserted a key card to enter the lounge. Heather glowered at him as he turned his back on her and gathered up her luggage again. A few steps through the door, Jason turned back, stopped Heather with a halt signal, and slammed the wonky wheel back into place with one precise thump. Heather lowered it to the floor and smoothly rolled it back and forth.

She nodded in thanks as they progressed into the impressive Alaska Lounge. It stank of luxury and exclusivity, a mix of leather and musk, and Heather looked around in wonder. The decor was in the mid-century modern style, which reminded her of the Warrens' amazing home before Dennis Burke had tainted it. It was disquieting in that way, but it didn't lessen her amazement at how glamorous the airport could be.

"Maybe I got into the wrong line of work," she said, half joking.

"Maybe you did," Jason replied.

He made a beeline for two women and two small girls who sat on a curved couch around an unlit fireplace. Heather recognized the older woman as the one who'd been covered in blood on the day of the shooting. All of them turned, expressing their happiness at seeing Jason with a variety of smiles, the younger woman's being the most restrained.

Heather increased her speed to catch up with Jason, and as he hugged the four, Heather stood awkwardly by the side. The older woman, who was obscenely beautiful, patted the seat next to her, and Heather awkwardly dropped down onto the red leather.

"Kathleen," she said.

"Heather."

"So you must be the woman who's going to find my husband," she said.

Jason's mother, Heather thought, finally placing who she was in the family. She still looked far too young, but upon closer inspection, Heather noticed the subtle facelift scar behind her right ear.

"I'll certainly try my best."

Kathleen waved her off. "Oh, bullcrap. You sound just like my husband. So modest."

Heather noticed the primly dressed woman, who she now placed as Jason's wife, staring daggers at his mother for cursing, something she didn't seem to notice or was purposefully ignoring.

"Better to be modest than overconfident," Heather replied.

"I don't know about that. I think I've been overconfident my entire life, and it's worked out pretty well. Maybe you should try it sometime."

"I'll think about it."

Kathleen cackled. "No, you won't. You're you till you die. I can tell. I bet your husband is the overconfident sort. Opposites attract and all that."

"He was," Heather agreed. "And they do."

Jason's mother clapped a hand to her mouth, and Jason's wife's displeasure greatened.

"Oh, I'm so sorry."

Heather flushed and waved her hands. "No, no. He's not dead. We're just divorced."

"Well, still... Shows me right for being overfamiliar," Kathleen said, smacking the back of her hand. "That's over-confidence for you. Though, like I said, opposites attract, so I reckon we'll get on just fine."

Heather could only offer a polite smile. "I'm sure we will."

Kathleen looked around. "Well, as my son seems to have no interest in introductions, these three are Natalie, Charlotte, and Marie. Say hello, girls."

Jason's daughters waved shyly, and Heather smiled and whispered hello. Natalie offered a strained simper and went back to whispering to Jason.

Kathleen tutted. "Right, Heather, I think these four have heard enough from me for today. So how about we go get a drink and get to know each other?"

Heather wanted to mention that it wasn't even midday yet, but one look at Jason and she knew it was highly recommended to comply with the request. For everyone's sake. However, as his mother eagerly jumped to her feet and squeezed past Heather, Jason grabbed his mother's wrist gently.

"Mom, remember that Heather is here on business. Please don't get her drunk."

"She's a cop, honey. A homicide detective at that. She's not going to get drunk off one little glass of wine. Are you?" Kathleen asked.

Heather looked at her blankly.

"No offense, but I have heard those in your profession like the bottle."

"None taken. The stereotypes exist for a reason," Heather said tightly.

"Hey, no judgment. Surgeons and ex-ballerinas are the same," Kathleen said with a wink. "Plus, you'll need at least two to face all those stuffed shirts at the CIA."

"Mom," Jason said sternly.

73

"What? I mean, Jesus, honey, but you intelligence officers aren't exactly a barrel of laughs, and if you step out of your bubble for a minute, you'll remember that you're also not especially welcoming to newcomers. Especially those who you think are beneath you. I remember your birthday party where your work friends met your college friends." Kathleen turned to Heather and gestured theatrically. "Disaster!"

Heather smirked as Kathleen linked her arm and dragged her upward toward the empty bar. She glanced back at Jason, who gave her an apologetic look before returning to his wife.

Kathleen released Heather, sat down hard on a stool, and spun around with her legs extended. Heather noted she wasn't wearing any shoes despite her beautiful, form-fitting sundress. Amused, Heather wondered if she'd already been drinking—a question that was answered when Kathleen whistled for the young bartender, who looked at her fondly and asked if she wanted her regular.

Kathleen shook her head and slammed down fifty bucks on the table. "I've had enough liquor for now. Two sauvignon blancs, please, and don't skimp on me."

"Of course, Mrs. Fleming," the bartender replied.

"Oh, and keep the change."

Looking at the drink's list, Heather calculated that the change would be three-fifths of the bill, which made sense why the bartender seemed keen on Kathleen.

"I must apologize for my son," Kathleen said, grabbing Heather's hand.

"You don't have to do that," Heather insisted gently.

Kathleen sighed as she let go to pick up her promptly served, frosty glass of wine. "No, I do. I have no idea how he ended up so rude."

"He's not rude … per se. Just straight to business."

Kathleen cackled again, a scratchy smoker's rasp on the edges. "Yeah, you can say that again."

"So he's not like his dad either?" Heather asked, sliding her glass of wine closer.

"Oh god, no! Christopher is even more delightful than I am," Kathleen enthused.

"That's hard to imagine."

Kathleen grinned and smacked Heather on the arm. "Oh, you, charmer, you. No, really. He's the life of the party. Everybody loves Christopher. The man has wit for days."

"Huh. I guess the apple fell far from the tree."

"Yup. And rolled down a hill. Don't get me wrong, I love that boy to death, but sometimes I wonder if we took home the wrong baby."

Heather smirked and sipped her wine. She looked at Kathleen and opened her mouth to speak, but as she analyzed the woman's face, she couldn't remember what she meant to say. It really was perfect. Almost unsettlingly so. Taught, lineless, poreless, plumped, and perfect. It was perfectly symmetrical while retaining uniqueness and character with her foxlike features and upturned nose.

"What is it, honey?" Kathleen asked, cocking her head.

"Sorry. It's just you look so young. You keep talking about Jason being your son, and it's not computing."

"Well, I wasn't thirteen when I had him, if that's what you're wondering, though I know it looks that way. Not to toot my own horn, but I'm looking good at forty-nine."

"I agree."

"Admittedly, I did have him when I was nineteen, but I have Christopher to thank for all of this."

"So he was the one that ... operated?"

"Of course! Who else would I let cut me open? My facelift, my nose, my fillers, my brow lift, my breasts, my tummy tuck, and my rear. He did it all."

Heather's eyes flitted around Kathleen's face. "He's clearly very talented. I almost couldn't tell you'd had anything done until ..."

"Until?" Kathleen prompted.

Heather tapped behind her own right ear. "The scar."

Kathleen looked as mesmerized by Heather as Heather was by her. "Well, that's a detective for you. Most people don't believe I've had anything done. My Christopher has a subtle hand."

"You must trust him a lot."

Kathleen patted her chest. "Oh, with my life. You know, I was the first face he ever stuck a syringe into. And when I looked into the mirror, I just knew he was going to be something great."

"Wow. You must be a great judge of character," Heather said, unapologetically buttering Kathleen up. "I was reading some articles about him. He's one of the best surgeons in the world."

"Damn right. That man could rearrange the spirals of someone's fingerprint if he wanted to," Kathleen joked.

"Did he have any enemies?" Heather asked, abruptly shifting gears after coasting.

Kathleen sipped her wine coyly. "Are you questioning me, Detective?"

"A little bit," Heather admitted.

"Great! Go ahead. I haven't spoken to a cop in twenty years."

Heather wanted to ask more about that but resisted. Instead, she repeated her question.

Kathleen shook her head. "Nope. None. As I said, everybody in the world loves my husband. My god, they love my husband. He lights up a room. He really does. He's witting and charming and never in a bad mood. I've never even heard him have a cross word with anyone. Not even people who deserved it."

"Okay, any money troubles? Debt collectors, loan sharks, that sort of thing," Heather queried, hesitantly testing the waters.

Kathleen, fortunately, didn't look offended by the question. "Not unless four million dollars in liquid, three houses, and no debt counts as money trouble?"

"No, it doesn't."

Kathleen looked thoughtful as she drained her glass. "Though I will say that although everyone we know loves Christopher, fame and wealth can come at a cost."

"What do you mean?"

"Well, there's a lot of people out there who need money, honey. Most of them don't kill ten people to get it, but there are all sorts of freaks in the world. I'm sure you've seen your fair share."

"Do you think someone could be targeting him because they've seen him on the news?"

"Or seen his face in magazines or his book on the bestsellers list. They'd also know that a surgeon probably isn't expecting something this like unlike all those poor actors with stalkers are. He's rich, easy to track down, but not famous enough for a security detail."

"So you're expecting a ransom."

"I'm hoping for a ransom. At least I can pay that, and this whole mess will be over."

Heather nodded and continued to drink. After a little more stilted conversation about Christopher, which Kathleen was clearly growing anxious about, Heather relinquished control and let Kathleen order another glass of wine and take command of the chitchat. The alcohol was going straight to Heather's head on account of her newly low tolerance, but as Kathleen reeled off anecdotes, Heather relaxed, pretending she was merely having drinks with an old friend instead of a stranger whose husband she was in charge of finding.

CHAPTER TEN

THE SURGEON

2018

CHRISTOPHER STARED AROUND AT HIS NEW OFFICE and leaned back in his chair. Though costly and inconvenient, the renovations had been worth the wait and more. The room was transformed beyond recognition, and if it wasn't for the familiar sounds of the same nurses chatting in the hall, he'd have thought he was in an entirely new building.

When he'd first opened his own private practice, the building had been clean and, above all else, functional. However, it had also been dated, dingy, and a little worn around the edges. A lick of bright white paint and brand-new linoleum fixed most of the glaring issues, as did the tasteful wall art and the pack of pretty nurses in flattering powder pink scrubs.

However, as everywhere else in the building advanced into the modern era on his dime, his office was left behind. This was his doing, of course. When in business of any kind, there were always priorities to be had. The first impression was crucial, the private rooms and surgical suites even more so.

Still, he'd always felt slightly embarrassed when his potential clients entered his stark, beige office. It made him feel less like an award-winning surgeon and more like an '80s principal about to award two weeks of detention, and he knew his wealthier clientele were put off by the drab offerings.

That was to be the case no longer. Not with his Japanese minimalism-inspired feng shui paradise. There were bunches of bamboo adorning the corners and a small water feature pressed against the wall, situated beneath a painting of snowy mountains. A *shoji* room divider gave patients privacy while they changed, a humidifier pumped out the scent of sandalwood and jasmine, and the dark teal walls were decadent but cozy.

After four weeks of using a separate, even drabber office, his was finally ready for the public. He straightened his bronze nameplate on the opposite edge of his desk and checked his schedule for his first patient. Looking at today's schedule, he noticed the date in the top right corner: June 12, 2018.

"Crap," he muttered, bolting upright and rolling his chair closer to his computer.

He and Kathleen were hosting a family dinner party tonight with Jason and Natalie, and though Kathleen usually micromanaged every detail of such events, this time she'd put Christopher in charge of flowers and desserts. He hadn't ordered either. He manically opened tabs, searching for flower and cake delivery places that offered same-day delivery. Just as he clicked on the first tab, he received a knock at the door.

"Come in," he called out, straightening up and composing himself.

In his panic, he'd forgotten to check who was on the other side and tried to recall the names on the spreadsheet as a young man entered. He was likely in his mid-thirties, handsome, and bore a grin that revealed him as the easy type of patient. The young man released a low, prolonged whistle as he looked around the room.

"Well, this is more like it!" he exclaimed, slapping his thigh, his Southern accent thick and unexpected.

Christopher chuckled. "Well, I'm glad you like it, though I'm not sure what you mean by 'more like it.' Have you been here before?"

"No, no, Dr. Fleming. I have never had the pleasure. As it turns out, you are an awful tricky man to get an appointment with. So, unfortunately, I was forced to resort to seeing some other highly recommended surgeons across the country. The thing is, when I walked into their offices—" the man paused to shake his head— "I hate to be rude, but I could tell that they were not the type of men I'd want carvin' into me. A man has to have standards, you know? And you can tell a lot about a man from his office. Yours tells me that you're a man of style." He stopped again to gesture up and down across his suit and around the room. "As you can see, I can relate."

Christopher followed the man's gesture. He wore a well-fitting three-piece suit in camel-colored plaid, a pale blue shirt, and a dark-blue tie. It looked expensive, and the color scheme emphasized his floppy blond undercut and sapphire eyes. He was stylish, yes, but he was also the best-looking man that had ever sat across from Christopher in his office—at least pre-surgery.

The man strode forward and extended his left hand, flashing a diamond-encrusted Rolex that put Christopher's admittedly costly watch to shame. Christopher suspected, from the man's loose grip, that he was, in fact, right-handed but had been keen to show off his watch. As juvenile as this tactic was to Christopher, it at least reassured him of his newest patient's financial situation.

"Clarence Dixon Jr. is the name," the stranger said.

"And what can I do for you today, Clarence?" Christopher asked, quickly shaking the man's hand, minding that he kept his wrist turned away from Clarence's aspersions.

Clarence grinned and sat in the opposite chair, never breaking eye contact. "I want to talk to you about facial reconstruction surgery."

80

Christopher hesitated, once again looking at Clarence's perfect, symmetrical features. Hollow cheeks; a defined jaw; a diamond-shaped face; high, arched brows; and flawless, unmarred skin.

"What kind of face reconstruction?" Christopher asked.

"The whole damn thing, Doc," Clarence effused. "I want you to tear my foundations down and build 'em back up again."

"I'm afraid I don't understand."

"I want you to give me a brand-new face," Clarence said, pointing a finger gun at Christopher's chest and then back at his enviable countenance.

"Mr. Dixon."

"Clarence, please."

"Clarence. Not only is that not a surgery I would recommend to anyone, but from a medical standpoint, you have a near-perfect face."

"Aha! *Near* perfect. See, how's about perfect? Going the whole nine yards. Complete renovation."

"I ..." Christopher stuttered.

"Well, how's about doing something just to see if it can be done? Surely you're just as interested in the challenge."

"I'll admit it's an intriguing prospect," Christopher mused kindly, wondering whether he should press the big red security button that resided on the underbelly of his new desk.

"Honestly, Doc. I'm bored."

"You're bored ... of your face?"

"Hell yeah, I am. I'm surprised more people don't get bored of their faces. I've been staring at mine for damn near three decades. Surely you're bored of yours?"

"I think about other people's faces far too much to pay my own any mind."

"Well, think about your office instead then. I can tell you've 'had it done,' so to speak. And maybe it looked fine before and had some nice features, but you knew it could be so much better than just okay."

"Respectfully, your face is a lot nicer than this office was."

"Well, that's mighty sweet of you, Doc. But it's not going to change my opinion."

Christopher tented his hands. "So what exactly is it that you want to be done?"

Clarence's grin widened, his eyes lighting up. "Well, I'll tell you. I want a straighter, narrower nose. I want more prominent cheekbones and a sharper jaw. I need all of my moles removed. My smile could do with a few more kilowatts. Oh, and I want the shape of my eye entirely altered."

Christopher cleared his throat. "Altered how?"

"They're too damn round. I want… what do you call it… almond? Yeah, I want them almond. And instead of these sad clown edges, I want them turned up like a cat. Less eyelid too. Something sleeker and less childish."

The changes were giving Christopher pause. Though he was faithful in his abilities, these extreme and numerous requests were begging for a botched situation akin to the infamous "Catwoman." It was too much to change at once, and it was clear that the man in front of him—put together and charming as he was—desperately needed a psychiatric evaluation, not a scalpel.

"I believe that's possible," Christopher said. "But—"

"That's what I like to hear!" Clarence said, ignoring the *but*. "I just knew you'd be the man for the job."

"Now, I'd like to clarify. I'm saying it's possible. However, it would be a very costly surgery, not to mention a long one with a difficult road to recovery."

"Not a problem."

"I'm talking extremely expensive. Six figures."

Clarence chuckled. "As I said before, that's not a problem."

"Not to mention the ethical issues."

Clarence waved him off. "Psh. Ethics schmethics."

Christopher furrowed his brow, bemused. "I'm curious. What is it that you do, Clarence? You mentioned that you're just shy of thirty, and you come in here with a watch that costs more than my first home and a suit that probably costs more than F-cup breast implants."

"Oil," Clarence said simply. "Good ol' Texan oil."

"Huh. So you're Dixon Oil. I've heard of that."

"Flattered. So how about it? Can we schedule a date?"

Christopher pawed at his face. "I—"

Clarence held his hands up. "Okay, okay. I can tell you're still unconvinced, so how about we continue this discussion over dinner tomorrow? I've heard Marcel's is good. Great even."

"It is."

"Well then. Come on. My treat."

"It wouldn't be very professional for a doctor and a patient to go to dinner together."

Clarence whistled again. "You are a tough nut to crack. Phewee. Okay, how about we think of this as less of a doctor-patient relationship and more like a business exchange. You have a service I wish to purchase for a large amount of money. Right?"

"I suppose."

"Okay then. Let me woo you as I would any other business partner."

Christopher hesitated. "Okay. We can go to Marcel's. The owner is a close friend from high school, and it's been too long since I've seen him. However, that doesn't mean I'll change my mind about recommending the surgery."

"Deal, but before I lay down on this, I'm going to throw this out there and see if you catch it. How about, whatever you'd charge for something like this, I pay double?"

Christopher scratched his beard. "Now, that *really* wouldn't be ethical."

"Oh, who gives a flying crud? Surely there's something you want. A new vacation home? A boat? A car? A trip to Cancun? Come on, tell me what you want."

Without thinking, Christopher's mouth answered for him. "I want to buy my son a house. He and his wife are expecting their first child. My first grandchild."

"Okay. Sold. I'll buy that house for you. Pick out a place, and I'll wire you everything you need, down to the cent, but only if you do exactly as I ask."

A knock sounded at the door, and Christopher lowered his voice. "Let's continue this conversation at Marcel's. Book the wine cellar room so no one can hear us talk."

Clarence stood enthusiastically and saluted. Christopher mirrored him without the latter flourish, and the pair shook hands again—this time with their rights.

Clarence made his way to the door and turned back. "Expect a car at your home at seven o'clock sharp tomorrow. A black sedan. He'll honk twice."

"Don't you need my address?"

Clarence paused, his face twisted in amusement. "See you tomorrow, Dr. Fleming."

Clarence pressed the green button by the door to unlock it, and the head nurse, Marie, stumbled in and flushed with embarrassment as she walked straight into Clarence.

"Oh my gosh, I'm so sorry!" Marie exclaimed, her mascara-laden eyes wide.

"Don't worry, ma'am," Clarence insisted before inhaling. "My, don't you smell nice? Is that Chanel's Coco Mademoiselle Intense?"

"It is," she stuttered.

Clarence nodded toward Christopher. "What did I say? This is a honey pot of taste and luxury."

Clarence gave a slight bow before ducking through the cracked door.

Once he was gone, Marie turned to Christopher. "Who the hell was that?"

Christopher shook his head in disbelief. "I have no idea."

Marie hummed, looking over her shoulder. "Well, your wife is on the phone. She wants to know if you want roses or tulips and if you think Natalie would prefer cheesecake or I brûlée."

Christopher sighed with relief, rolled, and closed his many tabs. "Tell her white roses and vanilla cheesecake."

"Will do. She also says you'll need to pick her dress up from the dry cleaner on the way home and that she put the ticket in your coat pocket before you left today."

"Thank you, Marie," Christopher said, eternally grateful for all the organized women who kept his chaotic life in check. He lowered his voice. "Please ensure Mr. Dixon doesn't wander around the building."

"Was that the guy who just left?"

"Yep. He's an odd duck. I have a feeling he might... linger."

"I'll keep an eye out."

"Thank you, Marie."

Once Marie was gone, Christopher rolled around the room, thinking hard. Natalie was due in six months. If he could perform Clarence's surgery in the next few weeks and acquire the money promised, then he'd have plenty of time to purchase the house before the baby arrived. They'd even have time to paint the nursery if everything went to plan.

As shady as Clarence's request seemed, and even though his conscience was screaming at him, Christopher had never been an idiot, and he knew it was far too good of an offer to pass up.

CHAPTER ELEVEN

THE DETECTIVE

BY THE TIME THE FIVE-HOUR FLIGHT FROM SEATTLE TO Washington, DC was finally coming to an end, Heather could hardly keep her eyes open. The large glasses of airport wine had caught up to her, and the numerous complimentary coffees had little effect on her alertness. All of a sudden, she was back in Seattle, nursing a flask of whiskey at work and trying to push her memories anywhere else. She didn't want to move, and at first, she struggled to remember how she ever operated while constantly hungover.

Then, as Heather's yawns had turned from occasional to consistent during the last hour of the flight, Kathleen had scraped the bottom of a bottle of red. She seemed completely fine, energetic even, and it was then that Heather remembered her old secret. Stay a little drunk all the time, and the aftershock would never catch up to you.

It was hard to tell if Kathleen was a full-time alcoholic. Though her tolerance was clearly astronomical, this behavior also seemed understandable in the wake of such a tragedy. Everyone had to cope somehow, and even though she was as withholding with her emotions as her stoic son, it seemed she required an extra something to stay in that state.

She wasn't alone. It was a pattern that Heather was familiar with and noticed even more now that she was on the other side of rock bottom. Gene, Beau, Nancy, and even Gabriel, to some degree. Whatever vice people had—whether it was gambling, drinking, smoking, or binge eating—exacerbated in the face of trauma.

In that regard, Jason was a breath of fresh air and a complete enigma. Heather knew he must have something that helped him cope, but whatever it was, it was a mystery. Maybe he was a meditator—an idea that made her smirk—or perhaps a sense of purpose was enough to keep him from falling apart. Now there was a concept that was elusive to Heather. To be so grounded, so sure you're doing the right thing, and so in control, was incredibly enviable. While Jason was safely in his bunker, she was being knocked around by the storm, unsure of how she got there or where she would be flung to next.

Today, at least, she knew where she was landing, and upon doing so, Heather followed Kathleen like a puppy through security, catching odds and ends of a story about Kathleen's worst celebrity encounter. Jason trailed behind with his family but kept a firm eye on his mother, assessing the area for potential drunken disasters. Fortunately, they made it through, and when two cars pulled up and Jason said goodbye to his family, Heather realized there would be no unpacking her suitcase in a guest room. They were going straight to the CIA.

The CIA headquarters—otherwise known as the George Bush Center for Intelligence—was a mere twenty-minute from the Washington, DC, airport. The drive went by in a flash after such a lengthy plane journey, and before Heather knew it, they reached the security checkpoint. This one was more intense than it had been at either airport, but Jason quickly procured Heather a guest pass lanyard with little back and forth.

The headquarters were comprised of several functional buildings made up of pale concrete and rows of narrow rectangular windows, some of which were tinted seafoam green. The size was admittedly impressive, but the iconic structures weren't as flashy as Heather had expected. This made sense when a quick search informed her that the last major renovations had been done in the '90s.

She was internally embarrassed to admit that she'd been taken in by action blockbusters and had thus been expecting something less practical and more superhero movie. In her mind's eye, she'd pictured swathes of glistening white, surrounded by supercars and gadgetry. Instead, it looked like the world's most secure high school. At least it was easier to pretend like she belonged.

"You're not impressed," Jason said, twisting to look at Heather in the back seat.

"No, I am," she insisted, an unsaid *but* at the end of the sentence.

"Heather. I am a US Intelligence Officer. I know when someone is lying."

"Sorry. I think I just expected it to be …" Heather waved her hand lackadaisically.

"Newer? More like a spy movie?"

"Yeah. A little more James Bond and Tony Stark, and a little less … community college."

For the first time ever, Jason barked a loud laugh. He looked at her in disbelief and shook his head. "Ouch."

"Hey, you told me not to lie."

"You could soften the blow."

"Well, if it's any consolation, it's nicer than the FBI headquarters. Better a community college than a prison."

Jason snorted. "Now you're just brown-nosing."

"No, seriously. That place sucks, and it's impossible to find parking."

"Yeah. That's definitely a problem we don't have."

Jason and Heather looked out at the massive expanse of parking. It was so immense that in the bright midday light, Heather could hardly make out the edges of it. Cars and windows glared at her, and she wished that she'd brought sunglasses.

"Okay, let's go meet the team," Jason said.

"Cool."

"Leave your luggage in the bag. Joe here will drive us home too."

"Am I staying with you guys?"

"How would you feel about staying with Mom instead? She seems to really like you and—"

"Sold."

A corner of Jason's mouth flicked up. "Don't get too drunk though."

"Don't worry, I'll turn in early."

"I appreciate you humoring her," Jason said as they strode into the building and crossed the marble CIA logo embedded in the floor.

"I wasn't, really. I enjoyed talking to her."

"Great. Well, once this is over, if you're looking for a new line of work, I'm happy to pay you to visit her. She needs someone to talk to when Dad's busy, and God knows Natalie and I don't know how to."

"Hey, no need to pay me. I'm dying to hear more crazy ballerina stories," Heather said, staring around at her illustrious surroundings.

"Well, she's got plenty of those." Jason snapped his fingers. "Hey. Put anything in your pockets in the basket."

Heather snapped out of it where she was. Ahead were two armed guards, a metal detector, and a conveyor belt X-ray machine. She put her wallet, badge, and a tin of mints in the plastic basket and stepped through the metal detector with her arms raised. As expected, no issues arose, but it was like going through the shoplifting detection systems while leaving a store. A part of her always worried she'd unconsciously stolen something.

As they progressed, Jason frequently flashed and swiped his badge, opening up hallways and layers of the enormous central building. People greeted him as they passed, but no one seemed to pay her any mind. Everyone's lack of interest—from security to peers—made her realize that Jason must be a higher-ranking officer than she'd first assumed. As long as she was with him, everything was fine.

On the sixth floor, after a seemingly endless amount of hallways, stairs, elevators, and doors, they reached a white wooden door with "Room 612—Board Room" written on its dull plaque.

Jason opened the door, and they stepped inside. Like the rest of it—excluding the lobby—it wasn't much to look at. Wooden paneled walls and dated carpet lined the room, and at the center was a long, glossy table surrounded by comfy-looking leather chairs. A small desk was propped beside a smart board, and a projector was at the far end. It looked like every board and meeting room she'd ever been to. An unimportant room in a tucked-away recess, perfect for a secret meeting.

Despite everything she'd seen thus far, she had still anticipated an internally illuminated circular desk with matte glass tops that underlit essential faces. Worst of all, she'd been picturing holograms and enormous touchscreens, a thought she dared not mention to Jason for fear of further humiliation.

Instead of any of that, a group of three well-dressed people around her age was gathered around the table, using Toughbooks that were certainly expensive but nothing Heather hadn't seen before. Two of them looked up as Jason shut the door behind them, and one—a decidedly feline-looking red-headed woman in a blue pantsuit—kept typing.

"Everyone, this is Detective Heather Bishop," Jason said.

"Hi," Heather said with a slight wave, wishing she sounded half as commanding as Jason had.

"Heather, this is Bonnie Anderson," Jason informed her, gesturing to the woman nearest to the door.

"Hi, Heather, it's so nice to meet you," Bonnie enthused.

"Likewise," Heather replied.

Bonnie beamed, and her expression was contagious. She had a slender but round face, dark skin, elegant stature, and cropped-short, curly brown hair. She wore a silk blouse, blazer, pencil skirt, and low practical heels, all of which looked expensive without advertising the fact.

"She's our Directorate of Intelligence," Jason continued.

"Sounds fancier than it is," Bonnie said. "I'm basically admin. If you need a file or contact details, I'm your girl."

"She keeps us all afloat," said the dark-haired man sitting beside Bonnie.

"And this is Takahiro Nakamura," Jason said.

Takahiro raised a hand. "Hi. I'm one of the many resident science, tech, and weapons nerds. If you need to use anything more complicated than a microfilm reader, I suggest you come to me. For example, if you need to set up cameras somewhere, I'll give them to you. You want night goggles? Hey, me again."

"Great. Thank you," Heather said. "As you can imagine, my precinct doesn't have much in the way of state-of-the-art equipment."

The red-headed woman snorted and finally looked up. "I'll bet," she said dryly.

The others pulled a face, and Jason sighed. "Heather, this is Jessica Malloy, Paramilitary Operations Officer turned Field Agent."

"Impressive," Heather replied.

"Yeah, it is," Jessica retorted. "Which is why I should be on the ground, not you."

"Jessica, we've been through this," Jason lamented. "Heather is on the ground because she won't attract suspicion. Not to mention she's the first one in this team—yes, I said *team*—to find a lead."

"Oh, come on, Jason," Jessica groaned. "If I'd been in Glen-whatever, I would've found it just as fast."

"Jessica, this isn't the time to have an ego fit," Takahiro said. "This is about finding Jason's dad."

"I'll give you an ego fit, Nakamura," Jessica growled.

Heather couldn't quite believe what she was seeing. Why would Jason recruit someone like this? Heather had seen plenty of live wires in her career, and as determined as they often were, they were not reliable team members. Determined to be the best, they constantly jeopardized cases by leaving others in the dark. And judging from this tense first impression, Jessica was even sparkier than most.

91

Jason looked at Bonnie and Takahiro. "Hey, how about you two take Heather to get some lunch. She had a drink with my mom on the plane, and I think she's got low blood sugar."

Jessica scoffed again. "Very professional," she sneered, though Heather hardly heard her over the rumble of Bonnie and Takahiro's chair wheels.

"Of course," Bonnie said. "You're in luck. The taco bar is open today."

"Great," Heather enthused, rising above Jessica's snide comments and following the other officers out of the room.

From a distance, Heather heard Jason close the door hard behind them.

"Don't worry about Jessica," Takahiro said. "You probably won't hear much from her anyway."

Pretending Jessica didn't exist, Heather asked, "So let's say I need those cameras, how do I contact you?"

"Well, because this isn't an official investigation," Bonnie whispered, looking around, "you can't just call us up. We're all tapped when we're inside. So contact Jason on his home phone. He can pass whatever you need to us, we'll figure it out, and get back to you."

"Though we do have our ways," Takahiro added. "If you get a call that says 'No Caller ID,' answer it. That'll be us. Or someone asking about your car warranty. But most likely us."

"Great," Heather replied, seemingly for the hundredth time.

"Don't worry. You're going to do great. We've been reading about you all morning," Bonnie said.

Takahiro nodded and whistled. "Yeah. The cases you've solved. Wow. Way more interesting than what I've done."

"Seriously?" Heather scoffed.

"Yeah," Takahiro insisted, wide-eyed. "We've never taken down a serial killer with our bare hands. The most exciting thing Bonnie and I do is look through files and footage and make the odd phone call. We're office plebs who stare at screens all day."

"But your work is important," Heather insisted.

"Yeah, I mean, it is," Bonnie said. "But we don't see a lot of action. I mean, Jessica and Jason do, especially Jessica, but taking down one of America's most prolific child killers? Now, that shit is documentary-worthy."

Heather took the compliments thankfully but hoped that neither of them had said any of this to Jessica. Though judging from the woman's hostile reaction, she feared they likely had.

CHAPTER TWELVE

THE AGENT

THE DOOR SHUT, AND JASON WAITED FOR THE FOOT-steps to recede before speaking. Jessica looked up at him, her arms crossed and her brows raised. It was the same scathing expression Natalie gave him when he had missed Charlotte's dance recital, but unlike his wife, Jessica didn't scare him.

Once he was sure Heather was out of earshot, he hissed, "What is your problem, Malloy?"

"That hick cop. Jesus, Jason, what were you thinking? We can't trust someone like that or bring them to visit. Do you know how easily manipulated they are? How easily bribed? Not to mention cops are loyal to the FBI, not us. Law enforcement sticks together."

Jason frowned. "That's a hell of a way to talk about the people who serve our citizens."

"Please. You know I'm right. At best, she's inexperienced and—"

"I knew it," Jason interrupted.

"Knew what?" Jessica sneered.

"You didn't read her file."

Jessica shrugged. "Why bother? All small-town cops are the same."

"Because I told you to."

"Well, as this isn't an official mission, you're not my boss. I'm just a friend helping out, and I'll read what I want."

"Don't be a child. This isn't about you and your grudges, it's about saving my dad."

"Exactly, and I think we could save him without getting tangled up with some cop," Jessica replied indignantly.

"No, we couldn't, and you know it. It's not like you can just take off work, fly to Portland, and sniff around for days or weeks. Even if you could, you don't know the local PD, so there'd be no backup, SWAT, forensics, APBs, nothing. And even if you somehow found these guys on your own, you don't have the power to arrest them. Heather does."

"So you're using her as a puppet?" Jessica asked, leaning back in her seat with a smirk.

"No. I'm not 'using her as a puppet.' I'm working alongside someone I believe can find my dad. I know the concept of playing nice with others is foreign to you, but—"

"Remember what happened last time we trusted a cop?" Jessica asked coolly.

"That was different, and you know it. In location, in expertise, in situation. It's unfair to paint everyone with the same brush because of one incident."

Jessica scoffed. "An *incident*? Wow."

"You know what I mean."

"I'm not sure that I do."

"Just read the damn file."

"Fine. I'll read your precious file about your new girlfriend."

"Jessica," Jason said warningly.

"Kidding," Jessica replied dryly as she opened her laptop. Her eyes flitted back and forth as she skim-read Heather's file, the boredom showing on her face. She paused and looked up at Jason. "Seriously? She joined the force at eighteen and became one of Seattle's youngest homicide detectives. Big whoop."

"Keep reading."

"Fine."

Jessica kept scanning and scrolling, and slowly but surely, the defiant look on her face was replaced with surprise. She tried to hide it, holding her eyebrows low, but Jason could see it in her eyes. She was begrudgingly impressed, and when she began to chew her cheek and slammed the laptop closed, he knew he'd won the argument.

"Impressed?" he asked.

"A little. For a cop, she's done some commendable shit. Putting that sicko Paper Doll Killer away should've won her the Medal of Valor."

"But?"

"*But* I still don't trust her."

"You don't have to trust her, but you have to help her if you want to stay on the team."

"Who says I want to stay on the team?" Jessica retorted. "Maybe I'll make my own team and—"

A knock at the door silenced the pair. Jessica went to continue her point, but Jason shushed her and opened the door. Heather stood sheepishly on the other side, her clothes crumpled from the long flight. He hadn't noticed until now, but he knew Jessica would and braced himself as Heather stepped into the room.

"Sorry to interrupt," Heather said. "I forgot my jacket, and Takahiro and Bonnie wanted to eat outside."

Jason twisted and saw the gray jacket hanging on the back of one of the chairs. He strode over, watching Jessica cautiously, ready for her to strike. Handing the jacket to Heather, they were still in the clear, but as the detective shucked it on, Jessica cleared her throat.

"I love your pantsuit, Heather. Where'd you get it?"

"Wal-Mart," Heather replied, dripping with sarcasm.

She looked at Jason with disappointment and stormed out of the room. It was clear that it wasn't just over the suit jab either. She'd been listening in. Jason shot a scathing look at Jessica—who seemed nothing but amused with herself—before taking off after Heather.

Heather quickened her pace, desperate to reach the elevator before it closed, but Jason caught up to her and grabbed her upper arm. She wrenched it from his grasp and spun around. He expected her to be furious, and she was, but more than that, she was hurt.

Thank God Mom's not here to see this, Jason thought, imagining the boxing his ears would receive, despite him being twenty-nine years old.

"I didn't come here to be mocked," Heather stated.

"I know. I didn't bring you here to be mocked."

"Did you know she'd hate me?"

Jason hesitated. "I didn't think it would be that bad."

Heather scoffed. "Why is she even on the team?"

"I know it might be hard to understand, but she is important to the mission. She's our best marksman, not to mention she's friends with all the Special Activities Center guys, who we'll need if anything goes sideways or if we need more hands on deck to take these guys down. They could be with a gang or have bodyguards. That is not something you, or your SWAT team, is equipped to handle."

"I'm sure the Portland PD will be completely fine. In fact, from the way you tell it, you need me and not the other way around. So if I'm going to be treated like the crap on the bottom of her shoe, maybe I'll just cut contact. Investigate alone. Or maybe I'll just kick it to the FBI. I'm sure they'll keep you in the loop."

The threat was significant, and he knew that it was far from empty. Heather was sincere and capable, and though she recognized that Jason and his crew were an asset, she didn't need them half as much as they needed her, at least for now. He thought to grovel but then thought better of his poor acting abilities.

"Your assessment is correct. And I'm sorry for Agent Malloy's behavior."

"I want to hear it from her."

Jason almost laughed. "I think that might be asking for too much."

Heather surveyed him with dark eyes, penetrating eyes. "Fine, but only because I want to bring these assholes to justice. But if she disrespects me again, either she's out, or I am."

"Understood, Detective. I—"

Heather's phone rang and, to Jason's immense relief, interrupted the pathetic apology he'd further crafted in his head. Still surveying him coldly, Heather took a few steps back, leaned against the wall, and answered the phone. Jason wasn't sure if she wanted him to leave, so he stayed to listen in.

"Hello, Detective Heather Bishop," Heather said flatly. Her eyes widened, and she straightened up, peeling away from the wall. "Oh, hi, Sally. How can I help you?" She paused to listen to the muffled voice and retrieved her notebook. She began writing frantically with the notebook pressed against the wall, and Jason moved forward to make himself useful by letting her use his open palms as a table.

"Uh-huh… okay," she said. "What about the other one… Okay."

What they were discussing, he had no idea. Her blatant refusal to put the call on speaker was part of his punishment, and though Jason attempted to read her scrawl upside down, her handwriting was indecipherable.

The elevator dinged, and he was relieved when Takahiro and Bonnie emerged. There he was, half-squatting, half-kneeling before Heather as if at the altar of an ancient deity. God forbid his superiors witnessed him not standing up straight.

The pair approached, confused, and Jason gave them a look that said to stay quiet. They did as they were told but chose to loiter and listen in rather than keep moving. Fortunately, they were in Heather's good books and thus were allowed to form an audience without any dirty looks being flung their way.

Heather smiled at the three and ended the call. "Great, thank you so much, Sally. Bye."

Everyone stared at her expectantly as the call ended, and even Jessica, with her batlike hearing, slunk out into the hallway. Heather held them in suspense for a few more seconds before exploding.

98

"I've got them. They're definitely in Northeast Portland near Sunshine Sally's."

"You're sure?" Jason asked.

"Sure enough to get North Portland PD to start patrolling. Sally just told me that a guy matching our description came in today asking for a new loyalty card. He said he'd lost his but was one stamp away from a free drink. She knew he was telling the truth because he's a regular, and he always hits on her when he comes in."

"Couldn't that be anyone?" Jessica asked.

"Hang on. I'm not done. Two weeks ago, he came in and bragged about his new work van and said she should come and hang out in it sometime."

"Sounds like a coincidence to me," Jessica said.

"Jess, shut up," Bonnie snapped.

"Thank you, Bonnie," Heather said. "Sally says his name is Joel. He also has a friend. A handsome guy with short blond hair, but she didn't know his name. Says he always loiters out the front while Joel buys for both of them."

"Got a last name?" Jason asked.

Heather's smile faltered. "No, not yet."

"Oh, great," Jessica said. "Now we've only got to hunt down a guy called Joel and a handsome blond in the twenty-fifth most-populated city in the country."

"Twenty-sixth," Bonnie corrected her.

"It doesn't matter," Jason said confidently. "Great work, Heather."

Heather nodded appreciatively. "I'll fly back to Glenville now. That way, when Portland PD calls me, I'll be ready to drive over. I'll call them on the plane and update them. They're already looking through traffic cam footage to try and pull a plate, but it'll take a while. Better to get officers to patrol the neighborhoods nearest the café."

"I'll join you first thing tomorrow," Jason said. "I'll make up some excuse. Take some time off for grief reasons. I'll stay at my parents' place. I need to supervise some repairs anyway."

Jessica looked bewildered. "Really? You're going to fly all the way across the country based on either a lucky guess or a total coincidence?"

Everyone continued to ignore Jessica, and Jason shook Heather's hand. "I'll see you soon, Detective."

"In Portland, I hope," she replied and turned to the other three. "Nice to meet you, Takahiro, Bonnie." She paused and stuck out her hand for Jessica to shake, which was, as anticipated, refused. "Absolute pleasure, Jessica."

Takahiro snickered as Heather strode away down the hallway but stopped when he caught sight of Jessica's glower.

"You're all idiots," Jessica hissed before storming away.

"Better an idiot than an asshole!" Bonnie called after her teasingly.

Jessica flipped her off as she pushed open the door to the stairs and disappeared from view.

"She might be right about us being idiots," Takahiro said. "But Heather is one sharp cookie."

"Jessica will come around," Bonnie assured him.

Jason rubbed his stubble, unable to care about Jessica or her temper tantrums right now. He was consumed by hope, though he tried not to be. They were so close. Soon this was all going to be over, but first, he had to break the news to his grieving family that he was leaving first thing tomorrow and had no idea when he'd be back.

CHAPTER THIRTEEN

THE DETECTIVE

COMBINING THE FORTY MINUTES SPENT GOING TO AND from the CIA headquarters, the ten hours in a plane, and the two-hour round trip from Glenville to Seattle, Heather had spent over half the day traveling just to end up right where she started. The effect of this was exhaustion to the point of delirium and a sickening ache behind her eyes. As the taxi pulled up to her house at ten past ten, all she wanted to do was shuffle inside and collapse onto her bed.

She'd had another glass of wine on the flight back, hoping it would counterbalance the ones she'd had in the morning, but instead, she now had no energy to eat, shower, brush her teeth, or even get undressed. That didn't mean she wouldn't though. She had recently become very good at forcing her body to do things it didn't want to do.

Not to mention, one of her many New Year's resolutions was to go to bed clean—not just bathed, but moisturized, brushed, and scrubbed. Her habit of drinking until she passed out had prevented this for the majority of 2019 to 2022. Though she'd always remedied it in the morning, waking up with a hangover and an unbrushed ashtray mouth was always morning-ruining, and it would take a lot more than a punishing day to ruin her six-month streak.

As the driver took off, a figure moved in the dark by her front door. The bulb for the automatic porch light needed replacing, something she'd repeatedly forgotten to do for nearly a year. She couldn't tell who it was, but she knew it was a man. Instinctively she reached for her favorite gun and realized she'd left it at home. So instead she grabbed her keys and shoved them between her fingers so that they protruded like bronze talons.

"Who's there?" she commanded, her voice more confident than she felt.

"Woah! Put the claws away," Gabriel said, holding his hands above his head. "Sorry, I should've turned my phone flashlight on, but I thought you would've seen me in the headlights."

"I honestly wasn't looking. I'm so tired I don't even know if my eyes were open when we pulled up."

"Guessing you don't want to watch a movie then?" Gabriel asked, his baleful expression lit up by the yellow streetlamp as he stepped closer.

"Crap. I totally forgot about movie night."

"That's okay, we can still have some food," he replied cheerfully and waved the condensation-soaked plastic bag containing chow mein boxes.

Heather shifted her weight from foot to foot and chewed on her lip. "I'm really sorry, but I think I just need to go to sleep."

"Oh. Okay. More for me, I guess. Or you can keep it in the fridge, and we can try again tomorrow?" He sounded so hopeful, and it broke Heather's heart to deliver another blow.

"Maybe," she said. "How about you hold onto it just in case?"

"Just in case of what?" Gabriel asked before waggling his brows. "Do you have a boyfriend you're not telling me about?"

"No."

"Girlfriend?"

"No."

"Meeting up with Dr. Julius Tocci?" Gabriel inquired equally suggestively.

"No."

"Your ex-husband?" he asked, more sincerely.

"Jesus, Gabriel, no!" Heather snapped.

Gabriel recoiled like a kicked puppy, and Heather sighed, rubbing her forehead. They both stared at each other for a while, both hurt and frustrated.

"So where the hell have you been?" Gabriel asked.

"I was in Virginia."

"Wait. Why the hell were you in Virginia? And why didn't you tell me? You know how superstitious my mom is about flights. She always burns a candle when loved ones are on a plane. When she finds out I didn't tell her, she's going to kill me."

"I'm sorry. I was distracted. I had a lot of people to meet."

"Wait. Virginia. Isn't that where the CIA headquarters is?"

Heather nodded.

"Did Jason fly you out to go to the goddamn CIA headquarters?"

"Yeah."

Gabriel's pouty tone was moving toward giddy, and his expression lightened. Gabriel was obsessed with TV shows about spies and US intelligence. *Alias*, *Jack Ryan*, *Homeland*, and even the less flattering *Wormwood*—he watched them all.

"Okay, you have to tell me all about it," he enthused. "Come on, you must be hungry. I'll go home once we've finished eating, I promise."

"Gabriel, you know I can't. It's classified information, not to mention what we're doing isn't exactly aboveboard."

"Oh, come on, Heather!" Gabriel moaned. "I'm not going to tell anyone!"

"I'm sorry," Heather mumbled, moving past Gabriel to her front door, her house key outstretched.

"No, you're not. You love this. You love being more important than the rest of the force."

Heather looked over her shoulder with a frown. "You know that's not true."

"Actually, I don't know. You moved here to get away from it all, but now you galivant around with the FBI and the CIA and check out dead bodies with Dr. Tocci, the best goddamn pathologist on the West Coast. That doesn't really sound like small-town living to me. That sounds like you're bored and you miss your old life. It's like you used us to heal, and now you're going to leave us all in the dust. First Virginia, next stop Seattle."

"I'm not going to leave you," Heather said sadly.

"You sure? Because aside from work, I barely see you. Gene says he hasn't seen you in weeks. Now, I'm not trying to sound needy, but everyone misses you. Maybe it would be fine if I thought you weren't suffering, but I think you still are. You've just replaced booze with running the skin off your feet and solving cold cases for Julius. You've transformed yourself from an alcoholic into a workaholic because you can't bear to be alone with your thoughts."

"That's not fair," Heather said quietly. "I'm just doing my best. Like everyone else."

Gabriel shifted his weight from foot to foot. "You don't need to isolate yourself. We're all here for you."

"I'm fine. Okay? I just like being busy."

"Beau says you haven't been to AA in two months."

"Crap," Heather hissed.

"Crap?"

"I forgot."

"Come on, Heather."

Heather paused. "Since when have you been hanging out with Beau?"

"This cool music venue called Sludge opened up."

"Sounds lovely," she retorted.

"Hey, you could be judgemental in person if you ever returned my texts."

"I don't have time to get drunk in dive bars that smell like urinals."

Gabriel looked at her in disbelief. "You used to. It's like you tried so hard to fix yourself that you've turned into someone else."

Heather softened, her face burning. "I'm still me. You just met me when I was down. This is what I'm like when I'm doing well."

Gabriel shrugged. "I don't believe you."

"I'm telling you the truth. Maybe you just don't like the real me."

"The *real* you seems a lot like an act to me."

"Gabriel."

"Whatever." Gabriel began to walk away toward the road. "Oh, by the way, Tina is pissed off that you missed work today. I just thought I'd remind you that Jason isn't your boss and that you're not unfireable."

"Good night, Gabriel."

Gabriel didn't reply, and when Heather turned around, he'd disappeared into the darkness of the night, his bag of Chinese food crinkling somewhere in the middle distance. Heather chewed her lip, trying to ignore the knot in her throat, until she tasted blood. Then came the pain. She sucked her teeth and wiped away the persistent beads with the back of her hand as she let herself in.

She was too angry to feel guilty. Between Jessica thinking she was a bumbling idiot and Gabriel—and seemingly everyone else in town—thinking she was an uncaring workaholic, her hackles were up. She felt alienated by both worlds, trapped in some sort of inescapable, unbeatable purgatory. Damned if she did, damned if she didn't.

She hated arguing with Gabriel, but that didn't stop her from continuing the debate with him—and Jessica—in her head. To him, she emphasized the importance of her work, how it came above fun and even friendship—how the town needed her, how Jason needed her, how Christopher needed her, how all those victims of all the cold cases needed her. To Jessica, she listed her achievements, but it didn't do any good. Neither of them was really listening. They'd made up their minds.

She paced the house, her dogs hot on her heels, their nails tapping against the wooden hallway and kitchen linoleum. She fed them absentmindedly and continued to pace, desperately trying to resist smoking the pack of cigarettes hidden in a trick drawer. Smoking and drinking were what she used to do when she felt overwhelmed, manic, angry, or upset. Now all that was left to do when she felt those things were work, run, or pace. It was too late to run, and she had helped solve Julius's last cold case awhile back, so pacing it was.

She thought about Julius some more and thought to call him. It was late, but she needed to speak to someone who understood who she was. She loved Gabriel, but he was cut from a different cloth. Most of the time, it felt as if she and Julius were not only made of the same fabric but had been sliced into shape by the same scissors.

Julius picked up on the second ring and answered enthusiastically. Heather could hear food frying in a pan only a short distance away as he laid the phone down on the counter. She'd never been to his bachelor pad but pictured a painted black kitchen with charcoal marble countertops.

"Are you busy?" she asked.

"No, no. Just finally making myself some food," Julius replied.

"Why so late?"

Julius chuckled. "Are you telling me you eat at a reasonable time?"

"No. I just thought I was the only one who didn't."

"Well, I'll admit that eleven is late. Even for me. But it's been a very long day."

"Same here," Heather groaned, plopping down on the couch.

"Tell me about it."

"You first."

"Awards ceremony," Julius replied. "I'm sure you remember those."

"Vividly. Did you wear a tux?"

"Of course. Black tie. It felt as macabre as usual. Dressed up to the nines. Trophies. Photographers. Champagne. All for slicing open bodies."

"I'm weirdly kind of jealous."

"Why? You hated those things. Wearing dresses made you irate, if I remember rightly, as did those little purses that couldn't even fit a phone inside. You said it was a bunch of pomp and nonsense."

"I don't know. Maybe it's just the day I had. Tiny fish, big pond. Then I get back to the tiny pond and feel like there's no room to swim."

"Maybe you've outgrown Glenville? Perhaps you're ready to return to Seattle?" Julius asked hopefully.

"I have changed way too much to move back to Seattle."

"Have you? That's funny because you sound awfully like a woman I used to work with." He paused thoughtfully. "Though perhaps nostalgia is merely getting the best of you."

"I honestly don't know anymore," Heather said quietly, each word draining more of her waning energy. "The city felt like too much noise, and for a long time, this felt better. Freeing. Now I don't know."

"So what did you do today to cause this identity crisis?"

"I went to the CIA. Now, there's a place I don't fit in."

Julius laughed. "I could have told you that. You're far too fun to be one of them."

Heather buried her head in her hands. "That's the problem. I got back, and my best friend says I've turned into a workaholic. That I don't have time for anyone anymore."

"Well, you seem to have time for me," Julius added.

"It's different. I think we're the same. I don't have to pretend to be anything I'm not."

"Well, I must admit I'm flattered that Washington's best detective thinks we're twin flames, but please don't let the sins of the present blind you to the horrors of the past."

"You're such a poet," Heather scoffed.

"I'm English and Italian, darling. It comes naturally. But seriously, please remember that being a shark in the ocean didn't bring you much joy either."

"What if I'm never content? What if I'm doomed to be constantly searching?"

"You'll figure it out," Julius assured her. "You're only thirty-three. These are the ups and downs that come with the territory. At least you're not a middle-aged divorcee with all his best years behind him."

"I'm already a divorcee."

Julius chuckled again, a little sadly this time. "Yes, I suppose you are. You're young though. You'll find someone else."

"You could find someone else too. Want me to wingman for you? Turns out I'm pretty good at it. Set up two locals, and they're engaged now."

Julius hesitated. "I'll think about it. Speaking of divorce, have you spoken to—"

Heather interrupted, quickly changing the subject. "Got any more cold cases for me? I could do with something to mull over while I'm working on this case."

"I do, actually. The Ribbon Killer. A friend in London sent it over. In 2017 a girl was found in Hyde Park lying on her back as if in a coffin. No footprints, no fingerprints. She'd been strangled with a ribbon that had then been tied around her neck as a bow. She was naked and otherwise uninjured. Actually, she was in remarkably good condition."

"Weird. Can you send me the files?"

"Are you sure? I don't want to overwhelm you."

"Oh no, please do. I like being overwhelmed."

Julius chuckled. "Perhaps your friend is right. But I'm hardly a pot that can call the kettle black. That's why I'm cooking the most bloody ridiculous meal right now when I could be eating instant noodles."

"What are you making? Describe it slowly," Heather teased, faux flirtatiously. "Turns out even the airplane food in first class sucks."

Julius snorted. "I'm making *cilbir*, which is basically poached eggs on top of Greek yogurt with a garlic chili sauce drizzle. And then, to go with it, I'm making *lahmacun*. Now, that's where the real challenge is."

"What is that?" Heather asked, her stomach grumbling. She moved to the kitchen to raid her barren fridge for cheese slices and olives and munched them down as Julius continued. She hoped with enough imagination, she might be able to taste what he described.

"It's a baked Turkish flatbread topped with minced meat, onions, garlic, tomatoes, chili, et cetera. It's going to be good, but I'm starting to regret not just ordering in."

"I wish I had the motivation to cook like you do. I'm getting better, believe it or not—"

"I believe it."

"—But cooking for more than forty minutes sounds exhausting and pointless. I eat everything in three minutes flat to keep the dogs away."

"It helps to think of it as a practical, productive form of meditation. I take my mind off work, but I'm not doing something as trivial as watching rubbish on TV. I'm learning a skill and looking after my body. It's more akin to working out. Though, I admit, I struggle to keep up with that one."

"Yeah, that's more my area of expertise. Gardening too, weirdly enough."

"Perhaps you can come up, stay for a weekend. You can teach me how to run and keep my herbs alive, and in return, I'll teach you how to enjoy cooking."

Heather hesitated. She could never tell if Julius was hitting on her or not. More than that, she also couldn't tell if she liked it. From an analytical standpoint, they were undoubtedly a good match, though perhaps there was something condemning about being too similar. As Kathleen said, it was all about opposites. With someone like Julius, it could be perfect or a horrible disaster, and even though it had been half a decade since her divorce, romantic conflict was the last thing she needed. Still, she had to admit it was nice knowing she was still attractive despite her lack of effort in that department.

"Yeah, maybe. Maybe we could work on the Ribbon Killer case together once I'm done with my current case," she said.

"Oh, of course. The shooting. I was sorry to hear about that. Dreadful stuff. Are you doing all right? Aside from the identity crisis?"

"I think I am, but if you ask anybody else, not so much."

"Well, I'm willing to take your word on it. Though please be careful. Don't blow out your own flame by moving too fast. I'd like to keep solving murders with you for many decades to come."

Heather yawned. "I'll try my best. Hey, Julius, I'm beat. I'll let you get back to your cooking."

"I'll send you a picture when it's done," Julius teased.

"Please don't. I think I'll die of hunger."

Julius chuckled. "I'll only send a picture if it goes horribly wrong and is inedible then."

"We both know it won't be."

"Even perfectionists can make mistakes. "

"Yeah, I'm well aware."

"Good night, Heather," Julius said kindly.

"Good night, Julius. Thanks for the chat."

Heather hung up, stood up, and grabbed her laptop. She was exhausted, but there was a new itch to scratch. She opened the lid and typed the name Daniel Palmer in the search bar. Just before pressing Enter, she looked at the liquor cabinet and all the framed photos and awards she'd recently decorated it with. At the center was her pride and joy—the Homicide Investigator of the Year Award, given to her at a low point in the aftermath of the Paper Doll case. The problem was not the memories associated. Receiving that award, with the dead girls' parents in the crowd applauding her, had felt like reaching the light at the end of the tunnel. No, the only problem was it was addressed to Heather Palmer, not Bishop.

She drummed her fingers on the table and closed the laptop lid. It was too late and the day too fraught. The last thing she needed right now was a social media stalking session. Her ex-husband had become blurry in her mind, and there was no need to sharpen the picture.

CHAPTER FOURTEEN

THE DETECTIVE

HEATHER WOKE UP ON THE COUCH TO BIRDS CALLING, her laptop open once again, and her staring at the porcelain face of a dead girl. Shortly after her call with Julius ended, and the steps to her nighttime routine were ticked off, Heather had fallen asleep wrapped up in clean sheets. However, as much as the conversation and hot shower had soothed her, neither could keep the bad dreams at bay, and she woke only an hour later in a cold sweat. She'd then spent many hours conscious before finally passing out. She calculated she'd had four hours of sleep all up—hardly a new record—and fortunately, her time awake had been productive.

During her fruitless nap, Julius had sent her the Ribbon Killer files. His friend in London who'd done the autopsy report was almost as thorough as Julius and even more long-winded. It was a perfect—if harrowing—way to pass a restless night.

Heather sat up and pulled the laptop closer to examine the notes she'd made. The victim's name was Lilly Arnold. Her body was discovered by a jogger in Hyde Park at five forty-five in the morning. She'd looked so peaceful that the jogger initially thought she was still alive, though upon trying to find a pulse, he realized she was definitely dead.

By the time Julius's pathologist friend arrived, her body was still warm and flaccid, indicating she'd been dead for under three hours. Specifically, he believed she was killed at around four-thirty. Aside from all the usual indicators, a prominent aspect in confirming the time of death was the thick, goopy layers of nail polish applied to her fingers and toes. When pressed, it was not yet fully dry and indented under the pressure of a nail edge. According to the pathologist's beautician daughter—who was soon ushered onto the scene—she approximated that the thickness of polish would take about two hours to completely dry.

Lilly was completely nude aside from the pink ribbon around her neck. Her eyes had also been closed, her hands were clasped as if in a coffin, and she wore smudged lipstick and an excess of blush on each cheek. According to her family and friends, Lilly usually wore very heavy makeup, including false eyelashes, but all that had been removed and replaced with what reminded Heather of an antique doll. Her signature hoop earrings, too, had been removed.

Lilly was eighteen when she died. Far too young. Still in university and working nights at a nearby pub, The Thistle & Pig, since turning eighteen seven months prior.

Her age made Heather shiver. The Paper Doll Killer's second victim—Sydney Benson—had also been eighteen, though she looked much younger than Lilly had. She was the only adult that he had ever taken, and Heather had always suspected he thought her to be a child.

No one thought Lilly Arnold was a child. In fact, witnesses say the attention she received bordered on the extreme. Older women often had to intervene as drunken men's flirting turned physical. One man in particular was questioned multiple times due to his obsession with Lilly but was eventually released because of his alibi.

Though Heather agreed that he was innocent, she believed a man had killed Lilly. The person who had strangled her had done so from a height advantage and with significant force, likely a large male, and there were obvious sexual motivations. The investigators at the time agreed, but the killer was never found.

It was strange. Something about the case felt familiar. It wasn't similar in nature to anything she'd ever personally worked on before, but still, there was a sense of déjà vu surrounding it. It was possible that Gabriel had told her about it. It was seemingly a rather famous case that often popped up on unsolved mystery subreddits—but she wasn't convinced that that was it either.

She stood to make a coffee, hoping whatever was at the back of her mind would emerge with enough caffeine, but as she did, a calendar notification popped up in the top corner.

Pick up suit.

"Pick up suit?" Heather asked, wracking her tired brain. The realization hit her like an eighteen-wheeler, and she jumped to her feet. "Pick up suit!"

Heather had ordered a suit from Schneider's Buttons & Threads—the local tailor owned by a shriveled mouse of a man named Arnie Schneider—and she was supposed to pick it up today. The suit itself was not the problem; the issue was its purpose. Nancy Ellis's fundraiser, an unmissable event, was tonight, and Heather had forgotten all about it.

The intention was to gather Glenville's elite and squeeze every last penny out of them to help those affected by the shooting and pay for the three locals' funerals. Nancy had even offered to pay for a statue to be erected in the park in their honor if the donations exceeded twenty thousand dollars.

Supposedly, Nancy had started preparing as early as two hours after the shooting on Friday, which sounded about right, and by Saturday lunchtime, anybody who was anybody had received an e-vite with a dress code. Heather had gone that same day after visiting the motel to Schneider's Buttons & Threads and then promptly forgotten all about it.

In the face of a big formal event, Heather couldn't help but feel her conversation with Julius about missing award ceremonies had jinxed her, and she realized she needed to get the lenses in her rose-tinted glasses adjusted.

She shut the laptop lid. "Not today, Lilly," she said before starting her morning routine.

The tailors didn't open until ten, so after feeding the dogs, Heather attempted to make an omelet, which was seemingly a success judging from the thumbs-up emoji Julius sent her in response to her pictures. Enjoying the praise and thinking about what Gabriel was saying about keeping people in the loop, she decided to keep the ball rolling and headed outside. She intended to take photos of her garden to send to Gene. She knew he'd be particularly jealous of her juicy, oversized heirloom tomatoes, but more than that, he knew he'd be wildly impressed.

As she lined up the shot, her phone rang. It was Howard Lewis from Portland PD, and Heather nearly dropped her phone in her panic to answer. She picked up, and before she could say hello, Howie began spouting a long series of enthusiastically delivered information that could ultimately be summarized by, "We know where the killer's van is."

One of their officers had found it coincidentally after getting lost in a lesser-known suburb while picking up his daughter from a sleepover. He spotted it next to an abandoned house covered by a too-small tarp while reversing and immediately called the station to send an undercover cop to watch the building. As of yet, no one had been in or out.

"So are you coming, or do you want me to send the SWAT team in?" Howie asked.

"I'm already on my way," Heather said, and it wasn't a complete lie. She was already back inside, pulling an outfit together and looking for her keys.

"All right. I'll see you at the North Precinct in two hours. If my guy sees movement in the meantime, we'll take action."

"I'll be bringing my specialist consultant with me. He's an ex-marine and weapon expert turned private investigator," Heather lied. She held her breath while she waited for the reply.

"Sounds like a helpful man to have aboard," Howie said without hesitation. "Tell him I say welcome."

"I will. Thank you, sir. See you soon."

As soon as she was done talking to Howie—who was incredibly organized and fastidious despite his borderline goofy personality—she sent a cursory text to Tina, Nancy, and Gabriel apologizing for her inability to attend the fundraiser. They all responded within a few minutes, but Heather let each message go unread. If they caught the killers, that was all that mattered. She was going rogue and keeping her boss in the dark, but it was easier to ask for forgiveness than permission. Not to mention if Tina insisted on coming with her, it could ruin everything for Jason and keep him on the benches, and Heather knew who she'd rather have by her side in a physical conflict.

Heather declined a call from Gabriel and instead returned to the main objective by calling Jason. He answered, sounding moodier than usual.

"What is it, and can it wait?" he asked. "I just reached Black Douglas, and there's a bunch of beer bottles and cigarettes in the driveway. Looks like some local kids have been playing with Ouija boards or something."

Heather sucked her teeth. "I told Tina to keep someone posted up here. I'm so sorry. Probably kids from out of town."

Jason sighed. "It's fine. Just need to clean it up. So can this wait?"

"No," Heather said. "Operation Silver Scalpel is a go."

CHAPTER FIFTEEN

THE DETECTIVE

D ESPITE HOWIE'S FIRM RECOMMENDATION, HEATHER and Jason decided to forgo the SWAT team, but they happily compromised and were followed to the scene by a van full of highly trained, heavily armed backup. In Heather's experience, real on-call SWAT teams—not the pretend Glenville kind—did not like to wait around. They would clear the house, and loudly too, destroying potential evidence with their stomping feet, kicked-in doors, and impatient trigger fingers. Having ordinary cops waiting covertly in the wings allowed Heather and Jason to carry out a stealth mission like spies rather than a hyper-macho militia.

Leaving the van a few meters down the road next to a bunch of overgrown roadside foliage, Heather and Jason parked on the other side of the road to the abandoned house. No sirens, no doors slamming, they exited their car, keeping their guns hidden so as not to frighten any nosy neighbors.

"You ready, Bishop?" Jason asked as they crossed the road. He'd never called her that before, and it was said with something that sounded a lot like respect versus the indifferent "Heather" and teasing "Detective."

Heather nodded, her eyes trained on the van, while Jason stayed focused on the front door. "Yep. Do you think there's a back entrance?" she asked.

"Two-story suburban house? I'd guarantee it."

"Let's move in through the back. Catch them by surprise."

"Roger that," Jason replied, picking up the pace toward the structure.

Once they were actually on the property, they slowed and ducked as they crept past one of the few intact windows around the side. Jason checked out the van as they passed it, looked back at Heather, and nodded. It was a positive ID.

The partly fenced backyard was overgrown and littered with beer cans, broken glass needles, and crack pipes, and much of the grass was ruined by burned-out fire pits. Howie had said the dilapidated building had been a problem for a while and was waiting to get torn down to repel the squatters and delinquent teenagers that frequently occupied it. Heather genuinely pitied anyone desperate enough to dwell in such a hovel but understood why the dangerous eyesore needed to go. Today, though, she was glad it was still standing. It was the perfect honey trap for criminals on the run.

They stepped up onto the back porch and froze as rotten boards creaked. No one seemed to stir inside, so they moved to the door, guns raised, backs pressed against graffiti.

"Ready?" Heather asked.

"Yes, ma'am."

"On my count ... Three, two, one, go."

On the word *go*, Jason pushed open the ajar door—which hung limply from its rusty hinges—and Heather followed him into the filthy kitchen. Flies buzzed around what appeared to be a rotting rat carcass in the sink, and pizza boxes were piled high. Heather stopped breathing through her nose, the smell of putrefaction overwhelmingly pungent, and they quickly moved through the doorway into the living room.

A moldy couch was pressed against the front door as a barricade, and wooden planks covered the two windows on either side. There were two broken deck chairs, and in the middle of them was a small coffee table sporting an empty bottle of cheap hooch and a broken radio. In the corner was a metal barrel filled with soggy but burnt newspapers that had once operated as a makeshift fireplace.

The house was narrow, and after checking the downstairs bathroom, there was nowhere else to go but up. Heather gestured to the staircase, which was missing several steps, and leading the way, she ventured cautiously up the flight.

On the landing, they were faced with three closed doorways, and despite their rather shambolic ascent up the decaying wooden structure, they still heard no movement.

"Left," Heather mouthed, and they veered toward the first door.

Once again, Heather counted down, and Jason entered first. She was hot on his heels, but after pointing their weapons around the dimly lit room, it was clear that it was empty.

Heather tilted her head, and they filed out onto the landing and tried again with the next room. Clear again. Just an old moldy bed and carpet that smelled decidedly of urine.

For the final time, they repeated themselves, and though Heather was losing hope, Jason remained the epitome of determination and focus as he opened the door.

Once again, it was empty, their final hope crushed. Then Heather looked down at the dated cream carpet and spied the large pool of congealed blood partly hidden behind the bed. Jason fell back, looking through the doorway with his gun still drawn, as Heather knelt by the patch of cruor. She dipped her finger in it and quickly retracted, wiping her finger on her pants.

"It's still fresh," she said, no longer lowering her voice. "Cold but wet."

Jason turned back and stared at the sticky omen, his eyes briefly haunted. "It could be from anyone or anything. I clipped that guy a few times, maybe he was bleeding out."

Heather stood. "Yeah. You're right. I'll get Howard to send in CSI. No point in jumping to conclusions." She pressed the button on her walkie and addressed the backup team. "The house is clear," she said. "No signs of the shooters or the victim. You guys can turn back, but tell Howard to send in CSI. There's a lot of blood here."

"Copy that, Detective," replied a deep voice.

"There would be no point in kidnapping him and then killing him," Jason added as if Heather had said anything to the contrary.

Heather knew that wasn't statistically true and that Jason would agree under different circumstances, but she thought better than to argue with him about his father's well-being.

"They probably just came here to sleep, swap cars, and ditch this one. The van is too recognizable," Jason added. "Maybe the flyers weren't a good idea."

"Maybe," Heather said though she disagreed. Without the flyers, they wouldn't even be here.

Something about the putrid, gory scene felt stranger than Jason's theory. Heather's gut churned as it had when she'd approached Dennis Burke's hut, and the longer she looked around the sizeable master bedroom, the more blood there was. Splatters of it could be seen on the bedding and the peeling wallpaper. From her expertise, whoever had been hurt was likely no longer alive.

Just as they were about to leave, Heather noticed something sticking out of the closed bedside table drawer. It looked like the corner of a piece of paper. Crimson fingerprints had marred and rendered it pasty and soft. Heather stepped over the puddle, opened the drawer, and retrieved a leaflet. It was in poor condition, and she touched it gingerly, not wanting to tarnish it with her own fingerprints before forensics got their hands on it. Despite the damage, she could see that it was for the Silver Falls State Park in Salem, Oregon, and upon carefully prying it open, she saw that one of the waterfalls was circled.

119

"What's that?" Jason asked, and Heather jumped. She hadn't heard him sneak up behind him.

Putting your time at The Farm to good use, she thought bitterly as she calmed her beating heart.

Heather tapped the circled waterfall. "There's a cave behind this waterfall."

"Do you think that's where they could be hiding?" Jason asked, sounding as if he was already sure that it was.

"It's definitely worth a look," Heather replied.

She believed what she said, though she noted internally that it seemed strange to leave behind something so "condemning." She knew they were amateurs, but while a loyalty card was one thing, an "X marks the spot" was another.

"What if it's a trap?" she asked.

"I'm sure the police department in Salem with be happy to escort us out there. They're only two guys, and lousy shots at that."

"Yeah, you're right," Heather agreed, though her stomach roiled.

Gabriel would've asked her about her gut and the hesitation in her voice, but Jason was laser-focused. He didn't care about how she felt as she looked down at the pamphlet or her woo-woo instincts. The man was made of math and logic, and this was the next rational step. Knowing Jason would go with or without her, she photographed the booklet with her phone before leaving it on the table for forensics.

Just as she was about to call the chief to tell him to bring in the CSI team, he called her first.

"Hello? Detective Bishop?" he asked.

"I'm here."

"I'm sorry that the suspects weren't present. I know that must be disappointing. However, I do have an interesting update about our suspect Joel, the one with the loyalty card. His mother just came into the precinct and filed a missing person's report for one Joel Schubert. Apparently, he told her he'd be away on a job for a few days but would be back home today."

"Huh."

"Penny for your thoughts?"

"There's a lot of blood here."

"Yes, the team informed me."

"Does Joel have any DNA on file?"

"Already looking into it. The CSO and her team are already on their way."

"Have you had any other missing person's reports? For a blond man, likely the same age?"

"I'm afraid not. The partner in crime, I'm guessing?" Howie asked.

"I'm wondering if he was less a partner and more of a boss. He's a much better shot. More expensive gear. Was smart enough to not go into the coffee shop and give his name."

"So our second man might be the mastermind of this situation?"

"Yeah. And I'm thinking maybe he and Joel had a … falling out," Heather said, making sure to not bring up the significant possibility that the blood could belong to Christopher.

"Don't worry, Detective. We'll have the team dig up the backyard just in case," Howie stated. "Did you find anything else?"

"Yeah. A pamphlet for the falls in Salem. It's covered in bloody fingerprints, and we think that Joel or his accomplice might be hiding out in a cave there. Can you contact the Salem PD and arrange for an escort?"

"Of course. The chief of police up there is a family friend. They'll be at your command and ready on your arrival."

Heather was taken aback by the professionalism. Nothing operated this quickly in a small town, and just like that, her big-city nostalgia returned despite the horrors.

"Thank you. We'll drive down now. The blood is recent. I think they're only a few hours ahead of us."

"I'll alert the park rangers. Get them to keep an eye out while you head down. We're not going to let these fuckers get away. Not in my state."

Heather ended the call, and she and Jason made their way out of the house through the way they came in. Back in Jason's car—which he'd insisted on taking instead of Heather's—they both looked back at the abandoned house.

"I think you're right, about the blond," Jason said.

"I'm not sure. But I guess we'll find out. If they are where we think they are."

"They're there," Jason assured her. "At least the blond is."

Heather nodded, wishing she was half as confident as Jason. "Ready to head to Salem?" she asked.

"As long as you promise we won't run into any witches," Jason replied flatly and started the engine.

It was a joke. This time Heather was sure of it, but her stomach was still in too much turmoil to muster up anything louder than a breathy snort. Jason didn't seem to notice as they tore off toward their next destination.

"Wrong Salem, I think," she finally said.

CHAPTER SIXTEEN

THE SURGEON

2018

"HOW ARE WE DOING TODAY, MR. DIXON?" Christopher asked, striding into the private recovery room with a smile and a clipboard. Clarence turned to look at him, his face wrapped up tight like an Egyptian mummy.

"Mighty fine, Doc," Clarence said with a pained grin. "In fact, I'd say I'm feeling downright peachy."

"Excellent. That's what I like to hear."

"Well, it's hard not to be in good spirits when getting routine sponge baths from beautiful women."

Christopher chuckled politely. Usually, he was more protective of his staff, quickly reprimanding any sexism or chauvinism that came their way. However, Clarence Dixon was no ordinary patient, and with an extra $700,000 in his pocket, Christopher opted to humor him. He could always give the nurses a handsome Christmas bonus to assuage his guilty conscience.

"Well, I'm glad you've enjoyed your stay," Christopher said. "We pride ourselves on our hospitality."

"Oh, that has not been lost on me, and as a Texan, I know a thing or two about hospitality. In fact, I might actually miss this place when you finally let me out of here."

"Well, today might be the day. I'm going to have a look at your face, and if it's still healing correctly and there's no more sign of infection, then you're free to go. I know that you had to stay a few more days than anticipated, but I'm feeling hopeful."

"Less talking, more unwrapping," Clarence said, rubbing his hands together eagerly.

"Of course. Please hold this." Christopher handed Clarence a handheld mirror. "You don't have to watch, but many prefer to."

"Oh, I'm going to watch. I paid more'n half a million dollars for this face. I want to see what your famous hands are capable of."

"I must warn you that it might not look how you're expecting just yet. You have many months of recovery ahead of you. Please expect some swelling, bruising, and redness. Though the scarring itself will be minimal and should soon become invisible."

Clarence looked up at Christopher with puffy, bloodshot eyes and grinned. "Are you scared of me, Doc?"

Christopher blinked rapidly as he looked down at his sterilized scissors in the plastic tub. "Of course not, Mr. Dixon. You seem like a fine young man."

"Then why are you always reassuring me?"

Christopher furrowed his brow. "I say this to all my patients."

"No, no, that's not it," Clarence said, waggling a finger. "I can tell when people are nervous, so I'm just wondering what's causing your jitters? Is it my face or me?"

Christopher faltered. "Neither, I—"

Clarence barked a laugh, his serious expression lifting. "I'm pulling your leg, Doc! Come on now. Keep going. Don't let a little fun stop you."

"Of course."

Clarence held up the mirror and held unblinking eye contact with himself as Christopher carefully snipped away at the bandages and gauze, peeling back yellowing, bloody layers. When the first patch of raw, pink skin was unveiled, Clarence gasped. At first, Christopher feared that the sound was one of horror but soon understood it to be an exclamation of excitement for how Clarence squirmed like an impatient child.

Then, much to Christopher's discomfort, the visceral reaction took a sexual turn. Clarence moaned with pleasure as more of his face was unveiled, and he didn't even seem to feel pain as gauze peeled away from scabs and pulled at sore skin. Christopher had never seen anything like it. It was primal, compulsive, and seemingly insuppressible. This man had wanted to be someone else for a very long time.

Christopher cleared his throat and raised his voice above Clarence's sounds of satisfaction. "As you can see, you now have a much sharper jaw, achieved via a combination of liposuction, Juvederm, and subtle silicone implants. I have also flipped your top lip to give you a fuller effect without needing injectables, turned the corners up, and added dimples for a perfect Hollywood smile."

Clarence was starting to calm down now that the unveiling was over, but his breathing was still heavy, and his pupils were severely dilated. He gave his new mouth a spin. It looked painful, but the effect it had was undeniable. That was a mouth fit for a movie star. He held it like that for as long as possible, examining it from various angles in the mirror before turning it on Christopher. Christopher smiled back, but when he relaxed his own face, Clarence kept going. He worried he might be stuck until Clarence finally fell back into neutral.

"Good work, Doc. That's one heck of a grin."

"You'll also notice that your eyes are no longer downturned at the outer edges and instead have a slight fox lift upturn. You also have less lid space, and the eyes' shape is much more almond. I also gave you an eyebrow transplant using hairs from the back of your head for a darker, more masculine brow."

"What about the cheeks? Somethin's different there too."

"Implants akin to the jaw and buccal fat removal in the cheek pads for that modelesque gaunt look you described."

"The nose?"

"Standard rhinoplasty. Straighter bridge, more even nostrils, and a pointed tip."

Clarence then noticed the bandages still on his ears and looked at Christopher with amused confusion. "What on earth have you done to my ears?"

"I noticed that they were a tad uneven in size and shape, so I've made them symmetrical and a little prettier. They have a rounder top, and the left no longer sticks out more than the right."

"I had never noticed that before," Clarence said, wide-eyed with awe. "See, I knew you were the man for the job. I said 'go to town, make me beautiful,' and you have."

Christopher couldn't exactly see the beauty that Clarence saw. Not yet. There were too many stitches, his eyes were surrounded by purple and yellow, and there was a shiny, swollen quality to his visage that resembled the outcome of a shellfish allergy and a dinner at Red Lobster. Still, beneath the ghastliness, there was good, clean work and a promising future for his face.

"I'll tell you, Doc. When you have the amount of money that I have, not much impresses you anymore. Especially people. Sure, the Grand Canyon or a well-trained lion impresses me, but a man? Not so much. You, however, are an impressive man," Clarence gushed.

"Thank you, Mr. Dixon."

"Clarence, please."

"Clarence. I'm glad you are happy with your face."

"More than happy, Doc. More than happy."

Christopher smiled softly. "We'll monitor your blood pressure, and if all goes well, you can leave at five."

"So soon? I'm starting to get cold feet about leaving."

Christopher laughed. "I'm sure your house is much nicer than a hospital room."

"Yeah, but my wife ain't half as nice as the girls here, and her cooking is way worse than the food. You know, I bet that Marie is a fine cook. Damn, if I weren't married, I'd whisk her away right now. Though she might not be interested after watching me piss into a bedpan." Clarence guffawed loudly, and Christopher graciously joined him, though he inwardly cringed as his patient's face contorted, the skin so taut and shiny it looked as if it might snap.

"Marie is a great nurse," Christopher agreed.

"Could you send her in here for me? I have a request."

Christopher balked. "What's the request?"

"I want her to shave my head. There's clippers in my bag."

"Shave your head?" Christopher questioned. "Why on earth would you want to do that? You have beautiful hair."

"I figure I've got the face to pull it off now. Plus, it seems a little silly to spend months losing weight, working out, and buying a brand-new face only to leave your hair precisely the same as it's been for the past decade."

"I think you'll regret it."

"It's only hair. It'll grow back."

"How about I shave it instead? I think Marie will be nervous about clipping your graft."

Clarence shrugged. "Whatever you say. Though make sure she comes to say goodbye before I head off."

"Of course, Clarence," Christopher said, feeling queasy for poor Marie and debating whether this entire procedure had been the right thing to do. The physique change, the haircut, the entirely new face. It felt less like a new beginning or insecurity than it did like a complete identity change.

As the golden tresses began to fall away and scatter upon the white sheets, Clarence watched Christopher's handiwork in the mirror with that same writhing excitement.

"You're almost as good of a barber as you are a surgeon," he joked.

"I'm not sure if that's true."

"Well, it's not patchy, so you're doing something right."

"I used to cut my son's hair into a crew cut every week. At his request. So I know my way around the clippers."

"Ah, a little soldier boy. Is this the son who's about to be a daddy?"

"It is. He's my only son."

"Sons are a blessing. I have three myself."

"Your wife must be exhausted."

Clarence smirked. "Not like she ever lifts a finger. No, that's the nanny's job. Got two of 'em. Mexican. Good workers." Christopher hummed in response. "Anyway. I do hope your boy enjoys his new house. I guess I'll never find out. It's funny. You've been under my skin, cut me open, sewn me back together again. Few things, if any, are more intimate than that. And yet this is likely the last time we will ever meet."

"Well, I'd agree with you, Clarence, if we didn't have three follow-up appointments."

Clarence's face fell. "Ah, of course. My mistake. Morphine makes me forgetful."

"Not a problem, just make sure to schedule the first one with whoever's on the desk on your way out."

"Sure thing, Doc."

The last of the hair fell to the ground, and Clarence admired his newly bald head. It was a striking look, and Christopher had to admit that the man was right: he finally did have the face to pull it off.

CHAPTER SEVENTEEN

THE AGENT

THE PARK RANGER MET THEM IN A SMALL PARKING LOT and guided them into a space despite his utility golf cart being the only other vehicle present. He was old, knobbly, and missing most of his teeth. His gray-and-green uniform hung baggy from his bony body, and his ill-fitting hat wobbled atop his head. When he stopped his incessant jabbering—despite the fact they could barely hear him over the engine—his mouth puckered, giving him the look that his head might invert if he wasn't careful.

Jason tried not to stare but found it difficult. You didn't get people like that in the city. To him, the weathered ranger was as fascinating as the excess of trees and wildlife that surrounded them. Despite the hindrances of rurality, he had to admit that Heather had a much more beautiful work environment. He thought to mention this to her, but the hour of silence was tough to break, and he didn't want to instill doubt by revealing how out of his element he was.

He imagined she had felt the same way at the CIA in her ironed clothes and stiff posture, though she did a much better job at fitting in than he did. Though she was a weaker marksman and lacked formal training, she was better than him at a lot of things, his point proven as she jumped out of the car and strode toward the man. She matched his bumpkin body language perfectly, and the ranger's face lit up. She could fake it, being a people person. He couldn't do that. He supposed he never needed to; his intimidating manner was all he needed to get answers. But out here, they needed to be people's friends for things to run smoothly.

He finished parking, joined them, and greeted the man with a nod. The words still weren't coming, but it didn't matter. The man didn't seem to notice him anyway. Why would he when Heather was there?

"So you haven't seen anyone?" Heather asked.

"Nope," the old guy said before spitting on the ground.

Jason frowned, but Heather didn't wince and waited for the man to continue.

"I walked there for the past hour. Checked the trail cams too. Saw a couple o' deer but no people. If they were ever behind that waterfall, they're still there."

"Well, we'll go have a look. Thanks for your help," Heather said kindly.

The man tipped his hat. "I reckon I'm due a nap, but there are a few more rangers around should you need any help. Though finding the fall should be pretty easy, there's plenty of signs and paths all over the place. That particular one is a little off the beaten trail, but if you stay left after the big one, you'll hear it."

"Thank you, sir," Jason finally added, holding out his hand.

The man took his hand with a surprisingly firm grip and looked Jason up and down with amusement. "What are you? Special forces?" he joked.

"My consultant," Heather corrected.

"Consultant, eh? Well, I hope your consultant knows how to use a firearm if those assholes are out there."

"Don't you worry about that, sir," Jason replied, patting his gun.

"Good man," the ranger enthused before departing on popping joints.

Once he was out of earshot, Heather said, "Backup is on the way, but they're going to keep their distance and stay hidden. If they hear shots after we enter, that's their cue to move in."

"Sounds good. Let's go."

They trudged off along the damp path, kept wet by tree cover, and didn't talk much as they made their way toward their destination. At first Jason thought it was because Heather was laser-focused on the mission, but something else was wrong. She was chewing her lip where there was already a scabby split, and while one hand was on her gun, the other was clenched. He decided to leave it alone, but after the first waterfall—which Heather stopped to take a photo of for her parents so she could pretend she was taking time off—he decided to broach the subject.

"You all right?" he asked.

Heather flinched and looked at him in surprise. "Yeah, I just hate the woods," she finally stuttered.

"What's wrong with the woods? They look pretty nice to me. Better than being surrounded by concrete."

"The last time I was in the woods looking for a killer, I found him, but it was too late."

Jason nodded. "Dennis Burke. That was a hell of a case. I ended up following it on the news."

"Yeah, it was."

"I feel the same about the desert," Jason said after an awkward beat of silence.

"Huh?"

"How you feel about the woods. I feel the same about the desert. Similar deal. Terrorists in a hut in the middle of nowhere. Got there too late to save a captive."

"Sorry."

"Thanks," Jason muttered. "Sorry about Alice Warren."

"Wow. No one ever remembers her name. Not outside of Glenville. It's all about Burke."

"I think it's important to remember the victims."

"I agree."

Heather looked at him as if she was trying to figure something out. Her eyes narrowed and her brow furrowed. Eventually, she relented and started to speed up, walking ahead of him as if she knew the place like the back of her hand. He wanted to tell her that he wasn't a robot, that he really did understand, but he knew it would be hard to believe without a heart-to-heart talk, and their professional relationship wasn't close to that stage yet.

As the sound of their destination built to a watery crescendo, he received a call and gestured for Heather to fall back as he answered. It was Bonnie. He decided to put it on speaker to save him and Heather from any further attempts at conversation.

"Hey, Jase," she said, and he cringed at the nickname while Heather smirked.

"Bonnie."

"So I dug up Joel Schubert's files. None of them are ours, but there are plenty in other databases. Namely law enforcement's."

"Okay."

"You're right. Petty criminal. He's been booked for robbery, grand theft auto, assault, the works. Never murdered or kidnapped, but he did shoot a guy in the leg in a burglary gone wrong. He's done a couple of months in the big house here and there, but nothing big enough to keep him away for long."

"So we're right. He's no criminal mastermind."

"Nope," Bonnie replied. "He's a semi-reliable gun for hire. You're looking for someone else."

"We figured as much. We think it's his partner. The blond."

"It's possible," Bonnie said. "The blond wanted your dad but realized he couldn't pull it off on his own."

Heather nodded in agreement with Bonnie's assessment and asked, "Has he ever been booked with a blond before?"

"Hi, Heather," Bonnie chirped. "Nope. He went down with a few different guys but no young Caucasian blonds. Mostly old crackheads and ex-cons."

"He's also missing," Jason said.

"Yeah, I saw that just now," Bonnie replied. "Maybe there were too many cooks in the kitchen. Any word from forensics?"

"Not yet," Heather answered, checking her phone just in case. "I guess we'll find out if it was his blood soon enough."

"Thanks for the information, Bonnie," Jason added.

"No problem. You two stay safe. Don't pull any of that hero shit, Jase."

"I'll keep you posted," Jason replied before hanging up.

Heather's phone pinged, and she took a deep breath. "Backup is in the trees. You ready to go?"

Jason adjusted his bulletproof vest. "Let's do this."

They pushed through some trees and came to a clearing surrounding a small waterfall. The water ran over a ledge, creating gaps at the side that they could sneak in through without getting soaked and consequently shot.

"I'll take the right," Heather said.

"Copy that," Jason replied, splitting away and moving toward his entry point with calculated determination.

He waited, with his back to the slimy rock, until Heather matched his movements on the other side. He was disoriented by the deafening roar of the body of water but kept his wits about him. They looked at each other across the gap, Heather mouthed a countdown, and on *go*, they rounded into the cave.

"Police! Put your hands on your head!" Heather called out, pointing her gun around the cave, her voice echoing back at her.

The flashlight attachments on their guns illuminated the small cave, and when Jason saw two figures—one brown-haired and one blond—he nearly fired on impulse. He didn't let his instincts get the better of him and kept his trigger finger slack though. Fortunately, no one took the opportunity to fire back. In fact, neither of the suspects moved at all.

"Oh my god," Heather said, her voice froggy.

133

She moved closer as Jason stayed rooted in a puddle, as if vines were bolting his feet to the freezing-cold floor. Once she was only a few feet away, her bright white light revealed everything. Jason tried very hard not to let the roar of rage rip out of his throat, but a strangled moan managed to sneak from between his lips like a wounded boar.

Two men were seated, propped up against the cave wall, their mouths slack and their throats deeply slit. Dark blood covered their clothes, and it was all Jason could do not to throw his gun in frustration as he truly realized and understood that he was looking at the corpses of Joel Schubert and his partner in crime.

Heather reached out and touched the blond's throat and retracted from the cold. She hissed, planting one palm hard on the floor. She looked over her shoulder and shook her head.

"They've been dead for a while. Rigor mortis is setting in. I guess forensics will figure out it's their blood at the house soon enough."

Jason didn't reply. He just kept staring into the lifeless eyes of Joel Schubert. He recognized them well from their clash at his Black Douglas. They'd been fearful back then, but now there was nothing there except for layers of dry tissue.

"So much for the blond being the one in charge," Heather muttered, heaving herself off the ground and falling back.

"Fuck," Jason whimpered in frustration.

He didn't bother to look around for his dad. He knew he was long gone. He'd probably never even arrived at the cave. These two were nothing more than effective bait for a pair of stupid fish.

Jason put his gun on the ground and began to pace. When his frustration reached a critical level, he extended an arm and punched the cave wall above the heads of the dead with as much force as he could muster. It was a mighty swing, and each of his knuckles split upon impact. Blood rushed down his arm, and he turned to see Heather hang up the phone.

"We're going to find him," she said.

Jason scoffed and squatted to pick up his gun. As he did so, the light shone once again on the men who would never see justice. He quickly moved the flashlight away, but Heather stopped him firmly.

"Look," she stated.

There was something grasped in the stiff hand of Joel Schubert. The pair moved closer with bated breath and soon realized it was an envelope. Heather released the barrel of the gun, moved toward Joel, and pried the paper out of his rheumatic fingers.

"It's addressed to you," Heather said faintly.

"Read it," Jason commanded.

"Are you sure you want me to—"

"Read it," Jason growled.

"'Dear Jason Fleming. I know this all must be awfully confusing for you. Exhausting too. You're not used to doing your own dirty work. Haven't been out in the field in some time. Your partner there, the pretty Indian, now, she's used to seeing bodies. I bet if you measured her heartbeat right now, she'd be as calm as a monk in a monastery. But you? You're like a rat in a maze. You sit in your office in a suit and tie, feeding intel to the Air Force, getting them to drop bombs and fire missiles. Every day you come home with blood on your hands that you wash off in the en suite of your suburban palace. I wonder how you sleep at night, but I bet it's cozy. Meanwhile, people out there, across the world, are terrified of men like you. But not me, not anymore. God, how I'd pay to see your face right now. But I'm afraid we're doomed to be star-crossed enemies.'"

Heather folded the letter back up and slipped it back into the envelope. Jason lowered the light, and Heather moved toward him. She was soft, almost motherly, like a parent picking up their child after getting into a fight at school.

"What are they talking about?" she whispered.

Jason ignored the question and snatched the envelope from her hand. He pulled it back out of the envelope and flipped the piece of paper over, revealing a flyer for Black Magic Pizzeria.

"Do you know where this is?" he asked her sternly.

"Let me look it up," Heather replied hesitantly. She typed on her phone, her eyes flicking between the screen and Jason's face. "Yeah. It's a couple miles away."

"Okay then, let's go. Now. No sleeping on it. No thinking about it. We're going."

"I—"

"I can go alone."

Heather stiffened. "No. You're not going alone. But doesn't this seem weird to you?"

"Weird?"

"He said you were like a rat in a maze. He said you'll never meet. What if this is a trap?"

"Even if it is, we're going. We need answers, and going home won't answer any of them."

"Jason, I have a really bad feeling about this."

"I don't operate on feelings. Are you coming with me or not?"

Heather sighed. "I'm coming with you. But so is backup."

"Fine. Let's go," Jason replied, stuffing the envelope into his pocket and keeping his gun firmly in his grip.

CHAPTER EIGHTEEN

THE DETECTIVE

A S THEY SPED TO THEIR NEXT DESTINATION, HEATHER stared at the rain-spattered window and watched the drops roll down the glass in jagged lines. She tried to guess the paths of each strand but had little success in predicting unpredictability. It was a boring game, but she needed something to occupy herself while not behind the wheel. Easily carsick and impatient, she hated being in the passenger seat at the best of times, and the dark only worsened her grievances. Though it was not yet nightfall—as Jason informed her when she told him to turn on the headlights—the world around them was rapidly dimming as gloomy, water-filled clouds consumed what remained of the sky.

It might have been the start of summer, but aside from the Sunshine Sally's Café logo, Heather struggled to remember when she'd last seen the golden orb or felt its warmth. Considering the success of her garden and her tanner-than-usual tone, it must have been recent, but she couldn't place when or where. Tampered with by her current emotions, her memories turned grayer the deeper she dived, casting even her ruby-red tomatoes in various shades of ash.

As the bitter black storm took hold, Jason finally turned on the headlights and grumbled as Heather taunted him with a silent "I told you so." Their surroundings were becoming dangerous fast—despite what his precious weather app said—and the road ahead was quickly covered in the core ingredient of a hydroplane.

It all felt like a bad omen, but if Jason didn't operate on feelings, Heather doubted that an even less tangible harbinger of doom would deter him. Though, as they passed a murder of crows picking at the remnants of what was once a raccoon, she wished it would.

She turned to Jason, considering making an excuse and forcing him to pull over. Travel nausea masquerading as food poisoning might give them some time to come up with a better plan. Just as she turned, one hand over her mouth and one on her stomach, Jason answered his ringing phone, completely ignoring her charade. Heather dropped the act as he proceeded to drive one-handed instead of putting the call on speaker. Her anxiety spiking as he swerved on the empty road, she glowered and felt pity for Gabriel, having been stuck in the passenger seat for the past year. Still, Jason gave no acknowledgment, and she returned to watching the droplets, pretending she was too absorbed in their pattern-making to hear Jason's conversation, but she knew from their proximity that she wasn't fooling anyone.

"Hi, honey," he answered.

Natalie, Heather thought.

"I know. I said I'd call. It's just… Yeah, I know. I'm sorry. You know I hate worrying you. Come on, honey, please don't. I just got caught up in… Yeah, of course."

Natalie seemed to be crying on the other end, and as the conversation became increasingly fraught, Heather willed her body to meld through the car door and onto the road. Unfortunately, her cells were uncooperative, so there she remained. Stuck fast and uncomfortable.

"No, the house was a bust," Jason added. "No, I'm not on my way back, we had to go to a second location. Honey, I'm trying to find my dad. I miss you guys too, but… Uh-huh… Listen, I'll let you know once we find these guys, and then I'll head home as soon as I possibly can. You know there's nowhere I'd rather be."

Jason sighed, and the hair on the back of Heather's neck rose as she felt his eyes on her.

"No, the second location was a bust too. Sort of. Honey, I can tell you all about it later, but I have to go." He paused as Natalie's buzzing voice was raised almost to the point of clarity, and Jason grew quieter by the second. "Please don't put the girls on right now. I'm just about to pull up… Natalie, come on… No, I don't know when I'll be back, but I'll tell you as soon as I do… I hope so, but I just don't know. I'm sorry, honey. I love you. Okay, bye."

Slowly Heather turned to face Jason, his eyes flitting between her and the road ahead. "Are you—" she started.

He thankfully interrupted her question, tactfully avoiding the mutual vulnerability. "Sorry you had to hear that," he said.

Heather threw her hands up. "Hey, don't worry about me. Honestly, I don't know how you do the family thing. Having three dogs is hard enough, but at least I don't have to apologize to them."

"Huh," he said.

"What?"

"I just pictured you more as a cat person. Low-maintenance, standoffish, prickly."

"Are you talking about cats or me?" Heather asked.

"You are definitely not low-maintenance."

Heather scoffed but didn't disagree.

"You're divorced, right?" Jason asked tentatively.

"Yeah, but not because I'm prickly and high-maintenance," Heather joked dryly.

Jason apologized with his eyes. "Was it because of work?"

Heather hesitated. She could see the anxiety in Jason's eyes about the future of his marriage, but she also knew he was as good at detecting liars as she was at sensing danger.

"It wasn't exactly the job," Heather said. "It was how I reacted to it. I yo-yo'd between being an insomniac workaholic and a depressed drunk. Neither worked well for a happy marriage, and eventually...," she paused, "*Dan* felt he had to leave. So it was the job, and it was me, and it was everything all at once."

"Makes sense."

"Do you and Natalie argue a lot?"

"Never."

"Then don't worry about it," Heather advised. "Especially not right now. Natalie is traumatized and wants you close to her. You're under a lot of pressure. What's happening between you is normal. You'll figure it out."

"Thanks."

"No problem." Heather cleared her throat. "Before we pull up, can I ask you something?"

"Shoot."

"What do you think that letter meant? I mean, do you have any idea who could've written it?"

"Nope. Not a clue," he replied.

"Do you think some sort of extremist is targeting you?"

"An extremist?" he questioned, his expression bewildered.

"Yeah. All the stuff about getting the military to do your dirty work and the mention of bombings and stuff. Maybe an anti-war protestor pushed to the extremes? Or someone affected by the drone strikes overseas?"

"God, I hope not. We have enough on our plates as it is without bringing domestic or international terrorism into the mix."

Heather balked at what she had to ask next. "Did you have anything to do with stuff like that? You know, ordering strikes?"

Jason surveyed Heather calculatedly, but there appeared to be cogs turning behind his eyes. "Even if I did, you know I couldn't tell you. Anyway, we're here."

Heather coughed and bobbed her head, her face burning, but her body chilled. It was unnerving to realize that while Jason knew everything about her and her career, she knew almost nothing about him or all that he had done in the name of protecting his country. She was starting to like the guy, trust him even, but she knew that her theory of not being able to truly know anyone was ten times truer for someone like him.

"Ready?" Jason asked gruffly.

Heather glanced in the rearview mirror, reassured as backup pulled up behind them, and then looked down the barrel of the run-down street to Black Magic Pizzeria. There was a faded hand-painted sign above the front door that featured three witches surrounding a cauldron and laminated menu items in the dark windows.

Dark, Heather thought, double-checking the opening hours.

"It's supposed to be open," she said.

"So?"

"So where is everybody?" she asked.

Jason looked around. "Most of the houses look abandoned, maybe the pizza place is too. They probably just never deleted their website."

Heather pursed her lips. "No. There was a new review posted yesterday on Yelp."

"Maybe they just decided to take the day off."

"Jason, this doesn't feel right."

Jason was already half out of the car and looked at Heather with that same cool expression. "Are you coming?"

Nothing was going to stop him, so "Of course" was the only answer she could give as she joined him in the cold world outside of the car. They walked toward the pizza place. Heather could see that the front door was propped open, and there was definitely no one inside. It had been awhile since her gut had screamed at her so loudly, but there was no turning back.

She looked back to see a group of six heavily armed police officers following them discreetly, a range of weapons aimed at the building. They may not have been a SWAT team, but they were city cops, and they were not only capable but ready. Still, it was a small comfort as Heather nodded at them for them to take their positions and they hid behind cars, leaving her and Jason to enter alone.

Jason moved in first, but Heather was hot on his heels, slipping through the partly-opened entrance. She braced herself for something horrible, but there was no explosion, no gunshots, no ticking, no beeping, no nothing. At first glance, it was just an empty run-of-the-mill pizzeria until she spotted the knocked-over stools at the counter and gestured toward them. A struggle seemed likely.

They split up to look around, carefully treading across sticky black-and-white linoleum tiles and scrutinizing each bit of turquoise and patterned plastic furniture with the lights on their guns. There were open boxes full of pizza atop several of the spray-streaked tables with half-eaten slices abandoned in both box and booth. One notable slice was on the floor, a skid mark of sauce to its left as if it had been thrown. She knew teenagers could be messy, especially around their friends, but this seemed like something else.

"Is anyone here?" she asked loudly after finding her left half of the room devoid of human life.

A banging noise answered her question as she turned toward a closed door kept shut by a tilted chair that had been obscured by the height of the central counter. Jason quickly moved to her side, and with their weapons aimed high, Heather removed the chair as Jason cautiously opened the door, keeping his body angled out of the potential firing zone.

When no gunshots came, they peered inside to see six people shoved inside a cupboard, bound and gagged. Two wore uniforms sporting the same witch-and-cauldron logo, and the others were dressed in casual clothes. All of them were young, just kids trying to do their job or catch a bite to eat.

"Oh god," Heather whispered, ungagging the nearest person, a young female employee, and then she moved clockwise to the others while Jason protected her back. "It's going to be okay," she assured them as she moved. "Are any of you hurt?"

"No. They didn't hurt us," said the uniformed young girl with short pink hair.

"Who's *they*?" Heather asked.

"Two men and a woman," the girl trembled. "They were dressed in black and forced us in here at gunpoint."

"What did they look like?" Heather questioned.

The girl stammered. "They were wearing masks."

"Like balaclavas?"

The girl shook her head. "No. Like human faces. You know, like those creepy masks of presidents."

"Were they of presidents?" Jason asked.

The girl's coworker shook his head. "I don't think so. Actually, one looked a lot like you," he said, looking up at Heather's face with an expression that made her skin crawl.

Heather instinctively stepped back and glanced at Jason, who looked equally confused. "Do you have cameras?" she asked.

"Yes, but they shot out the lenses and took the tapes," the young man replied.

"Tapes?" Heather groaned. "When did they leave?"

"I think fifteen minutes ago. That's when I last heard the door creak," the girl said, glancing at the wall clock.

Shit, Heather thought, realizing her efforts to avoid the pizzeria had ultimately screwed them out of finding who they were looking for. But what she couldn't figure out was why they'd stopped off here in the first place. Was it to throw them off the trail, or was there more here than six terrified young people?

"Okay. It's okay," she assured them. "We're going to get you out of here. Now, I'm going to untie you, but I want you to stay here until we're sure it's safe to leave. Don't move unless one of us gets you."

She was met with nervous nods and tried to smile, though her muscles strained against the attempt, causing an unsettling leer. Their expressions far from comforted, she gave up, and after setting them free, Heather apologetically shut the door. She turned to Jason, only to find he'd disappeared. Looking around, she briefly panicked before spotting a swing door with a porthole window still oscillating from interaction and followed him through it. She found him in the modest kitchen staring despondently at a closed pizza box on the counter.

"It's addressed to me," Jason murmured.

That's why we're here, she thought, staring at the lonely box in the tidy kitchen.

"Don't open it," Heather warned. "That's the trap."

"Step back then," Jason warned her with a growl, his fingers on the edge.

Heather didn't budge. "Jason, I'm serious. We need to call in the bomb squad, and—"

It was too late. The lid was already being pried ajar, and as two officers pushed their way into the room, Heather screamed at them to move. With a flicking motion—as if overturning something that you saw a spider crawl beneath—Jason flung the cover open and jumped back, and Heather scrunched up her eyes. When another bout of nothing occurred, she opened them and craned to see a normal—though topping-heavy and incredibly greasy—pizza inside the box. Then they both saw it: something was stuck to the lid.

Heather crept closer and saw that it was a maze—one of those types given to children at restaurants, along with a box of off-brand Crayola, to keep them occupied and quiet while their parents tried to relax. But this one did not inspire any feelings of tranquility. In the middle, situated in a dead end, was a prominent red dot drawn in crayon. Next to it were the words, "You're Next."

"End of the road," Heather said quietly, and Jason looked at her accusingly. "Sorry," she added hastily. "I've just seen something like this before."

She turned to the two officers as Jason stayed focused on the pizza and told them to do a sweep. She specified the bathrooms and prayed they wouldn't find Christopher dead in the bathroom as she'd found that little girl all those years ago when she, too, had received a token signifying the end of a terrible game.

"What's on the pizza?" she asked, returning to the dumbfounded Jason.

To her shock and horror, Jason picked up a piece and bit into it. He chewed, swilled, and then frowned. "Lamb, onions, garlic, peppers… saffron. I think."

"Impressive palate. Do you think it means anything?"

"Probably," Jason said, pinching his bridge. "But I have no idea what. I just know it's time to go home. Whoever this is, they're right. We are at a dead end."

"Yeah, maybe," Heather replied, looking up the ingredients on her phone. After only finding recipes for a few Spanish recipes and *kabob koobideh*, an Iranian type of kebab, she abandoned her attempt to find meaning in the food. She figured someone out there was probably just frustrated, awaiting their dinner to arrive.

The officers returned, having cleared the building. Heather asked them to call in CSI as Jason pocketed the note, and they moved toward the front door. Just as she slipped outside, she told one of the officers to remain with the captives, gather their statements, and then call in more officers to escort them home.

Jason still had his gun raised, and just as Heather was about to tell him to lower it—not wanting to worry the few inhabitants any further—a loud bang rang in her ears. At first, she'd thought Jason had fired, but when she saw his face staring past her, she followed his gaze to the other police officer who'd been in the building. There was a smoking hole in the forehead of his helmet.

"Shooter!" Heather cried out. "Everybody, get down!"

She and Jason ducked behind a car just in time as another shot rang out, and the car mirror was desecrated by the impact. Several car alarms began going off, disorienting the entire crew, and Heather looked around frantically for the source of the violence.

"Where the hell are they?" she muttered, and then she looked at the downward angle of the shot and realized, whoever was shooting wasn't on the ground. "Sniper," she said into her walkie and looked up.

What appeared to be a woman was lying on her stomach atop the building to their left, wearing motorcycle gear and a mask that looked frighteningly like Heather's face. It wasn't just Jason who was being toyed with anymore. Heather held the bile at the back of her throat and told backup where to point.

"Who has a clean shot?" she asked.

"I do," a slightly grizzled woman's voice replied.

"Take the shot," Heather commanded.

Bang.

Heather watched as the rifle was knocked from her doppelganger's hands, and the woman scrabbled back and out of view. They all waited for her to reemerge but were soon met with the revving of a motorcycle coming from the back of the building. Heather was quick to command the officers to follow the sound but knew that whoever had killed the officer was long gone, the engine already roaring in the distance.

The officer, she thought, getting to her feet and sprinting toward the man.

"Officer down!" she repeated. "Get an ambulance out here!"

However, much like the woman on the roof, she knew it was already too late. She gently removed his helmet as Jason hovered above and revealed the face of a middle-aged man with a large black mustache and wide-open eyes. His mouth, too, hung slightly ajar as if mid-sentence. He had been dead before he hit the ground.

Heather dropped down onto her rear, water soaking through her pants, and stared at Jason in horror. "What do we do now?"

"We inform the CIA," Jason said confidently, dragging Heather effortlessly to her feet by the armpit. "An Intelligence Officer is under threat, that makes it our territory now."

Heather agreed blankly, finding that she no longer wanted to be chief and commander as the other officers crowded around their deceased colleague. Jason patted her back before leaving her shell-shocked to head to the car. He had plenty of calls to make, and though Heather may have been needed, she stayed right where she was as her fellow police officers displayed their grief.

CHAPTER NINETEEN

THE AGENT

HEATHER ENDED UP STAYING BEHIND TO HELP CLEAN up the mess they had made, and though Jason had half-assedly volunteered to stick around, it was clear he wasn't needed. Heather went so far as to insist he head home to his family. It didn't feel right to do so, but he had nowhere else to go and nothing else to do.

Not only was his boss unhappy—to say the least—with Jason's unprofessional conduct, but a thirteenth dead body had just joined the proliferating pile of murder victims. Worst of all, every single one of them had been killed because of his father— his hero—and seemingly himself. What they'd done to trigger such heinous acts, he had no idea, but the guilt was still heavy on his aching shoulders. Sure, he had worked with the military as Heather had suspected, but he was not a major player in the sector. In fact, it was unfathomable to Jason that he was remotely important enough for somebody to murder others because of him. He'd only been with the CIA for seven years, and though he'd climbed the ranks fast and had had a hand in some significant missions, he was far from being one of the big dogs. So if the family fortune wasn't the motivation, why him and not his boss? He feared that if it really was the end of the road, as Heather had put it. He might have to live the rest of his life without the answers he craved.

His phone rang, and he hesitated before flipping it from its face-down position. He feared that Heather, his boss, or his wife would be on the other end with more bad news or further tears. Fortunately, it was only Bonnie, but it still took tremendous force to answer, despite reminding himself that he'd assembled the team for a reason, even if their efforts had proved futile thus far.

"Hi, Bonnie," he said flatly.

"Hey, Jase. How goes it?" Bonnie chirped, ever eager.

"I'm flying back to Virginia."

"So… it went?"

"Bad. It went bad, Bonnie. Joel Schubert and his partner in crime are dead, their throats slit by their boss or another layer of lackeys."

"Crap," Bonnie huffed.

"That's not all. A local police officer was also killed by a sniper, and these freaks are running around wearing masks of our faces to commit their crimes."

"Ew. Creepy. How the heck would they even… You know what? I don't want to know."

"Me either. And it's a little worse than creepy," Jason chastised. "Did you miss the part about the dead cop?"

"Yeah, I did. Sorry, my brain is short-circuiting."

"It's fine. Well, you're fine. It's not fine. This whole thing is a mess, and I think it's my fault."

Bonnie hummed. "How do you figure?"

"Because there was a letter addressed to me. I'll get into it when I see you, but let's just say, whoever this is, they're targeting me. Which is why I've had to bring the case to the official attention of the Agency."

Bonnie sucked her teeth. "Did you get in trouble?"

"What do you think?"

"Fired?" Bonnie asked with bated breath.

"No."

"Phew. Suspended?"

"Somehow, also no," Jason replied. "And don't worry, I kept your names out of the mix," he informed her, hearing the unsaid question in her voice.

"Well, that's something, and maybe it's for the best that it's not a secret anymore. We can actually ask for help now."

"It's a small consolation for having a target on my head and the blood of thirteen people on my hands. Not that Joel and his companion were good people, but they were still…"

"Yeah. People, I know. Well, hey, another upside is, I can now organize the best possible protection for your family too. Should I send some agents over now to watch your house?"

Jason rubbed his face. "Yeah. I didn't even think about that. Tell them to be subtle though. I don't want to scare Natalie."

"Sure thing. And if it helps, I also have some new information. About Schubert's partner and a possible suspect, though if now's not a good time…"

"It's as good a time as any. We need new leads and fast."

"Okay, so Joel Schubert's partner was named Wendell Bates. Takahiro hacked the cameras near Sunshine Sally's and found the van when it still had plates on. They bought it from a used-car lot for cash and registered it under Wendell's name. I thought it was likely a fake name, but when I ran the name through the system, lo and behold, who should pop up but a handsome blond who lives in Portland? The rest matched too: ex-bouncer, assault charges, robbery charges, manslaughter. He was also notably a paranoid schizophrenic who'd been institutionalized several times. Had a lot of opinions about the government, and a prior search of his computer in his home found that he was an active user of the Tor browser—"

"The what?"

"The thing you use to get on the dark web. He also was an active participant in a lot of insurgent, extremist forums."

"So Heather was right about the extremist," Jason groaned, keeping his voice low and hoping that everyone in the first class had their headphones on and earplugs in.

"She was right about the *what*?"

"Whoever wrote the letter mentioned the CIA using the Air Force as puppets. Clearly, whoever has taken my dad hates the government, and if Wendell was a radicalized insurgent, maybe that's how he met whoever's doing this."

It made sense, and he was realizing there was something to Heather's method of reading between the lines instead of relying on finite data.

"Huh. Hang on, Takahiro is flailing around. I think he's found something. I'll hand you over."

"Sure," Jason said, not sure he was prepared for the incoming energy.

"Hi! Jase! Are you there?"

Jason uttered a strained, "Yeah."

"Great. Listen, man, I know you've had a hell of a day, but I was just going through some files to help Bonnie out. Mainly, I was looking for crimes of a similar nature in Portland, CCTV of Joel and Wendell and the people they've associated with, etc., but nothing was jumping out."

"Okay."

"But just now that we know the kidnapping isn't for financial gain, I decided to go in a different direction and run your dad's name through the system. See if there's anything more to the motive than getting back at you."

Jason shifted in his seat, pressing the phone closer to his ear. "I'm listening."

"Well, it turns out he actually contacted the CIA back in 2018 to offer intelligence about a terrorist named Clarence Dixon Jr."

Something flickered in the back of Jason's mind, and he strangled out a sound that only faintly resembled the question he meant to ask.

What?

Takahiro repeated himself, louder this time, "Your dad provided intel about a terrorist. His name was Clarence Dixon Jr. He bombed the MI6 in December 2018. Killed one person and severely injured another."

"Clarence Dixon… That name. Why is it so familiar?" Jason asked, trying to read between the lines but finding that the words were covered with black rectangles. Redacted, redacted, redacted.

"He was all over the news at the time, or maybe your dad mentioned him to you?" Takahiro asked. "I mean, I've never heard of him before today, but you know I only think about tech stuff."

"No, it's not that. I'd remember if Dad told me he was going to talk to the CIA," Jason said, wondering why his dad would keep something like this from him and how he managed to go behind his back at his own workplace. He was starting to doubt his credentials as an intelligence officer, but his father had always been an adept liar. It was why Jason had believed in Santa until he was twelve. "Does the file say how he knew Clarence?"

"Sure does. He was a patient, apparently. Total face reconstruction."

"Total face… Was this before or after the bombing?"

"Before. In June."

"So he changed his face, bombed a major government building, and then disappeared?"

"Pretty much. Not to quote Scooby-Doo, but he would have gotten away with it too. No way anyone could've IDed him without your dad's description of his new face. His older photos and the composite drawing look completely different. Not that his testimony helped beyond putting a name to a face, they still never found him."

"So he's in hiding," Jason realized. "That's why he's getting other people to do his dirty work for him. My dad ruined his new identity."

"So maybe that's why took him? To punish you both? Two birds, one stone, you know? He hurts you and the guy who stabbed him in the back in one go?"

Jason's stomach churned. It was bad enough to be held hostage on account of someone else's actions, but to have screwed over your captor on such a colossal level diminished any hope of fair or accommodating treatment. Before, he'd pictured his dad in some basement somewhere, sleeping on a mattress, but now the vision bore chains, torture, and grievous bodily harm.

He cleared his throat with some sparkling water and changed the subject. "Whom did this Clarence guy kill at the MI6?"

Takahiro clicked and typed loudly before answering. "An intelligence officer. Ruby Norris."

Jason scratched his face hard, catching his cheek with a chipped nail. "I know that name too."

"Sorry, can't help you there. Even I don't have the clearance to access her files in London. All I can see is that she worked alongside the CIA on a couple of occasions, but all the information is redacted. Did you work with her?"

"I don't… can't remember."

"You're under a lot of stress," Takahiro countered. "Get some rest, I'm sure whatever you've forgotten will come to you."

"Yeah, give it time. You've always had the worst memory," Bonnie chimed in from a distance. "It's your only flaw."

She was wrong about it being his only flaw, but she was correct that it was a glaring one. At least as far as work was concerned, if it was in the past, it was gone. Today and tomorrow were all he knew, and until now, not lugging his history around had served him well. Now, despite how much it clearly pained her, he envied Heather's visceral, expansive recollection abilities.

The names provided bugged him. They crawled under his skin, itchy lumps squirming and crawling up to the tip of his tongue, where they pinched the muscle with sharp mandibles. It itched, pulsed, and zapped, but nothing revved inside his mind.

He ended the call, clearly frustrated but verbally thankful. A probable suspect was a game-changing lead, and despite his mouth and brain having run dry, he called Heather with the good news. He could tell she was defeated and guilt-ridden when she answered, and something roiled within. She sounded on the verge of tears and close to hanging up because of it. Despite wanting to, he didn't apologize. He couldn't undo the damage, but he could make it count for something. This man, Clarence Dixon Jr., and his father's testimony, at least meant that the officer who had died did so in the name of inevitably catching a dangerous international threat rather than for another tragic murder case turned cold.

He told her everything with as much brevity as he could muster, and when he was done, Heather breathed quietly into the receiver. It took her at least thirty seconds to say, "It's good. It's really good. I'll let Howie know. He's pretty devastated. It might help him to know we're moving in the right direction."

"When you speak with him, please tell him to inform Officer..."

"O'Brian."

"O'Brian's family that I will cover his funeral costs in full and be happy to help them with anything else they need."

"That's kind of you," Heather said quietly.

No, it's not, Jason thought. Kindness would be going back in time and taking his place. Kindness would be doing something that didn't assuage his guilt as a bonus.

"It's the least I can do," he stated.

Heather sniffed, and Jason hoped it was only from the evening air. "I'll let you go," she murmured.

Click. Silence.

Three hours on the plane to go.

Back at home—after greatly surprising his daughters with both his presence and plush toys and tiny purses from the airport—the girls were sent away to play with their presents while he dived into another hushed argument with Natalie. Not that *argument* was exactly the right word for what occurred. He said very little, and while Natalie was upset, she wasn't angry. She'd never been a foam-finger-waving fan of his line of work, but her distaste for the danger had only grown with the birth of each of her children and her decline in financial independence.

Fortunately, she ran out of steam quickly, clearly more grateful that he was home than upset that he was late, and they were all summoned to the dining room to say grace and eat a delicious beef casserole. It was nice, it was warm, and it was devastating. There was a man who wouldn't be going home to his family tonight, and Jason tried not to imagine what this room would look like right now if Natalie had been the one to get that dreadful call instead. Warm, yellow, illuminated by candlelight would be replaced by stagnant blue, the shadows hard to swim through, and muffled sobs coming from the rooms above.

He was distracted through dinner, his daughter's stories of school and backyard worms barely registering. Natalie noticed, and instead of scolding Jason for not paying attention, she took the girls to bed early and left her husband to sit and finish dinner alone.

When she returned after a lengthy story-time session, she found Jason crouched on the living room floor, surrounded by the carefully labeled plastic storage tubs that usually occupied the basement. He was flipping through a large hardback book at a maddening pace, and Natalie approached cautiously, perching her dainty body on the arm of the family-sized couch.

"Jason, honey, what are you doing?" she inquired, keeping her voice steady.

"I'm looking through my yearbooks."

"Why?"

"There's this name. Clarence Dixon Jr., I recognize it from somewhere, but I can't find it. I thought maybe I went to school with him, and that's why he knew me, but I can't find him. His pictures online don't ring a bell either."

Natalie pressed a worried hand to her decolletage. "Jason, what's going on?"

Jason looked up at his wife and realized he'd said too much. "Nothing, honey. Just something to do with my dad's case."

"Jason, does someone dangerous know who you are?"

Jason stayed silent.

"Is our family in danger?" she asked in a hushed tone, looking up the stairs behind her for peeping faces between the banisters.

Though it pained him to admit it, Jason nodded. "Maybe, honey, maybe. But don't worry. Please don't worry. I'll make arrangements. The CIA will keep you safe, I promise."

"Will we have to leave our home?" She analyzed her husband's face and closed her eyes, moving her hand to her forehead. "What about school?"

"It's only temporary."

"And what about you?" she asked, moving both hands to her lap and balling the fabric of her skirt into her fists. "Are you going to come with us?"

He shook his head. "I can't, honey. I have to find this guy. I think he has Dad."

Natalie's eyes welled with tears, and she tightened her grip. "When do we leave?"

"Tomorrow. To be safe. Mom will go with you. I'll put my best agents on the case to safeguard, and I'll call you whenever I can."

"What about visiting?"

"I can't know where you are. If I get…" He didn't finish the thought aloud, but Natalie got the gist and began to sob.

He held his arms out for her, and she stood. He feared she might run to the bedroom, but instead, she walked toward him and lowered herself into his lap. He wrapped himself around her and rubbed her back gently.

"It's going to be okay."

"No, it's not," she whimpered. "We're going to have another baby."

He squeezed her, feeling joy wash over him despite everything that had happened. "Honey, that's great. I can't tell you how great that is."

She shook her head. "I can't—I *can't*—look after and support three children on my own."

Jason's heart plummeted, and he tightened his grasp and stroked her hair. "You won't. I promise it's going to be okay. You'll see."

It didn't sound like a lie, but he prayed to a God to whom he hadn't always been faithful, to make his assurances come true.

CHAPTER TWENTY

THE SURGEON

2018

A S CHRISTOPHER FLICKED THROUGH PHOTOS OF HIS latest patient's tummy tuck for the website and congratulated himself on the quality of the results, somebody tapped lightly on his office door.

"Come in," he said and swiveled to face forward, a smile on his face.

The door opened, and Marie stepped inside. "Good morning, Dr. Fleming," she replied.

"Good morning to you, Marie," Christopher enthused. "How may I help you?"

"I just wanted to let you know that I don't think Mr. Dixon will be attending his appointment today."

Christopher furrowed his brow. "Really, why's that?"

"Nobody at reception can get ahold of him. The calls ring out, and the e-mails bounce back."

"Hmm. Perhaps I'll try to give him a call. We've mostly been communicating via my private number. Maybe he doesn't recognize the clinic's."

Marie gave him a strange look but, fortunately, didn't press the matter of why he would be contacting his patient in such a manner. She forced a polite smile, as she always did, no matter the challenging nature of a client or coworker, and said, "Let me know if you get ahold of him."

"Of course. Will do, Marie. Please delay whoever is in the waiting room by ten minutes to give me a chance to contact him."

"Of course," Marie replied, glancing at his work on the turned screen and nodding approvingly before leaving.

Christopher leaned back in his chair and scrolled through the long list of contacts on his phone until he reached Dixon. They hadn't spoken since the discharge back in June, but Clarence had contacted reception to cancel and reschedule, so he held onto some degree of hope. Yet just as Marie had said, the phone just kept ringing with no sign of being answered. He waited until the beep only to be informed that the user's voice-mail box was full. Still in good spirits, Christopher tried again and again, hoping the third time would be the charm. It wasn't, so he resorted to sending a text. It tried and failed to send for a few seconds before the blue bubble turned green and sent as a text message instead of an instant one.

Maybe he's somewhere without a signal, Christopher thought. *Out checking his oil fields for more liquid money.*

It wasn't illogical, and Clarence had never struck him as being particularly organized. In fact, "away with the fairies"—a phrase Kathleen enjoyed—seemed an astute observation.

So he let it go and returned to the photographs of his work while waiting for his next patient. It was nothing to worry about, he was sure. Patients missed appointments all the time. Sure, it was strange that Clarence had avoided the clinic for the past six months, but he wasn't the first ultra-rich client Christopher had had who flouted their appointments. Not to mention Clarence lived far away and had a private doctor to attend to his healing. No, the main problem for Christopher was not the avoidance or lack of contact. It was having performed the best work of his career and having nothing to show for it, and as the biggest surgical convention of the year was coming up, he was growing desperate.

———

At home, Kathleen and Christopher curled up on the couch together, savoring a particularly delectable bottle of red wine—gifted to him by a recurrent client—after enjoying their ritualistic Friday takeaway. Tonight it had been a platter of sushi from the brand-new place around the corner. It was impressive and would undoubtedly make its way into the rotation, and though Christopher feared he had overindulged from the heaviness of his eyelids, he was utterly content.

When their DVR recording of the latest rendition of *Swan Lake* by the illustrious ABT had come to an end, Kathleen moved to take her emotion-stricken bubble bath, leaving Christopher to flick to the news as he did every night. He didn't like to dwell too much on the darkness of the world—his son did that enough for the entire family—but he thought it only right to stay informed and educated. If only to be able to make conversation with Jason.

His hopes that nothing too heavy had happened in the last twenty-four hours were quickly crushed by a news presenter informing the audience that there had been a bombing in London at the MI6 and that an unnamed intelligence officer had been killed. It chilled him more than most stories, considering his son's profession, a career path that had already given him and Kathleen much grief. He was proud of Jason, of course, but couldn't he have chosen something less dangerous? At least that provided something they could agree with Natalie on.

Then an extremely blurry—*why is it always blurry?* Christopher lamented—clip of CCTV footage was shown, along with a plea for information from the audience. The man in question's face was distorted and grainy, but after operating on it for eight hours, Christopher would know it anywhere. The man in the footage was Clarence Dixon Jr.

"No, no, no," Christopher muttered, the color draining from his face.

He looked around and could hear Kathleen singing in the bath, fortunately wholly unaware. He'd known that the surgery was wrong, but he never thought it would come to this. Now he had proof that his instincts were right, and he was complicit in an innocent person's death because he'd ignored them for financial gain. He had helped this man, this *terrorist*, change his identity so extremely that he could blow up a building and get away with it.

"Not on my watch," Christopher muttered. He might not have had a photo of what he had done, but he did have a photographic memory and the language to describe what he remembered. He would contact the CIA as soon as possible and tell them everything. The tricky part, however, would be keeping the atrocity his scalpel and hands had wrought upon the world from his family and friends.

He turned the TV off after he played the clip again, confident that he was correct in his assessment. No sooner had the screen gone dark did Kathleen return to the room, dressed in her favorite robe with her long hair piled into a towel. She was carrying two fresh glasses of wine and offered one to her husband before pulling back, placing both on the table and putting her hands on her hip.

"What is it?" she barked, scrutinizing him.

"The news," Christopher replied flatly. There was no point in trying to lie entirely.

"I keep telling you not to watch that stuff! It only upsets you, and you can't do a goddamn thing about it."

Except for once I can, Christopher thought ruefully but nodded to keep up the charade.

Then Christopher remembered that every nurse in his practice, not to mention the anesthesiologist, knew Clarence's name and knew exactly what procedures had been performed. He knew most of them watched the news or at least read the paper in the breakroom, and soon enough they would all know what had happened and how they all played a part. Especially their trusted boss. He buried his head in his hands, his skin feverishly hot and ears turning pink. He'd have to pay handsomely for them to keep it to themselves and toss in the possibility of a HIPPA violation for an extra guarantee of silence, and even then, he might only dig himself a deeper hole and get dragged to court for bribery. It was all getting so complicated so quickly, and he knew he had already failed to fool his wife.

"My love, what in the hell is going on?" Kathleen asked, sitting next to him, one brow raised as high as the Botox would allow.

Christopher looked up at her and knew she would see right through anything but the truth. "I've done something terrible, but you can't tell Jason."

He expected her to look terrified, the worst thoughts racing through her mind, but she kept her glass steady as she plucked it from its coaster.

"Tell me," she commanded, sinking back into the couch and bringing her legs up to sit cross-legged.

"I had a patient. Weird guy. Oil tycoon. Richer than God. He asked me to completely reconstruct his face. I mean, from the ground up."

Kathleen rubbed her foot absentmindedly and sipped from her glass. "Yeah. I remember you mentioning that. It was a long surgery. You were exhausted."

"It was the most extreme surgery I've ever done. And it was a total success. I wanted to take photos, but the guy kept blowing us off and eventually went no contact."

"Okay," Kathleen replied, digging her thumb into her right arch.

Christopher stared at his thumbprint on his glass. A biometric, just the same as a face. A part of what made them all human.

"I just turned on the news. There was a bombing in London. At the MI6. An officer is dead." He looked up at his wife, who calmly continued to drink and waited for him to continue. "It's the same guy. Clarence. He used his new face to commit an act of terror and get away with it."

"Okay. What are you going to do about it?"

Christopher faltered, removing his spectacles and running his fingers through his hair. "I'm going to try to keep the girls at work quiet, and I'm going to tell the CIA everything. Tell them his name, give a detailed description of his new face so that they can catch him."

"Why not tell Jason? It might be helpful to have him there with you."

"I don't want him to be ashamed of me."

Kathleen took a slow, thoughtful gulp and looked at the black screen. "Okay. I'll keep this secret for you. Just this once. Though, if you want my two cents, you should tell him. Regardless, I'm glad you're doing the right thing by going to the CIA."

Christopher pulled Kathleen's wine-holding hand to his face and kissed it repeatedly. "Thank you for not judging me, my love."

Kathleen surveyed him like a lion eyeing up a zebra as he groveled, her posture still dancer-perfect. "Did you have any suspicions at the time?"

Christopher let her hand drop. "Yes," he said sadly. "I did."

"Reservations?"

"Yes, those too."

"So why did you go through with it?"

"He offered to buy Jason a house," Christopher admitted, feeling smaller than he ever had.

Kathleen sighed and pulled her hand back toward her mouth. "You are a wonderful father and a perfect husband. The best I could have ever hoped for, but like all men, you're weak when it comes to money. Don't let it happen again."

"I won't," he assured, trying not to choke on the copious amount of nervous saliva.

"I love you," she said and leaned over to slap his cheek lightly before kissing it.

"I love you too. Are you sure you're okay with not telling Jason?"

"Telling Jason what?" she asked convincingly, batting her lashes before handing him his glass of wine.

Christopher nodded, feeling his throat constrict with emotion. Kathleen didn't mind others crying, but her tear ducts had been sealed over by sharp tongues and wooden rulers in ballet school, and he always felt silly showing such intense emotions in front of her.

Kathleen snuggled back up to him and pulled the blanket back over them. "Let's watch something fun. Whatever you like."

Christopher eyed his Blu-Ray cabinet thoughtfully. He wasn't taken by any of it but knew he needed to relax before the long day of being questioned at the CIA ahead of him.

"Let's do *Rocky Horror*. I could use a hum along."

Kathleen lit up and jumped to her feet before plucking the collector's edition from the shelf. They'd been to see it more times than Christopher could count, and each of them possessed a variety of "naughty" costumes, which embarrassed their son to no end. Despite being veterans, every time they attended, Kathleen would pretend to be a "virgin" just so she could perform the Time Warp splendidly in front of a crowd.

She returned and started the movie up, and Christopher allowed himself to be comforted by the familiar film, his wife, and the numerous photos of their newborn baby granddaughter that covered the walls and mantle. He was sure it was going to be okay. One person was dead, but he could stop all this before anyone else got hurt. He was a villain and a hero of his own making, but at least he was walking toward the light, and soon Clarence Dixon Jr. would never haunt them again.

CHAPTER TWENTY-ONE

THE DETECTIVE

THE FAMILIAR CALL OF THE CUCKOO CLOCK CALLED Heather's attention, and she glared at the little man in lederhosen as he silently blew into his alphorn. She hadn't slept, not a wink, and as each sleepless hour passed, the wooden figure's cheerful, rosy face grew increasingly mocking. She flipped him off as he spun on his perch and was relieved post-impulse that his back had been to the gesture. The guilt caused by insulting her tiniest friend burned hot. After all, it wasn't his fault that she couldn't sleep. He was just doing his job and couldn't help that he had a much cushier gig than her own.

Heather slapped her cheeks. "You're losing it," she stated loudly, waking up the slumbering animals that were coiled in the corners of the furniture. "Sorry," she whispered, and one by one, they nestled their heads back into their warm circles. She rolled her eyes as one of them huffed. As if a spoiled dog had anything to complain about.

Snapped out of her hypnotized focus on her corkboard by the interruption, she moved back to her laptop and swept a fingertip across the mousepad. It had been inactive for so long that she had to type her password in again, and in her exhaustion, she got it wrong twice before she finally cracked the code: *FiBeTu!*.

Her laptop hummed in protest at being disturbed, and Heather was vividly reminded of exactly why she'd gotten so little done in the three hours she'd been home. Still, she wasn't going to give up on her trustworthy companion so easily. The poor thing just needed some TLC.

"Come on," she said, tapping the laptop three times above the camera with increasing intensity. To her immense surprise, the smacks worked, and the endless loading symbol vanished. "Go figure," she said and dived into what the limitless depths of the internet had on Clarence Dixon Jr.

As it turned out, not much. It soon became apparent that Mommy and Daddy, or whoever ran Dixon Oil, had done an outstanding job at burying anything unsavory about their most-wayward family member. Of course, they couldn't scrub it completely, so the London bombing was still easy to find. However, after that, he became a ghost, his dirty secrets ushered from public spectacle with fat wads of hush money.

So she decided to go back before the events at the MI6 headquarters and found herself transported to 2015, staring at who this mysterious man used to be. It was strange, if not downright unsettling, to witness the static snapshots of a life before chaos. The old photos of him—smiling with his family, cutting ribbons, on the grill, at the rodeo—were so normal. In them, he appeared, at worst, to be a somewhat-eccentric billionaire with his enormous cowboy hat, wrist bling, expensive cars, and mostly-silicone trophy wife, but that wasn't surprising. What man with that amount of money wasn't at least a little strange? There was also plenty of good there. His smile reached his eyes; he did charity work; he was, at least at face value, a good father and a great businessman. In fact, Dixon Oil's profit margin almost doubled when he apparently took over in 2014. Nothing about him caused Heather's guts to tie themselves into knots, unlike the photos of other once-"normal" monsters she'd seen.

Then in early 2016, the articles and photos decreased until Clarence once again disappeared altogether.

"What happened?" Heather asked herself, placing photos of Clarence in December 2015 and May 2016 side by side for comparison. In both, he was cutting ribbons, one for a community center and the latter for a mini-mall. In the older photo, he was all shiny teeth, bright-blue eyes, lustrous golden hair, and triumphant posture. Then in 2016—though he was still incredibly handsome—there was something dull and sullen about his countenance. All that sparkle he'd possessed in spades was gone.

Though she couldn't put her finger on what had caused the light to go out in Clarence's eyes, she knew that his On switch had been turned off with a firm finger. Despite all that he'd done, Heather couldn't help but feel sorry for the man in the photos. She was sure if you compared pictures of her before and after the Paper Doll Case, they'd be similarly juxtaposed.

"A psychotic break?" she wondered. "A rocky patch with the wife? What was it?" She drummed her fingers on the coffee table and sipped her now-room-temperature tea. She knew that something terrible had happened, and she was going to find out what.

Knowing that Jason woke up at five, she thought to call him and ask if he could find the contact details of Clarence's family on the off chance that they knew something. Just as she was about to press Call, her phone began to vibrate. Jason had beaten her to it.

"Hi, Heather," he said. "I know it's early, and—"

"It's okay, I'm wide awake."

"I figured you might be. Find anything on Clarence?"

"How did you know I was looking?"

"What else would you be doing?" Jason asked.

Heather didn't have an answer for that. "Yeah. Bits and pieces. I think talking to some of Clarence's family might be valuable. Unless the CIA already has?"

"You're not a psychic, are you?"

Heather snorted. "Unfortunately not. Why?"

"Shame. The CIA is looking for one."

"Seriously?" Heather inquired incredulously.

"Sorry. Classified. Anyway, I was actually going to ask you for a favor."

"Okay?"

"I know you hate leaving Glenville, but hear me out. 'We' apparently interviewed Clarence's mother and wife after the bombing on behalf of the MI5. But as you might imagine, we didn't manage to pry much information out of them. They reacted … poorly to our agents. Probably worried they were at risk of going to prison themselves by association."

"Figures," Heather said, trying and failing to not sound like a know-it-all. "You get pulled into the CIA for an interview, and you're going to be looking over your shoulder for men in black for the next few months."

"Yeah, Mom was right about us not being the warmest people."

"Or the least intimidating," Heather quipped.

"That's why we need you. Unfortunately, Clarence's mom suffers from early-onset Alzheimer's and is in a home under lock and key. His wife, however, still lives in the same family home, and when I called her pretending to be *The Washington Post*, she was highly interested in doing an interview. Seems pretty desperate to salvage her own name and that of the company."

"Jesus, poor woman," Heather sympathized. "Must be hard finding out you've married a monster."

"So?" Jason prodded.

"So what?"

"Will you do it?" he asked.

Heather frowned. "Do what?"

"Go down to Texas and interview Clarence's wife, Prudence Dixon, and see what you can find out. Dig into his history, see if there's somewhere he might go to hide."

Heather leaned her head back and rolled it around her shoulders. More long flights were far from gracing her list of desires. "Why me? Why not one of your agents?"

"You just said we're intimidating."

"You are."

"Exactly. And also because, for whatever reason, people like you."

Heather laughed at the backhanded compliment. "Okay. So I go down there, pretending to be, what, a successful journalist? I can hardly string a sentence together in my notebook."

"You don't actually have to write anything. It's all just acting, and I've seen you do that."

"I...," Heather began, trying to figure out how to get out of this assignment and coming up blank.

"There's a package heading your way. It'll get there around ten. Inside is a disguise and anything else you might need."

"A disguise?"

"You've been on the news before. We don't want her to figure out that you're a cop. Can you do a Southern accent?"

"Why?" Heather groaned, fearing the likely answer but hoping she was wrong.

"I told her you're originally from Dallas. That's where she was born. Thought it might win you some brownie points."

"Great," Heather said sarcastically and cringed as the cuckoo clock announced the passing of another hour.

"That's the spirit. A car will pick you up for the airport at twelve. The ticket is already paid for. Your meeting with Prudence is at five."

"I didn't say yes," Heather retorted.

"I could hear it in your voice. Talk soon, Bishop."

He was gone before she could argue, and Heather tossed her phone onto a faraway armchair and rubbed her eyes with her palms until she could see stars burst behind her lids. Once again, she was getting shipped out across the country and leaving Glenville behind. Not that they were struggling without her. The varying unanswered texts on her phone had informed her that Tina was doing a great job managing the media, Nancy had raised all the money required, the force was tamping the mass panic, and the three funerals would be done by the end of the week.

Despite the tragedy occurring on her turf, Glenville didn't need her, though this knowledge did little to alleviate her guilt for abandoning them once again. This worsened when she checked her calendar. Penciled into today's slot was another movie night with Gabriel—a back-to-back creature feature at the local cinema they'd organized over a month ago—and a much-needed catch-up lunch with Gene. Worse still, if she also didn't make it back by nine o'clock tomorrow, she'd miss yet another AA session. She hoped Beau was doing okay and was still attending the sessions without her.

She crossed the room and texted Tina.

Heather: *Need to interview shooting suspect's wife in Texas. Will not be in again today. Will keep you updated on my findings.*

The typing bubble popped up and stayed up for a long time.

Tina: *I asked you last night if you'd find the local bike thief.*

Heather couldn't believe her eyes and had entirely forgotten about the ridiculous request. Sure, she could spend the day finding some teenage asshole. Not like there was the pressing matter of a domestic terrorist to attend to.

Heather: *Sheriff, the CIA has requested that I attend this interview. It's very important.*

Not even thirty seconds passed before the reply came like a missile.

Tina: *You don't work for the CIA, you work for me.*

Heather ground her teeth as she typed.

Heather: *Right now, we're working alongside the CIA, so actually, I work for both of you. Anyone else can find the bike thief, and I'm sure you realize it's not even half as important as this.*

Tina: *I'm sure someone else from the CIA could also interview the suspect's wife.*

Heather: *They want me.*

More typing bubbles. They appeared, disappeared, and appeared again, like some twisted game of Whack-a-Mole that infuriated Heather and made her sick in equal measure.

Tina: *I am beginning to doubt your loyalties to Glenville and would prefer you be upfront with me if you're thinking of leaving the force.*

Heather's jaw dropped, and she nearly threw her phone again.

Heather: *I'm not leaving the force. I'm working with the force and the CIA to stop the man who is responsible for ten people being killed in our town. I am breaking my back for this town and its citizens.*

Tina: *Fine. Go to Texas. I hope you find something worthwhile.*

Heather turned her phone off. She couldn't understand why Tina was being so painfully obstinate. Jealousy? Stress? Concern? It was a mystery, but just like the bike thief, her boss's anxieties and neuroticisms were not a priority right now.

Angry, she returned to her research for four increasingly fruitless hours until the knock at the door announced the arrival of her disguise. She thanked the man—who was clearly a disgruntled CIA field agent tasked with a mission far beneath him—and disappeared back into her dark, drawn abode.

She nearly laughed as she tore into the box. Inside was an ash-blonde wig with a dark, grown-out parting, a hairnet, lace front glue, a smoky-eye makeup kit, oversized blingy sunglasses, bangles, denim flares, and a spaghetti-strap tank top in gaudy leopard print. It was an ensemble Heather would never wear, not even as a teenager, and Jason knew it. That's why it was perfect, if a tad ridiculous.

Sitting in front of her laptop, she watched video after video on how to correctly apply and lay a lace front wig. Her thick head of hair only added to the difficulty, but after many, many frustrating and sticky attempts, she finally succeeded. It was far from perfect, but it was convincing enough, and after plucking at a couple of hairline strands, she was confident that it would pass the test under the scrutiny of daylight.

Then it was time for the makeup. While easier than the wig, it also came with its fair share of pitfalls, especially in the form of liquid eyeliner, which she ran sloppily across her upper lid over the sparkly black eyeshadow. The line grew thicker and thicker, but when she achieved symmetry, she let it lie.

Once dressed in her outfit—which somehow fit like a glove—she looked at herself long and hard in the mirror. It was disconcerting to see someone so unfamiliar looking back, but she knew there was no way that anyone, not even her parents, would recognize her. At least not from a distance.

"Hey, y'all," she drawled, trying out her temporary accent. She grimaced. It would be something she'd have to work on in her head during the flight. At least it was a more productive task than watching crappy blockbusters.

She snapped a low-res photo with her phone and considered sending it to her mother as a joke but decided better of it. Her mother might well have a heart attack if she believed, even momentarily, that her daughter had taken chemicals to her precious matrilineal Indian hair. So Heather kept it as a private keepsake of a very strange life.

CHAPTER TWENTY-TWO

THE DETECTIVE

AS HEATHER STOOD IN THE PICKUP ZONE AT THE ARID Dallas airport and batted away flies, she waited nervously for a black car to appear as it always did. When a few minutes passed and there was still no sign of her ride, she worried that Jason had forgotten to organize the Texan end of affairs. It wasn't like him to skimp on the details, but he was under a lot of pressure, and perhaps his grasp was beginning to loosen.

It took her a few more minutes to piece together what Jason probably thought was evident, especially to a detective. No car was coming because what kind of journalist turned up in a black sedan with a private driver? Maybe some big-shot editors did, but not thirty-three-year-olds in Forever 21 outfits.

That left her with one option. Calling a taxi. The idea didn't thrill her, especially as Jason had failed to provide cash or credit to accompany her new identity. Aside from the new driver's license, everything in her wallet was the same as it had ever been, and she hoped that no one—especially Mrs. Dixon—would have the opportunity to look too closely at her faded debit card.

Just as she was about to press Call on a local taxi service, she caught sight of something white and enormous rounding the corner toward her. She looked up at the grumbling machine in disbelief. It was one of her favorite cars ever made—an immaculate 1959 Cadillac Eldorado Biarritz Convertible in Olympic white with red leather interiors. The gleaming aluminum trims made her thankful for her sunglasses, though the pale-gray sky was still devoid of the sun.

The soft top was up on account of the gray skies above, and as Heather let out a low whistle to herself, the shadowy driver rolled down the passenger window. She looked behind her as she looked at her, expecting someone a lot more glamorous to emerge from the airport exit.

"Ms. Knight?" the man called out.

It took Heather a moment to remember that she was no longer Heather Bishop but Violet Knight, a slightly younger woman with a completely different backstory, birthday, and personality. Violet was a bubbly, fun-loving party girl with a Persian cat, an advice column, and a blog about beauty trends. Jason had even gone so far as to have fake articles put up in her name, thanks to a friend of his mother's.

"That's me!" she exclaimed, snapping into character, waving and trotting forward in her never-before-worn high-heeled sandals with a big, glossy grin.

"Mrs. Dixon sent me to pick you up. She doesn't like uninvited taxis coming onto the property, plus she figured after a long journey in coach, you might like to travel in style."

She'd flown first class, thanks to Jason—something she was going to sorely miss once all this was over—but chose not to take the assumption as a slight against Violet's perceived class status. It was apt to assume that was the case, if a little condescending.

"Mrs. Dixon figured right," Heather said, leaning down to face the man. She was starting to lean into her Southern accent but kept it subtle to avoid hamming it up. The driver didn't look at her strangely, so she allowed herself the delusion that she was nailing this acting gig.

"Well, hop in. Let's not keep Her Majesty waiting," the driver joked.

Heather laughed politely and did as she was told, though the nickname gave her pause. It was the type of moniker one usually used for a tyrant of a boss, though it was conceivable that he and Prudence were close enough that ribbing was permitted, if not encouraged. Heather hoped for the latter possibility, not wanting a repeat of trying to squeeze information out of the shrewd, wealthy, and impatient Nancy Ellis. Especially with the limited allotted time, she did not have the time to work her way into anyone's good books, nor would there be any opportunity for a do-over.

She dropped down into the passenger seat, and the man—who was plump with a pencil mustache and a black curtain of hair surrounding his bald dome—shook her hand eagerly. His palm was sweaty, but she detected no nervousness.

"Name's Jim," he informed her. "I've been driving for the Dixons for three decades now, but I must admit, it's been awhile since I've picked up any guests. Especially none as pretty as yourself."

"Well, consider me honored. Is this your car?"

Jim shrugged, a coy expression on his flushed face. "Technically, it belongs to Her Majesty, but considering she can't drive… Well, I reckon this filly might as well be mine."

"Well, you're a lucky man then. She is mighty fine," Heather replied, her accent strengthening.

Fortunately, Jim didn't seem to notice the fluctuation and nodded enthusiastically. "Just you wait till we're out on the highway. She handles like a dream. What kind of car do you drive, Ms. Knight? A fashionable woman like yourself must have a beautiful car."

"A 1977 Ford Granada," Heather replied too quickly and cursed herself. Her car was as far from as famous as she was, but she had to be careful to keep her feet firmly planted in Violet's uncomfortable shoes.

"Huh," Jim hummed. "I had you pegged for more of a Fiat 500 type of woman. Maybe a Mini Cooper."

"It was my dad's," Heather clarified, which seemed to assuage any suspicion. It had been far too long since she'd been undercover.

———

Jim was right. The Cadillac did handle like a dream, and although Heather was disappointed to abandon the cushy interior, she was easily distracted from the letdown by the breathtaking Dixon estate ahead.

Situated in a quarry at the base of a cliff of reddish rock and sitting upon bright green grass that certainly cost a fortune to maintain were several large barns, garages, staff facilities, and five enormous mansions—all of which were painted the same shade of lustrous alabaster. The central mansion was much larger than the four flanking it. Security personnel clustered around the behemoth dressed in uniforms the same shade as the paint, making their black automatic weapons stand out like the sharps and flats of a piano keyboard.

"What's with all the houses?" Heather asked.

"Well, there was a time, back in the good old days, when the entire Dixon family lived on the same property. The last arrangement, prior to Prudence taking over the big one, had Mr. and Mrs. Dixon Sr. holed up in the center, their daughter in the one to the right, their son in the one to the left, Mr. Dixon's parents in the one on the far left, and his aunt and uncle in the one on the far right."

"Sounds nice," Heather said. "Having such a communal living situation. You know, in DC, I don't know any of my neighbors beyond them keeping me up at night."

"Well, no offense, miss, but that sounds awful to me."

"None taken, but you know what city folks are like. Unfriendly, untrusting. I have to admit I miss living out here. Rural."

Jim nodded gravely. "Maybe you should move back? Work for Prudence. She's always looking for cleaners and the like."

Heather smiled politely. "I'll keep that in mind. So did the kids move into their houses when they turned eighteen?"

"No, they lived at home until they got married. Then they got given the houses as wedding presents."

"Kind of like the royal family in England?"

Jim chuckled. "Well, out here, the Dixons are the royal family. Or at least they were. Everyone's gone now except Mrs. Dixon and the four kids. Though at least we have them to carry on the legacy. We might see another golden era yet."

They parked, and Jim turned to her, his voice lowered and eyes darting.

"Now, I must warn you. Mrs. Dixon hasn't been herself as of late. She's as nice a woman as I've ever known, but she's… sensitive. Just be careful with your questioning. I'd hate to have to pick up the pieces."

Heather didn't know whether he meant Mrs. Dixon's pieces or her own, but she nodded as if the warning would alter any of the questions she'd have to ask. After thanking him, she left Jim behind and approached the big house unescorted, her fake driver's license and press pass at the ready. As she crossed the enormous plot of land, walking poorly in her heels on the soft, cushy ground, she looked at the other four houses. They were in good condition, but their rows of glass eyes were hollow and dark, implying vacant interiors, white sheets, and a thick lamina of dust. It seemed a waste, and if she'd thought Nancy Ellis's home to be too big and too empty, these were something else entirely.

After passing through the brusque security and getting patted down by a young Middle Eastern woman with a severe black bob, Heather was ushered silently and without greeting into the house by a man she presumed to be some sort of butler.

He didn't turn to look at her as he led her through the ostentatious and very Texan interiors, allowing Heather to marvel and gawk at the gaudiness of the intricate wrought iron, white stone, glistening marble, cowhides, and exotic hunting trophies until they finally came to a stop by a sheer curtain-covered archway. A pair of stuffed zebras flanked the entrance and watched Heather with glassy gazes as the butler cleared his throat.

"Come on in!" a woman's voice slurred beyond the veil.

In response, Heather was thrust inside with a firm, flat palm on her back, and she stumbled down an unexpected step and into the room. She managed to right herself just as Prudence Dixon turned to look at her, a colorful cocktail in hand and a slack, uneven expression on her makeup-laden face. Prudence didn't seem to see nor hear the blunder and clapped her hands in delight and collapsed back onto the cow-print couch.

"My god!" Prudence exclaimed, propping her elbow on her thigh and her chin on her palm. "And here I was expecting some stuffy old prude wearing a brown pantsuit and baggy stockings to ask me questions. But my god! What a knockout! My husband would have simply *loved* you." Prudence spoke quickly, almost breathlessly, but there was no bitterness, no jealousy. It was simply a fact. Clarence Dixon Jr. would've found Heather attractive. The idea made her itch a little, but she blushed at Prudence's wondrous expression.

"Thank you, ma'am," Heather said, cautiously moving closer.

"Oh, good lord, darling. Please, don't call me 'ma'am.' I'm only thirty-four."

Strangely, despite her beauty, Prudence looked far older than thirty-four. At first Heather wasn't sure if it was the '80s pageant do, heavy makeup, fuchsia bandage dress, or square-tipped French manicure that was causing this middle-aged *Real Housewives* effect. Then as Heather neared, she realized it was the copious amount of plastic surgery impairing the accuracy of her age-ometer. Sure, Prudence looked good—smooth, snatched, and poreless—but the dozens of tweaks created the illusion of someone decades older desperately attempting to cling to their distant youth.

"Do you mind if I sit down?" Heather asked, nearing the couch.

"Of course not! Please sit! Do you want a vodka? A cocktail? Marg? Any of the above? Come on, don't make me drink alone," Prudence begged, clinking ice against the sides of her glass.

Prudence was reminiscent of Kathleen—wealthy, beautiful, and drunk—but she was somehow a pale imitation. A mask of glamour hiding something painful. Where Kathleen was self-assured, this woman was a shaking chihuahua, all bulging, watery eyes and bundles of nerves too close to the skin.

Heather hesitated. If she wanted anything, she wanted bourbon, her old faithful, but Violet—the Texan party girl— was one for something a little wilder. Heather disliked tequila and downright hated mixers in her liquor but requested a fresh lime margarita with an eagerness that implied it was not only her favorite drink but she was here for something more akin to a social call.

It was the right decision, and Prudence clapped again, placing her glass between her thighs and enthusiastically ringing a little bell placed on the side table. The butler emerged, took their orders, and vanished without saying a word.

"You know…," Prudence said, extending the drunken hand of a girl at a party desperate for a tearful, meaningful chat— Heather met her grasp and allowed her knuckles to be squeezed together—"I so appreciate you doing this for me, Violet. Can I call you Violet?"

Heather smiled politely but couldn't even squeeze in a response before Prudence kept rambling.

"No one's ever been much interested in my side of the story. Not in the papers anyway. If there were any stories, they weren't flattering. I married a monster, so what sort of idiot must I be? But what no one realizes is that people can change like that." Prudence retracted to snap without sound.

Heather nodded. "I hear this all the time from women writing to my advice column."

"Do you really?" Prudence exhaled, relieved.

"Yeah. Good guys turned into wife-beaters overnight. That sort of thing."

"Well, to his credit, Clarence was never a wife-beater. Nor did he lay a hand on the children despite his daddy's love of cuttin' a switch. If he did, I would've left him then and there."

"So how did he change?" Heather asked.

Prudence paused. "Aren't you going to write this down?"

"Oh, of course," Heather said, rummaging around in her bag for her fresh new notepad.

Prudence looked approvingly at the pen and pad and continued, "Well, I better start at the beginning. So I met Clarence when I was nineteen. My god, fifteen years ago now. Can you believe that? Though I, of course, don't count the last five," she clarified hastily. "I haven't seen him since he left for London, and he was mostly on the couch by that point."

"Tell me about the early years. It'll help the reader to sympathize if they know why you fell in love in the first place."

"Wow, you really know what you're doing, don't you?"

"I believe in helping other women," Heather replied.

"No, you're something special. I can tell. You know, I have been praying for something like this," Prudence cooed, returning her hand to Heather's.

Guilt chewed Heather's insides as the butler entered once against with drinks on a silver tray accompanied by a tasty-looking selection of cheeses and crackers. Prudence once more released her viselike grip to blob some melted cheese onto a water cracker. It was then that Heather noticed the shakes, the poor spatial awareness, and the limited control of her slender digits. Then it clicked. She wasn't drunk; she was high. Sedated. Heather eyed the guards out of the corner of her eye and hoped that it was nothing more sinister than a little pill-popping problem.

"You should try some of this," Prudence enthused, and Heather obliged by plucking a chili-stuffed olive from a bowl before picking up her tall glass topped with a lime slice.

"So the early days?" Heather prompted.

Prudence nodded, covering her full mouth. "Oh yes. Oh, they were perfect... I mean, a real fairy tale. Which, of course, makes it all the more painful. Clarence was beautiful and charming and adventurous and an old-fashioned gentleman all rolled into one. And he was sexy. Phew, was he sexy. We have four kids for a reason, you know," she paused to laugh, and Heather joined her. "For a while, it seemed like the passion would never stop. We were just so obsessed with each other."

"So what changed?"

Prudence sighed and gathered up more snacks to stuff into her mouth. "What changed?" Prudence asked herself. She sipped the mysterious cocktail to wash it all down and became abruptly somber as she ruminated on her answer. "What changed was the death of Clarence's father, Clarence Dixon Sr. They were very, very close. Enviably so. Best of friends, really. Though the important bit here is not so much the death itself but how he died."

"How did he die?" Heather asked, scribbling in her notebook.

"Drone strike. Would you believe it? In Iran. He was over there trying to strike up a deal with some other oil tycoon, but it just so happened that there was a terrorist hiding out in the town where they were having dinner. *Boom*. No more Daddy Clarence. Then, my poor husband, he became completely obsessed with finding out who had ordered the strike and became totally... um,"—Prudence searched for the word and clicked clumsily again—"radicalized against the government. Met some guys who felt the same on some weirdo forums and just slowly but surely lost his mind. He stopped going outside and just sat in that damn basement 'researching.' Honestly, I never thought he'd do anything so extreme, which I know seems hard to believe."

"Hindsight is twenty-twenty. I'm not here to judge you," Heather said, humoring her interviewee by grabbing a cracker and oozy chunk of some sort of French wheel. As she bit into the cheese, something came to mind. The pizza. The ingredients. The Iranian kebab recipe. Another little jab, which only helped to confirm that Clarence was the man they were looking for.

Prudence closed her eyes and sighed happily. "Thank you, Violet."

"You're welcome. So you said you haven't seen Clarence since he left for London?"

Ever so briefly, Prudence opened her eyes and flicked between each of the guards. "No. I have not. Which is a real shame because I'm dying to give him a piece of my mind because God knows I won't be able to in heaven."

"Do you have any reason to believe he's reentered the country?"

"I don't, though it wouldn't be hard. A bribe here, a bribe there, a private jet. Plus, it took a few days for them to identify him, he could've gotten back through even without all the extra effort."

"I know it's a strange question, but have you ever heard of the name Christopher Fleming?"

Prudence's face lit up. "I have! He did my breasts and nose. I actually recommended him to Clarence. You know, I *must* go back and get my lips done by him. I'm afraid no one else compares. At least not in America."

Heather nodded, not wanting to break the bad news or alert Prudence to any more of her husband's crimes. She seemed to be suffering enough as it was. Instead, with all her questions answered, she continued drinking and asking Prudence a few questions about herself to keep up the charade and placate the poor woman.

They dived deep into motherhood, fashion, hobbies, the business, but eventually, Prudence's already lazy eyelids closed, and Heather was escorted away by the security guards in the corner of the room.

CHAPTER TWENTY-THREE

THE DETECTIVE

THE ARMED GUARDS WATCHED HEATHER INTENTLY AS she approached the tail fins of the Cadillac. While keeping her distance, the young woman with the black bob of glossy hair paced parallel to Heather until her hand was on the passenger door handle. It seemed less of an escort and more of a request to leave immediately. Heather had no problem obliging the woman and opened the door. As soon as she was back in the comfortable passenger seat, she looked behind her at the watching, predatory eyes and was grateful when Jim pulled away over the cattle grid and through the golden gates.

Back on the main road, another wave of endless summer storms rolled in. Gray clouds and a green tinge beckoned rain, thunder, and lightning, and as soon as they roared down the empty highway, the torrent began.

"Crap," Heather said, looking up at the roof and thinking Jim should've picked a more waterproof vehicle.

"Yeah, it's not looking good," Jim replied. "Better check the website for cancellations."

Heather groaned. As much as she didn't want to endure another long cross-country flight, she also didn't want to be stranded somewhere so far from home. Unfortunately, upon opening the website, it became quickly apparent that she had no choice but to wait the weather out.

"Canceled. Canceled. Canceled," she groaned, reading the list of flights to Seattle.

"Don't you worry about a thing. I know a great hotel nearby," Jim assured, reaching over to pat her denim-covered thigh.

Heather cringed and grew ever grateful that her disguise hadn't entailed wearing a dress.

"Is it expensive?"

"For you? Not at all. Free of charge, and get what you want from room service."

"Are you sure?" Heather asked hesitantly, and as Jim's hand lingered, she feared his version of free might be very different from her own.

"Yes, ma'am. Mrs. Dixon owns the place, and after your kindhearted visit, I'm sure she'd be happy to put you up for as long as you need."

Heather relaxed, knowing Jim wasn't the one offering to pay. "Well, hopefully, it'll only be for one night, and please let her know how grateful I am."

"I'll be sure to do that, Ms. Knight," Jim said with a smile and a wink.

The hotel was beautiful in that same gaudy, over-the-top way that the Dixon estate was, and the service was truly top-notch from the moment she set foot in the glistening lobby. Since she was well acquainted with cheap motels and microwave meals, there was something to be said for the perks of this wealthy and glamorous lifestyle, but as the staff fussed and businessmen gawped, she also knew that Violet's wasn't a life she could endure for long. Aside, of course, from the first-class flights.

Photos of the Dixon family—dating back to the invention of cameras—lined the hallway in a neat row. As she neared the end, she saw there was a disproportional gap in the even spacing where another photo had once been, followed by a brand-new image of Prudence and her four blond children. It made sense to eradicate Clarence from such places, but Heather wondered if they could've done so in a less eerie fashion.

In the room, free from onlookers and possible spies for Mrs. Dixon, Heather liberated herself from her uncomfortable disguise and changed into the cozy spare clothing she'd fortunately brought along for the journey home. She had also luckily remembered the wig glue and eyeshadow, just in case she needed to reapply. It looked like she would have to if Jim took it upon himself to drive her to the airport in the morning.

She lay back on the enormous circular bed with the pearl-colored clamshell headboard and plucked and pulled at the remaining glue along her hairline. She needed baby oil and hoped the expensive hotel conditioner would do the trick once she worked up the energy to shower. She listened to the storm wage war against the historic building and figured she should clean up before the power went and took the hot water with it.

She shifted, and her stomach called out to her in a rumble that rivaled the thunder. *Order first, then shower,* she decided, picking up the dainty receiver from the golden rotary phone and dialing for room service.

Despite all that was offered on the laminated menu on the bedside table, she opted for a beer and a cheese pizza. She didn't want to be rude by running her tab up into the hundreds but also desperately craved something that tasted of home. She instructed the staff member to leave the tray outside her room so she wouldn't have to put her disguise back on and finally rolled from the bed to shower.

The gold-and-pearl bathroom was just as impressive as the rest of the suite, and she kept her eyes open while she washed, mesmerized by how the other half lived. In doing so, she caught sight of herself in the enormous oval mirror and laughed at the state of her hair and face. The former was glue-covered and crimped from the braids she'd put it in, and the latter—as well as the upper half of her forehead—was covered in a goopy layer of smudged black. She scrubbed with water, then, remembering the waterproof labels on the eyeliner and mascara, resorted to body wash to remove the remnants. Then her eyes began to itch, and she promised them that come tomorrow, the only thing they'd be wearing would be sunglasses, with the makeup palette held at a safe distance in her purse.

Wrapped in a towel, she sat eating pizza with her damp hair around her shoulders and enjoyed some reality TV about real estate agents with the volume down. Despite the obviously scripted drama, she was really getting into it as two women who heavily resembled Prudence fought over obtaining the listing of a Spanish-style mansion in Beverly Hills. Just as one woman moved to strike, the lights flickered, and then everything went dark. She sighed and lay down her slice before reaching for her phone. As predicted, the phone lines were also down, which meant that updating everyone about her findings would have to wait. She just hoped no one was up late worrying about her well-being while she sat eating carbs in her palatial room.

After another two slices—consumed in the white light of her phone flashlight—she dropped her towel, pulled on the men's white tank top and boxers that sat in a pile by the bathroom doorway, and crawled into bed to get an early night. She attempted to read a few chapters of a book on her phone, but her eyes drifted in and out of focus, so she placed it within reach on the other pillow and closed her lids. Between her hazy vision, the comfortable bed, her full stomach, the beer, and the sounds of rolling thunder, she thought sleep would be easy to obtain tonight. Instead, despite it all, she was even more restless than usual. Her gut was trying to tell her something, and it had

185

nothing to do with the excess of cheese consumed throughout the day.

It's the blackout, she told herself. But she wasn't convinced by the angel on her shoulder today. This allowed the devil to speak louder, and the tiny horned figure told Heather to watch her back.

Heather tossed and turned and changed position a thousand times, but nothing helped. Every sound was too loud. People coughing in the room down the hall, cars driving past, and the rustling of shrubbery out the front—all of it was crystal clear and burrowed in through her ears and rubbed her brain raw.

Then one sound pierced through the rest. A doorknob rattling. *Her* doorknob. She turned on her phone flashlight, kicked off the covers, sat bolt upright, and stared at the door. On any other day, she'd assume it to be someone from the bar downstairs with the wrong room or a housekeeper mistaking the room for unoccupied, but today she knew there was nothing innocent about this attempt to enter.

Carefully, quietly, she slipped out of bed, stuffed pillows under the comforter, and placed the wig atop the plush log, creating a blissfully ignorant decoy Violet. Then Heather snuck into the bathroom and hid around the corner of the double-sink cabinet. She cursed herself for not bringing her gun. She'd toyed with the idea: applying for a permit, putting the weapon in a locked hard case, and transporting ammo in a separate checked bag. It seemed simple enough, but then why would Violet Knight have a gun? She never intended to stay in a hotel, so she'd have to take the gun with her, and none of the above would have fit in her albeit-large designer purse. There was also the security-laden home of Mrs. Dixon to contend with, and in the end, it just didn't seem worth it.

Hindsight really is twenty-twenty, she thought bitterly, insulting her past self viciously in her head.

She looked around for an escape, but the bathroom faced into the building, rendering it windowless, and the only potential weapon within reach was a toilet brush. Its handle was fortunately made of metal, so it would do in a pinch, and she was eternally grateful that upon pulling it from its porcelain holder, it only stank of bleach.

A key turned in the lock, and the door to the suite creaked open quietly. Heather held her breath and returned to her hiding place as someone padded into the room. They were light on their feet, and when they came into view—occasionally illuminated by the flashes of light coming in through the semi-drawn curtains—she saw the figure of a woman not much bigger than herself dressed in black form-fitting clothing.

The woman on the roof? she wondered. *Has she followed me all the way to Texas?*

Her relief at being evenly physically matched was soon crushed as she watched the woman raise a gun, point it at "Violet's" head, and fire three silenced shots. They might have weighed the same, but a gun held a huge advantage over a toilet brush handle.

Had the pillows been stuffed with cotton, it might have bought her some time, but the flume of feathers ruined her ruse, and knowing she was doomed if she didn't move, Heather began to crawl out from the bathroom and toward the open door. The darkness was on her side, as was the slam of rain against the glass, but without light to guide her, she turned too soon and collided with the wall. The hollow plaster thumped loudly, and from behind, she heard her would-be murderer turn to face her.

Jumping to her feet, Heather spun on her bare heel, swung the toilet brush hard, and knocked the gun from her attacker's hands with a loud smack. It flew across the room, and as the woman scrambled after it, Heather took the opportunity to run out of the room and down the hallway. With no pockets available, she tucked her phone into the waistband of her unisex y-front briefs and hoped the tough elastic would be enough to hold it there as she ran.

At least you're getting your steps in, she joked as the phone jostled, racking up the count on her exercise app.

Another shot hurtled past her head, missing her in the pitch-blackness as she zigzagged from wall to wall. Eyes adjusting, she spotted silver and dove behind a room service trolley, picked up a heavy metal tray, and held it in front of her as she jogged backward toward the fire escape. The next shot landed but merely dented the sturdy slab instead of piercing its steel hide. She thanked whoever was in charge of the material's invention as she pressed the bar down with her elbow and stepped out onto the cold concrete landing.

She spun, grating the pads of her feet, and ran down the stairs using only judgment to guide her. The door slammed open moments later, and she held the tray above her head, hoping to at least preserve her skull as bullets rained down. None made impact as she skittered down the sharp-edged steps, and feeling strangely untouchable, she struggled to hold in a contemptuous, hysterical laugh.

Hand on the rail, she swung around another corner, her eyes having adjusted enough to tell her when to turn. She grated her heels in the process and envied Kathleen's hardened ballerina feet as she continued to chafe, cut, and stub with each misplaced step. Still, the adrenaline soared as another bullet missed, and she finally released an insuppressible guffaw.

As if in answer to her frenzied hubris, a bullet landed in the center of the tray, and the second bark of laughter caught in her throat as her arms gave way to the impact. The metal slammed into her skull, and she let out a trembling moan as she stumbled down several steps onto another landing. The skin was broken, there was blood, and the pain was unbearable, but she kept going. There was no other choice.

She turned, and realizing there were no more steps, she knew she had reached her destination and threw herself through the door and into the lobby. There were guests everywhere, trapping her pursuer in the stairwell, and she ran past them to the front door. The businessmen gawked, as they had earlier, but she knew it wasn't because of her skimpy ensemble. It was because of the blood pouring down her back.

She dropped the tray as she entered the carousel doors and panted as she pushed, her body giving up on her with each added exertion. Finally, she exploded out onto the wet street and skidded through a puddle to the curb. Spotting a taxi, she ran toward it, hoping it wouldn't speed off at the sight of her. It didn't, and she jumped in the back and pulled her phone from her waistband.

"Airport," she said breathlessly.

"I'm sorry, darling, all the flights are—" he stopped talking when he turned around. "My god, what the hell happened to you? Has somebody hurt you?"

Heather caught sight of herself in the rearview mirror, blood careening down from her scalp. "Please just drive."

"Yes, ma'am."

As they took off toward nowhere, the streetlights flickered into life one by one, and soon the surrounding buildings joined them. Heather checked her phone. Two bars were good enough, and with her waning consciousness, she called Jason, not caring what the driver could hear of their conversation.

"Heather? What's going on?"

"Somebody just tried to kill me," Heather wheezed. "Clarence has people watching the house, or Prudence is in on the whole thing. I don't know, but I managed to escape. I'm on the way to the airport or the hospital, I don't know."

"Hospital," the driver chimed in.

"Are you hurt?" Jason asked.

"I'm bleeding pretty bad."

"Okay. I'm texting you an address. Go there instead. My people will pick you up with a medic on board. Storm be damned. We'll get you back to Glenville. I know there's an airstrip there. Once you're stitched up, you're going to pack your things, and then we'll get you somewhere safe. You're going to be okay," he insisted.

"Okay," Heather murmured.

"Heather, can you get there?"

Her phone buzzed with the address, and just before everything went black, she told the driver where to take her.

CHAPTER TWENTY-FOUR

THE DETECTIVE

HEATHER CAME TO IN THE DARK AND FOUND HERSELF unable to move. For a panic-stricken moment, she feared she might be dead until the pain started. Fortunately— or unfortunately, she couldn't quite decide—she had yet to shuffle off this mortal coil and carefully began to wiggle her extremities. Nothing seemed to be broken or missing, which was a good start, and it seemed that most of her mobility limitations were caused by the weighted blanket on top of her. She inhaled deeply. The blanket smelled familiar: her forty-eight-hour, exercise-proof deodorant, and Fireball's sleepy corn chip scent filling her nostrils.

She sat up despite the weight on her chest and the pain blooming across her scalp and looked around. It might have been dark, but she'd know her bedroom anywhere. What was disturbing was not her return to comfort but her inability to remember a single second of the journey. Had she flown? Had she been driven? Who had changed her clothes? Who had tucked her in? Who had washed the blood from her body?

Blood, she thought, remembering how it had careened down her shoulders and back. Tentatively she touched the back of her head and sucked her teeth as she ran a finger along the stitches. She couldn't remember having her head sown back together either, but the severe head wound was undoubtedly the answer to her information blackout.

There was movement outside the door, and she froze with fear as the door rattled and then stopped. It was happening again; it was going to happen again. Her heart pounded, and her head throbbed, and she pushed her back against the wall beside her bed, too exhausted to fight anymore.

Knock. Knock. Knock.

Three polite wraps on the door preceded Bonnie's voice, who asked, "Heather? Are you awake?"

Heather whimpered in disbelief as all the alarms stopped ringing inside her mind. "Yeah, I'm awake," she said, her voice hoarse. "Come in."

Bonnie entered the room with a soft, tired smile. "How are you feeling?"

"Like somebody just tried to kill me," Heather said, pulling the blanket up to her neck, not caring how childish she appeared.

Bonnie frowned. "Yeah, I'll bet. You were in rough shape."

"What are you doing here?"

"Well, I happened to be in Dallas visiting my grandma when Jason called me, which meant I headed your rescue mission. Divine intervention, I guess, especially as somebody also tried to break into my house at the same time as they tried to kill you."

"Jesus. Do you think they were trying to kill you too?"

Bonnie grimaced. "He had a hammer. So I'd say, yeah."

Heather shuddered. For some reason, that choice of weapon was so much worse than a 9mm pistol. At least her death would've been quick. "That's awful."

"Yep," Bonnie replied, much more clipped than usual. "So I guess I'll be coming with you to the bunker."

"The bunker?"

"Yeah. One of many. You, me, Takahiro, Jason, and Jessica will be staying at this one together to stay safe. Our families will be shipped off to some other undisclosed location too."

"My parents?"

"All taken care of while you were sleeping. They're at an undisclosed safe house somewhere. Personally, I think they're unlikely targets, but Jason insisted. I guess it's better to be safe than sorry."

"Can I call them? They must be terrified" Or, more accurately, at least in her mother's case, filled with fury at being uprooted because of her daughter's poor choice in career.

She hoped for the agents' sake that the safe house had cable because God help them if she missed out on whatever period drama she'd recently sunk her teeth into.

Bonnie smiled again. "Yeah. Of course. You'll have plenty of time on the plane."

Heather wanted to scream. More planes? She should've seen it coming, but even first class was getting old by this point. All she wanted was her bed. Yet she kept her mouth shut and her expression grateful. She was lucky to be alive—not everyone was—and complaining about another cushy bout of travel seemed awfully insensitive.

"What about my friends?" Heather inquired. "Do they also need to go into hiding?"

"Not as far as we're concerned. Only your family is linked to you publicly. I doubt Clarence or his crew would have any idea of whom you socialize with outside of blood relatives. He's probably only known who you are for a couple of days, and you've hardly been here."

She made a good point, and though Heather was still worried about her loved ones, she knew that Bonnie was probably right about them not being of interest to Clarence. They knew nothing and would continue to be kept in the dark until all this was over.

Bonnie sat on the edge of the bed and patted what she must've thought was Heather's leg but was actually a balled-up section of blanket. "Everything and everyone's going to be okay."

"Do you just think that, or do you know it?"

Bonnie frowned, and Heather felt guilty for challenging her. Clearly she was mostly self-soothing rather than trying to comfort Heather. She needed to state her beliefs out loud to make them come true. Heather had been there before.

"He's after Jason," Bonnie reasoned. "And he didn't want us helping him. I doubt he cares about our friends or family. Now get dressed and pack a bag. We leave in ten."

"Okay," Heather said quietly, the creaking bedsprings drowning out her response.

Bonnie paused in the doorway. "Hey, I'm really sorry about all of this. I hope you're okay."

"I'm okay," Heather replied, unsure whether it was a lie.

"I'm glad. Let me know if you need anything. I'll be in the living room."

Just as Heather heaved herself out of bed and turned on the light, a knock sounded at the front door. She moved out into the hallway and watched as Bonnie opened it before Heather even had a chance to step into the living room. She looked down at herself and realized she was only wearing an oversized T-shirt and the same men's boxers from earlier but failed to duck back into her room in time.

The early-morning breeze brushed over her bare calves, and she stared back at a bewildered Gabriel. So fixated on Heather—who realized she must look as bad as she felt—he jumped as Bonnie held out her hand.

"Hi, I'm Heather's cousin, Bonnie Anderson," she informed him, only semi-convincingly and making the rookie mistake of using her real name.

Gabriel seemed reluctant to reciprocate as he continued to stare ahead, but his politeness took hold, and he offered a quick shake.

"On which side?" he asked, subtly testing the stranger who, for innumerable reasons, did not look remotely related to his best friend. Chief among them was that Bonnie was African-American and Heather was Indian-British-American.

"Her dad's side," Bonnie replied with a chipper grin.

"Her English dad's side?"

Bonnie's shrugged. "Yeah, I know. Hard to believe. Technically, my mom is his half-sister and moved to America before I was born."

Nice save, Heather thought, genuinely impressed at her ability to skirt several issues at once. Gabriel still didn't look convinced but left it alone as Heather approached the front door. Bonnie muttered something about coffee getting cold as Gabriel stepped inside and awkwardly headed for the kitchen.

"Hey, Buster," Heather said quietly.

"What's going on, Heather? You look…"

"Like crap? I know. My dad's mom—Nana—just died."

"Doesn't your Nana live in England?"

"She and Pop moved over here last year to be closer to Dad, what with the cancer. Bonnie happened to be nearby, so she's going to drive me up to Seattle." Lie after lie, each one settling like a rock in her stomach.

"What, right now?" Gabriel asked. "It's five in the morning."

"Yeah, well, Dad needs me right now. Speaking of which, what are you doing here?"

"One of your neighbors called the cops. Said you told her to feed the dogs while you were away, but then she saw a bunch of strangers pulling up to your house. She was worried you were being broken into. I said I'd check it out."

Heather shrugged and frowned, looking around the street and her empty living room. "Huh, that's weird. It's just me and Bonnie here. I guess she is going senile after all."

Gabriel narrowed his eyes. "You're lying to me."

"Gabriel."

He threw his hands up. "You know what, I don't want to know. So when are you going to be back this time?"

"I'm not sure. No idea when the funeral will be yet. Can you feed the dogs for me while I'm away and let Tina know what's going on?"

He rubbed his forehead. "Yeah, of course. But, Heather—"

"Yeah?"

"Never mind. I'm sorry about your Nana," he added as an obvious afterthought, just in case she was telling the truth. In fact, both sets of her grandparents lived overseas, and not a single one of the four of them had ever had cancer. She was pretty sure Gabriel knew that from passing mentions, but he wasn't confident enough to risk being unsympathetic.

"Thanks, me too," she said, looking down at her feet to sell her grief.

That was a mistake. Gabriel took a sharp inhale of breath and stepped toward her. "What happened to your head?"

Crap, she thought. "I slipped."

He put a hand on her shoulder. "Heather, I'm worried about you. Are you being held hostage?" He lowered his voice, putting his other hand on his gun. "Blink twice if you need me to get you out of here."

She looked up at him and didn't blink, though the outside air dried her eyes.

Gabriel removed his hand and sighed. "You'll call, right?" he asked. "Check in when you get there?"

"I'll try to. Might be a bit chaotic, knowing my parents."

He cursed under his breath in Spanish, and apologetically, Heather stepped forward for a hug. He fortunately accepted but quickly retracted as Bonnie re-entered the room and cleared her throat.

"Heather, we have to go soon," she pushed gently.

Gabriel retreated through the doorway. "I guess I'll let you go. Give my condolences to your dad, and let me know the funeral location so I can send flowers."

"Will do. Thanks, Gabriel."

Gabriel nodded, turned, and walked away to the sad song of the morning birds, his body cast blue by the light of dawn. Heather chewed her lip, shut the door, and looked at Bonnie.

"That sucked."

"Yeah, it did. But you'll make it up to him when this is over. Look on the bright side. At least he's the kind of guy who'll stick around. I think the guy I met on Tinder two months ago will probably have found a replacement by the time I get back to the real world."

"He's not my boyfriend," Heather clarified.

"Even better. A friend like that is there come hell or high water. Now, come on, I'll help you pack."

CHAPTER TWENTY-FIVE

THE DETECTIVE

THE BUNKER'S LOCATION WAS UNDER LOCK AND KEY past the point of the Washington, DC, airport, and once loaded into the van, they had endured the long, bumpy journey blindfolded. Heather figured it must be near enough to the CIA headquarters for Operation Silver Scalpel to be able to be summoned at a moment's notice. After all, no one expected them to rescind their duties and stay holed up full-time in a bunker until somebody else caught Clarence. They were still in charge. They just needed a well-guarded place where no one was going to assassinate them while they slept.

After what felt like two hours—making it, to her estimation, around one o'clock in the afternoon, though who knew with all the jetlag—the van came to a halt, and the two women were ushered through what sounded like a thick metal door, down a long flight of stairs, and then through another door before the blindfold was finally removed.

As her eyes adjusted to the bright lights, her jaw dropped, and she glanced at Bonnie and found her in a similar state of shock at what lay before them.

This is more like it, Heather thought.

Unlike what she'd been permitted to see of the CIA headquarters, the state-of-the-art bunker looked as if it had been ripped directly from a sci-fi movie set. Her high expectations for what she'd expected from the boardroom were far exceeded by the chic, futuristic world of glistening white, clean lines, glass surfaces, and the plethora of screens and technology. It wasn't cozy by any means—and she feared that one tumble might shatter the entire setup—but it was breathtaking and, undeniably, excitingly cool.

Sitting at one of the shiny, underlit tables were Jessica and Takahiro, who appeared to be playing a pretty boring game of Go Fish. Jason was nowhere to be seen, but considering the past twenty-four hours, she imagined he was enjoying an unconscious break from the world. She knew he was an early-morning guy, but today seemed like an exception to the rules, especially in the timeless void that a windowless underground fortress provided.

She could do with some winks herself after only managing an hour on the plane, but her brain was overloaded and her anxiety was at an all-time high. She reached into her pocket for her phone, a bad habit when nervous, and found that it was gone. She looked at Bonnie.

"Oh yeah, they would've taken that when you got on the van. Sneaky hands." She wriggled her fingers. "Can't have anyone finding out about this place, and not just for our sake. Let's just say this joint is mostly occupied by guys a lot more important to the government than any of us. You'll get it back whenever we leave."

"What about if they need to call me?"

Bonnie hummed. "They can still e-mail you. The computers use state-of-the-art VPNs."

"I guess that's something."

Heather stepped further into the room, and Takahiro greeted them warmly.

"Come, pull up a seat. We just started a new round. I can easily add two more players. In fact, I'm dying to. This game is no good with two people. Plus, I think Jess is cheating, and I need your detective skills to back me up."

"Nakamura," Jessica growled.

Takahiro groaned. "Come on, Jess. I'm dying of boredom."

"Fine," Jessica said, kicking out the seat next to her at the four-seater table. "There's food and crap in the kitchen if you want anything."

"I'm good, I had food on the plane. Any beer?" Heather asked.

Everyone looked at her strangely.

"It's one o'clock," Jessica retorted, a wry laugh caught in her throat.

"Oh yeah, of course. Haven't really slept in over twenty-four hours on account of an attempt on my life," Heather snipped pointedly. "Kind of disoriented. I was thinking I might have a drink and go to sleep."

"Well, there might be some alcohol," Takahiro offered. "I know the guys up top like their brandy, but I haven't checked. None of us really drink."

Jessica nodded in agreement. "Yeah. Too busy, you know? No offense."

Offense taken, Heather thought, resenting the sentiment and burning hot with irritation despite the powerful AC. She was busy, and she was *here*, wasn't she? The same as any of them.

Though it was childish, she looked around the room with her hand flat above her brows and immediately landed on what was obviously a liquor cabinet. It was situated next to a semicircular gray couch that surrounded a circular table sporting an ashtray and what seemed to be some sort of ventilation tube above it, and her inner rebellious teenager wished desperately for a pack of smokes to supplement what she was about to do.

She could practically hear Jessica's teeth grind as she marched over to the lounge area, pulled the cabinet door ajar,

199

and relished in the frosty blast fog of what turned out to be a state-of-the-art booze cooler. Heather hid a pleased smile from the others and retrieved an open bottle of high-end brandy, two cubes of ice, and a crystal glass. She poured herself a triple, even though she disliked brandy, and swaggered back to the table, kicking off her shoes as she went. When she arrived, she was all smiles in the face of Jessica's vexation and sat down hard on the kicked-out chair, even though it was likely designated for Bonnie.

"Right, so what are we playing? Go Fish?" she asked between sips, rubbing her hands together and cracking her neck.

"Yep," Jessica said sourly.

"How about playing rummy?" Heather offered, trying to be enthusiastic. "I whip ass at that."

"Don't know how to play," Jessica replied flatly, and the other two concurred with nods.

"How about poker then?" Heather prompted but received a similar response. "Guessing you guys have never been to Vegas then."

"Not allowed," Takahiro said. "No gambling, no drugs—"

"No binge drinking," Jessica added.

"Right," Heather said, feeling like she'd won the Guinness World Record for World's Trashiest Woman. "So Go Fish it is then. Let's do it."

Takahiro dealt the cards quietly, and Heather changed tact, trying to find some common ground with her new roommates.

"I'm sure going to miss my morning run," she said.

"There a track down a floor," Jessica said. "I've already been for mine. I wake up at five."

"Me too," Takahiro added. "Even us nerds have to stay fit."

"I get that. So what else do you guys do for fun?"

"Running isn't fun," Jessica laughed incredulously. "It's work."

"Yeah, of course," Heather responded, though she disagreed. "But seriously, on your perfect Saturday off work, what would you do?"

"I like spending time with my family," Bonnie offered. "Maybe cooking up some dinner."

"Oh, cool," Heather enthused. "I've just gotten into cooking after living off microwave crap for years. Made deep-fried chicken burgers last week and managed to not burn my house down."

Bonnie looked at her strangely. "Oh, I don't eat anything deep-fried. It's so bad for your arteries."

"Sure, but I think it's all about balance. A salad in exchange for a cigarette," Heather joked.

Jessica curled her upper lip in disgust. "Got any queens?" she asked Takahiro, who'd replied with a tap of the Go Fish pile.

"What about you, Takahiro?" Heather asked. "What do you like to do?"

"I'd probably build a computer if I had some time off," he replied.

"Like for gaming?" Heather asked excitedly. Gabriel liked video games, and even though she hadn't played anything since she was in her teens, she knew a lot about the modern world of gaming through him and had greatly enjoyed watching him play *Red Dead Redemption 2*.

"No, just to see how powerful it can be," Takahiro replied. "I'm not really into games."

"Oh, okay... Jessica?"

"I don't do days off," Jessica snapped. "So I'd be training and making myself useful. Probably down at the gun range."

The conversation was running dangerously dry, and after a few futile attempts to see if they watched any of the same TV shows or movies—they didn't—Heather decided to abandon ship. She'd anticipated being the odd one out, but considering her high-powered background, she'd hoped that she'd soon blend in with their shiver of sharks. Instead, she was a fish out of water, rapidly running out of air and wondering if she'd ever swam cohesively with any school.

As she lost another round of Go Fish—and figured out that Jessica was definitely cheating but kept it to herself—she mentally transported herself to Glenville and stood outside of the graffitied doors for Sludge. Though she'd initially blanched at the idea of attending—knowing a night of hedonism and indulgence awaited her beyond those doors—she now craved nothing more than a carefree evening and a hungover morning. As she had said, it was all about balance, and with the recent influx of tedium, disrespect, and abject misery, hadn't she earned a little fun? After all, she didn't want to end up resembling the sharp-toothed thing that Jessica had molded herself into.

CHAPTER TWENTY-SIX

THE AGENT

JASON WAS AWAKE WHEN HEATHER AND BONNIE arrived, as he had been when Jessica and Takahiro made their entrance. He'd heard them all mention him in passing, assured he was asleep, all the while he was working his way through two tiny triangles of a bland ham-and-cheese sandwich in complete darkness. His mouth was dry, but he knew if he got up to get water, then he'd have to hang out, and he certainly didn't feel like playing Go Fish.

Not that being in bed was much better. He felt like he was in the hospital and that a nurse would come in with a cup of pills and a blood pressure monitor any minute now. Fortunately, they didn't, but the sensation made it hard to settle, as did the conversation happening outside of his door.

Poor Heather was desperate to bond, but all her efforts resulted in was making Jessica angrier and Jason cringe. Bonnie and Takahiro were as friendly as ever, but he knew that as long as she avoided serial killer talk and stuck to the world of media and entertainment, her attempts to click would be futile.

If only his mother could've stayed in the bunker with them instead of going with Natalie and the girls. He expected their dwelling situation was equally antagonistic, especially under such fraught circumstances. But he supposed his mother being here would come with its own issues, such as ripping the costume off the wretched wolf playing nice among the sheep and teaching Heather to hunt alongside her.

As Heather made yet another tentative movie reference that nobody understood, including Jason, he decided to put in some earplugs and get some rest. He'd rather listen to the voices in his head—namely Natalie crying and yelling—than listen to another second of Heather grasping at straws.

They'd argued again before he left, he and Natalie, resulting in waterfalls of tears and a night spent on the couch. Natalie had spent a lot of her time crying lately and had been talking about going to stay with her sister with growing sincerity. It felt like they were standing on the edge of a precipice, and she was backing toward the ledge despite how much he begged her to stop moving.

It wasn't that she hated him. Quite the opposite. She loved him, their daughters, and the unborn baby so much that she couldn't bear him doing this job anymore. He could justify what he did in a million different ways, shine a thousand additional lights on the situation, and make promise after promise, but a switch had been flicked in her mind. Now nothing could flip it back. His job was too dangerous. That was that. So it was quitting or moving entirely to desk work, and he feared that even the latter might not be enough of a compromise. So they were at an impasse. He was in peril, she was losing her mind, and both of them were being forcibly kept apart with minimal contact. He knew tensions were exceptionally high because of the baby and the accompanying hormones, but he knew he couldn't pin all his hopes on the birth solving their problems.

He must have fallen asleep because a knock at the door stirred him awake despite the earplugs and he found himself far from his family, wrapped up in cold sheets. He blinked, removed the foam plugs, and beckoned whoever was outside his bedroom to come inside, even though he really wanted to tell them to do the opposite.

When Jessica opened the door, he nearly voiced this desire but swallowed his preemptive irritation and kept his mouth shut. He really wasn't in the mood for snarky comments, unhelpful opinions, or complaints about Heather or otherwise. However, they hadn't even been in the bunker for twenty-four hours, and he refused to be the first to start an argument. Especially as it was his fault that everyone was here in the first place.

Jessica turned on the overly bright overhead lights and hissed before apologizing. "Sorry, I didn't realize this was a dentist's office." She shuffled forward and tapped the bedside lamp, which was fortunately much dimmer. "That's better. This place is giving me a headache."

Complaint number one, Jason counted, though he couldn't disagree. "What's that?" he asked, inspecting the bowl in one of Jessica's hands. It looked to be some sort of rice noodle dish. Pad thai perhaps?

"Oh yeah, I brought you some actual food. Drunken noodles. Good stuff. You into it? 'Cause if not, I could happily go for round two."

"Hand it over," Jason instructed, grabbing the hot bowl like a greedy child. He looked down. The presentation left something to be desired, but the smell was mouth-watering. "Did you make this?"

"God, no. You know it's cold salads for me or hoping my latest 'houseguest' knows her way around a kitchen. No, luckily, Heather got bored with us and decided to take out her frustrations in the kitchen. It's a war zone in there—literally, I mean sauce and oil everywhere—so she's no pro, but I'll admit it, the bitch can cook."

Jason took a bite and concurred. "She can, but please, don't call her a bitch."

"What? It's a term of endearment between us girls."

Jason glowered. "Jess."

"Fine. She's not a bitch, and if she keeps to the kitchen, we'll get on just fine. Frankly, I just need Anderson and Nakamura to do the same and also leave me alone with the files."

"How about you not bully the team away from doing their job. Especially Heather, who risked her life for information."

Jessica gasped, mockingly defensive. "I'm not bullying anyone!"

"Come on, Jess, I mean it," Jason said sternly before taking another big bite of the delicious food. "How is she anyway?"

"Don't know, didn't ask. But she can't be that concussed if she can cook for a bunker of people."

Jason sighed. "How long are you going to do this for?"

"Do what?" Jessica asked, batting her lashes.

"Blame everybody else for what happened?"

Jessica gritted her teeth and looked at the door as if she might storm through it. Instead, she lowered her voice into a growl. "Listen, if that hick cop hadn't blabbed at the bar, then Sara would still be alive. I'd be married, maybe have some kids and a white picket fence. Instead, because of a cop…" she trailed off, her voice still cracking after all these years.

It always made Jason uncomfortable hearing such pain from such a strong woman's mouth.

"You're forgetting an important part of that story," Jason said kindly.

"What, the part where you saved my ass? No, dude, I'm not. That's why I'm here right now in this godforsaken bunker. Because I owe you one."

He shook his head. "Before that. Before I showed up with the helicopter. Who took a bullet for you and ended up in the hospital for a month?"

Jessica pursed her lips. "Nicolas Alvarez."

"Who was a…?"

"Cop, god damn it. He was another local cop. Okay, I know. I remember. And I get your point."

"Do you?"

"Yes," Jessica hissed. "Your point is to be nice to Heather or whatever."

"Not exactly," Jason started but looked at Jessica's expression and turned away from continuing his lecture on cops. "But close enough."

"You know, it would be easier for all of us, especially Heather, if you stopped moping and came out of your room. Listen, it sucks. Nobody's denying that. But none of us want to be here, and the sooner we track down Clarence, the sooner we get to leave."

Jason rubbed his forehead. "Yeah, okay. You're right. I'll be out in a minute."

"You better be," Jessica said, snatching his empty bowl and slinking out of the room.

He heeded her advice, but instead of joining her and the other two in the living area, he walked past them with a wave and entered the kitchen to check on Heather. He found her scrubbing the counters with a sink full of hot, soapy water at the ready for the mountain of dishes.

"We have a dishwasher," he informed her. "Two, actually."

Heather looked around and cursed as she spotted the artfully camouflaged appliances. "Dammit. Guess I might as well wash them now. Don't want to waste water."

"We're not going to stick you with the bill. Plus, if you cook, you don't have to clean. That's their job. That's how this works."

Heather shrugged. "I don't want to start enforcing chores like I'm their mom. Jessica already acts like a resentful teenager."

"Fine, from now on, as team captain, I'll do the enforcing. But today, I'll help you with the cleaning and leave them to it. But we're not handwashing anything that can fit in the dishwasher." He eyeballed the piles again. "How the hell is there so much to wash already?"

She pointed at the individual elements, breaking the heaps down for another member of the "can't cook" crew. "Saucepan, wok, pot for the noodles, colander, chopping boards, and bowls for everyone on the team and the entire security detail. It stacks up."

"No kidding," Jason replied, abruptly and painfully guilty over not being home early often enough to get to the dishes before Natalie. Worst of all, he kept forgetting to replace the broken dishwasher. Just as he was about to ask Heather if she thought that would make a good birthday present for his wife, he pictured her outraged expression and thought better of it.

He loaded the dishes into the dishwasher as Heather washed the wok and strainer, and when he turned to say there was a little more space left for another bowl, he caught sight of the back of her head. She clearly hadn't washed yet, her hair pulled into a low ponytail and matted with claret, same for the fluffy hairs on the back of her neck, and his already-malignant guilt spread from his heart to his lungs.

Last night he'd feared the worst when he couldn't get ahold of her, and when that dreaded call came, the relief was short-lived as she slurred and proceeded to pass out in the taxi. Worst of all, the driver—clearly worried she was dead and not wanting to be culpable—drove off after dropping her in the field, leaving her on death's door, half-naked, soaked through, and bleeding profusely. It was a miracle she was here, talking, smiling, scrubbing plates.

"You doing okay?" Jason asked, grabbing the last of the bowls.

"I've had worse. I think the emotional fallout is worse than the physical, and thank God for that dinner tray. Otherwise, I'd definitely be lying on the slab right now."

"So how are you feeling… emotionally?" Jason forced himself to ask, his delivery a little stilted but genuine.

Heather raised her eyebrows and screwed up her mouth. "You really want to know?"

"Sure."

"I don't think I'm going to have a good night's sleep for a long time."

Jason nodded. "I'm sorry I sent you down there."

"Don't be. It was worth it."

"It was?" Jason asked, lighting up despite himself.

"I'll tell you all about it when I'm done talking about my feelings," Heather scolded, placing the wok in the drying rack.

Jason nodded gravely. "You can … keep talking. If you want."

Heather chuckled. "I'm kidding. Plus, you really don't want to know what's going on in my head. You've got enough horrors going on on your own without doing a trauma exchange, I'm sure."

"I don't think anything going on in my head is half as bad as the Paper Doll Killer. I don't know how you ..." Jason trailed off.

"Yeah, me neither," Heather said, her voice turning crackly when it got low. "Though it's worse for you. You have daughters. You can put yourself in the parents' shoes. I can live with it because I can't, and I won't."

"I can't imagine living without children," Jason replied, hoping he didn't sound unkind. "So you don't think you'll ever ..."

"I don't know. Probably not. Might need a lobotomy first," Heather laughed. "Not to mention a second husband."

"Well, maybe it won't be so painful one day."

"I hope so."

"I'm surprised you didn't quit after that."

"Would you have?" Heather inquired. "Quit your job after that?"

"After *that*? Maybe."

"Huh. I figured you were made of tougher stuff than me."

"I think you might be underestimating yourself in that case."

The corner of Heather's mouth flickered and then fell. "I nearly did quit. Ran away from Seattle for the quiet life. Ironic, isn't it? All I wanted was peace, but now I'm catching terrorists with the CIA and filling all my spare time with cold homicide cases."

"Cold cases, huh?" he asked. "Why would you do that to yourself?"

"For the same reason you run five kilometers a day and work for the damn CIA. Compulsion. The inability to stop." Heather paused and dried her hands. "Speaking of. After this is all over, would I still be able to, you know, access files now and again? Might help me out on occasion."

"That depends. Do you want to join the FBI and become privy to that level of information?"

Heather barked a scratchy laugh. "I'll get back to you on that one."

CHAPTER TWENTY-SEVEN

THE DETECTIVE

AFTER THEY'D FINISHED THEIR EXTENSIVE CLEANING, Jason and Heather returned to the living area, where the others had long abandoned cards and were busy rifling through physical files and clicking away on supercomputers.

"Found anything?" Jason asked.

"Not yet," Bonnie said. "A little bit about the Dixon family here and there, but they were all pretty clean aside from a shady uncle and a little tax fraud in the late '90s."

"Well, that's where I can help," Heather said, pulling up a seat at the table. "So when I was digging for dirt on Clarence, I noticed that he basically vanished around early 2016 and didn't reappear until 2018—when the MI6 bombing occurred. What was weird was just before he disappeared the first time, he looked different. Not plastic-surgery different yet, but hollowed out. Dead behind the eyes, you know? It was like you could see him go from a normal family man to a monster overnight. Takahiro, could you bring up pictures of him from December 23, 2015, and May 2016. He cut the ribbon at a community center and a mini-mall. Shouldn't be hard to find."

"Is this where you try to justify his actions with trauma?" Jessica snapped.

"Jess," Jason warned, but Heather stopped him.

"No, I'm not. I'm trying to explain to you, a member of this team, what this man's motivations are and were so that we can profile him. That way, we can get inside his head, predict his next move, and catch him. Make sense?"

Jessica nodded tensely. "Sure. Whatever."

Takahiro brought up the photos on his computer and whistled. "Wow, Heather was right."

"Show the class," Jessica barked, gesturing to the numerous screens that plastered the walls.

Takahiro nodded sheepishly and projected the "before" and "after" around the room, and even Jessica seemed taken aback by the stark contrast.

"Jesus," she said. "It's like somebody ripped his soul out." She looked at Heather, her attention finally hooked. "What did his wife say?"

"She told me the only thing that made sense for him to go from that to that." She paused for suspense, glad to finally have all eyes on her, "His dad died on April 5, 2016. And not only were they very close, but what killed his father, Clarence Dixon Sr., was a drone strike while he was on a business trip in Iran."

"Do you know where?" Bonnie asked, left fingers itching to type and right hand ready to broadcast her findings to the group.

Heather nodded. "Yeah, it happened in a small town near Bushehr called Sarzeh. Clarence Sr. was staying in a hotel there near his contact's oil field. Unfortunately, someone else was also staying in Sarzeh—"

Bonnie cast a file onto one of the screens in between duplicates of Clarence's before and after.

"A terrorist by the name of Saeed Golshani, who had radicalized, kidnapped, and later murdered his young English wife."

"Yeah, I remember hearing about this," Takahiro added, throwing more files onto the wall. "They'd been looking for him for a while, so when the Air Force found his location, they took the shot, despite the civilians."

"Which begs the question of why he's after the MI6 and CIA when the army made that call."

Jason cleared his throat. "Actually, it was me who made the call."

Heather and the others nearly snapped their necks to stare at him. Heather analyzed his every movement and knew that he wasn't even close to joking.

"What do you mean you made the call?" she asked, dumbfounded.

"In 2016, I was assigned to a team that was initially looking for the young woman Saeed Golshani had kidnapped. We were working alongside a team at MI6 because, despite the girl being English, she was officially taken in California while on 'holiday.'"

Heather faltered and stumbled, visible anger mounting as she tried to get her words out. "Why didn't you tell us?"

"Because I couldn't remember," Jason pleaded earnestly, his suddenly pathetic tone grating on Heather's nerves like a violin bow.

Despite this, Heather did believe him. She knew what it was like to have a wall up and have one word, one trigger, kick a hole through the brick and send it all tumbling down.

"Okay. Fine. You couldn't remember. I believe you. The part I'm having trouble with now is that you found out the location of a terrorist—sure, okay, good job—and then you nuked the place without, I don't know, checking for civilians? I mean, I'm sitting here asking myself whom I have been working beside." Heather panted.

Feeling hot, she stood from the table but kept her palms glued to the glass top.

"I nearly died for this case, only to find out you..." she trailed off, her voice growing hoarse. "You lit the first match in this goddamn *dumpster fire!*"

The others looked taken aback, but no one was quite as wound up as Heather, so she peeled her sweat-stuck hands from the table, leaving foggy imprints behind, and stalked back to the liquor cabinet. This time she grabbed a sealed bottle of scotch from the back and shrugged off the pained expressions on everyone's faces as she twisted the top and poured herself a neat double.

"Heather, please sit," Jason asked. "Let me tell you everything, then you're free to judge me and even leave if you want."

"Fine. Go ahead," Heather said, falling backward onto the gray couch and putting her feet up on the coffee table.

Once Jason—ashen and nervous—was sure she would stay quiet and listen, he began and told the entire story of how he knew Clarence Dixon Jr. from beginning to end.

It was December 2015, and Jason had been with the CIA for just over one year but had quickly climbed the ranks to a moderately high-ranking officer position. It had helped, of course, that a great-great-uncle on his mother's side had been a valuable agent during multiple wars both before and after the founding of the Agency, but mostly it was because—as Jessica interrupted and phrased it—Jason was just that good. Despite her irritation, Heather avoided calling him a nepotism baby and chose to believe Jessica's praise.

After continuing to prove himself time and time again, both on the field and in the office, he was finally invited to join the big boys in finding and taking down Saeed Golshani. It was clearly a test, an opportunity for him to cut his teeth among his experienced yet churlish peers. Some officers didn't take his skyrocket to success well and decided to slack off, assigning him several vital duties, including communications with the Air Force. Despite their intentions to send the runt running back into his mother's arms, Jason succeeded on every level, and soon enough, he, the Air Force, MI6, and the few team players in his crew managed to roughly locate Saeed.

Jason was on top of the world until the missing girl's body turned up in a nearby river along with her newborn child.

His superiors were greatly disappointed at the loss of such a critical component in the mission, and though they recognized such a new recruit should never have had so many responsibilities, it was still, in part, his fault. Fortunately, they didn't fire him, and his severe scolding only drove Jason more. He was going to make it up to them, the dead girl and her poor baby.

So when he finally pinpointed Saeed in Bushehr, he and his superiors at both the CIA and MI6 decided to order a strike on his location, lest he should escape again. They, of course, tried to clear out the small oil town, but they were hasty and didn't want to tip Saeed or his men off. Though Jason was assured that the province had been cleared of civilians, he would soon find out it was a lie after being given the critical task of making the call.

Saeed died, as did several of his men, and the rest of them were rounded up. So at first, it seemed like a success until the rest of the rubble was searched. There were also four civilian casualties. Two locals, a local oil tycoon, and one American citizen: Clarence Dixon Sr. If it had gotten out, it would be a black stain on the CIA, MI6, and the Air Force, and though they managed to keep it from the papers for a long time, keeping Clarence Dixon Jr. silent was a nearly impossible task. They eventually succeeded but not without a great deal of financial and legal heavy lifting.

"So that's where I know his name from," Jason said, ending the harrowing tale. "I only spoke to him directly once when he managed to break into the lobby. I think he got arrested that day for threatening bodily harm against one of my bosses. I can't believe I forgot. I mean, I killed his dad."

Nobody said anything because he had—and here they all were, dealing with the repercussions of that button push. Heather wanted to tell him that it was okay, that he didn't mean to, that he was just doing his job, and that his superiors manipulated him, but ultimately, it didn't change the fact that he was right. His actions culminated in the deaths of four innocent people. Julius was right about perfectionists making mistakes, but this was an insurmountable blunder with fitting repercussions.

"Did you ever apologize to Clarence?" she asked, already knowing the answer. Jason opened his mouth to speak, but she elaborated. "Not with money. Not with excuses. Just 'sorry'?"

"It sounds like you're blaming him for the actions of a murderer and a terrorist," Jessica said, bristling. "Lots of us lose our dads, but we don't blow up buildings and kill people because of it."

Jason interrupted. "No, she's right. I didn't. I was twenty-two and sure that the greater good came with casualties. Now, I can't help but think, what if I'd handled everything better?"

Heather shook her head fervently. "No. Ignore me. It's not helpful to be critical of the past. Seriously. You take that 'what if' and throw it away, crush it under your boot, throw it outside through the air lock. Thinking it won't change anything, and you falling apart over this won't help anything. We're here now. And Jessica is right. It would be one thing if he was just coming after you, but he's killed over a dozen people in the last week alone, and—"

"He's going to kill him," Jason exclaimed, eyes wide. "Oh my god, he's going to kill him."

"Kill who?" Jessica asked.

Heather stood from the couch at the same time as Jason stood from the table, and they looked at each other, horrified.

"His dad," she whispered. "An eye for an eye."

The others looked shell-shocked and remained mute as Heather rejoined them, swilling her drink around and watching the tornado as she thought.

"He's not going to kill him quietly. In order to punish you, you'll need to be watching in one way or another. That means he's still alive, and if we can get to Clarence before the big show, we can safely extract your dad."

"So he's on death row, and we have to get the keys to the Huntsville Unit before the needle arrives?" Jessica asked, seemingly looking to Heather for guidance.

"That's not how I'd put it," she replied hesitantly, "but yes."

"Can we draw him out?" Bonnie offered.

"Yeah, like with his kids or his wife or something?" Jessica asked, glancing at Jason before he protested. "Not hurt them, of course. Just bring him to us. His wife for your dad."

"No," Jason said firmly. "I've done enough harm to his family. We do this right. We hunt him down like Heather does. Using detective work."

Jason also looked to Heather expectantly, and though she appreciated the sudden faith everyone had in her bloodhound skills, she needed a moment to think. She sipped her whiskey and gulped it down with an excess of saliva, her hand developing a slight shake.

She nodded after half a dozen paces across the room and spun toward the group on her socks, nearly losing her balance in the process.

"Okay, so he clearly has eyes everywhere. That's how he knew I was in Dallas, what room I was in, everything. Probably saw right through my disguise from the beginning. I also don't think he does his own dirty work and would never stay too close to a crime scene. Which rules out his location being in Washington, Oregon, or Texas."

"Great, so that just leave the other forty-seven states and the rest of the world," Jessica moaned. "For all we know, he could be in fricking Tijuana right now."

Heather lowered her brows and shook her head as she took another sip. "No. He's not. He's in Virginia."

"How do you figure?" Jason asked.

"He's hunting us just as much as we're hunting him. He's been setting traps and straight-up tried to have me and Bonnie killed."

"Me too," Takahiro added. "The shed I used to live in at my parents' place burned down last night."

Jessica looked thoughtful. "I did have this really weird thing driving home last night. I thought he was just trying to drag-race, but..."

"So he's trying to thin the herd and single Jason out," Bonnie added.

Heather nodded. "Exactly. He wants to get rid of us and lure Jason in for the final show before killing him too."

"So how do you figure he's in Virginia?" Jessica asked.

"Because he wants it to be easy enough for Jason to find him on his own. And after last night, I think he's getting impatient. A hungry predator circling his prey. The kicker is, I bet he knows we're in Virginia too. We're both just waiting for the other to emerge first."

"How confident are you about this?" Jason asked.

"As much as I can be," she replied truthfully.

"Great. Then we get the CIA and everyone else we can to scrape the whole state. Top to bottom," Jason commanded. "Bonnie, you get in touch with everyone you can. Police, FBI, private investigators. Takahiro, you're on cameras, security systems. Anything that seems weird. Jessica—"

"Special Activities Center. Got it."

Jason finally sat back down and exhaled. "Heather, you're on brainstorming. Use your cases to your advantage. Where do killers usually hide?"

"Abandoned places. Plain sight if they can. Warehouses. Fishing shacks."

"Write it down," Jason demanded but with upbeat enthusiasm.

Heather nodded, and just as she moved toward her room, she asked, "Hey, do you think I could get a corkboard in here?"

CHAPTER TWENTY-EIGHT

THE AGENT

"HEATHER," JASON BLURTED LOUDLY, ENTERING her room without knocking.

To his surprise, she was slumped over herself and snoring, her hair wet and dribbling onto a pile of printouts on the bed. Ahead of her, propped up on top of the chest of drawers, was a brown corkboard, overgrown with Clarence Dixon Jr.'s life thus far. His childhood, family, marriage, children, and successes were laid out in lush detail across the left side, and on the sparser right were labels like "high-functioning psychopath," "post-traumatic stress," and "paranoid personality disorder" stuck to articles and psychological studies.

In the middle of the board, she had listed Clarence's possible locations with the warehouse thickly underlined. Jason shook his head in disbelief. She had been right on the money. Of course.

"Bishop, come on. Wake up," Jason said, shaking her shoulder.

Heather stirred awake with a snort and looked around wildly as Jason stepped back and threw a high-tech bulletproof jacket at her.

"What's going on?" she asked, scraping her wet hair back.

"We already found him. Well, technically, Takahiro's software did. Facial recognition stuff. It's above my pay grade, but basically, he ran the composite drawing of Clarence through the remotely accessible cameras of Virginia, and less than twenty-four hours later, boom, it makes a perfect match.

"Where is he?" Heather asked, now forcing her thick mane hair into a slicked-back bun.

Jason couldn't help but smile. "He's in a warehouse. By the docks in Richmond, Virginia. Congratulations, Detective. You were right on both counts."

Heather looked at him blankly. "Are you serious?"

"Deadly. I've already got two agents heading in to watch the place while we get over there with the SAC guys."

Heather could hardly suppress her grin as she shook her head in disbelief and pulled on the bulletproof vest over her black T-shirt. "How far away is it?"

"Forty minutes. I guess you were right about Clarence knowing where we are. He got close, but we've gotten closer."

Heather nodded and reached for her pants. In his excitement, Jason hadn't noticed she wasn't wearing any and turned to face the door.

"What does your gut say?" he asked. "After the pizzeria incident, let's just say I trust your instincts a lot more than my own."

Heather jumped up, and he could hear the buckling of her belt as she said, "Show me the video."

Jason nodded and turned back as Heather grabbed her jacket, boots, and gun. She shoved the latter into her belt and approached the doorway as Jason exited the room.

"We can give you something better than that," he offered, referring to her almost-antique weapon.

She looked at her third-generation Glock 19 with its worn grip and tarnished exterior and shook her head. "No, it's me and her until either one of us bites it."

Jason didn't try to argue, though he intended to press her to take an automatic rifle as a backup before they left. He knew she'd be unable to resist the allure of the armory, even if it meant being a little unfaithful to her old reliable.

They emerged into the central area, and Jason nodded at Takahiro, who cast the video of Clarence onto the walls. Though you could only see the back of his hoodie-covered head, Jason could see Heather's eyes light up. The Takahiro pressed Play, and the man turned, just once, toward the camera, before entering the run-down brick warehouse.

"Play it again," Heather said.

Takahiro rewound and pressed Play, and at the moment when the man turned, he paused. Heather furrowed her brow and stepped closer to the screen. Though he was sure of what he saw, Jason waited with bated breath for her answer. At least a minute passed before Heather finally turned and nodded.

"So it's him?" he exhaled.

"As far as I can tell," Heather replied, her brows still heavy and knitted. "Is there any better footage?"

"Unfortunately not," Takahiro replied. "The warehouse belongs to a pretty run-down marina called Donahue's Docks. I'm surprised their cameras are even connected to the internet."

"So are you in?" Jason prompted.

"Yeah, I'm in," Heather said, a lot less enthusiastically than he would've liked.

"Are you sure?" he pushed.

She turned to look at him, her lip bloody from being chewed. "Yeah, it's him, and I'm sure."

Jason didn't believe her, and he knew she didn't believe herself either, but they were both sure it was him, no matter her doubts, which meant they had to move.

—

After only thirty minutes, the roller coaster of a journey was at an end, the peaks and valleys of rural Virginia successfully traversed in record time. Organs unsettled by the repeated jolts, lifts, and landings, Jason, Jessica, and Heather eagerly ripped off their blindfolds and let their vision stabilize their equilibrium as they waited to be released from the van.

Jessica let out a shaky breath as the doors unlocked, and Jason hoped it was just because of the journey and that Heather's sixth sense wasn't catching. He looked at each of them, trying to detect doubt but seeing none. They had a strategy, they had weapons, and they had plenty of backup. There was no reason to get cold feet now.

Heather stood, crouched, and hopped out onto the cobbled street surrounding the three-story redbrick building. She didn't shake, tremble, or retreat, but he noticed her grip tighten on her gun, so he did the same.

The building was surrounded by the SAC, and Jessica shook her head.

"So much for a covert entrance," she growled. "It's that new asshole in the SAC division. He just loves going against my orders."

"It's fine. He's here. He's trapped. We don't need to sneak up on him," Jason assured himself and the others before approaching the nearest unit to lay out their plan of attack.

While he and Jessica would enter through the doors picked up on the CCTV, he wanted a pair of officers at each exit, ready to move in at his or Jessica's command. If they did move in, they were to apprehend Clarence without killing him at all costs and should endeavor to do the same to the rest of the organization. Stern, his back straight and head held high, Jason asked if he had made himself clear.

"Yes, sir," came the unanimous response.

"Move out," he told them and turned, allowing them to organize amongst themselves who should go where.

After thirty seconds of coded discussion and walkie beeps and hisses, he twirled a finger in the air, and everyone, including Jessica and himself, moved into position.

Heather approached the door with them, and Jason shook his head. "Bishop, I need you to hang back."

"You wouldn't even be here if it wasn't for me," she protested.

Jessica shrugged. "She's right."

Jason gave up immediately. She was right, and if Jessica trusted her enough to be on the front line of this takedown, then so did Jason.

"At least get behind me," he added. "If anyone's getting shot, it's me."

"Nobody's getting shot," Jessica hissed. "And I should go first, I'm the best marksman."

"We've been through this," Jason growled. "Now, Bishop, get behind me, and, Malloy, get the door."

Unhappily the trio triangulated, and once Jason was sure that the angles were optimum, he raised his voice, allowing Clarence the opportunity to come quietly.

"Clarence Dixon Jr., this is Jason Fleming of the CIA. Come out with your hands up. We have you surrounded."

Jason pressed a button on his watch, and for two exact minutes, everyone waited in silence. When the beeps came, Jason banged his fist against the metal door.

"Come out with your hands up. This is your final warning."

Everyone dangled from tenterhooks this time, sure that Clarence would emerge from one of the doors at any moment. He didn't, and there was no reply nor sound of any kind from inside.

"He's not coming out," Heather said. "If he hasn't already, then he never will. He'll wait us out for weeks."

Jason agreed and nodded at Jessica, who counted down from three, before throwing open the unlocked door. On the other side was a vast, dark, and seemingly empty room that must've once stored boats but now was only occupied by the scurrying of rats and the persistent dripping of salt water from a hole in the roof. Jason pointed his flashlight at the slimy concrete floor covered in a thin layer of stagnant salt water and pond sludge and told everyone to watch their step as he took the first step inside.

Jessica was next inside, and after mere seconds, she cried out and shoved him to the side. Just as he was about to question her, a deafening shot fired from across the room, peppering the brick behind them. It missed them by such a large margin that Jason figured whoever had fired had to be blind or dying.

"Stay back, Heather," he said. "There's a shooter in here."

"Gladly," she replied, hiding outside.

"Who's there?" Jason called out, his light not quite reaching the source of the shot.

Click. Boom.

Jason flinched, expecting to be blasted full of buckshot, but the sound hadn't been another shot. It was the sound of a spotlight turning on, illuminating the far wall and their attacker. A man was sitting slumped on the ground like a rag doll, his legs stuck out straight in front of them, his jeans half-soaked with sediment. His right arm was crooked, his finger on the trigger of a shotgun, whereas the other was as stiff as his legs, holding the barrel.

He pressed down again, but neither Jessica nor Jason moved this time as he sent the slug flying in the same direction as before, missing them once again. From a distance, it was clear that this man was Clarence Dixon Jr., but something wasn't right. In fact, something was very wrong.

They walked toward the man, calling out repeatedly, but the only response they received was the raising and lowering of his arms. Eventually, they reached him and stood on either side of the man in the hoodie. Jason reached out and, without any protest from the figure, turned on the shotgun's safety and cautiously touched the man's hand that was wrapped around the barrel. His fingers were covered in super glue, and his flesh was cold.

Jason called out to Heather. "Bishop, get in here. You need to see this."

She responded with echoing footsteps and the hiss of a curse word as she stumbled.

"I told you to watch your step," Jason said.

"No, there's a goddamn trip wire in the doorway."

Jason looked down at the man again, at his fingers, his hands, his gun, and moved his flashlight up. Fishing wire, and plenty of it, was attached to pulleys and contraptions on the wall and ceiling above, leading all the way back to the trip wire. It was a booby trap, which meant that, despite his face, this wasn't Clarence.

He dropped into a crouch, and his two companions joined him. They cocked their heads at the eyes, unblinking and unmoving, sunken behind a layer of what looked like skin.

"It's a mask," Heather said, leaning forward. "Silicone. A perfect recreation of Clarence's face."

"You're kidding me," Jessica groaned.

"Nope," Heather replied, pulling gloves from her pocket and snapping them on.

Tentatively she pried the cover away to reveal a man in his sixties with a double chin and curly salt-and-pepper hair. Heather reached out and touched his throat, but it was very apparent to all of them that he was dead from the small bullet hole in the center of his forehead. Heather snapped several flash photos before standing.

"Who is that?" Heather asked, staring around.

"I have no idea," Jason said.

"Don't look at me," Jessica replied.

"Let's get the police department in here," Heather commanded. "We need CSI in here, and we need an ID on this guy. Figure out who he is to Clarence."

"Tell the SAC to do a sweep first," Jason said to Jessica. "Don't want any locals getting shot if Clarence has any crew hiding out."

Jessica nodded and left the room, and Heather carefully stepped around the barrel of the gun to Jason. She placed a hand on his back. "We'll find him," she promised.

Jason didn't reply, but he shook Heather off, stood, and strode out of the room and back into the cold, gray light of the dock. Heather was quick on his heels, and it was a good thing too, because a man in a stained red T-shirt was held back by the SAC and begging for a cop.

"Hey, are either of you two cops?" he called out.

"I am," Heather replied, striding forward, her badge at the ready.

"Hey, can you tell me what's going on here?" the man pleaded. "My name's Danny. I own this joint."

"Danny Donahue?" Heather questioned.

The man shook his head. "No, Danny O'Shay. Mr. Donahue is who I just bought this place off of."

"Let him go please," Heather instructed the SAC and beckoned Danny forward to come walk with her by the edge of the docks.

Jason followed discreetly and listened in on their conversation.

"So, Danny, you got any proof of you owning this place?" Heather asked, adopting a subtle East Coast cadence and posture that informed Danny that she was tough but fair.

It seemed to work, and Jason could see the man relaxing.

"Yeah, of course, I do, but those goddamn feds wouldn't listen to me. What are you doing running around with all these army guys anyway?"

Heather held out her hand. "I'm asking the questions here. So show me."

"All right, all right, jeez," Danny replied, fumbling with his phone and opening his gallery. He clicked on an image, zoomed in, and handed it over. "Those are the papers I just signed yesterday."

"All right. That checks out," Heather replied, handing him his phone back.

"So can you tell me what's going on here and why my new place of business is being surrounded by the feds?"

"Well, Mr. O'Shay. We have just found a dead body on your property. You wouldn't happen to know anything about that, would you?"

Danny began effing, blinding, and sweating profusely through his already-dampened shirt. He assured her over and over again that he "didn't know nothing about that," and though she believed him, she let him sweat until she was sure.

Eventually, she interrupted his anxiety attack by pulling out her own phone. "Are you squeamish, Mr. O'Shay?" she asked.

"Nope. Worked in sewage for twenty years."

Heather nodded and flipped her phone around. The color drained from Danny's face.

"Do you know this man?"

"Jesus, Mary, and Joseph," he moaned, reeling back. "That's Larry Donahue. The one I bought the marina from."

"Is Larry associated with any criminal organizations? "Heather asked.

"God, no. Larry is—was—a religious man. Devout. Gives to charity. Runs the soup kitchens at Christmas. Nicest guy I've ever known. Eight kids, twenty-somethin' grandchildren. Always has time for each of them. God, his poor wife."

Heather nodded and whistled for an officer to escort Danny O'Shay away from his own property. Once he was gone, she dropped the act and looked near screaming. She loosened her bun and unleashed her hair, only to comb it back together again with her fingernails. It looked and sounded painful, and Jason felt like he could practically feel her pain until he realized he was digging his own nails into his palm.

Clarence had killed another innocent man for nothing. For a cheap trick. For Jason.

CHAPTER TWENTY-NINE

THE DETECTIVE

INSTEAD OF IMMEDIATELY RETURNING TO THE BUNKER, Jason insisted they head to the CIA to speak to his superiors and pick up some mail. Though Heather was desperate to get back to the drawing board and figure out where she'd gone wrong, she agreed to tag along. It was all she could really do as the only cop involved: buckle up and ensure the train stayed on the tracks.

As they crossed the marble threshold and made it through security, Jason spoke for the first time in over an hour.

"Well, I guess we can strike Richmond from the locations list," he said numbly. "Or maybe Virginia altogether."

"Hey, at this rate, maybe we can find him through the process of elimination," Jessica drawled, stepping through the metal detector.

Heather didn't say anything, humiliated that her instincts had been so wrong. With each misstep, she could feel control of the case slipping away and into the hounds of faceless CIA higher-ups.

"I don't know how you two do this," Jessica said. Heather looked at her questioningly, and she elaborated. "All the planning and the research. I'm the person who finishes the job. I get told where to go and whom to kill. No waiting around. No 'getting in the mind of a killer.' No bullshit clues. Just coordinates and a gun. This waiting around is making my skin itch."

"Mine too," Heather said. She might have been more adjusted to playing the long game, but this one was really dragging its feet.

Jessica veered off to talk to the head of the SAC, and Jason disappeared behind a glossy wooden door for the better part of an hour, leaving Heather on an uncomfortable maroon chair in the hallway. At least she had her phone back, but she dared not turn it off airplane mode, wanting to avoid the barrage of texts until she felt emotionally equipped to handle them.

Jason emerged, looking apologetic, and pressed the button on the elevator across from Heather. It dinged and opened, and he stepped inside, keeping his hand across the edge of the door until Heather pried herself from the leather and shuffled inside.

"I know, I want to get back too. Just let me grab my mail, and we can go."

"Do you normally get mail delivered here?" she asked, not bothering to inquire about his meeting because she knew he'd never tell.

"Sometimes. It's usually internal. Pay slips or bonuses. That sort of thing. Or information that needs to be shredded after reading. Occasionally, that's from the Bureau or the government."

"Huh. The only mail I get is from the Home Shopping Network," Heather replied.

Jason looked at her strangely. "The what?"

"Never mind."

They entered Jason's office, which smelled like beeswax polish and was a lot nicer than the boardroom, though it was just as dated. It had a *Mad Men* energy about it, and she nearly made a Don Draper joke but realized it would be for her amusement only. Just another pop culture tidbit that would fly high above Jason's head. She tucked it away in the back of her mind for Gabriel, to whom she owed at least some CIA secrets, even if they were only in the form of oak furniture.

There was a letter at the center of Jason's desk, and he paused before moving toward it. He picked it up gingerly by the corner, examining it with a frown. It was a standard envelope, but all it had on it was his first name in scrawled handwriting and no stamps.

"Guess that's not standard procedure?"

"No, it's not," Jason muttered, cautiously feeling the envelope with the very tips of his fingers. He blanched and threw the envelope down onto the desk.

"What is it?" Heather asked.

Jason shook his head in horror and picked it back up, much to Heather's dismay. He tore open the sealed flap, leaving the edge frayed, and tipped the envelope upside down. A silver scalpel skittered onto the table, and Heather gasped as she saw that the tip was covered in dried blood.

Heather inhaled sharply. "Oh my god. Has he been listening to us? About Operation Silver Scalpel?"

Jason looked at her, eyes wild. "He can't have. It's impossible. We always check for bugs."

"Then what?"

"It's my dad's. It's his scalpel. Or the brand he uses, at least. He never shut up about how good they are."

"Shit. Do you have forensics—of course you do. Get them to test the blood and the saliva on the envelope."

Jason didn't reply as he noticed something Heather hadn't and pulled a letter out. He unfolded it, cleared his throat, and read it aloud.

"'The wonky wheel goes *tick, tick, tick,* amongst the hum of the future in a dark-gray hallway. There I am, riding in the cloth, ready for constantly cleaning hands to put me in my final resting place. The clock with an agenda goes *tick, tick, tick* amongst the chemicals as the door swings shut. There I am, hiding in plain sight, ready for you."

Jason looked at Heather dumbfounded, but Clarence was not the first killer Heather had met who was fond of riddles and puzzles.

"Evacuate the building," she urged, darting forth to snatch the letter and reread it. "I think he's planted a bomb."

"That's impossible," Jason said. "The security—"

"Please trust me," she begged.

Jason paused and then nodded. "Of course," he replied like a soldier before his captain, picking up an official-looking black phone from his desk.

He dialed a short number and spoke clearly into the receiver. "Code red. Get everyone out. I believe there is a bomb on-site."

A muffled voice responded, and the alarms began.

Jason plugged his available ear and yelled, "No, I don't know where it is."

Heather reread the letter for the umpteenth time. "Gray. Concrete. Dark. Cloth. Chemicals. Sounds of the future." She looked up at Jason and shouted, "Are your janitor's closets in the basement?"

"Yeah, I think so," he replied just as loudly.

"What about servers? Like computer servers."

"Yeah, probably. Can't think of anywhere else they'd be." She waited for it to click and watched the information click into place behind his eyes. "It's in the basement in a—?"

"Janitor's closet!" she answered, increasing her volume again as the sounds of chaos crescendoed and the room's lights began flashing red.

"Janitor's closet," Jason informed whoever was on the phone.

"Disguised as cleaning supplies or something!" Heather added.

Jason repeated the information down the phone before hanging up.

"The bomb squad is on their way to the basement. You should leave."

"What about you?" Heather asked.

"If this bomb goes off, I'm not having innocent men die instead of me."

Heather crossed her arms. "Well, I'm not leaving."

"Fine," Jason said, surprisingly unargumentative.

Heather figured he now knew her well enough that he'd just be wasting time and his breath if he tried to stop her.

"Come on, let's get to the basement. Put your detective powers to the test."

"How many janitor's closets are there?" she asked as they began to run toward the elevators.

"You don't want to know."

"No, I really do."

"At least twenty. So we better move fast."

In the basement, the bomb squad was waiting for them, accompanied by several dogs—Belgian Malinois and German shepherds—who were chomping at the bit, yanking against their harnesses and wearing down their nails on the concrete floor. Though Heather appreciated the help of their height-ened senses and years of training, as the group took off down the long hallway and moved past endless basement rooms, it turned her stomach to think that these animals could be blown to Kingdom Come with the rest of them. Just more innocents to add to the pile.

"What can they detect?" she asked one of the handlers.

"Pretty much anything," one of the men replied. "So you're thinking it's definitely in the janitorial sector?"

Heather nodded, thankful that the maze was arranged into easy-to-find clusters as they came to a fork and everyone who worked there turned left. At the mouth of the new, wider hallway, the dogs were released, and everyone watched as they zigzagged with their noses to the ground, sniffing at each and every door.

Heather felt the hum of technology in her feet from the colossal server room to their right at the center of the fork, and she felt her heart pound in the wound at the back of her head.

"It's here," she said, her gut pulling her forward with as much strength as the dog's nose.

Halfway up the hall, she spotted one of the dogs—a graying German shepherd with cataracts—who began to whine and paw at one of the doors. Before she could take another step, the bomb squad ran past her on light feet and pushed toward the wall as if their wall of bodies would save her from any potential blast.

That was when she really realized where she was: facing a bomb designed by a highly intelligent psychopathic terrorist. One wrong move, or one second too slow, and it could be lights-out forever. She wondered if she died right here, right now, whether her family would ever be told the truth about what happened. Probably not, which was even worse. No closure for anyone. Her body splattered beneath a building, never to be retrieved or buried.

The men opened the door, and Heather noticed a look of surprise on their faces. Despite Jason tugging at her arm to stay back, she tiptoed, and when they moved forward, she did too. Eventually, she saw it. Right in the center, on the middle shelf, was a pink boxed present wrapped up in ribbon. There was a label hanging from it. It was addressed to Jason. And to her.

Then she really did fall back, her fingers tingling, and she didn't realize she was beginning to hyperventilate—her life flashing before her eyes—until Jason placed a firm hand on her shoulder. It was too late to run, and the ticking emanating from the box filled her ears despite its low volume.

"It's okay," he said calmly, and she wondered if he was a religious man. She'd never asked.

Did he believe in heaven and that he and his family would be reunited there with certainty, or did he—like Heather—fear what was on the other side? Where had all those victims of all those killers gone? She often asked herself late at night. Were they safe and warm, or were they gone in the dark?

One of the bomb technicians cut the ribbon, and she scrunched up her eyes as she heard them lift the lid. For all they knew, doing so would pull some type of pin, and then it would be over. Or it was just another joke, and there would be an alarm clock at the base lying on a bed of rose-colored tissue paper.

"Jesus," one of the men muttered, and another man joined him with a tool kit.

The proceedings were obscured by their bodies, and Heather felt Jason's grip tighten. For a small eternity, as Heather tried to stay conscious and questioned her entire existence up until this fatalistic moment, the men muttered and worked. All the while the bomb ticked, and Heather began to use them to count down from one hundred, sure that it was about to blow up anytime.

When she got down to thirty-two, thirty-one never came. Instead, the bomb fell silent, and the squad turned, not smiling but relieved. They showed Heather and Jason the mess of cut wires and electronics and tapped the digital clock face in the center.

Five seconds remaining.

It didn't drop to four, and Heather let out a long breath. Jason slapped the front of her collarbone and sternum and helped her to her feet. She could've hugged him but decided against it and instead just did her best to smile as he said, "Good work, Bishop."

One of the men on the squad spoke up. "No kidding, good job. This is RDX. They demolish malls with this shit."

So definitely not a prank, Heather thought, catching sight once again of the label on the pretty pink box.

CHAPTER THIRTY

THE DETECTIVE

WHILE JASON RETURNED TO THE SECRET WORLD behind the glossy wooden door to talk to his superiors about Clarence's elevated threat level, Heather was tasked with solving the formidable mystery at hand: How on earth had Clarence gotten the scalpel and bomb past security?

Fortunately, the former had an easy answer, though it ended her brief love affair with steel as a material. As it turned out, steel had a very low magnetic field; that way, as long as the object was small enough to pocket, you could take it through the metal detector without being flagged.

However, it seemed odd to Heather that it wouldn't have been noticed during the pat-downs that were administered more often than not, especially to newcomers. Heather herself had received one today, and it was certainly thorough. Still, it was hypothetically feasible, and if a scalpel was the only foreign object at hand, she'd settle on that theory and tell security to turn the frisking up a hundred percent.

However, the scalpel was not the only inexplicable intruder today, and there was absolutely no way anyone was getting a bomb past the metal detector, the X-ray machine, or the far-reaching hands of the security guards. So how had they done it?

She thought back to the riddle Clarence had written and remembered the mention of a wonky wheel in the gray hallway and constantly cleaning hands. A janitor's trolley. That's how it had been transported. The janitors must've had another entrance that they used.

Using the glass elevator at the end of the hall, she watched the thousands of panicked people outside, grouped into writhing swarms, and tried to estimate how many lives had just been saved. She thought it would feel better than it did, but instead, she felt a pang of churning guilt, and an all-consuming "what if" suffocated any happiness she could hope to conjure. What if the bomb had gone off and upwards of ten thousand people had died because of her and Jason?

You bury that out back in the dirt, she thought in Gabriel's voice. She would, eventually, but she would hold it in her skull and in her fist for a little while longer.

On the ground floor, she headed to security—the only people who had returned to their post—to determine the answers to all her numerous questions. At the booth, she began to fire off queries to a tall black man with a shiny bald head, deep forehead wrinkles, and a perfectly groomed goatee. He was kind and patient and agreed that she could be right about the scalpel and that she was undoubtedly right about the impossibility of getting the bomb through security.

"All right, that leads me to my next question. How do the janitorial staff get in and out with their trolleys? Do they push them through the metal detector, or…?"

"They don't go 'in or out,'" he said, confused, using his fingers to quote her. "They only stay in. As in, all the trolleys and products are kept in the basement, and the staff gets in and out the same as everyone else."

"Right," Heather said, tapping her notepad with her pen and her foot against the same floor in a synchronized beat.

"Actually," the guard replied, scratching his facial hair, "they do have to come to clean the entrance here on the other side of the security barrier. They take the trolley through that gate there so the metal doesn't set off the alarm. It never goes through the front doors, and security watches the entire time."

Heather lit up. This was something, she was sure of it. "And did anyone take it through the gate yesterday or this morning?"

"Yeah. The lobby gets cleaned at night after everyone goes home. So last night, the guy came up in the elevator, I let him through, and he cleaned."

"Okay. Did anything unusual happen during the cleaning?"

"No, but the elevators shut down for some reason, and he—an older guy named Eryk Sadowski—didn't want to take the trolley down the stairs. So I told him to leave it in the lobby and just grab it first thing in the morning. Then we left at the same time and let the night shift guys take over."

"And did he collect it in the morning?" Heather asked.

The guard continued to rub at his face. "Yeah, I think so because the trolley wasn't here when I arrived. I was late today," he elaborated. "Flat tire, even though I had new ones put on last week. Can you believe it?"

Heather could. "So who had your shift this morning?"

"Same guy that took over for me last night. New kid. Training him up."

"Is he trustworthy?"

The guard cocked a brow. "Ma'am, this is the CIA. What do you think?"

"Of course. So what time is his shift?"

"Ten till ten. Has been for a couple of days now."

"So you left at, what, 9:00 p.m., with Eryk, and arrived at 11:00 a.m.?"

"Yeah, that's about right."

"Okay, and how long has this 'new kid' been working for the CIA?"

"About six weeks."

"So he's probably not been around long enough to recognize all the staff by their faces alone?"

The security guard let out a rumbling laugh. "Ma'am, I've worked here for thirty years, and even I don't know all the staff off by heart. Have you seen how many goddamn people there are here?"

Heather looked over her shoulder at the mob in the parking lot and spotted a nervous-looking man dressed in tweed with a clipboard and a sodden handkerchief. She turned back and thanked the guard profusely, hoping that her next interviewee wouldn't blow any holes in her fragile theory.

"Lots of people," Heather called out as she stepped through the automatic doors, interrupting the man's muttering and startling him in the process.

"You're telling me," he squeaked.

"Guessing you're in charge of the count?"

"I am," he said, puffing out his chest but quickly deflating. "One of many," he added.

"Anyone unaccounted for?" she asked.

He turned, his watery gray eyes narrowed behind wire-rimmed aviator glasses, and he adjusted his too-tight tie that hung crooked beneath his brown jacket and above his cooked-salmon-colored shirt. She'd added suspicion to his clearly monumental stress levels, and it oozed out of his forehead, dampening his red fluff of receding hair and dripping into his thick mustache. His handkerchief was struggling to keep up with the deluge, but Heather was glad that he didn't stop trying.

Then it stopped, and he smiled, revealing tiny little teeth. "Oh, you're Officer Fleming's friend. Nice job on saving all of our lives."

"Yeah, that was a close one."

"Well, disaster averted. And to answer your question, in my section, there are nine unaccounted for, but eight of them are sick or on vacation. There's only inexplicable disappearance, but I'm sure if I cross-check with the gate guards—"

"Is our missing person Eryk Sadowski by any chance?"

The man cocked his head. "No. Lionel Green. He worked late last night and left at around 11:20 p.m. but didn't show up today, and no one can get ahold of him. How did you know about Eryk?"

"So he is on the list?"

"Yes and no. He was here this morning but clocked out early and texted his supervisor complaining of a migraine."

"I'm going to need to see the CCTV footage," Heather informed him. "Do you know anyone who can help me with that?"

"I can," the man exclaimed overenthusiastically. "Please, come with me..."

"Detective Heather Bishop," she said, holding out a hand to shake.

He thoroughly wiped his palm on his brown pleated trousers before accepting the gesture, and even then, it was still moist. Heather didn't let on. After all, she couldn't blame him; it was hot despite the gray, and the threat of a bomb would make anyone sweat.

"Everyone calls me Collins," he said.

Heather wasn't sure if it was his first or last name and never got a chance to ask before Collins moved in with his own questions.

"Detective, eh? What kind?"

"Homicide."

Collins whistled. "That must be fascinating."

"What is it you do?"

"I am an archivist. Looking after the old. Turning it into digital. So I spend a lot of time underground waiting for someone to visit," Collins joked. "But all us basement dwellers stick together, so I know the CCTV guys pretty well. They're still outside, but I know my way around their room well enough to find what you're looking for."

They made their way back through security—where Heather received yet another pat-down, though this one was apologetic—and approached an elevator. Collins stepped inside without issue, but Heather struggled to force herself through the invisible barrier and return to the dark floor below. If Collins noticed the struggle, he didn't mention it—a returned favor for her ignoring his nervous sweats—and waited patiently for her to push through.

In the basement, Collins chattily guided her along the halls, generating an adequate amount of distracting white noise as they passed through the janitorial sector. She was learning a lot about how being an archivist worked as they power-walked to their destination, and though she was sure none of it would stick, she prompted him when needed, knowing he needed the conversation as much as she did.

Eventually, they reached a short hallway with a black-windowed door at the end, and Collins fumbled with his ring of keys before letting them inside.

"Here we are," he said, gesturing around. "The digital security hub."

The room was exactly as she pictured it: desks, screens, spinny chairs, and lunch still on the tables. There was a pack of cards too. She supposed monitoring the CCTV at the CIA was mostly a pretty dull occupation because who would be stupid enough to try to break in, much less plant a bomb?

"So what are we looking for?" Collins asked giddily, sitting down on one chair and patting the one beside him.

Heather lowered herself, finding her body stiff from residual anxiety. "The lobby. Late last night and early this morning."

"All right. Easy-peasy."

Collins tapped around through a few numbers and dates until he brought up the entryway at 10:00 p.m. the night before. There was the security guard and the cleaner in question, just as she'd been told.

"Is that Eryk?" she asked.

"Yep. That's him. As I said, I know everyone on this floor," Collins chirped proudly, happy to be of assistance.

He fast-forwarded through Eryk cleaning and mopping the marble floor, then stopped when the old man abandoned the cart to leave.

"What's that about?"

"Security said the elevators weren't working."

Collins furrowed his brow. "Just the elevators?"

"I think so."

"Strange," he murmured.

"Why?"

"Well, if there wasn't a mass blackout, someone would have to have disabled the elevators manually."

"Huh. Who would have access to that?"

"Maintenance guys. Technicians. "

"Like Lionel?"

"Yeah, like Lionel," Collins said hesitantly, beginning to pick up on what Heather was putting down. He continued to fast-forward, just in case.

"Wait, who's that?" Heather asked, pointing to a man being let through the security about half an hour after Eryk left. He was wearing a black face mask and a beanie.

Collins squinted at the screen. "I'm not sure. I can't get a good look at him. Let me pull up the gate's security logs. See who left last." He did so and scrolled through the list until he saw Lionel, who, as he said earlier, left at 11:20 p.m.

"Did that look like Lionel?" she asked.

"No, Lionel is a short guy. Pudgy."

"Hypothetically," Heather said, "if somebody stole somebody else's key card and swiped it at the gate, it would show up as the key card's owner, correct?"

"Yes," Collins said gravely.

"Show me the footage from this morning. Around nine."

Collins nodded and clicked on a new file just as the door creaked open behind them. Heather froze and turned slowly in her chair to see Jason towering in the doorway.

"Boo," he said.

"Hi," Heather replied, beckoning him inside.

"What have I told you about wandering off?" Jason asked, using his best dad's voice.

Heather rolled her eyes. "Put me on a leash if you're so worried. But for now, you'll be glad I did." She looked back at Collins. "Press Play."

Collins did as he was told, and they watched as a man entered wearing a janitor's uniform, a hooded coat, and a backpack. He collected the trolley and rolled it right into a blind spot behind a marble pillar. After a few seconds, he reemerged. He put the bag on the convey belt, pushed the trolley through the gate, and stepped through the metal detector. A young security guard patted him down and waved him through. All clear.

"That didn't look like Eryk either," Heather said, unable to see the man's face but knowing from his hands and posture that whoever it was was not an elderly man. In fact, he looked strikingly similar in the figure to the man who left, pretending to be Lionel, the night before.

"No, it did not," Collins confirmed.

"So what's the theory, Bishop?" Jason asked.

Heather tented her fingers and rocked back and forth. "A man pretending to be a technician named Lionel Green snuck past security early yesterday. Then near 10:00 p.m., he deactivated the elevators and waited for a janitor called Eryk Sadowski to abandon his cart—because of the elevators—and leave. Then he turned the elevators back on and left himself. Nobody noticed he wasn't really Lionel because the security guard on shift was new. So as long as he had the right pass and lanyard, he could slip right past. Then the same man, pretending to be Eryk arrived in the morning, put the bomb and the letter in the trolley, pushed it through the nonsecure gate—because it had never left the property—planted both, and checked out early, texting his manager using Eryk's phone that he was sick, and all before the head of security arrived at work, who coincidentally was late because somebody let the air out of his tires."

"You see any faces?"

"Nope. Whoever it was, he was careful not to face the camera, but even if it was who I think it was, I'm pretty confident he'd be wearing a mask anyway."

Jason paced back and forth. "Okay, I buy it. I mean, it's complicated. Genius even. But it's definitely possible. My question now is, where are Eryk and Lionel?"

Heather paled. "I don't think anyone is going to like the answer to that. Collins, welfare check for Eryk and Lionel?"

"On it," Collins said, shakily rising from his seat and scurrying out of the room.

Jason took the chair, and both he and Heather looked at the man in the baseball cap, frozen and grainy, for a very long time. Then Heather copied what she'd seen Collins do and skipped forward a couple of frames. The man in the baseball cap tilted his face just enough that the profile was showing, and there it was, the edge of a mask and a nose and brow that looked an awful lot like Jason's.

CHAPTER THIRTY-ONE

THE SURGEON

2023

W ITH A SUFFOCATING SACK STILL PULLED OVER HIS head and tied tightly at his neck, Christopher was pushed down hard onto what felt like a reasonably expensive couch. His hands restrained, he touched the soft fabric—the most pleasant thing he'd felt in a small eternity—and let the texture distract him from his condensation-filled microprison. He breathed in and out through his mouth, though it only worsened the problem he was avoiding—the putridity of morning breath and stale champagne. Though the party had been, to his estimation, only a few days ago, he had not been permitted any luxuries—showering or brushing his teeth included—turning his own body into his torturer.

He'd been allowed to use a toilet, of course, in between being handed off from person to person and vehicle to vehicle, but only under duress, the flashlights shining through the material covering his face. Still, he was thankful, at least, for the small mercy of clean underwear.

This state of moderate cleanliness was nearly soiled when the sack—to which he'd become acclimatized sometime back—was wrenched roughly from his head and revealed Clarence Dixon Jr. standing over him.

He took a cold, spluttering gulp of air and felt a sense of bliss he never thought he'd feel again, accompanied by a piss-your-pants-worthy injection of fear into his adrenal system. But he had to admit, Clarence's new face looked great, perfect even, and on any other occasion, Christopher would have been glad to see his handiwork.

"Well, hey there, Doc!" Clarence exclaimed. "How you feelin'? A little rough, I expect."

"I've been better," Christopher coughed, his voice almost gone from lack of use.

Clarence pouted. "Yeah, well, as it turns out, your hospitality far exceeds my own. But if you look around, you'll see that I've made an attempt."

Christopher's eyes were blurry without his glasses, but even still, he recognized the room. It was his Virginia living room, except smaller. Details were missing, the plants had a plastic sheen to them, the wall art was missing texture, and yet it was unmistakable in intent. A half-hearted copy of his favorite place in the world.

"Where am I?" he asked.

"Well, you're home, Doc," Clarence said, grinning with that perfect mouth. "I figured it might make you feel more at ease while you scratched my back a second time."

"What are you doing, Clarence?" Christopher lamented. "People are dead, I—"

"Shhhh," Clarence hissed, putting a finger to Christopher's lips. "You know me. I am not a secretive man. I'll tell you everything if you just sit there and let me. Can you do that, Doc?"

Christopher nodded.

Clarence continued to grin and pulled up an ottoman to perch upon. "Well then, let me start by apologizing. Now, I never meant for anyone to get hurt. Honestly, I hadn't realized how popular you were. And I certainly didn't realize you had so many people willing to take a bullet for you. But hey," he said, clapping a hand to his chest. "That is my bad for hiring god-damn amateurs. But more than that, it's their bad for being so trigger-happy. So you'll be happy to know that their corpses are rotting away in some cave in Oregon."

Christopher opened his mouth to speak but closed it again, looking down at his knees.

"Huh. I'm taking it you're not an eye-for-an-eye man?"

"And I suppose you are?" Christopher inquired, feeling much like Dr. Frankenstein as he looked back up at his creation.

"I suppose I just don't care much about the whole world going blind. I mean, have you seen the world? Well, I know for a fact you watch the news, because how else would you have tattled on me?" Christopher asked, wagging his finger.

"Clarence, I... you killed a woman," Christopher whispered.

"I did, and I gotta tell you, Doc. That was a real wake-up call about my efforts in bomb-making. One death and one para-plegic? I mean, come on! For what they did? And what they continue to do?"

"They're human beings, Clarence. How can you not see that?"

Clarence gave a smug chuckle. "I'm finding it hard to see that flock of reapers as people. I mean, they sure as shit don't care about killing. At least I think about the people I hurt—their families, their lives, their afterlives, or lack thereof—but these monsters just go home to their children after pressing buttons on bombs."

Christopher went to bury his face in his hands and realized he was still restrained. He held his wrists out to Clarence, who leaped to his feet, retrieved a key, and freed the doctor from his shackles.

"Here you go, Doc. I mean, no point in restraining a man who doesn't want to get even."

"Thank you," Christopher murmured, trying to remain on the good side of someone who had clearly lost any semblance of the mind he'd once had.

"You are very welcome."

"So am I here because you want to kill me too? I mean, I must've ruined all of your plans."

"Doc, if I wanted you dead, I would've snuck into your house in the night and put a bullet in you myself. No, you are far too important to kill. Instead, you're going to make it up to me."

Christopher thought and sighed, finally burying his face in his hands successfully. "You want a new face."

"Smart man," Clarence enthused. "New face and bye-bye fingerprints. Graft over them, whatever. I want my biometrics gone."

"And if I do this, you'll let me go?" Christopher asked.

Clarence shrugged. "Sure. Why wouldn't I? So long as you don't go blabbing about face number 3, you're a free man. Though fool me once, shame on me, fool me twice... I won't be so forgiving. Be sure of that."

"So what am I supposed to say to the authorities?"

"Tell them what you like. Tell them I took you, beat you, and changed my mind about killing you or whatever fits. Heck, say you outwitted me or charmed me to death. Just don't mention the surgery. I'll clean this place up well. There will be no sign it ever took place."

"Okay," Christopher said without hesitation.

"Okay?" Clarence asked, jumping to his feet with glee. "Now that is music to my ears."

"But only if you promise me that my family is safe. I want evidence. Better yet, search their names right now, in front of me. If I see an obituary, then the deal is off, and you can kill me instead."

"Sure thing," Clarence agreed, retrieving a phone from his pocket and dropping down beside Christopher on the couch.

Christopher watched as his captor searched for Kathleen, Jason, Natalie, and the girls in turn. He went to their Facebook pages and scrolled through the news section. They were mentioned in the coverage of the shooting, but it was clear that they were still alive.

Christopher cleared his throat, stifling a relieved sob. "Okay. The deal is on, but I want to ask you a few questions first."

"Shoot," Clarence replied, standing again and making his way to the whiskey decanter next to the faux fine china.

Christopher was admittedly impressed with the detailing on this cheap biopic TV series set of his life, but more than that, he was unnerved. Had Clarence been inside his home? Did he have cameras there? If so, were they recent, or had they been there ever since this all started years ago? Had he watched Kathleen in the bath or seen them make love? His stomach churned, and he decided not to ask any of those questions.

Instead, he asked, "Why, Glenville? Why not take me from Virginia?"

"One, small-town cops are a lot more useless than big-city ones. I figured it would be easier to give them the runaround and throw them off the trail. Two, in Virginia, especially with the FBI and CIA so close by, I figured whomever I hired— and they would've had to have been the best—would've been caught within the hour."

"Okay. And where are we now?"

"A warehouse. Not abandoned, mind you. Cops are all over desolated buildings. No, this is a new business but highly unattended, storage for those cheap tiny houses for liberal vegan hipsters. Probably going down the shitter."

"What state?"

"Now, you know I can't tell you that," Clarence said wryly.

"What state?" Christopher pushed.

Clarence relented. "Well, I guess it doesn't really matter. Not like you can call for help. We're in Virginia, ironically. I know it's risky, but I've got a deal at the marina here. Got me a boat. And once my new face is done, I'm gone. Never to be seen again."

"Well, I like the sound of that," Christopher said.

"As do I, Doc, as do I."

"So when are we doing the surgery?"

"In a couple of days. I want to do it the day before I set sail. Avoid the risk of getting this new face caught on camera. Plus, I gotta round up an anesthesiologist to make sure this is done right, which is a whole other can of worms. So sit tight, and don't be afraid to make yourself at home. You can't get out, but my friends are your friends too. If you want a cheeseburger or a beer, just ask. There's a phone in the kitchen that leads straight to them and nobody else. Just in case you thought about calling 911."

"I won't."

"Good man," Clarence said, coming toward Christopher with his hand outstretched. They shook, and Clarence clapped him on the shoulder with a powerful slap. "Looking forward to working with you again, Doc. I'll be seeing you real soon."

Clarence moved to leave, and Christopher called after him, "What about your new face? What do you want it to look like?"

Clarence paused. "I'll leave that up to you. Just make it unrecognizable, and don't worry about beauty. These past few years have taught me a thing or two about vanity."

He left through the front door, a gloomy warehouse, and a crowd of armed soldiers on the other side and left Christopher alone to the pale imitation of his home. Unbound, he got to his feet, stretched, and poured himself a whiskey, not really caring if it was poisoned or bottom-shelf.

As it turned out, it was an expensive bourbon, as expected from a Texan oil magnate, and Christopher downed the rest and poured himself another. He had nothing better to do than get drunk until the surgery rolled around, and hopefully, it would help to pass the time.

He hadn't been lying about performing what Clarence wanted. It was immoral, sure, but he would do whatever it took to get Clarence far away from him and his family. He'd prefer him to be dead or behind bars, but a different country seemed just as good. Out of sight, out of mind. Somebody else's problem.

Then an idea hit him. A "two birds, one stone" type of idea. What if he made a mistake during surgery? It was possible, especially considering all the work Clarence had already had done. So much under his perfect face was in the wrong spot, shifted around with lifts and implants. It would be easy to cut the wrong part, nick a misplaced artery, or burst an implant. It would be just as easy to conspire with whoever the poor anesthesiologist would be. That was what caused most surgical deaths after all. Or perhaps get Clarence drunk, or slip drugs in his drink and cause a nasty reaction.

The problem therein lay with what would happen to him if Clarence wasn't around anymore. Would his men let him go, or were they crueler captors than their boss? He would be ridding the world of a dangerous scourge, but could he happily risk his life to do so?

A plan so dangerous would require some thinking and a lot more whiskey.

CHAPTER THIRTY-TWO

THE DETECTIVE

HEATHER SAT WITH HER HANDS WRAPPED AROUND A cold cup of coffee, occasionally blowing on the surface as if it was still steaming. The others were seated in similar states around the central hub of the bunker. Takahiro was mindlessly tapping on the keyboard of a dead laptop, Bonnie was picking at the remnants of the pasta she'd made for lunch an hour ago, and Jason was sitting with his back to them, his eyes glued to a bland landscape painting on the wall.

He'd gotten off the phone with someone from the CIA about forty minutes ago, his expression beyond grave when he hung the receiver on the hook. It wasn't surprising to any of them what Lionel's and Eryk's fates had been. Heather, in particular, had been convinced of their demise ever since Collins had mentioned the sick-day text from Eryk. Still, the confirmation was devastating, especially for those who knew them.

Lionel Green had been found stuffed into the trash chute of his apartment building with his throat slit. They might've not discovered him at all, far in and stuck as he was, if it weren't for the blood pooling in the dumpster out back. It took the fire brigade three hours to get him out, traumatizing absolutely everyone on the block in the process, including his elderly mother with whom he lived. That imagery was going to stick with all of them for a long time. As was what happened to Eryk.

Eryk Sadowski was found in his gardening shed, crumbled to the floor, a tulip bulb in one hand and a trowel in the other. He'd been shot in the back of the head from the open doorway, his interior matter splattered across the potting bench before him. His wife had heard the shot from the kitchen and moved to the window to see a man dressed in off-white tactical gear run off into the trees. When the coast was clear, she moved toward her husband, but he was already gone. A forty-year marriage, over in a flash.

It revolted Heather. Gnawed at her. Here was a person so poisoned by his grief and subsequent radicalization that he'd do anything to get revenge. Four innocents had died in that strike; in turn, he'd killed at least fifteen. To her, the math wasn't adding up. His anger over his father's death was, and always would be, justified, but couldn't he see that he'd become what he hated: somebody willing to kill innocents for the greater good? His bottom line was the same as the government's, just in reverse. Instead of being right, he was worse than they were: a hypocritical, cowardly monster slitting throats and shooting old men in the back of the head and Public Enemy Number 1. But she imagined, he probably liked the sound of that last part.

The thought of it was making Heather's blood pressure rise. She didn't have words for her frustration, her heartache, and what an awful week it had been. Of course, it would've been much worse if everyone at the CIA headquarters had been blown to smithereens, but it still didn't feel like a win. How could it be with two elderly women having their lives ruined right toward the very end?

Bonnie rose from her seat, clearly having had enough of pretending to eat her food. "Would anyone like a cup of tea?" she asked. "There's green, black, and chamomile."

It had nothing on Foster Ellsworth's collection, but Heather managed to request a chamomile and pry her hands from her mug to hand it to Bonnie. It might help. Probably not, but it might. She knew what would really help was the liquor cabinet, but she wasn't returning to her old ways, not just yet.

Takahiro followed Bonnie as she moved toward the kitchen—a loyal, heart-eyed puppy—and turned to Jason, Jessica, and Heather with a weak smile.

"I'll make some food," he offered. "Chicken soup. Something comforting. Early dinner for early turn-ins."

They muttered their thanks, and Jessica pulled up a chair next to Heather but didn't speak. They'd all run out of words. She reached for the pack of cards, dealt them ten each, and placed the rest face-down aside from the card on top. Heather looked at her questioningly.

"Rummy? I thought you didn't know how to play."

"I lied," Jessica said. "Also, I like to drink two beers every Sunday that the football is on, and my favorite movies are *The Breakfast Club*, *When Harry Met Sally*, and *Pretty Woman*."

"Why are you telling me this?"

"Because we both nearly died today, and the only reason we didn't is because you're good at what you do. So maybe I don't want to scare you off anymore."

"Thanks," Heather replied, picking up her hand. "Though I still don't think the CIA is for me."

"Anything I can do to change your mind?"

"Magically turn into a small-town operation?"

Jessica shook her head. "You're wasting your skills over there."

Heather shrugged. "I don't know. I think I've had my hands pretty full."

Jessica tilted her head back and forth and laughed weakly. "Yeah, I guess you're right. Just being selfish, I guess. It's a major sausage party in my sector."

THE HOUSE ON THE LAKE

The phone on the wall interrupted their game and conversation, and they turned to look as Jason approached the insistent buzzing. It was strange. Jason had answered several calls today, and yet this one seemed different, more urgent in its shaking and sound. Jessica must've felt the twisting in her gut too—or however her gut instinct manifested—because as Jason answered, her lips shaped around the word, "Don't." Heather, on the other hand, wanted him to answer, needed him to answer, but she knew that there was something terrible on the other end.

"Hello?" Jason asked, his mouth already curled downward at the corners.

Then the creases between his brows appeared, as did the singular line on his forehead. Then he began to argue with the caller, disrupted stops and starts peppering the audible side of the conversation. Eventually, he gave up, his hand wrapped around the phone so tight Heather thought the plastic might splinter. He turned to her, held it out—the coils in the wire straightening—and said, "It's for you."

Heather didn't bother to ask questions and scurried to the phone in her socks, grabbing it from Jason's hand as he backed away. He faced Jessica, tapped his ear, mouthed for Takahiro, and remained by Heather's side as she spoke.

"Hello?" she asked as he had done.

"Is this Detective Heather Bishop?" asked a female voice in a sultry purr.

"It is. Who is this?"

"My name isn't important."

"When you call a secure CIA bunker, I'm pretty sure it is. So who are you, and how did you get this number?"

"You're wasting time, Detective," the woman responded. "As I said, my name isn't important, but his is."

A scuffle on the other end ended with the receiver knocking hard against what sounded like teeth.

"Say it," the woman's now distant voice snarled.

"Gabriel," said the muffled voice.

It was him. Heather could tell it wasn't a trick. Not AI. Not a recording. Not an impersonator. Him. She looked to the others—who were already listening in with headphones—with a panicked expression, and they looked back in horror.

"Gabriel?" she asked, her question met with a pained wheezing. She closed her eyes and exhaled slowly through her mouth. She pictured him covered in bruises, with one of his eyes swollen shut from the knuckles of a fist and his teeth chipped from the butt of a gun. "Talk to me, please. Are you okay?"

"I'm alive," he gurgled. "But I won't be for long unless you give Jason to her."

Heather inhaled shakily, looked at Jason—who lowered his chin somberly—and said, "Okay. Tell her I'll bring Jason as long as she doesn't hurt you any further. We'll be there in five hours. Tell her not to answer the door for anyone but me. I want to keep this quiet."

Gabriel reiterated the information as best he could and eventually said, "It's a deal."

"Where are you?" she asked, gesturing for Bonnie to bring her shoes over.

"Your house. I was feeding the dogs and watering the plants as usual when she broke in. I let the dogs run away through the back door, sorry."

"Don't be. You did the right thing. Hold tight, and I'll see you soon. I promise."

"Okay."

"I promise," she reiterated.

Crackling, crumpled sounds followed, and the woman spoke again. "I'm glad we could come to an agreement so easily. I'll be seeing you soon, Heather. Come with Jason and no one else. If I see cops or CIA, I'll slit your precious pal's throat. I'm sure you've seen enough of my handiwork to know I'm not lying."

"You're not."

"See you soon, Detective," the woman cooed.

The line went dead, and Heather's organs somersaulted in her cavities as she failed to hang the phone up with a badly shaking hand. Jason helped her to her destination, and Heather looked up at him, ready to apologize.

"You did the right thing," Jason said. "We'll fly directly to Glenville, just us and a pilot. They'll be watching the airstrip,

I'm sure. At the same time, Jessica and the SAC will fly into Seattle and drive down discreetly." He paused. "Call your boss. See if you can get the police department to check for anyone suspicious in the streets. Send out a few patrol cars, see if we can make them crawl back into hiding."

"Sure," Heather murmured, forgetting how to blink or dial a number from the bunker's secure line.

"Jessica, SAC," Jason commanded. "Bonnie, you tick the boxes and get this approved. And Takahiro, you get into Glenville's cameras, specifically by Heather's house. See if you can see something the police can't."

Then he leaned forward, typed in the private network six-digit code, and let Heather type in the rest.

"Hello, Glenville Police Department," Tina answered on the first ring.

"Tina, it's Heather—"

"Heather?" Tina questioned, more astounded than angry. "Heather?" she repeated, her voice thick like she wanted to cry. "Where the hell have you been? I've been trying your phone for days. Gabriel said you had to rush off to some funeral, but I don't believe a word out of that boy's mouth. Is something wrong?"

"Tina, I'm sorry. I can't tell you everything right now, but I really, really need you to listen to me," Heather begged.

"Okay," Tina said, her voice hushed. A door closed, likely to her office, and she encouraged Heather to continue.

"The terrorist who killed those ten people—"

"Terrorist? What are you talking about?"

"It … hasn't been on the news?" Heather asked and glanced at Jason, who shook his head. Of course it wouldn't be.

"Has what been on the news?"

"Don't worry about it," Heather said hastily.

"Don't worry about it?" Tina asked incredulously.

"It's confidential information. I'll be able to tell you about some of it one day, maybe, but for now, I need you to do me a favor. I'm coming into town with Jason Fleming, and we think some people might be on the lookout for us. It would be better if they weren't able to easily do that."

"You want patrols?" Tina asked, thankfully understanding the gravity of the situation.

"Yes. But keep it subtle. I don't want to tip them off."

"Heather, I... I'm sorry," Tina replied, the words sounding foreign. Heather knew they didn't have time for this, but she let her boss continue. "I had no idea that... Jesus... I was just worried that I was losing my best detective—"

"Your only detective."

"Well, exactly. I wanted you here, with us. With all that's been happening in this town, we don't know how to cope without you. Selfish, I know. I mean, I had no idea this was some sort of national emergency, and I don't understand how you've gotten yourself tangled up in this, but still, I'm sorry. There, I said it. And if you have to leave us, I understand."

"Apology accepted," Heather rushed as Jason tapped his watch. "We'll be in Glenville in five hours, so start staggering the patrol out over the next few."

"All right. Please, stay safe."

"I'll try," Heather promised and hung up the phone.

CHAPTER THIRTY-THREE

THE DETECTIVE

O N HEATHER'S STREET, SHE STOPPED JASON WITH A hand on his chest just before they were illuminated by the streetlight hidden by a large pine tree. She looked around to check that the coast was clear. It was, and she tilted her head to the right to the other side of the street where the houses of varying ages sat in a disjointed row.

"Let's go up that alley," she whispered, gesturing to the gap between the two houses to the right of her own. "The one between mine has a bunch of crap in the way. Then we'll go through that middle house's backyard and into mine. There's a secret entrance into the laundry room through the crawl space under the house. Don't ask me why, I didn't put it there, but only Gabriel and I know about it."

"Sneak attack? It's risky."

"Yeah, but it's our best shot. I'm not letting anyone die tonight, but I'm also not letting you get dragged away to your execution. This is my town, my house, my family. We're doing it my way."

"Yes, ma'am."

"Let's go."

Carefully they crossed the road, grateful for the cover the light rain provided their footsteps, and snuck up the side of one of her neighbors' houses. It belonged to an eccentric elderly woman who insisted Heather called her Baba and delighted in looking after Heather's dogs. Fortunately, she had no dogs of her own to trigger the alarm, and as she skulked through the overgrown garden, Heather was glad that she also had no fences or floodlights, making their journey seamless.

They paused by the back-left corner of the house with Heather's hand on the lichen-covered drainpipe and scoped out Heather's own adjacent backyard. There was no one outside watching the back entrance, but she made sure to not trigger the automatic light by keeping close to her neighbor's wall as they rounded the corner. They inched along, Jason copying Heather's every move as if mimicry was an art form, until Heather spotted the broken bit of lattice and dropped to her knees. Together they crawled through the dirt, pulled the lattice aside, and made their way through the insect-infested crawl space.

Heather pulled spiderwebs from her face and tried to keep calm as she brushed a large black spider from her slicked bun. Jason was an army-crawling pro, undeterred even by the recently shed snakeskin stuck to his elbow.

Finally, they came to a dirty incline and a small trapdoor on the roof, which Heather slid open as quietly as she could, though it was impossible to stop the wood from scraping in its socket. They paused, and no one seemed to notice, so they progressed through the black hole.

The laundry was dark, but the doorway was haloed in a golden glow. The hallway light was on, and from the two patches of black at the base, it was clear that someone was standing with their back to the door.

Heather looked to Jason, and he stood, nimble despite his size, and approached the door. Heather raised her gun but lowered it in awe as she witnessed him open it, grab the man with a chokehold, and silently yank him down onto the laundry floor. He was out like a light in five seconds.

He, Heather thought, *was definitely not who I heard on the phone.*

Whoever she'd spoken to had backup. Of course she did; no matter how armed or skilled, it would be downright idiotic to make such a vital trade without some heavies to hand.

Noticing the absent man and the ajar door, a set of heavy footprints ran down the hall toward them. Heather took aim at the base of the door, and as another man rounded into the laundry, she fired into his shin, sending him crumpling to the ground. Adrenaline kicked in, and she launched herself at him, kicking swiftly under the jaw and knocking him backward onto the kitchen linoleum. He faintly stirred but didn't move, and a shot flew down the hallway past Heather's nose.

She turned left toward the living room to see the Middle Eastern woman from the Dixon estate—and likely the woman from the rooftop and the hotel assassin too—pointing a gun at her, her chest heaving and her eyes wild. Behind her, Gabriel was gagged and bound to one of the dining table chairs. He was rocking and pleading behind the cloth in his mouth. He was in as bad shape as Heather had feared, and despite the gun trained on her face, she couldn't stop staring.

Jason tackled her and launched them both into the kitchen, stepping on the other man in the process.

"Get it together," he yelled, his gun out.

Heather bobbed her head and quickly scrambled toward the kitchen window. She knew it looked like she was running away, but Jason didn't question her as he stood, shoulder to the edge of the doorway.

She was thankful for the trust, lifted the wooden frame— which was fortunately loose from the cold and made no sound—and slipped through, narrowly avoiding kicking over dirty dishes in the process. Just as she landed on the other side, she heard Jason fire a shot down the hallway, hoping his aim was as sharp as she believed, considering Gabriel was smack-dab in the middle of the firing range.

She ran around the side and perched beneath the window by the front door. It was unlocked, and as Jason fired again, she saw her opportunity to slide it open and take fire herself. She didn't aim to kill; they needed intel, and this woman was their best bet at not losing Clarence altogether. So she fired a shot into the woman's right arm, not initially realizing that she was left-handed. Still, it stunned her enough that Jason ran forward and tackled her to the ground.

It seemed they had the upper hand until Heather saw how the woman's arm was crooked. She had a clean shot at the top of her skull into the parting of her sleek black bob. She didn't take it. She couldn't take it. Jason wouldn't want her to take it. Right?

The woman fired into Jason's gut, and he reeled back. He was wearing the world's most expensive bulletproof vest, but at close quarters, the pain would be immense, and he faltered, his arm limp, allowing the woman to punch him one, two, three times in the face. Blood on her knuckles, she raised the gun, but just like they needed her alive, she clearly needed Jason alive. As she fought with her killer instincts with Jason kneeling at her mercy, Heather slipped in through the window and snuck up on the woman as best she could.

It wasn't good enough, and at only a foot away, the woman turned and, in an impressive display of skill, kicked the gun out of Heather's hand and circled back around to smack her in the face with the heel of her thick-soled boot.

Heather slammed into the couch at a breakneck, whiplash speed, and barely held herself up as her mouth filled with blood. Her vision was bright and dark all at once, distorted as she tried to right herself. Then the woman ran at her and, using a surprising amount of strength for someone more petite than Heather, picked Heather up as if she was a mere child and tossed her over the couch. Heather landed on the unvacuumed floor, dog hair sticking to her face, and moaned.

With blood pouring from her fingertips, the woman rounded the couch, grabbed Heather's head in both hands, raised it up, and held it above the coffee table. She pried her mouth open, lined up her teeth with the edge, and Heather readied herself for the dentist bill that would come with a makeshift curb stomp.

She struggled and thrashed, making it as hard as she possibly could for the woman, and when the impact never came, and the woman released her, she fell forward, lightly smacking her head. The mixture of colors in her vision grew brighter, and hand to her forehead, she turned to see Gabriel, somehow free from his chair, with his belt looped around the woman's throat. He yanked her backward, and Heather—using what remained of her depth perception—kicked the gun from her hand and darted back from the strike zone.

The woman audibly choked, and Gabriel, short and strong as an ox, continued to drag her, the belt tightening all the time like a pit bull on a choke chain. He yanked her up into the chair before quickly moving the belt to her arms and narrow waist and fastening her against the chair. Ignoring the pain and her unsteady legs, Heather jumped up and grabbed Gabriel's handcuffs that had been placed on the side console and helped to further secure the woman.

After they added the zip ties that were buried in their attacker's alabaster pocket, all she could do was rock from side to side until she fell to the side and hit the carpet with a thud. She screamed obscenities, but they ignored her to look at Jason, who gave them a thumbs-up.

Heather sighed with relief and looked down at the screaming woman. She placed a boot on the side of her face and added pressure until she fell silent.

"Is there anyone else in the house?" Heather asked.

"No," the woman spat.

"Is Clarence Dixon in town?"

"Junior," she emphasized, the adoration apparent.

Having seen it before in Gustavo Molina and Francisco Medina, Heather saw her for what she was. Clarence's right-hand man. The killer puppet.

"Well, is he?" Heather prompted, pressing down harder.

The woman laughed coldly and didn't answer the question. Instead, she tilted her face upward, the left of her lips beneath Heather's boot. She was beautiful with her high cheekbones and a noble Roman nose, but her magnificence came with a warning, like a coral snake behind glass or a jaguar pacing the boundaries of its zoo exhibit. Give a little, and they'll take a lot. Your life included.

Heather pouted and pulled the woman's lips to the side with her sole, revealing a sharp canine.

"Well, if you don't answer me, maybe you'll be more willing to speak to the CIA. I'm sure they'll treat you real nice."

The woman didn't answer but surveyed Heather with disgust.

"You know, I bet they'll have to keep a long, long time. You might never see your precious Clarence again. Even if we don't catch him, I'm sure he'll move on to some secret location that you'll never find."

"He would never leave me behind," the woman hissed. She was panicked, revealing her soft spot to everyone in the room.

"He's going to leave without you, isn't he?" Heather coaxed. "Tell us where he is, and we'll take you to him. That way you can say your goodbyes before you both get carted off to different prisons."

"Or before we run away together."

"Either way. One of us wins. Seems a lot better than ending everything tonight, don't you think?"

Overtaken by what seemed to be love or obsession— whether solely for Clarence or what he believed in too—the woman spoke quietly, "He's at a warehouse in Virginia."

"We're not falling for that again," Jason said, massaging his chest as he stood.

"No, really," the woman insisted. "He's in the same town. The one you went to was a decoy. We figured you'd never think he'd stay so close by and give up on the area."

"Give us an address," Jason demanded.

"Take me there instead. Hold up your end of the deal."

Heather looked at Jason. "Call the team in. Let's take these three to Virginia. See if we can get answers out of the two in the kitchen and laundry and a location out of this one."

"Yes, ma'am," Jason said, glaring at the woman on the floor as he pulled out his phone.

Heather removed her boot from the woman's face, put an arm around Gabriel, and picked up the baseball bat beneath the console before leading him to the bathroom to fix what she could of his face.

CHAPTER THIRTY-FOUR

THE DETECTIVE

THE CHOICE OF VEHICLE WAS A STROKE OF GENIUS ON Jessica's part, opting for a modified people carrier—complete with a roll cage and bulletproof glass—whose clunky silver exterior would blend in at any little league game. It was almost identical to the car Heather's mother had driven when she was a child, and she sat in the middle back seat as she had back then, needing to look through the front window to avoid car sickness.

Behind them was the far-less-covert tactical vehicle, an all-black tank that took up more than its side of the narrow road, sporting what was essentially a tiny jail cell on the back. She supposed subtlety didn't matter so much on their way out. Though their brief tour through suburbia before getting onto the main road out of town would have certainly earned the wagging of local tongues.

Gabriel sat beside Heather, slumped against the door and using a melted ice pack as a pillow, and only remained conscious due to Heather's vigilance. Like herself, he was probably concussed, and sleep could come when they met the medic at the nearby airstrip. Jason, who was riding shotgun, seemed to have no trouble staying awake despite his injuries, his eyes scanning the dark for danger as if he had natural, built-in night vision.

Heather nudged Gabriel again and removed her own ice pack to carefully press her fingertips against her badly swollen jaw. It didn't feel like much, thanks to the painkillers in her bathroom cupboard left over from when her face had last had a run-in with something hard. It must've looked horrific, however, because Gabriel shook his head with disbelief despite his own set of terrible facial injuries. Not wanting to give her brain stimulus to overreact to, Heather opted not to look in the rearview mirror and enjoyed the numbness while it lasted.

"If you keep going like this, you're going to end up with no teeth," Gabriel said so quietly she could barely hear it.

"Speak for yourself," Heather replied, tapping her front tooth.

Gabriel ran his tongue over the chip and threw himself backward. "Goddammit."

"I'll pay for that," Jason said, pulling himself away from his surveillance to turn and look at the pair in the back seat. His already-serious expression fell. "It's my fault you lost it," he murmured, turning away again.

Gabriel waved him off. "It's all good, man. I've got insurance."

"Wait, even dental?" Heather asked.

Gabriel looked at her quizzically. "You've been a cop for what…?"

"Fifteen years."

"Fifteen years. And you didn't know that we get dental?"

"I don't go to the dentist. I've got perfect teeth."

Gabriel scoffed. "You're out of your mind. You have to go to the dentist."

"Fine. Once all this is over, we'll go together. Happy?"

"Not really," Gabriel grumbled, continuing to prod at his incisor.

Teeth on her mind, Heather tongued her own mouth and squirmed when she felt something wriggle. A molar with a crack in it, one half lifted from the gum. She cursed loudly and returned what remained of the ice pack to her face.

"Uh-oh," Gabriel said. "One down, thirty-one to go."

Heather flipped him off, but despite the pain, she smirked a little on her uninjured side. Despite the unpleasantness of their reunion, she was glad her surrogate baby brother was there to tease and commiserate with her.

She nudged him with her shoulder. "You did well today."

Gabriel shrugged, shying away from the compliment. "No biggie. I'm getting used to saving your ass."

Heather swooped her left fist around to punch him lightly in the arm, and he mouthed silent howls of pain as he clutched his bicep. Heather resisted laughing, knowing that it would hurt terribly.

"You really did do good today," Jason added. "Color me impressed. I think even Jessica might have to admit she was wrong about small-town cops."

"Let's not go that far," Jessica muttered, focused on the road ahead. "But in taking those three down, we now have a location for a high-threat level domestic terrorist, so as far small-town cops go, you have certainly earned your badges. To the point, I think you should be carrying something with a little more weight around in your pockets."

"CIA?" Gabriel questioned.

"FBI," Jessica replied quickly. "I'd rather not have you on my turf."

Heather heard the wink in her voice and finally laughed but immediately moaned in pain. Gabriel reached out, concerned, but before he could speak, a large van came into view in the headlights. Sitting in the center, it took up the entire road, making it impossible to pass.

Jessica slowly came to a halt. "Who's this asshole?"

Heather looked out the window, and when she saw the missing plates, she yelled, "Back up!"

Flanked by trees, there was nowhere to turn, so Jessica began to reverse, and luckily, the van behind also got the memo. They moved fast, Jessica putting even Heather's NASCAR-style driving to shame, but as the vehicle ahead revved, Heather knew they were doomed if they couldn't find a place to pivot.

Crash.

The minivan's rear made contact with the van behind them, and all four turned to see another vehicle turned sideways behind the SAC, forming a barrier on the narrow road. They were trapped.

Doors opened and slammed ahead, and they turned back to see two figures dressed in cream raise semiautomatic weapons and point them at the windshield. Heather's heart pounded in her loose tooth and swollen face, and before Jessica could yell, "Duck!" she was already unbuckled and squashed into the foot well.

A dozen bullets splintered the bulletproof windshield into a kaleidoscope of busted glass, and though none of them passed through, it wouldn't hold forever.

"Heather," Jessica said, "under the seat, there's a box. Gabriel, yours too. Grab them and pass them forward."

Heather and Gabriel rummaged and retrieved the large plastic cases. They were heavy, and Heather immediately knew what was inside them. AR-15s. Heather had never used them outside of the gun range but knew that they were every paramilitary operation's weapon of choice. They passed the boxes forward, and Jessica and Jason assembled and loaded the weapons while instructing Heather to press the center console buttons to roll down the driver and passenger windows.

"Be our eyes," Jason said to the two in the back seat as he crawled out of hiding.

Heather stayed flat in the center, eyes focused through the one section of unbroken glass at the center base. She watched the two men lower their weapons, say something to each other, and take a step forward.

"They can't see us through the glass," she reported. "Their guns are down. I think they're trying to figure out if we're hit."

Jason and Jessica looked at each other, moved to their respective windows, and hung out, keeping their heads low and within cover. With a series of cracks and bangs, they fired along the ground, making the attackers dance and retreat. One screamed out in pain as several bullets destroyed his foot, and his companion abandoned him, leaving him to scrape the road with what remained of his foot before eventually jumping back into the roaring vehicle.

"They're inside," Heather said. "No guns."

Jason and Jessica fired again, this time shattering the windshield of the opposition. Theirs wasn't bulletproof despite the tactical appearance, and a bullet impacted the driver's skull, sending his head flying back into the headrest. His eyes and mouth open, he was dead on impact, and another man dragged him out of the seat and took over. He chose to reverse instead of charge, and Jessica resumed her seat, punching out a section of glass in front of her with the barrel of the gun, sending it sliding down the hood.

She revved and passed the gun back to Heather. "You know how to use one of these?" she asked.

"Yeah," Heather said with more confidence than she felt. It had been a long time, but as she handled it, her muscle memory showed her the way.

"Good," Jessica growled. "I am not letting these assholes get away."

Pedal to the metal, Clarence's death squad failed to outpace Jessica in time, and she rammed them one, two, three times. The opposition, in return, put their vehicle in drive and pressed up against the minivan, as if adding more pressure would help anything. Like two angry bulls let loose in the rodeo ring, they pushed back and forth, locked and stubborn. Smoke rose up on both sides, and the smell of burning rubber was suffocating.

From what Heather could see of the driver, it was apparent that he was terrified. His young face was stretched to extremes by panic, his associates were screaming at him, and his knuckles were white to the point of splitting skin. Jessica, on the other hand, was full throttle, her growls pitch-matched to those of her van. It was almost as if, through sheer determination, she began to get the upper hand; and after one long, squealing push, the opposition lost their footing and skidded back at an angle.

The hood crumpled and their lights smashed, Clarence's soldiers began to reverse again, and just as their slight angle was about to tilt them into the trees, White Forest ended and became sprawling livestock fields. Fortunately, the cows were all safely asleep in their barns as the van careened off the side and over the barbed wire fence at breakneck speed.

Jessica stayed still as the others ground their gears in the mud, turned, and began driving alongside the road, tearing up the grass and leaving two perfect muddy lines behind them. She was giving them a head start. Then, as soon as the other vehicle had veered back up onto the road, it was go time.

They took off, zero to sixty in no time at all, and Jessica called out over the roar of the road, "Blow out their wheels!"

"Yes, ma'am," Heather muttered, almost stepping on Gabriel to line up her shot from the left window while Jason took the right.

It was clean and easy, despite the potholes and accompanying jostles, and paired with Jason's acumen, both of the rear wheels were blown out in seconds, along with the rear window. Their pursuers slowed significantly, sparks flying as metal ground along the tarmac, but continued to try to drag the slowly dying corpse of their van along the main road. They must've been going about seventy—too slow to outrun Jessica but too slow to stop—when Heather spotted it.

"Deer!" she screamed.

Jessica slammed on the brakes just in time as the vehicle in front swerved to avoid a doe standing idly in the middle of the road. It ran off in the other direction as the van lost control, hurtling off the side of the raised highway. They must have come off the steep three-foot precipice at the wrong angle because they flew before flipping. They rolled again and again, each sickening crunch worse than the last, and Heather couldn't peel her eyes away. When it finally came to a standstill, she expected it to explode, but instead, it just smoked and hissed while those inside remained utterly still.

"Do you think they're dead?" Gabriel asked.

"The SAC is about to find out," Jessica said, referring to the eight Special Activities Officers who had pulled up behind the minivan and were now running toward the destroyed vehicle with AR-15s by their sides.

Heather watched unblinking, her hands still on her own automatic assault weapon, as they pulled six bodies from the wreck. After checking pulses, one of the men held up two fingers at Jessica, who nodded.

Those that were alive were dragged to the tactical SAC conveyance and placed in the temporary jail cell with Clarence's right-hand woman, her two bodyguards, and whoever had been in the blockade and survived. From the look of the CIA officers, Heather bet it was likely a fifty-fifty situation.

Then Jason and Jessica hopped out to deal out orders. Heather heard snippets. Police. Barricade. Fire brigade. It was going to be a mess sorting all this out, and Heather rubbed her eyes, knowing they would be stuck there for a while, and the painkillers were rapidly wearing off.

To her immense surprise, Tina pulled up ten minutes later in her custom Sheriffmobile and tilted her head for Gabriel and Heather to get in. Slowly they dragged themselves from the badly damaged car and shuffled into the back seat. Tina looked at them and frowned at their faces but didn't look shocked or horrified.

"I think," she said, "you two have an extra week of paid vacation days I've forgotten to give you. Sorry about that."

Gabriel rolled his head to the side, his cheek pressed against the headrest, and looked at Heather. "I could do with a holiday. What do you reckon?"

"Yeah, but not with you."

"What? Why?" Gabriel pouted.

"Because I'm not going to goddamn Disneyland," Heather said with a smile before closing her eyes as Tina took off toward the airstrip.

CHAPTER THIRTY-FIVE

THE DETECTIVE

WHILE THE CIA EMPLOYEES AND THEIR DETAINEES flew off toward Langley, Virginia, Gabriel and Heather were sent off in a small luxury plane that would take them to the bunker—or at least as near the bunker as they were allowed to land.

Gabriel, seemingly having put the day's events to one side, was having the time of his life, but the cramped quarters reminded Heather a little of Roland Ellis's Beechcraft Bonanza. Fortunately, this pilot seemed a lot more reliable than the late mayor, and the roomy, first-class-style lounge seats and top-up on ibuprofen and paracetamol set her at ease. As long as

Clarence didn't have shooters in the air, they would be fine for the next five hours.

Once they were given the okay from the pilot through the intercom, Gabriel unbuckled and raided the mini-fridge. It was full of food and water, which Heather thought was a nice touch until she spotted the mini bottles of champagne and realized the refreshments had not been provided with her and Gabriel in mind. Yet as Gabriel rummaged for a wrap that took his fancy, Heather didn't stop him. They'd more than earned a snack, and the CIA could easily afford to replenish the provisions for the dignitaries and executives who would next use the plane.

"Throw me that tuna sandwich," she said.

Gabriel turned and wrinkled his nose. "Tuna? Really? In the one place where we can't open the windows?"

Heather shrugged with a wicked expression, and Gabriel sighed dramatically before throwing the packaged triangles at her. She tore it open, and he dramatically retched as she bit into it.

"You better eat that quickly," he warned.

"Or what?"

"Or I'll throw it out of the airlock."

Heather laughed, sending a wet crumb flying in his direction, which only furthered the dramatics. "You wish you were strong enough to open that damn door."

Gabriel flexed. "Don't try me."

"Anyway, don't worry. This'll be gone in ten seconds flat."

She wasn't lying, and as Gabriel sat on the floor munching on a chicken-and-avocado wrap, they began a sort of eating competition, and both finished within three minutes of opening the packaging. Heather finished ten seconds before Gabriel and laughed again, to his dismay.

"You're the world's fastest eater," he said, a little jealous and a little more awestruck.

"Three dogs," she explained. "Gotta be quick if I don't want them taking it."

"Wanna wash it down with a little of this?" Gabriel asked, plucking a mini champagne bottle and two plastic cups from the fridge. "I don't know if you feel like celebrating, but ... I do."

"Sure," she replied, glad she'd turned down the opiates.

He popped the cork and sat back in his seat, filling the cups up on the plastic tray. He passed her a glass, and in exchange, she threw a balled-up blanket at his chest. He winced when it hit him, and she whispered apologies, wondering what the damage was like under his shirt. At least there was no blood.

"Don't worry about it," he said, rubbing his sternum. "Thanks for the blanket. Is this cashmere?"

"I have no idea, but I know I want to be under it with champagne in hand."

"Me too," he replied, adjusting himself for maximum comfort. Legs up, tucked in, drink in hand, he twisted his body toward her. "So can you tell me what's going on yet?"

Heather nodded. "Yeah, Jason said so at the airstrip. You'll have to sign some paperwork at the bunker, but yeah."

"Bunker," he said in disbelief. "Lucky my parents are in Mexico for the week. They won't even notice I'm gone if I don't tell them."

Heather thought of her own parents and sipped her drink. He had no idea just how lucky that was. "Well, if this lead is what we think it is, you'll be back home in forty-eight hours."

"Fingers crossed. So what do I need to know?"

"Where to start?"

"You've told a story before, right?" he teased.

She had, so she started at the beginning, watching Gabriel's eyes widen as she filled him in on Clarence's facial reconstruction, the prisonlike Dixon estate, the dead bodies of the shooters in the Salem cave, the sniper at the Black Magic Pizzeria, the attempt on her life in the hotel, the near bombing of the CIA headquarters, the murdered employees, and the drone strike that started it all. It took an hour and the entire bottle to explain it all, but Gabriel stayed completely silent aside from the popping of a second.

"And that's pretty much it," she said dryly as if she hadn't just explained the craziest week of her life bar none. And Gabriel knew better than anyone that Heather had had some crazy weeks.

"Holy shit," was all he could say in the end, and Heather thought that about summed it up.

"I'm sorry—" she started, but he quickly interrupted her.

"No. Please. Don't be sorry. Here I was complaining about stupid movie night, and you nearly died. Several times."

"Movie night isn't stupid," she said softly.

"Yeah, it is. And that's fine because I enjoy it. But it's not important."

"I think lots of things are important. Just in different ways. All of this has me thinking about my... I don't know..."

"Mortality?" Gabriel finished.

"Yeah, I guess. And I think you were right about me working too much."

Gabriel shook his head. "No. You told me that you're happier. This is you when you're happy, and if you're happy, I'm happy."

"I don't know if I'm happy. It's hard to tell when you're so busy, which I guess is the point. I was just being defensive. You sounded so much like my ex-husband, and I was just determined to prove that I wasn't that person again, that I'm not doomed to repeat the past over and over again."

"I don't think you're doomed," he said, topping up their drinks. "But my therapist says that the past we outrun, we're doomed to repeat."

The sentiment hit her bruised body like a ton of bricks. "Jesus. Maybe I do need to see your therapist."

"Maybe. Maybe not. But as good as you are at running..."

"Maybe I could do with slowing down?"

Gabriel tilted his head back and forth. "Something like that. I know it's hard with all the... awful crap. But last year, when I was pretending that Dennis Burke never existed, he just grew more powerful in the back of my head. Like I was spending all my energy avoiding him and feeding the fear in the process."

Heather could tell he'd talked about this a lot in therapy, but she wasn't sure she was ready to let the Paper Doll Killer or her failed marriage catch up to her just yet. It had been too long, and it all had become too monstrous over time. He was right; she had fed the beast by denying it wasn't there. But at least it was caged and unable to roam free in her psyche.

"As you say," Gabriel continued, it's all about balance. Run. Stop. Deny. Accept. Relax. Work. Just make sure you're not tipping the scales too far either way."

"Well, on that note, let's start with a drink."

"We're already having one," he chuckled, waving his cup around.

Heather smirked. "No, when we get back. I want to check out Sludge and see your band. Take the night off."

"You're going to hate it," he warned. "It's dirty, loud, and crowded."

"Hey, I'm not some eighty-year-old woman. I can get down."

"You can *get down*? Jesus, how did we end up friends?"

"I don't know, but I'll tell you what, I'm glad we are. You have no idea how boring these people are." Then she threw a hand up. "Okay, that's unfair. They probably have their hobbies and friends, but they work more than I do, and to say I don't fit in would be an understatement."

Gabriel barked a laugh. "So you're not running off to the CIA or FBI?"

"Not anytime soon."

"Great. I can put my 'fear of change' chat with my therapist on hold then. But seriously, Heather—" he looked at her with puppy dog eyes "—don't let me hold you back. I'm going to be in Glenville until I'm an old man. If one day it doesn't fit, move on."

Heather arched an eyebrow. "Oh, you think I'm sticking around for you, huh? Better talk about that narcissism problem with your therapist next, Buster."

Gabriel snorted and sipped his drink. "All right, so tell me about these stuffed shirts. Do they wake up at 5 a.m., drink egg yolks, and go to bed at 8?"

"You have no idea how right you are," Heather chuckled, reclining her chair and twisting her body to her best friend, and laid the strange world of CIA out for him until they were both half asleep, empty cups in hand.

Eventually, after some gentle mutual ribbing, he said, "You know what, they sound pretty cool."

"I know. They are. And they really saved my ass."

"And you've saved theirs," he insisted. "They couldn't have done this without you."

"Yeah," she said quietly, retracting from the praise.

"You ready for tomorrow?"

Heather chewed her lip and slowly nodded. "Yeah, I'm ready."

"Great," Gabriel responded, turning away and closing his eyes. "Let's get this bastard."

Yeah, let's, Heather thought as sleep took her too.

CHAPTER THIRTY-SIX

THE DETECTIVE

THE WOMAN WITH THE BOBBED HAIRCUT SAT IN THE back seat looking far more disheveled than she had the night before. She wasn't bruised, per se, but without her makeup and dressed in beige scrubs and slip-on prison shoes, she'd lost much of her striking ferocity. Heather wondered what had happened to her during the night. She was sure it was a lot worse than a boot pressed to her cheek, whether verbal or otherwise. Still, whatever they'd done, it was like pulling blood from a stone, and she hadn't even given them a drop of moisture aside from her name—Parisa Shah. An Iranian woman. Heather put two and two together without even needing to look up the names of the other three deceased civilians from the 2016 drone strike.

So here Parisa was, gleeful and humming with excitement, getting her way and guiding them to her master. Initially, Parisa's immense joy at leading them to Clarence concerned Heather. Surely it must be another trap, she thought, but as the woman babbled, it became clear that this was a case of derangement or possibly a form of Stockholm syndrome. This woman, this devoted follower, clearly, for whatever reason, had no idea that terrorist organization leaders usually didn't look kindly upon rats. In fact, she feared for Parisa's life far more than she did her own.

Still, she was grateful for the clear directions, and soon six vans packed with SAC officers and a culmination of CIA agents, officers from every agency Heather could spell and several she couldn't, and the local police followed Jason, Heather, Jessica, Gabriel, and Parisa to a warehouse that was also owned by poor Danny O'Shay.

As they surrounded the building, sniffer dogs, attack dogs, bomb squads, tech specialists, EMTs, and anyone else they needed had arrived, and the building was thoroughly surrounded by at least three barriers of people, weapons, and vehicles. This was it.

With Parisa in tow, they exited the car and suited up, ready for entry. Gabriel had been advised to stay back, and though Jason watched him warily, he had saved their lives, and if he wanted to come, everyone seemed willing to oblige him. But he was warned to stay back, stay covered, and not do anything stupid, which Heather hoped he took on board.

"So this is the place?" Jason asked, prompting Parisa.

"This is it," Parisa answered eagerly, almost salivating at her proximity to her Clarence.

It was definitely the right place. They just had to hope that despite his apparent knowledge of her capture, Clarence wouldn't expect her to turn on him so quickly and that he was still situated inside these four walls.

"Great," Jason enthused, patting her on the shoulder and manually turning her to face two SAC officers. "Keep her here."

"Wait…," Parisa stammered. "That wasn't the deal. You said you'd let me go to him."

"Be glad we're not," Jessica retorted. "As soon as he figured out that you're the reason we're here, he'd shoot you just as he would anyone else."

"Not me," Parisa whispered. "He loves me."

Jessica scoffed. "God, honey. You need to get better taste in men."

She loaded and cocked her gun and looked at Heather, Gabriel, and the five SAC officers that would be joining them through the main entrance. "You ready?" she asked with a smile, spitting her gum onto the concrete.

"You seem chipper," Heather replied, checking her own gun, surprised she was being allowed to enter at all.

"We're about to end this thing. And it's all thanks to you," Jessica said. "Is your boy toy ready?"

Gabriel slapped his bulletproof vest and pulled on his helmet. "Ready."

"This is going to get messy, I can promise you that," Jason assured them gravely. "But we have the upper hand. They know we're here, and they know they're outnumbered."

"Let's do this," Heather said, locked and loaded and ready to go.

With the rest of SAC ready at the other entrances, some prepared to burst in and some to guard, the group of nine moved to the main entrance and took their positions. Jason, central, gun held straight out, informed one of the officers to kick the door down on his count.

Three, two, one, Heather thought in time, squatting, her gun at an angle, ready to take the left side of potential attackers.

Go.

Bang.

The man kicked in the flimsy door with a clean kick, and several flashlights illuminated the small space. No one fired. There was no need to. No shots, no sound, no movement. However, the room was far from empty.

"Oh my god," Jason murmured, entering the room first despite Jessica's cutoff protests. He kept moving forward, and though the SAC—trained for battle, prepared to die—moved in behind him, the other three hung back, waiting for an explosion or another killer human puppet.

When there was none, they straightened and entered the room, checking every corner and concrete crevice before focusing on what had caught Jason's attention.

The room had been turned into a surgical suite, a rudimentary one, but there were tools, lights, and a table. On the table was a body covered by a sheet and bloodied in various places.

Jason turned to Heather, his eyes bright, and she knew they were thinking the same thing. Clarence might have taken Jason's father for revenge, but he also needed a new face. The old one wouldn't cut it anymore, not anywhere in the world. So if he wanted to get away, he needed a brand-new identity, and who better to give it to him than a plastic surgeon. Unfortunately, it looked like the proceedings had gone horribly awry.

"I think it's Clarence," Jason said. "That's why it's empty. He died during surgery, and everyone left."

Though Heather was content with everything culminating in Clarence Dixon Jr., she feared for Jason's father. If he'd killed the man on top, even accidentally, was he in the ground somewhere or in another new location altogether? And would they ever be able to find him if they didn't know who they were now tracking?

Heather stepped toward the body. "Do you want me—"

Jason shook his head. "I'll do it."

Carefully, he grabbed the edge of the cloth, and Heather's stomach lurched. She almost slapped it out of his hand, but it was too late, and Jason peeled the sheet away from the bloodied body. Heather recoiled as a terrible noise escaped his throat, and he fell to his knees.

Christopher Fleming was lying on the slab. Multiple stab wounds decorated his body, and a shiny steel scalpel was laid upon his chest.

Heather turned to Jessica, whose hand was clasped to her mouth, and whispered, "Call it in. Christopher Fleming is deceased."

"Yes, ma'am," Jessica trembled, showing true horror behind her facade for the first time ever.

Heather put a hand on Jason's shoulder as Gabriel approached and looked at the body with a tight expression.

"Is that ... ?" he asked.

Heather nodded gravely and looked around the room for something, anything useful. Then she spotted something in the far-right corner next to some metal cupboards and locked double doors.

"What the hell is that?" she asked, and Gabriel turned to look.

While she stayed planted beside Jason, her partner approached, gun and flashlight raised, and cautiously he reached out to touch it. He turned back around.

"I think it's a 3D printer," he said.

"Wait, what?" Heather asked.

Gabriel opened the cupboard beneath the machine and pulled out a mask. A mask of Heather's face, which was soon joined by Jason's, and two more belonging to people she'd never met. Rose, who'd worked at MI6, perhaps? A virtual death mask. It was all another part of the game. Another toy for the man with the ever-changing face. A testament to his obsession with disguise and a sick in-joke for him and him alone. Thousands had been spent on unnerving the rats in his maze, and it had worked because as Heather stared back at her own eyeless countenance, all she wanted to do was scream.

"What the fu—" Gabriel started, but then the shots started, and they all ducked for cover, aside from Jason, who stayed kneeling, his hand on his father's cold forearm.

The shots weren't coming from inside the room. They were coming from deeper inside the warehouse and outside as well. Over the walkies, people yelled orders and declared men down, and Heather jostled Jason out of his fugue state.

"Jason, you have to get up," she begged.

Fortunately, she didn't have to tell him twice, and he carefully covered his father's face and leaned into his unhearing ear to say, "I love you."

"We'll come back for him," Heather promised, leading him and the crew to the next doorway. Clear-minded, she was in control now, and with her hand on the lock, she glanced around and asked, "Are you ready?"

"Of course," Jason answered, his voice tight.

Heather looked at Gabriel, clicked the lock, and counted down, "Three, two, one, go."

The door slammed open, and the nine moved through and quickly took shelter behind barrels, furniture, and stacks of timber. Gabriel joined her on the left by the planks, whereas the others split up in pairs or threes. Gunfire rained down on them, but none were hit by the exposed members of Clarence's organization. Clearly realizing they were outnumbered, the members of Clarence's organization began to run for cover in what Heather recognized as flimsy tiny homes. It was surreal to witness. An entire village of two-room houses littered around the biggest warehouse on the block, filled with people holding death machines.

"Cover me," Jason and Heather said to Jessica and Gabriel as they darted forward, safeguarded by their respective partners' unrelenting fire.

Heather tailed Jason as he kicked in a frail white wooden door—complete with wreaths and a welcome mat—and entered a small, stylish house. Jason looked around, almost as horrified as he'd been at the sight of his father's body, and Heather asked, "What is it?"

"It's my parents' house," he murmured, spinning around. "Not literally. It's a copy. That's how their kitchen looks, and ..." He turned to the right, facing the chic living room dotted with fake plants and cheap china. "That's their living room."

A man popped up from behind the couch, but he wasn't able to even pull the trigger before Jason landed three shots into his chest. Blood poured from the holes instantly; whatever vest he'd been wearing not even close to the standards the CIA could provide.

Without needing to be asked, Heather helped him clear the house, hoping she wouldn't have to kill anyone. She knew they were bad, but the whole thing was beginning to remind her of a cult and its leader. Brainwashed, malcontent youths who were probably ordinary people once before the Internet and the charisma of a monster ate them from the inside out.

After clearing the entrance and the singular bedroom, Heather found Jason in the kitchen, his gun trained on a kneeling young man who had his hands above his head. Heather didn't know if he would shoot, but she would never find out because whatever he intended to do was interrupted by Jessica's voice on the walkie.

"Clarence is on a boat! No one saw him leave. Look for a trapdoor. Something that would take him onto the dock without being noticed."

Heather saw Jason's finger on the trigger and moved forward, pulling her Glock from her belt, pistol-whipping the young man unconscious.

"Come on," she said. "Let's go find Clarence. Leave the rest for the SAC."

Jason sucked his cheeks and curtly nodded, moving through into another room while his would-be prey lay breathing on the floor.

The less blood, the better, Heather thought, and she followed Jason through the small circuit of a house.

It didn't take long for them to find it. It was sticking out from beneath the sectional couch, its lid the same material as the carpet but with a slender moat surrounding it. It was clearly usually locked based on the torn fabric around the keyhole, but today, in Clarence's haste to escape, it was open. Jason pulled the lid up and looked down into the dark.

For whatever reason, of which there were multiple possibilities, he hesitated, and Heather shoved past him.

"Ladies first," she said and, before he had the chance to protest, dropped down into the hole, not checking to see how deep it was before taking the plunge. Fortunately, it was only a story, and she landed on a pile of silt without collapsing and looked up at him with a thumb raised.

Jason followed suit and jumped down, landing on one knee like some sort of superhero, and looked straight ahead along the dank concrete passageway that led directly onto the wooden docks ahead.

They both inhaled—sucking in mold and damp—as they saw him. Clarence. Standing, facing them, waving on the back of a large speedboat with two of his men. He was wrapped up like a mummy, but it was undeniably him, and as he set sail, his bandages blew in the wind as the Virginia weather lashed and screamed along the river to the ocean.

Jason and Heather ran for their lives onto the dock as two special forces operatives jumped down behind them. The four made it onto a boat, and Heather stepped back as Jason got them going. Her family was not outdoorsy, nor were they rich enough to own a boat. Thankfully, Jason's parents were, and with the key still thankfully in the ignition, they took off after Clarence, peppering his boat fruitlessly with bullet holes.

Clarence was undeterred, standing there, dodging every bullet and continuing to wave. Heather had the shot, but though she asked if she should take it multiple times, so transfixed was Jason that he became mute, his gun in his lap. It was only when the man to his right was struck in the chest and fell back hard did he stand and aim his rifle right at Clarence's head. He had an even better shot. A perfect shot. He knew it. Clarence knew it. And they both, as well as Heather, knew he wouldn't take it.

"Fuck," he hissed, increasing the speed. "Aim for the motor on the back."

Four guns trained on the speedboat motor, and after only a few well-aimed hits, it exploded with an echoing bang and soon clouded the boat with a veil of thick black smoke. Then, once it had run out of natural thrust, Clarence's vessel halted on the still water.

Despite their proximity, no more shots were fired as Jason pulled up beside Clarence, who only turned his head, not his body, to look at them. His eyes were blackened around the edges, the sclera bloodshot, and his lips were pulled taught. He looked demonic, like a sleep paralysis monster, or something ripped straight from a horror movie.

Then he turned—his legs first, then his upper body—and held his gun out. Except he didn't point it at Jason, Heather, or the two SAC officers. Instead, he pointed it at the two men dressed in alabaster who sat on the row seats.

Bang. Bang.

Clarence fired rounds into each of his faithful follower's skulls and pushed each motionless man overboard with a hard shove. He watched them blankly as they sank before looking at the other four in the adjacent boat.

"I want to be alone with Jason and Heather," he said calmly.

Without hesitation, Jason looked at the two officers and commanded them to take the boat back to shore before dragging Heather to her feet and onto Clarence's boat.

"'Atta boy," Clarence cawed as Jason sat before him, rocking the boat with his weight.

Cautiously, Heather joined him, and Clarence cocked his head like a dog hearing a high-pitched whistle. The seats were bloody, and Heather made the mistake of wetting her hand in the pool.

"Sorry about that, darling," Clarence cooed. "But I knew they would never leave my side. And I'm afraid I needed to talk to you privately." Clarence stuck a hand out to her, taking the bloodied one unflinchingly before turning to Jason. "So you are the famous Jason," he said. "My, my, you don't look much like your daddy. I wonder if your momma wasn't playing around."

Jason took his hand, despite the burning hatred in his eyes, and shook it firmly. "And you're Clarence Dixon Jr.," he replied, emphasizing the latter aspect. "You look a lot like yours."

Ignoring the goad, Clarence sat down opposite the pair with a smile. "I am. You know, I've been wanting to meet you for a long time."

"I'm aware. And I want to apologize to you."

Clarence cocked his head. "You do?" he barked. "Now, I did not see that coming." He slapped his leg and bared his teeth. "You know, I didn't take you for the apologizing sort."

"What sort did you take me for?"

"The ruthless, bloodthirsty type. I have to admit, I'm a little disappointed. Never meet your heroes, huh?"

"Hero?" Jason questioned.

"Well, perhaps *nemesis* would be the better word. Every great man needs one, and I'm sure you can agree that we are both great men."

"I'm not sure if I see it that way."

"Well, you haven't had your eyes opened yet. And you know, I'm awful good at doing that. You know, you two could come with me. I need people like you to rise up against our oppressors."

"And who, exactly, is oppressing you?" Heather snapped. "Spoiled little rich boy, blessed by his wealthy white birth. You know you're one of the richest men in North America, and instead of giving to the poor, fighting for what's right, you've murdered innocent people."

Clarence hooted, hollered, and doubled over with laughter before straightening up to meet Heather's unflinching scowl. "Phew. Wow. Now, I'm sorry for laughing, darling. But *you* might actually be my hero. That is just the type of revolutionary thinking I'm looking for. Now, I bet you were a punk back in your day. Short hair. Fighting slimeballs. Kicking ass and taking names. The problem is, you've picked the wrong leader. You need someone like me to tap into your true potential, just as I did for Parisa."

Heather spit a wad of nervously generated saliva right into his eyeball, and Clarence laughed again, but there was an edge of frost to it this time.

"I'll get back to you in a minute, but, Jason, I want you to know that I'm a forgiving man. And though you might not believe it, I forgive you. Do you forgive me for killing your daddy?"

Jason stayed silent.

Clarence continued. "'Cause the way I see it, we're square. I killed. You killed. I stay on this boat, you swim back to shore, let me take the girl, and I'll be on my way to Cuba, never to cause trouble again. Cross my heart and hope to die. So do you forgive me?"

Jason continued his silence.

"You know no one has to die," Clarence said, standing again and pointing his gun directly at Heather's forehead. "So once again, do you forgive me?"

"Yes," Jason said.

Clarence clicked his tongue and turned the safety off. "You know, I can abide a man being a lot of things, but a liar isn't one of them."

Clarence moved his pistol and fired a shot into Jason's shin before grabbing Heather and pulling her onto his lap, his gun pressed hard against his temple.

"Now, Jason, I recommend you get to swimmin'," he said. "Or else I'll do worse than take Heather here with me to Cuba."

Jason struggled back to his feet, despite his likely shattered shin bone, and pointed his gun at Clarence's head. "I can't let you go."

"Come on, Jason. As I said, we're even, and I forgive you. Don't make this harder than it has to be."

For a microsecond, Jason's eyes moved to Heather's, and she nodded. She saw the muscles in his jaw tighten like thick cords beneath the chiseled surface, and he fired. Blood and brain matter splattered the third row of seating behind, and Heather struggled free of the dead man's grasp. She'd heard a click, but he'd died before the trigger was pulled, and she staggered toward Jason.

After a few deep breaths, they moved toward Clarence, his legs still propped up on the seat, the rest of his body on the wet ground. Jason hopped the row, stood above the man who'd taken so much from him and others, and unwrapped his face. Heather kneeled and watched, her breath caught in some unknown crevice of her body as the sore, unhealed face was revealed.

The man staring at the gray sky with glassy eyes was completely unrecognizable. Gone was the beauty, the character, replaced by something so neutral that he was devoid of humanity. She felt if she blinked, she'd forget what he looked like, so she kept staring. The only things that she could hold on to were the subtle scars and blooming bruises. Had he had the chance to heal, he wouldn't—couldn't—stand out in a crowd. No one would look twice at a person so devoid of personality. He was no better than a shadow of a man. It was an act of genius on his and Christopher's part, but one that would haunt her for a long time to come, his ghost's face nothing but a blur in the corners of dark rooms.

"So that's it then," she said.

"Almost," Jason said quietly, lowering himself into the footwell beside Clarence.

He was too big, ungainly, and yet somehow as dainty as a ballerina and as delicate as a surgeon as he closed Clarence's eyes with his forefinger and thumb. He rested an elbow on the seat and propped his head up with it.

"I'm sorry," he whispered to the dead man before straightening up and clambering toward the engine.

The apology was true, despite it being addressed to a man who'd taken everything from Jason, and its genuineness tied Heather's throat in a knot. The boat took off toward shore, and she turned away from Jason, bracing herself against the salt water and watching as the worried faces along the dock grew closer.

CHAPTER THIRTY-SEVEN

THE DETECTIVE

B Y THE TIME HEATHER AND JASON REACHED THE SHORE, she was done for the day and detected that he was too. She felt limp and tense in all the wrong places, and all the exhausting days and restless nights caught up to her as soon as she attempted to leap from boat to dock. She lost her footing and was saved only by Jason's reflexes. She looked at him, her knees weak, and they both knew it was time to go home.

First, however, were the celebrations. After handshakes and hugs, and more handshakes and hugs, Heather and Gabriel began to hint at the idea of wanting to leave. No one had any arguments beyond the team being sad to see them go. Clarence was dead, as were several of his loyal followers, and those who had survived were cuffed and contained. There was nothing more for them to do; the pencil-pushers and local cops had it from here. So after some bittersweet goodbyes, the pair was escorted to a car that would take them to the airport, and Jason followed them over.

"So this is it," Heather said as Gabriel hopped in the back seat but kept the door open.

"I guess it is," Jason replied.

"Well, thank God for that."

Jason nodded. "Yeah."

"Are you going to be okay?" she asked.

He didn't answer her directly but cleared his throat and looked at the warehouse. "I'll send you an invite to the funeral, both of you."

"We'll be there," she assured him.

"Yeah, of course," Gabriel chimed in.

"Give my condolences to your family," Heather added.

"Will do," Jason said, his voice tight. "They'll be okay. We'll get through it. I think I'll take some time off to spend at home."

"They'll be glad to have you back."

Jason smiled softly. "Yeah, Natalie especially." He held up three fingers. "My eldest two are about to become very jealous."

Heather beamed. "Congratulations."

"Thank you."

"This isn't the part where you tell us you're naming your kid after one of us, is it?" Gabriel asked. Heather rolled her eyes and moved to smack his arm but missed by a wide berth. "What?"

Jason chuckled. "No. Natalie's spoiled younger sister is named Heather. Don't want her getting the wrong idea."

"Excuses, excuses," Heather joked.

"Plus, I have a feeling this one is going to be a boy."

"So you're telling me Gabriel is still on the table?" Gabriel pushed, and Heather couldn't hope but smirk.

"I hope for your sake it is. Three girls, whew. Now that's a handful."

"Tell me about it. Though it's a shame that Dad won't be here to meet them. Having grandkids was the highlight of his life."

He sounded as if he might cry, and Heather looked away tactfully and stared out across the water. "I'm really sorry about your dad."

"Thank you. And thank you both for trying so hard to save him."

"It's my job."

"Still," Jason insisted, "you went above and beyond. If I was in charge of handing out medals—"

"No need for any of that."

"Compensation?" he questioned.

"Nope," Heather insisted.

"Come on. There's no way you get paid enough in Glenville," he teased.

"Probably not, but I'm not exactly the flashy sort."

"New car?"

"Hell no."

Jason chuckled again. "So even though I can't offer you medals, and you don't want compensation or a new car—"

"Hey, *I* didn't say anything about—" Gabriel started, and Heather landed her smack this time, silencing him.

Jason continued, "What I can offer you, if you take the course, is a place at the CIA. Officers, field agents, whatever you want. My word is worth a lot around here, and I know you both have what it takes."

Heather hesitated and looked at Gabriel. "You know, I'm thinking I might be a small-town girl after all. Don't get me wrong, it's been amazing working alongside all of you, but honestly, I miss my life. A lot more than I thought I would."

Jason looked disappointed but smiled softly. "I thought you might say that. You have my number if you change your mind. Gabriel?"

Heather turned to Gabriel, expecting him to repeat after her, but instead, he said, "Can I have your card?"

Jason fumbled around in his pockets and came up empty-handed. "Heather, send him my number. And my email address."

"Thanks," Gabriel said, unable to contain his excitement.

"How many languages do you speak?" Jason inquired, suddenly stiff and professional, his voice dropped half an octave.

"Two fluently."

"What's your education situation?"

"High school diploma."

Jason rubbed his stubble. "Make that a bachelor's degree, and you're in. I'll even fund your education if this is the direction you want to go in."

"Seriously? Thank you, man. I don't know what else to say," Gabriel exhaled in a burst of excitement.

"Don't worry about it, now I gotta go over there and schmooze. I'll see you guys at the funeral."

He held out a hand to each of them, and they shook it gladly before pulling away and turning back to the mob of police, CIA, and other emergency services. She just hoped he managed to escape before the media arrived. Once he was far enough away that she was sure he wasn't coming back, she shoved Gabriel over and clambered into the back seat.

"What was that all about?" she asked, a bemused smile plastered on her face. Though she'd miss him if he joined the CIA, a chance at an all-expenses-paid education was undeniably exciting.

Gabriel shrugged. "I think the past twenty-four hours showed me that I'm not as afraid of change as I thought. Like it was totally terrifying, and I'm really sorry about Jason's dad, but I can't deny that my heart's pounding in a good way right now." He paused. "Why did you say no?"

"Because I think, at least for right now, I'm happy being a small-town detective in a crappy car."

"For someone who's happy being a small-town girl, you seem to get into a lot of big adventures," Gabriel joked.

"Yeah, I think I might be a chaos magnet."

Gabriel shrugged. "Maybe the universe is telling you you're destined for something bigger than Glenville."

Heather hummed. "Maybe. But for now, I'm not going anywhere."

"Yeah. We'll see about that."

"I guess we will."

An agent interrupted them as she jumped in, cheerfully congratulated them, and turned on the engine. Gabriel—not half as exhausted as Heather—made polite conversation before jumping right into interrogating the woman about her life as an agent. She seemed keen to comply, and though Heather initially tried to listen, she soon turned it out and closed her eyes. As the vehicle rolled forward, removing them from the large shadow cast by the enormous building, she sighed in relief as she felt the sun's warm rays pour in through the windows and settle on her face.

CHAPTER THIRTY-EIGHT

THE AGENT

JASON PULLED UP AT HIS PARENTS' QUAINT VIRGINIAN colonial home and looked up at the American flag waving against the perfect, cloudless summer sky. The lawns were overgrown, and the gutters were full of leaves, but he was grateful to have daytime tasks to complete during his time off. He'd never been good at doing very little, especially when there was grief to contend with. He also knew his wife and mom were exactly the same, which meant there'd be little to do in the world of the indoors.

Two undercover guards sitting on the porch bench nodded and greeted Jason as he made his way up the pathway and wiped his filthy boots. He waved but didn't stop and let himself in through the unlocked front door. He had been informed that his family was here, but they didn't know he was coming, and a flicker of excitement pattered in his chest as he called out down the hall.

"Hello? Anyone home?"

"Daddy!" came a pair of high-pitched shrieks, followed by little running footsteps.

Their little voices nearly broke him, but he held it together as he braced himself for impact. Soon the girls' footsteps grew louder, and they appeared in the kitchen doorway at the end of the hall. Screaming louder once they saw him, they skidded across the floorboards in their matching polka-dot socks and landed into the crooks of his spread arms.

"Hello, my little ladybugs," he murmured, kissing the tops of their heads before holding them back at arms' length. "Wow, I think you've both gotten taller. How is that possible?"

Charlotte turned and hollered down the hallway, "I told you!"

Natalie appeared in the doorway with a serene smile. "Yes, you did," she said happily.

Jason kissed the girls again and tickled them till they ran squealing away into the living room to the left. He stood slowly, the pain in his body needling away at his brain. It must've shown on his face because Natalie's expression dropped, and she ran toward him, arms outstretched and reaching. She wrapped herself around his and stood on tiptoes to bury her face in his neck.

"I've been so worried about you," she whimpered. "No one would tell me anything until an hour ago. I'm so proud of you for stopping him."

Jason didn't reply but rested his chin on top of her head.

"What's wrong?" she asked, her grip tightening.

"Dad didn't make it," he whispered.

"Oh," Natalie whimpered. "I can tell the girls if you want."

"Thank you, honey, but I should be the one to tell them. I just need to talk to Mom first. Where is she?"

Natalie unleashed her husband but chastely kissed him before speaking. "She's upstairs."

"Okay. I'll be back in a minute."

Natalie shook her head. "You take your time. We'll be here."

"I love you," he said firmly.

"I love you too," she sniffled, smiling through the escaping tears. "I'll go make some tea and let them play."

Happy despite the pain, Jason winked at her before dragging himself up the stairs, and she blew him a kiss before padding slowly toward the kitchen. Once she was out of sight, he paused at the third-to-last step, but the soft laughter of the girls gave him the strength to reach the landing and knock on his mom's bedroom door. While he waited for her to answer, he looked around at the decor, remembering the duplicate that Clarence had created, and shuddered. That was a memory for the vault and nobody else.

The door swung open, and Kathleen stood on the other side in a dressing gown, a large glass of wine in hand. Her lips were stained purple, which meant it was not her first, but she looked at him with sober eyes as she stepped back to let him in.

Still silent, she glided to the padded seats that lined the bay window and exhaled as she sat. Her mouth occupied by wine, she patted the seat beside him, and once he, too, was seated, she laid her head briefly on his shoulder and squeezed his hand.

"He's gone, isn't he?" she asked matter-of-factly.

Jason turned to her, bewildered. "How did you know?"

"I felt it. Last night sometime. It was like a candle blowing out. Almost unnoticeable if you're not looking right at it, but of course, I always was. A little hiss, then a fizzle, then all that's left is smoke and darkness," she said, lighting a smoke with a match before blowing it out.

"I'm sorry," he choked.

She turned to him and shook her head. "My love, you have nothing to be sorry for. Just because his story ended sadly doesn't mean it didn't have a great beginning and middle. Your father was a fortunate man. He was loved, he was successful, and he made all of our dreams come true. We should all be so lucky."

"But it's my fault," Jason insisted, feeling so small, like a child waking up from a nightmare.

"Now, how on earth is it your fault?"

"I killed his dad. It was an accident—a drone strike gone wrong at the start of my career—but I still killed him."

"Okay," Kathleen said.

"Okay?"

"You made a terrible mistake. But it was a mistake. This man killed so many people on purpose. I mean, honey, the guy was a monster."

"What if I am too?" Jason asked, tears welling for the first time since his youngest daughter was born.

"Well, do you feel guilty for killing his father?"

"Yes, of course."

"And do you feel guilty for killing him?"

"Yes," Jason said without thinking. It was the truth; they could both hear it in his voice. That distinct and pained remorse that would, and always should, come with the burden of taking a human life. No matter how evil that human was.

"And do you think he felt anything about all the lives he took?" she asked.

"No."

"Well, there you go. Case closed. He was a monster, and you are a man, and that guilt you're feeling only means that there's hope for you yet." She squeezed his hand again as she took another sip. "There's not a soul in the world—certainly not in this house—that blames you for what happened to your father. And one day, when you're very old, he'll be able to tell you himself. But for now, you'll just have to take my word for it."

Jason wanted to speak but couldn't, for lack of words and lack of voice. Instead, he began to cry, and his mother pulled him to her shoulder and rubbed his back.

"Let it out," she said, her own voice constricted. He felt wetness on his forehead as she let out a shaky breath. "Do the girls know?"

"Not yet. I thought we should all be together."

"Quite right. A united family is the strongest thing in the world. And that's what we need in these difficult times."

"Yeah," he whispered.

Kathleen pushed him upright, laid her glass on the table, and extinguished her half-smoked cigarette. "Now, that's enough of feeling sorry for ourselves. We wouldn't want your father to see us in such a state, would we? Plus, how can we be sad with another Fleming on the way?"

Jason cleared his throat. "So no more day drinking?"

"No more day drinking. I'll wait until at least 7:00 p.m. to drink like a normal person if you can reserve the evenings for feeling sorry for yourself?"

"Deal."

"Good boy. We have a lot to do and limited time to do it, but it's okay to assign a little part of the day to hurt. Compartmentalize."

Jason nodded and stood. He held out a hand to his mom and helped her to his feet, and together they descended the stairs to where Natalie was waiting with a tray of tea.

"Ready?" Natalie asked, her lip wobbling ever so slightly.

Jason nodded and entered the living room with his arms wrapped around Kathleen and Natalie. The girls were playing with their enormous dollhouse, completely oblivious to what was coming. It felt cruel to rip their innocence away, but it had to be done.

The three adults took their places—Kathleen on the couch, Natalie on an ottoman, and Jason kneeling on the floor—and Jason cleared his throat. The two girls turned, their smiling faces and gleaming brown eyes faltering as they saw tears falling across their mother's puffy face and their father's serious expression.

"We have something to talk to you girls about," Jason said.

They were only young, but they could sense the energy in the room, and Charlotte began to sniffle as Marie crawled into her father's lap.

"Come here, baby," he said to his eldest, and she joined her younger sister in being held. "I'm sorry to have to tell you this, but your grandpa is with the angels in heaven now," he told them, holding them close to his beating chest.

"You mean he's dead?" Charlotte asked, always so smart. They'd lost the family cat the year prior, and Jason was glad that this concept was at least not new to her.

"Yes, honey. That means we're not going to see him again until we also go to heaven."

This opened the floor to a barrage of questions from both children, and as the three adults took turns answering, the concept finally started to click, and the tears began. Tears turned into wailing, and they all huddled together as the girls screamed their pain out into the open. It was confusing, and it was going to be hard, but Jason's eyes dried in being held by his family.

He felt everyone's pain, rocked them to and fro, and looked up at a photo of his father on the mantle. He thought of all the innumerable good times they'd had and plucked some stories from his hazy memory to tell over tea when their grief grew quiet enough for the girls to listen. There were so many amazing ones, and he was excited to tell them. As long as he had the ability to speak, his father was immortal on both earth and in heaven.

CHAPTER THIRTY-NINE

THE DETECTIVE

FORTUNATELY, THE FANFARE UPON ARRIVING HOME IN Glenville was muted. Aside from a couple of waves from people on the street—Amber and Bobby being the most enthusiastic of the greeters—Heather was able to pick up her dogs from the shelter, say goodbye to Gabriel, and make it home with minimal interference.

Once situated on her couch, she cuddled up by her pets, tucked herself under a blanket, and braced herself as she turned her phone back on after several days of radio silence. Her parents, Tina, Gene, Karen, Julius, and even Beau had texted and attempted to call multiple times. She felt guilty, of course, but more than that, she felt exhausted as more messages rolled in, and she groaned thinking about all the video calls and meetups she'd have to organize over the coming days. This would also entail lying, something she hated doing at the best of times.

For now, she sent all of them a likely infuriating "I'm alive" text and turned her phone back off. It was all she felt up to, for now, pushing any mutual interactions to tomorrow after a good night's sleep in her own bed. Though perhaps *good* was getting her hopes up too high, she had her fingers crossed for some satisfying REM.

"No more trips for a while," she promised her dogs. "And definitely no more planes."

They wagged at her and panted as if they understood, and she thanked them for not disappearing forever with treats from the coffee table drawer and an abundance of scratches.

She tried to fall asleep then and there, surrounded by large protective animals, but found herself instantly restless. She cursed her brain for the way it was and the way it had always been. Always thinking, always anxious, always nocturnal.

In trying to avoid thinking about Christopher and Clarence, she remembered what Gabriel had said about outrunning her past and how exhausting it must be. He was right, and how would she ever find peace, or balance, or know where to go next if she was always holding herself and the life she had lived at a distance? She'd run to Glenville but was still jogging in place, one eye open, ready to run once again.

What would happen, she asked herself, *if I just let it catch me?*

The answers ranged from something horrible—a deep, inescapable depression that would eat her whole—to obtaining life-improving peace. Though the bad was really bad, she no longer felt she had a choice not to try for the good. She was running on empty, and what would happen when she ran out was no more pleasant than the possibilities that came with giving the past a try.

So she decided to make the logical step and do what everyone had been asking her to do. It was time to check in on her ex-husband. Though their divorce had been messy and the separation painful, there was more good there than bad. Thus the perfect baby step.

She pulled up her laptop, typed in his name, searched, and quickly looked away from the results to grab a drink to settle her pounding heart. She was trying hard, every day, not to self-medicate, but some wounds called for a little rubbing alcohol.

Daniel Palmer was a good man and an even better husband. He was charming and polite, and Heather suspected he was much better liked than herself—even by her parents. She was never jealous though. It was understandable. There was a river of kindness that ran through him that never dried up and nourished everyone in abundance, especially her.

She had been the problem. The drunk. The workaholic. And back to the drunk again. Never visibly disastrous enough to worry her family or her co-workers, but certainly chaotic enough to aggrieve her constantly worried husband. He wanted her to go back to who she'd been at the start before becoming a homicide detective. However, despite knowing that girl was still inside her, it was impossible to dig her out. Too many hands had been dealt, too many cards stacked, and it was impossible to know which one to pull without the entire house falling down.

Late nights led to distrust, outbursts at dinner parties led to embarrassment, and hangovers and drunken nights led to a lack of intimacy. This growing tumor snowballed as she rolled down hill after hill until one day her problems were too big for him to melt anymore. So he left, and aside from divorce proceedings, the pair hadn't spoken to each other once in the past five years.

She returned to the laptop with closed eyes, took a sip, and opened them. A whimper escaped her lips, making her dog's ears perk as she skimmed the news articles about her perfect ex-husband.

Seattle Engineer Lead Suspect in the Tragic Murder of Fashion Model Katy Graham

With shaking hands, Heather clicked on an article, revealing a selfie of her ex-husband, Daniel Palmer, and his late fiancée, Katy Graham, at the Grand Canyon. Heather and he used to go to the Grand Canyon for the anniversary, which was beside the point but added an extra dagger to the knives twisting into her gut.

She turned on her phone, impatiently waited for the old piece of garbage to turn on, and called Julius, who once again picked up despite the time.

"Hello?" he asked, concern causing a waver in his voice.

"Julius?" Heather croaked.

"Heather, what's wrong? Where have you been? Are you okay?"

"I'm fine. I'm at home."

Julius exhaled. "Thank God. I've been so worried about you. What's wrong?"

"Dan. I… I looked him up. What the fuck? Why didn't any of you tell me this was happening?"

Julius sighed. "I'm so sorry, Heather. I should have told you, I can see that now. I wanted you to find out on your own terms, but no, this is cruel. You've been bombarded by the bloody Internet, which is far worse than me coming to you as a friend."

"Do you know what happened? All these stupid articles are so goddamn vague," she snapped, clicking madly as her laptop froze.

"Well, I did perform her autopsy," he said. "I really shouldn't, but I will send you the report. Please take your time reading it. It's unpleasant, and you seem overwhelmed as it is. Though when you do, don't hesitate to call. I'd be happy to answer any of your questions."

"At least tell me the cause of death," she demanded.

"Heather," Julius said softly. "Are you—"

"Yes! Just tell me."

"Strangulation. Not uncommon in crimes of passion."

Heather's mouth fell open. "I can't believe this," she moaned. "Is he going to prison?"

"No. Not as of yet. He's actually at home on bail, as far as I know. He's, of course, the main suspect as he's the fiancé, but beyond having a weak alibi, there's no evidence that he did it."

"He didn't do it," Heather declared firmly. "I can feel it."

"Perhaps give your heart time to settle before probing your gut. Your old affections might be interfering."

"What the hell does that mean? Do *you* think he did it?"

303

"Honestly, Heather, I don't know. He never seemed the type, but I'll admit, Veronica and I did go to dinner with him and Katy before the divorce, and they did seem a bit strained."

"Me and Dan were more than a bit strained, but he never killed me. He never even raised his voice at me!" Heather hissed.

"You're right. Heather, I'm sorry. This isn't the time for my opinions. It's only going to confuse you. Plus, I really didn't know him that well. Please talk to me, tell me how you feel."

"I don't… I don't know," Heather said, starting to hyperventilate and deeply regretting letting her past get close enough to deliver such a sharp sucker punch. "All I know is that he would have never done this. Not the Dan I knew."

"I think you're having a panic attack," Julius replied. "Should I come down? I have the day off tomorrow. I can be there in an hour."

She wanted to say yes—was actually dying to say yes—but letting the good parts of her past catch up too was too fraught. Whether in words or actions, she knew it would lead to some sort of mistake, and she was all out of capacity for disaster and complications.

Using the TV to square-breathe, she composed herself enough to say, "No. Thank you though. Really. But I think I'll just go to bed."

"Are you sure? I'm going to worry about you."

"I'm fine. I promise. It's just been a really, *really* long week, and this is just the rotten cherry on top. Seriously, I just need to sleep."

"Promise me you'll call me in the morning or at least answer my texts."

"I promise. Good night, Julius."

Julius sighed again. "Good night, Heather. I hope you feel better."

She clicked the red button, and the tears flowed. It had been a long time since she'd had a good, deep sob, and she let it all out. All her homicide cases. All the dead girls like Katy Graham and Lilly Arnold. The Paper Doll Killer, Dennis Burke, Alice Warren, Roland Ellis, Gustavo, Christopher

Fleming, and now Dan. She let it all hit her like a freight train, and she battled to drink her whiskey as it rolled about in the glass like the ocean in a storm.

When she could feel her extremities again, she stood and made her way to the spare room, which was still covered, after all these years, in taped-up and poorly labeled moving boxes. She unearthed one from beneath a moth-eaten blanket named "Photo albums" and tore into it with only her nails, tearing her pinky in the process.

Inside were several thick photo albums, ranging from her wedding up until things went sour between her and Dan. She picked one at random—2017—and flicked through. It was grounding, and despite everything, she found herself laughing and smiling at their adventures. Hiking, museums, picnics, the beach. Then there was a photo of Dan sleeping on a plane, his mouth ajar, his dark skin smooth and perfect, and Heather stopped smiling.

She flicked to the next page, and there was a photo of Dan standing in front of a red phone booth, next to the Queen's guards, and the pair of them in a horse-drawn carriage going through…

"Hyde Park," she whispered.

Hesitantly, she flipped to the last page and saw a photo of the pair of them standing outside a pub, having asked a passerby to take a photo. Behind them was the black-and-white Thistle & Pig, and there—standing outside the front entrance, wearing heavy makeup and hoop earrings, and smoking a cigarette—was Lilly Arnold.

AUTHOR'S NOTE

Thank you for joining Heather on her journey and delving into the mysteries of Glenville in *The House on the Lake,* the third book in this mystery series. Your decision to continue on this adventure means the world to me. In return, I have a little secret to share: the next book in the series, titled The Bridesmaids, is already in the works!

As a new indie author, I am incredibly appreciative of your support. Your reviews and word of mouth recommendations fuel my passion for writing and for bringing these stories to life. If you could spare a few moments to leave a review for *The House on the Lake,* it would make an immense difference. Your thoughts and feedback play a crucial role in shaping my creative process, enabling me to craft an even more captivating reading experience for you in the future!

Are you feeling up to another mysterious and thrilling adventure right now? Don't miss out on my other series, the *Mia Storm FBI Mystery Thriller* series. Set in beautiful Hawaii, this series kicks off with, Murder in Paradise. Join Mia Storm, a freshly graduated FBI agent who is thrown into a twisted murder case in an affluent neighborhood. Each victim is left with mind-bending riddles and puzzles as the only clues, and the killer seems to be playing a sick game. Mia must crack the case before the killer strikes again, but with each clue, the stakes get higher and the puzzle more twisted.

Thank you again for your support, and I hope you continue to enjoy my books in the future!

Warm regards,
Cara Kent

P.S. I will be the first one to tell you that I am not perfect, no matter how hard I try to be. And there is plenty that I am still learning about self-publishing. If you come across any typos or have any other issues with this book please don't hesitate to reach out to me at cara@carakent.com, I monitor and read every email personally, and I will do my very best to rectify any issues that I am made aware of.

Get the inside scoop on new releases and get a **FREE BOOK** by me! Visit *https://dl.bookfunnel.com/513mluk159* to claim your **FREE** copy!

Follow me on **Facebook** - *https://www.facebook.com/people/Cara-Kent/100088665803376/*
Follow me on **Instagram** - *https://www.instagram.com/cara.kent_books/*

ALSO BY CARA KENT

Glenville Mystery Thriller

Book One - The Lady in the Woods
Book Two - The Crash
Book Three - The House on the Lake

Mia Storm FBI Mystery Thriller

Book One - Murder in Paradise
Book Two - Washed Ashore

An Addictive Psychological Thriller with Shocking Twists

Book One - The Woman in the Cottage
Book Two - Mine

Made in the USA
Las Vegas, NV
17 July 2023

74847865R00180